in memory of

GUNDA BURGESS

1998

a bitter feast

by s. j. rozan

a bitter feast

s. j. rozan

st. martin's press
new york

Library of Congress Cataloging-in-Publication Data

Rozan, S. J.
    A bitter feast / by S.J. Rozan.—1st ed.
      p. cm.
    ISBN 0-312-19259-2
    1. Chinese Americans—New York (State)—New York—Fiction.
I. Title.
PS3568.099B58   1998   98-21558
813'.54—dc21   CIP

First Edition: September 1998

10 9 8 7 6 5 4 3 2 1

For Bubbe and Zayde
and all the immigrant *mishpocheh*
mine and not mine

And for Mok Sim Tsang
from the little boss

With gratitude to

Steve Axelrod, my agent
Keith Kahla, my editor
even more than usual

Fay Chew Matsuda at the Museum of Chinese in the Americas

Carl Goldberg, Betsy Harding, Royal Huber, Barbara Martin,
Jamie Scott, Lawton Tootle
anything they didn't do isn't their fault

Nancy Ennis and Helen Hester
anything they didn't do is my fault

Deb Peters
definitely one of us

David Goldberg, who still, I hope, has the dollar

and
The Carmelites
have you eaten yet?

a note on chinese names

In Chinese usage, the surname comes first. Most Chinese people have two given names, presented here with a hyphen; although not the modern way, it's easiest on Western eyes. Many Chinese people in America have an American given name as well. When Lydia Chin speaks or thinks in English, she uses the English order and the American name: "Peter Lee." Speaking in Chinese, she uses the Chinese order and name: "Lee Bi-Da." Most Chinese people in this book follow this pattern of speech. The exceptions are recent immigrants, who even in English use the Chinese order of names. Don't worry. You'll get used to it.

o n e

You really think there'll be trouble?"

I stood on the corner where Canal crosses the Bowery in the middle of a morning in the middle of May. The sun was bright and the sky was one of those radiant blues that people who paid more attention in high school English than I did probably know the name of. As I turned to Peter Lee, standing beside me, the soft breeze mussed my hair, but good-naturedly like a boyfriend, not pesteringly like a brother.

Peter, who to me is neither, just a Chinatown lawyer I've known since first grade, shrugged his broad shoulders at my question. "Not if we're lucky," he said, taking a gulp from the cup of tea loosing trails of steam from his hand into the fresh spring air. "But anytime people get arrested, there could be trouble."

I sipped at my own tea, handed to me by Peter when I'd first arrived. This was my reward for giving up part of a beautiful spring Sunday to stand on a noisy, traffic-scented street corner as a potential witness to potential trouble.

The tea was delicious, and perfect for the day: an astringent, fresh-tasting green. I didn't recognize it, but I knew the cup: it came from Ten Ren, a classy tea importer on Mott Street. Say what you will about Peter, about his distracted approach to his clothes (mismatched) and his car (wheezy), about his weakness for lost causes—he's an immigration lawyer, mainly—but this is a man who knows his tea.

"Look," he said in the unexcited and matter-of-fact voice he used to use, when we were kids, to propose the most outrageous mischief. "Here they come."

I peered where he pointed, down the slope of the Bowery, past the woman frying scallion pancakes in hot oil on a cart and around the jade-and-Rolex vendors yelling their broken English into the crowd. Kaleidoscopically shifting groups of people swarmed the sidewalks, but through them, three blocks away, I could see what Peter wanted me to see.

A small but purposefully moving platoon of men carrying a banner and a large black box were parting the sea of startled pedestrians as they marched up the sidewalk in our direction. The men were dressed identically, in black slacks and white shirts; one of them pounded a red-lacquered Chinese drum. I could hardly hear the eerie rhythmic thump of the drum over the traffic's roar, over the honking horns and rumbling trucks around me, but I could sense it, up through the soles of my shoes. It felt like the early beginnings of an earthquake, the first small but undeniable hint that soon everything will change, enormously and irrevocably.

People in the path of the marching men stared from in front, beside, and behind them, trying to make out the words on the banner and the meaning of it all. The men were Chinese, the banner was red, and the brush-painted words were Chinese, too, at least on one side. As the men advanced, the wind picked up, flapping the banner around. Then I could see the English on its other side: JUSTICE AND A LIVING WAGE, it said. The Chinese, though as usual more poetic, was similar. At the bottom of the banner, on both sides in both languages, were the words CHINESE RESTAURANT WORKERS' UNION.

I stared, too, but not at the banner. My attention was mostly on the box. It was a coffin.

I've seen coffins before, of course. I've even seen one or two dead bodies, which is one of the things my mother hates most about my job. She doesn't think people should be around dead bodies; she doesn't trust the dead, not one bit. This coffin was empty; I knew it was, Peter had told me. Still, seeing it move slowly up the Bowery to the beat of a soft, deep drum sent a shiver up my spine in the bright May air.

"Do they really think this is going to work?" I asked Peter, surprised to hear myself whispering.

He glanced at me, lifted an eyebrow. "It's working on you already."

I made a face at him for being right and went back to watching.

The men with the drum and the banner and the coffin crossed the street to the block we were on. They brought themselves to a halt a few doors down. In front of the glittering marble-and-chrome entrance to Dragon Garden, a hugely popular dim sum restaurant and banquet hall, they took over the sidewalk. They stood in ranks, twenty men in four neat rows, with the banner whipping in the breeze. The drum kept up its steady, pulsing beat as the pallbearers detached themselves from the rest. They carried the coffin as far as Dragon Garden's doors and stood it upright against the plate glass window beside the entrance.

The pallbearers returned to their ranks; then the men spread out. They held their banner high, they established a circle, and they began to march. One intense-looking young man with wire-rim glasses and hair so short you could see his scalp lifted a megaphone and led some slogan shouting while they handed flyers to passersby. People took the red-paper flyers and read them; but even people without flyers were staring at the coffin, at the restaurant's doors, pursing their lips, and walking on.

"Would you look at that," I said. "It's working. When you told me about it, I wasn't convinced."

"Really?" Peter flicked his eyes from the marching men to me and back again. "Your mom has an altar at home."

"Well, sure. And your Uncle Liang has one in the shop. But that doesn't mean . . ." I let my words trail off as a bent old woman grabbed the hand of the little girl she was walking with and pulled her over to the curb, as far away from the coffin as they could get without plunging into the Bowery traffic. I wasn't sure what it didn't mean.

We're a superstitious bunch, we Chinese, putting our faith in signs and wonders and the helpful and unhelpful interference in our daily lives of a teeming multitude of gods and ghosts. Not that anyone in my generation really believes any of this, of course, especially not ABCs like Peter and me, American-Born Chinese, as American as the next guy. Even some of my mother's friends scoff at the old ways—the different gods for different needs and the different tricks to get in touch with them and win them over. But still, my brothers and sisters-in-law and niece and nephews and I all troop out to New Jersey with my mother to sweep winter's debris from my father's grave at Qing Ming, and people bring one another oranges on New Year's Day.

Just in case. It's all just in case. And the Chinese Restaurant Workers' Union was gambling that, just in case, no Chinese person, food-obsessed though we tend to be, would deliberately cross in front of a coffin just to get some lunch.

And it was working. A well-dressed, heavyset Chinese couple whispered to each other, smiled maybe just a bit shamefacedly, and walked on. A large family, grandma in that two-piece heavy silk outfit westerners call pajamas, held an agitated sidewalk conference in which grandma did not participate but only stonily shook her head. They walked on, too. Even a young, hip, uptown Chinese man—he could have been one of my brothers—took his slim blond girlfriend by the elbow and, over her pouting protests that the food was so *good* here, gallantly but firmly guided her away. Another relationship doomed, I thought to myself.

A few of the potential Dragon Garden customers drifted only as far as Happy Pavilion Restaurant, another enormous dim sum palace down the street. Others went farther, as though no restaurant on a block with a coffin was good enough for them.

I looked at Peter, impressed. He looked at his clients, waiting.

This was a job action; this was a picket line; this was a strike.

4

Well, no, not really a strike: there were only two men in this marching, shouting circle from Dragon Garden, and they no longer worked
there. They'd been fired, according to Peter, for trying to bring the
muscle of organized labor to the busboys, waiters and kitchen help,
dim sum ladies and dishwashers, even the chefs at Dragon Garden.
They'd been fired by the restaurant's owner, H. B. Yang, for organizing on behalf of the Chinese Restaurant Workers' Union, and the
Chinese Restaurant Workers' Union—tiny, newborn, and untested
though it was—was a client of Peter's.

The wait was not long. "Look," Peter said, still deadpan,
echoing himself. "Here they come."

This time, "they" was the police.

They didn't come roaring up in squad cars; the Fifth Precinct
was only two blocks away, and even the police have trouble maneuvering cars through the streets of Chinatown. Four local cops, one
of them Chinese—Kenny Bao, a Division Street kid so spectacularly
skinny we used to call him "Bean Thread"—came quick-walking
around the corner, swung right past us, and planted themselves between the pickets' circle and Dragon Garden's doors. The sergeant
among them ordered the marching men, whose chants of "Living
wage!" and "Union yes!" had grown louder at the arrival of the
police, to remove the coffin from the premises and move the whole
picket line in an orderly fashion back to the curb, where last week's
picket line had been, so as not to interfere with the lawful conduct
of business.

He shouted that twice, in a voice that sounded like he was
calling through an invisible bullhorn. He turned to Kenny Bao, who,
looking uncomfortable but determined, repeated the order in Cantonese. When the circling, chanting men responded not at all, the
sergeant nodded to one of the junior cops, a policewoman who spoke
into a police radio.

Briefly, nothing happened. For what was probably a minute,
the men continued to march and the cops continued to watch them.
Peter and I continued to watch everyone. No one touched the coffin.

Then, from down the hill, from the same direction on the
Bowery where the marchers had first appeared, an NYPD bus, wire

mesh over the windows and black smoke puffing from the tailpipe, came rolling toward us. Kenny Bao stopped traffic so the bus could U-turn in the middle of Canal Street and pull to a halt at the curb by Dragon Garden.

"That was quick," I said.

"What was?" Peter was preoccupied, his eyes on the police and his clients.

"How fast that bus got here. You'd think it was just waiting around down there."

"It probably was. The cops knew these guys were coming. They said they'd be back last week as they dispersed."

"Dispersed. Only a lawyer would actually say that word in a sentence. Anyway, Peter, last week they dispersed. How'd the cops know they wouldn't *disperse* this week?"

Peter's eyes roved the scene as though looking for something. "They probably got the word that this was going to be bigger. In fact, I wouldn't put it past one of our guys to have leaked it to them."

"Why would they do that?"

"To impress our guests with all the police attention. Although our guests don't appear to have shown up."

I squinted at Peter in the sunlight. "Guests? What guests?"

"The New York Labor Council," he told me, still looking around. "The CRWU's been courting them for months. They were going to come today, to see what the CRWU could do."

"Why?"

"The CRWU is lobbying to get to be a local of some other union that's already a member of the Labor Council. Or at least to ally with the council."

"Why?" I asked again.

"Clout," Peter said simply. "You ally with someone allied with the Teamsters, for example, suddenly the restaurants have trouble getting deliveries if your members aren't happy."

"Makes sense," I said. "That's what this was really all about?"

He nodded. "The council doesn't want to be involved with

losers. This was as much for them as for Dragon Garden, to show them the CRWU's legit and serious. But they didn't come."

I looked around, as though maybe the New York Labor Council people were in disguise and I could spot them for Peter. "Well," I said, when I couldn't, "maybe they'll catch it on the eleven o'clock news."

"Something tells me we won't make that, either. But that's why I wanted you to come: insurance, so I'd have a civilian observer in case they didn't show."

The four cops made short work of the twenty men. They were ordered once again to move, and once again they didn't. The bullhorn-voiced sergeant yelled their rights at them, translated into Cantonese by Kenny Bao and into Fukienese by the young man with the megaphone and the wire-rim glasses. The three junior cops moved among them, cuffing them with the disposable plastic handcuffs the NYPD always brings to mass-arrest situations. Some of the men, looking unsure, glanced at the megaphone man as if for instructions. In sharp, to-the-point Cantonese, and again in Fukienese, he shouted, as Kenny Bao was handcuffing him, that they should cooperate with the police but tell them nothing except their names until their lawyer arrived. Then he snapped something at Kenny Bao, maybe about the handcuffs, and pulled away from him, and I thought, What happened to 'cooperate'?

The cops loaded the men onto the bus. The bus shifted gears with what sounded like a groan of complaint, maybe at having to work on such a beautiful day. Before it could pull away, the sergeant rapped on its closing doors. Two of the cops—not including Kenny Bao—carried the coffin across the sidewalk and shoved it into the bus.

As the bus stood idling, still pluming smoke into the spring air, my eye was caught by a glint behind the restaurant's glass doors. A man stood looking at the cops, the waiters, the bus. Bright reflections half obscured his face. He was dressed in a serious gray suit, white shirt, red silk tie, with a gold tie clip, gold ring, gold watch. He didn't smile and he didn't move.

I nudged Peter. "H. B. Yang," I said.

With a lurch that brought my attention back, the bus rolled away down the Bowery. The cops headed home, toward Elizabeth Street and the Fifth Precinct. The sergeant looked grimmer than the others, but he was probably the one who was going to have to do the paperwork.

The crowd that had gathered to watch the action disorganized itself into a sidewalk full of pedestrians again within seconds. Beside me, Peter sighed a sigh of resignation. "Well, I guess I'd better get downtown and see if I can start getting them out."

"I was certainly useless," I said.

"No, you weren't. The cops would probably have beaten all their heads in if you hadn't been here watching, putting the fear of a civil suit into them."

"Uh-huh, I can just see Bean Thread Bao beating people's heads in. And does Mary know you have such a low opinion of cops?"

Peter is dating Mary Kee, my oldest friend, who happens to be a Fifth Precinct detective. I take a certain pride in having gotten Mary and Peter together—well, okay, they both had to come and rescue me from a bad situation, but anything for a friend's romantic life—and so I give myself license to tease Peter about it. Though he blushes so easily when I mention Mary that it's no challenge at all.

"Well, Mary's pretty broad-minded," he answered evenly. "Like she doesn't mind at all that some of my friends are private eyes."

I made another face at him. "Okay," I said. "Now, listen, Peter, and be serious. Doesn't it make you nervous to be going up against H. B. Yang?"

Peter gave me a wry smile. "Why, you have a problem with H. B. Yang?"

"Me? We live in perfect harmony—he has no idea I exist and I like it that way. Peter, do your guys know what they're getting into here, messing with him?"

Peter shrugged. "You have to start somewhere. Dragon Garden's huge. It's popular with the tourists, so it's a visible target. And it's rolling in money, so they can't complain that paying four-fifty an hour would put them out of business. If the union can crack Dragon Garden, they'll have a shot at the rest of the industry. It's worth a try."

He grinned the funny grin again, the one that, when we were kids, meant he'd brought two loaded water pistols to school so *I* could shoot the gym teacher, too. "Besides, it's not a bad time for this. H. B. Yang has other things on his mind."

"You mean politically? Oh, Peter, you sneaky rat. You're thinking H. B. Yang might prefer not to be embarrassed in his new role as the mayor's adviser on the East Point project?"

"Well, if he's going to keep the kind of power he's always had in Chinatown, given the way things are now, he's going to need help. It trumps the new guys that he got next to the mayor on East Point, but if he makes Hizzoner look bad, it's all over."

"The new guys" were the Fukienese power structure now blossoming in Chinatown as Chinatown spread in all directions beyond its decades-old borders to absorb the new flood of immigrants, many of them Fukienese. The new guys had their own family and village associations, their own customs, and their own leaders. They had their own dialect that we Cantonese didn't speak. Chinatown's traditional power wielders were finding, in the past few years, that the unquestioning respect they were used to from the community wasn't automatically theirs any longer from the immigrant-on-the-street; and, worse, that the politicians outside Chinatown, when they had favors to ask or offer, did not necessarily go where they had always gone.

It was war, in a smiling, bowing, back-stabbing sort of way, and an important skirmish had been fought over the position of Mayor's Adviser on Community—read, Chinatown—Participation in the East Point Project. East Point was a planned commercial development on the East River, more or less under the Manhattan Bridge, which once wasn't Chinatown but is now. Because funding for the project was coming from the state and federal governments as well as the city, the mayor wanted the community solidly behind it, no protests, no objections, no "Give us a park, not commercial high rises"; and his choice of H. B. Yang for adviser was a clear signal

9

that he thought H. B. Yang could deliver. The face H. B. Yang would gain by buddying around with the mayor would go a long distance to maintaining his position in the community, but with it would come the responsibility, which New York politicians take very seriously (though they usually phrase it differently), of providing the mayor with some big face, too.

This responsibility would not be fulfilled by job actions against the Mayor's Adviser's restaurant by workers claiming to be making a dollar an hour.

"You've driven some of H. B. Yang's customers into the arms of Duke Lo," I said to Peter. "I saw a bunch of them going to Happy Pavilion."

Duke Lo was one of the new guys, being watched closely by those who watch these things as Most Likely to Succeed. Happy Pavilion, down the street from Dragon Garden, was his base of operations, his entry in the dim sum palace horse race.

Peter shrugged, but I saw a tiny smile at the corners of his mouth. "It's a free country."

"It'll drive H. B. Yang crazy," I said. "Not only to be losing customers, but losing them to Duke Lo."

"I can't help where people have lunch."

"You haven't changed since second grade," I said. "Still refusing to speak English when the principal comes around."

"If Miss Peters had given the class Mars Bars the way I suggested, that day wouldn't have gone like that," he answered, unperturbed.

"Peter, but really, H. B. Yang doesn't worry you?"

He scratched his head and moved his broad shoulders again. "No. It's not like it used to be. Tongs and hatchet men and all that. Now men like H. B. Yang are community leaders and hang out with the mayor. It's all done in court these days. And I'm a lawyer." He looked off in the direction the bus had gone. "Listen, I have to get down there before Warren ends up with six months for contempt."

"Warren who?"

"Warren Tan. From the Clinton Street buildings. The one with the megaphone. You know him?"

I thought. "Jeremy Tan's little brother?"

"Right."

"What's he doing working in a restaurant? I thought he went to Yale."

"He did. Honors in twentieth-century American history, with his thesis on the labor movement after World War II."

"I can see this coming."

"Right. Came back and got a job as a dishwasher at the Peking Duck House and helped found the CRWU. He's the strategist for actions like this and for long-term operations. Dedicated to the struggle for workers' rights." Peter raised his head, suddenly sounding like a stirring documentary film. "Will stop at nothing until the battle's won! No sacrifice too great!" He dropped his voice back to normal. "The rest of them will keep quiet, but he'll be on a hunger strike to protest prison conditions inside of five minutes."

"Never pass up an opportunity. Except, wait a minute. Isn't there something wrong with him—his heart or something?"

Peter nodded. "Apparently he's been on borrowed time since he was two."

"Is this kind of thing good for him?"

"His feeling is, he'll do whatever he wants as long as he can. It's better than worrying all the time, he says. Luckily for the union, he's brilliant. This coffin thing was his idea. Listen, I have to go. Thanks for coming. Give my love to your mom."

"And mine to yours, and to Uncle Liang."

Peter was already walking away; he waved without turning back. He'd be spending a good part of the rest of this gorgeous day in the dingy corridors and sweat-scented rooms of Central Booking, bailing out his clients and arranging for their court appearances. As I watched his large form shambling down the Bowery I reflected, for a moment, on how lucky Mary was.

Then I turned and walked the other way, thinking about tongs, and hatchet men, and how things were really done these days.

two

and I thought that was it for the waiters. I'd done what Peter wanted, been his witness at an event that hadn't needed much witnessing. If he wanted a P.I. for anything else that had to do with the Chinese Restaurant Workers' Union, he'd call me, but the kind of lawyering he was doing for them wasn't the kind that required any investigating of anything. So the waiters and I were through.

That was how I thought about it, and that was how I conducted the rest of that glorious day, and the days that followed. I whizzed along through Battery Park City next to the river on my Rollerblades, catching the scent of the river and of the beach roses they've planted there. I read the paper and went to my brother Ted's oldest son's fifth grade play. I called other P.I.s I know, and a few lawyers, in the hope of getting some work, and when there wasn't much work I went to the dojo and practiced my roundhouse kick. I bought groceries and brought them home to my mother.

I was sitting in the living room with my mother, in fact, about a week and a half later, watching the Cantonese early-evening news, when Peter called. My mother always had high hopes for Peter: he's

Chinese, a professional, and breathing. So she handed me the red kitchen telephone and watched me through narrowed eyes as we spoke, even though she knows he's dating my oldest friend, but also because our conversation was in English, which she believes Chinese-speaking children only use to hide things from their mothers.

"Lydia? I think I have a big problem," Peter said to me.

"You think you have it, or you think it's big?"

"Both. Can you come down?"

"To your office?" I glanced at my mother. "Ma has this chicken—"

"Tell her you're eating with me."

"Am I?"

He sighed. "If that's what it takes."

"She'll be on the phone to Mary's mother before the door shuts behind me."

"I'll fix it later. Will you come?"

"You know I can't resist riding in on a white horse to rescue a desperate lawyer."

"Please, Lydia." He sighed again. "If I'm right, this isn't funny."

"I'm sorry. Are you all right?"

"Me? Sure. Meet me at the office. We'll go around the corner."

So I slipped on my leather jacket and kissed my mother on the cheek, her complaints about her chicken only perfunctory in the face of my having been invited to dinner by a living unmarried Chinese male.

Peter's office was on the second floor of a building on the corner of Mott and Pell, above his Uncle Lee Liang's crammed import shop and about three steps from our apartment on Mosco Street. He was stacking papers and turning off lights when I got there. Jacketless in what I thought of as the cool of the evening, he locked up and followed me back down the stairs.

When Peter says "around the corner" he means "down the block" at No. 8 Pell Street, a restaurant with no more name than that. Why do you need a name, the owner, Shen Chiang, had asked totally rhetorically when he set the place up, when your address is a lucky number? Peter had helped him with the endless paperwork it takes to open a restaurant in New York, at a time when Mr. Shen needed all his ready cash—and all his cousins' ready cash—to get the establishment going. The agreement was that Peter would take it out in trade, and though I was sure that by now Peter had eaten his way through an entire restaurant chain, Mr. Shen not only welcomed him and his guests with glowing smiles every time he went but actually appeared offended if he ever heard that Peter had eaten somewhere else.

No. 8 Pell Street has another peculiarity, too. Along with the various city licenses that grant a business permission to operate, Chinatown has another set of required permits, unwritten but just as vital. The entire neighborhood is carved up, divided into turfs. Gangs—sometimes tong related, sometimes not—are the acknowledged holders of these territories. The gang controlling the turf your place is in acts like a feudal lord: your loyalty, expressed in protection dollars, guarantees smooth daily operation uninterrupted by pipes that mysteriously burst in your basement or armed men who mysteriously burst through your front door. If your uncle is a city councilman you might be able to avoid paying cash, although you will carry, then, a different kind of debt; but otherwise, everyone belongs to some feudal lord, and everyone pays.

With a very few exceptions. Because, among the various lords, disputes of various natures can't help but arise, it's useful to have a place to sit down and discuss things before deciding whether the Uzis and AK-47s are called for. No Chinatown gangster trusts another, so dropping in on one another is out of the question. Thus has arisen the need for places with no loyalties—not to the gangs, and not to the police, either.

No. 8 Pell Street is one of maybe half a dozen Chinatown eateries that fills this need. Interestingly, in a neighborhood with as many basement and second-floor restaurants as street-level ones, all the neutral places open directly onto the sidewalk and have huge windows. No one owned No. 8 Pell Street except Shen Chiang, and no one was turned away.

Which might be just as well, I reflected, if Peter's union succeeded in organizing the restaurants of Chinatown. At least Peter would still have a place to eat.

At No. 8 Pell Street, handshakes and greetings and long-time-haven't-seen-yous were exchanged, Peter and I were seated, and the first blue-and-white pot of jasmine-scented tea was rushed to our table.

"I heard my mom dialing Mary's mom as I left the apartment," I told Peter while he poured me a cup of tea. "Actually, she calls about once a week to sympathize with Mary's mom about how you'll never be a partner in a major firm or make a lot of money or anything."

"I won't?"

"But tonight," I said, "you can bet she's offering her sympathy that things aren't going so well between you two, and such a nice boy, that Lee Bi-Da." I gave Peter's name the full treatment, as though I'd been speaking Chinese. I wasn't; in spite of all the years of Chinese school and the need to speak Chinese at home, Peter and I are both more comfortable in English.

"Between me and Mary? They're not going well?"

"Well, obviously they're not, or you wouldn't be out to dinner with me."

Peter nodded, put down the teapot, and perused the menu, which I was sure he must have memorized by now. Mr. Shen came over to recommend, beaming as though he'd harvested them himself, the particular freshness of today's scallops. So we ordered them, along with a platter of sauteed watercress with fermented tofu. Then, munching on the crispy strips of noodle and the inch-long, deep-fried, pepper-sprinkled strings of dried fish No. 8 Pell Street gives you for starters, we got down to business.

"One of my guys has disappeared," Peter told me.

"One of your guys?"

"From the union. One of the organizers, the only one they still had inside Dragon Garden."

"I thought they'd been fired."

"Two of them. They hadn't caught on to the third one yet. His name's Chi-Chun Ho. He's been here about three years."

"What do you mean, disappeared?"

"He hasn't shown up for work for the last two days."

"Umm." I dipped a pinch of tiny fish into Mr. Shen's fiery mustard while I thought. "He couldn't just have gotten another job?"

"The union had a strategy meeting Tuesday night; he wasn't there. No one had seen him, and when they tried to call, no one answered."

A slight pause in Peter's voice before "no one answered" made me look up. "No one?"

"He lives in a basement apartment in Elmhurst with three other men from Dragon Garden, two other waiters and a busboy. Named"—he pulled a scrap of paper from his shirt pocket—"Yuan Lee, Song Chan, and Gai-Lo Lu. Not with the union, just men who work there. Anyway, no one answered."

"And the others—?"

"Haven't been to work either."

"Oh," I said. "But, Peter—"

I stopped as our oil-dipped scallops, glistening in a plump white mound and surrounded by thick slabs of black mushroom, were settled on our table next to a platter of emerald watercress. A clay casserole full of fragrant, steaming rice and a Chinese beer for Peter followed, and then the tide of waiters receded and we were alone again.

"Peter," I said, "what do the cops think?"

Peter placed serving spoons in each dish, all their handles pointing in my direction. I reached for the rice, dolloped a mound into the center of my plate.

"Nothing," he said.

"They think nothing?"

"There's no crime. Four immigrants not showing up for work; they're not impressed."

"You called Missing Persons?"

"Sure, but all they could tell me was that he's not in the morgue. No Asians this week at all."

16

Peter and I both knew what that meant: nothing. Missing Persons doesn't look; they just keep track of the unidentified dead who've been found. If there weren't any anonymous Asian bodies in the morgue, it only meant that none had been turned over to the NYPD for ID if possible. If ID wasn't possible, then they'd be buried, courtesy of the city, on Hart Island, that breezy place in the East River where all the unknown dead spend eternity together.

"What about Mary?" I asked Peter. "I mean, dating a cop must have some advantages."

"It does," he agreed, helping himself to mushrooms. "She asked the local precinct out there if they'd send someone around this afternoon, as a favor, just to check the place, and they did. But they said everything seemed normal."

"They got inside?"

"No. No one was there to let them in, and they didn't have a warrant or probable cause. They wandered around, looked through the windows. Everything seemed in order."

"That was it? That's an investigation? Didn't they even ask the landlord to let them in?"

"No one answered the landlord's doorbell upstairs. Though one of the cops swears someone was home."

"Well, but maybe it's an illegal apartment and they thought the cops had come to arrest them for that. The landlord's Chinese?"

He nodded.

That made sense. Although twenty years ago Elmhurst was Archie Bunker territory, now it's one of New York's most ethnically mixed neighborhoods. New immigrants—Chinese, Dominican, Colombian, Pakistani—flock there and live three or four to a room in illegal apartments in what are supposed to be one- or two-family houses. Renting these apartments is a big business in Elmhurst, and it's an ethnic business; both landlords and tenants seem to feel safer speaking the same language. You can think of it as middle-class oppressors preying on their newly arrived countrymen, or as the first generation giving a vital though societally unacceptable boost to newcomers, whichever suits you.

"And the four of them," I said to Peter, "including your guy, are they illegals?"

"My guy isn't, and one of the others. I didn't ask about the other two."

"Hmm. In my experience, lawyers only don't ask a question when they already know the answer and they don't like it."

Peter raised his eyebrows but didn't deny my point.

I popped a piece of scallop and a slice of mushroom into my mouth. I could taste the ocean, bright and wide and salty, in the sweet silkiness of the scallop, and the chewy thick mushroom was redolent of the dark, musty earth.

I said, "You're afraid something bad's happened to Ho because Dragon Garden found out about his union work?"

Peter shook his head as he swallowed some beer. "Not exactly. I told you, it's not done that way anymore. Violence is messy and hard to explain away. I don't think they'd bother. It's too easy just to fire people and then blackball them so they can't work. Then they leave town and you don't have to worry about it anymore."

"Then . . . ?"

"Well, Chi-Chun Ho might not know that. He might have been threatened, and the other guys with him just because they room together. They might have disappeared because of that."

"No violence, but threats?" I asked skeptically.

"The antiunion forces," Peter said, delicately not mentioning any names, such as H. B. Yang, for example, "would know that a guy like Ho wouldn't know that. If that happened and that's why they disappeared I want to know about it. It'll help our side. And maybe the poor guy's on the run when he doesn't have to be."

"But the other two organizers at Dragon Garden were fired, you said. They weren't threatened, were they?"

"No."

"Then why would Ho have been?"

"I don't know. I don't know if I'm right to be worried. That's what I wanted to talk to you about."

I went for some watercress, scooped up some chunks of vinegary bean curd with it. "Okay," I said.

Peter looked up over his glasses. "Okay, what?"

"Okay, I'll check it out."

"No," he said. "Wait. That's not the point."

"What's not?"

"For you to get involved in this."

I gestured around our table, at the diminished mounds of scallops and watercress, the depleted bowl of rice. "I thought it was exactly the point. You buy dinner; I find your guy."

"Lydia, come on. Mary would kill me if I hired you for this."

"You hire me all the time."

"But this—Lydia, these guys have disappeared. I don't think it means anything bad, but we have to consider that it could. This could be dangerous. You might . . ."

He trailed off, so I finished for him. "I might go chasing out to Elmhurst and get myself killed?"

"Well, Lydia, it wouldn't be—"

"Don't start. I did you and Mary a major favor that time."

"Mary would be the first to agree. She just wants to make sure you come to our wedding before we go to your funeral."

I stopped, a mushroom halfway to my mouth. "Wedding?"

"Hey, just metaphorically. Just in a manner of speaking."

Oh, sure. And the sudden burgundy flush of Peter's face behind his thick glasses was just a reflection off the neon sign in the window. And his sudden consuming interest in his glass of beer was just idle curiosity. And I was the Monkey King's uncle.

"You know," I said, "you're lucky your problem intrigues me more than your love life. Though not very much more, I might add."

"Please. Can we leave my love life out of it?"

"Fat chance. But we can put it off long enough for you to tell me what it is you *do* want me to do."

"I want *you* to tell *me* what to do."

"About your love life?"

"Lydia! About Chi-Chun Ho."

"And what do you mean, tell you what to do?"

"To find the guy. How would you go about it? What should I do next? Should I hire someone? Should I—"

"Peter." I put down my chopsticks, spoke slowly to my old friend. "Peter, who exactly would you hire if you didn't hire me?"

"Well, I . . ." The wine tint was back in his face, but the reason was different this time. "I guess I hadn't gotten that far."

"Uh-huh. And why exactly, if you did hire someone, would it not be me?"

"Oh, please, Lydia." Behind the glasses Peter's eyes looked panicky. "Mary—"

"Mary. My best and oldest friend. And I'm sitting here with possibly my second best and certainly my second oldest friend. And you asked me here to get advice on what I would do if you hired me to do what I do so you can go get someone else to do it?"

"Lydia, don't look at me that way."

"Peter, you're kidding me, right? I'll just decide you're kidding me."

I nodded in a satisfied sort of way and went back to my watercress and my scallop-sauced rice.

"Oh, Lydia . . ." Peter trailed off, unhappily, and drank some beer. I kept eating. "But . . ." he said. I kept eating. "I . . ." More eating.

"Okay." He sighed. "I know when I'm licked."

three

I left Peter among the ruins of our dinner and headed over to the Mott Street address he'd given me. Propriety demanded he spend some time chatting with Mr. Shen, and under normal circumstances I would have stayed and done the same. But I had a case to work, albeit for a client who had to be steely-eyed into giving me the address of *his* client and practically strong-armed into calling over there to say I was coming. It was already a few minutes past eight, and I didn't want to take the chance of finding no one there.

Although according to Peter it was a small chance: Warren Tan, twenty-two-year-old honors Yale grad, dedicated organizer, brilliant union strategist, was always there.

And he was when I arrived. The chipped plastic directory nailed to the side of the Mott Street building listed the occupants of the basement space as "Restaurant Workers" in English, the Chinese characters adding "Chinese." No one mentioned "Union." I went down the areaway stairs and knocked on the only door I found there, a scratched painted-steel thing with a tiny peephole.

It was opened, after my second try, by a thin young man with wire-rim glasses and buzz-cut hair. He seemed to be bouncing on the balls of his feet, not quite standing still, as he said, "Yes?"

"I'm Lydia Chin," I told him. "You're Warren Tan, right? Peter Lee called to say I'd be coming over?" I added, "I know your brother Jeremy."

"You're the detective?"

"That's right."

"Can I see some ID?"

So brother Jeremy's not enough, I thought, as I took my license from my wallet and handed it to Warren Tan. Of course, if I were lying about being Lydia Chin, I might be lying about knowing Jeremy, too.

Since most people have no idea what a New York State investigator's license looks like, I always wonder why they ask for it; I could show them anything. Sometimes I do. In this case, however, I handed Warren Tan the real thing, and he ran his quick eyes over both sides of it, actually reading it, expiration date and all.

"I had to check," he said—by way, it seemed to me, of explanation but not apology—as he handed it back. His words were quick, too, as though, having thought of them, saying them was just a mechanical necessity to be gotten out of the way as fast as possible. "I think I remember you, actually. You were in chem lab with Jeremy in high school."

"That wasn't my fault," I said hastily. "He was the one who wanted to see what happened if you added the yellow stuff to the blue stuff."

Warren Tan's face lit with a grin. "Funny," he said. "Jeremy always said it was you. Come on in." He stood aside so I could enter the offices of the Chinese Restaurant Workers' Union.

The place was a single small, low-ceilinged room, with a painted concrete floor and one too many glaring overhead lights. The battered file cabinets, chairs, and desks looked like refugees from a used-furniture dump. Not that you could see most of them, covered as they were with files, papers, newspapers, and white take-out containers, which scented the air with stale garlic and yesterday's sesame oil. My mother would have sniffed that this was what happened when

22

men set up housekeeping without women. In my heart I tended to agree with her, although her solution—that I should marry one of them and civilize him—was not, to me, the logical next step.

Warren Tan lifted files off a folding chair for me, one of four around a table that had probably seen more mah-jongg games than someone's old auntie could count before it was donated to this cause. His eyes darted around for a place to put the files; then he gave up. Sprawling in an even more rickety chair than mine, he balanced them on his lap. His shirtsleeves were rolled up above the elbow; he had, I noticed, well-muscled forearms.

"What can I do for you?" he asked.

I said, "You know I'm here because of Chi-Chun Ho."

"Yes."

"I just wondered if you had any ideas where he and the others might have gone."

He shook his head. "Sorry."

"Or why."

Warren Tan cocked his head and, as though reminding me of the obvious, said, "Ho's a union organizer."

"You think what Peter thinks, then? That they ran because they were threatened or something?"

"That's what Peter thinks," he corrected me. "I think 'ran' is too big an assumption."

"You think something's happened to them?"

He met my gaze directly as he said, "It's always a risk being in at the beginning of a union. Here more than most places."

"I don't know," I said, glancing around the paper-blizzarded, too-bright office. "Peter says it's not done that way anymore."

Warren Tan gave me the quick smile again, this time with an ironic tinge. "Peter's great," he said. "He thinks the law can out-maneuver the bad guys. And in the end," he said, shifting in his chair, keeping the files in his lap by some fast grabbing, "he's probably right. I think we'll win, because we have to. But for now, the bad guys have a lot of moves."

"Including threats?"

He gestured around the office with a sweep of the hand that

took in the room, the union it housed, Chinatown. "Most of these guys are new here, some without papers. They're in pretty desperate situations, a lot of them, and even the ones who're legal are used to the way things were done in China. You can see them being intimidated, turning tail and running, even if Peter's right and the threats are empty."

"And you're not so sure he's right."

"No."

"Has the union been threatened?"

Warren Tan nodded. "Sure. Every major restaurant owner would like to see us disappear. One of them offered to chop me up and serve me as shiu mai."

"But he didn't."

"I don't think so." He grinned.

"Anyone in particular making threats lately?"

He pursed his lips and shook his head. "I don't imagine we're real popular with H. B. Yang these days. But he doesn't have to be direct anymore."

"He doesn't? Why not?"

"With this East Point thing, he's under the covers with some serious heavies. Peter must have told you about the NYLC?"

"The what?"

"New York Labor Council. We've been talking to them for months. They were all set to take us on. Now suddenly they won't even take my calls."

I remembered back to the sunny street corner, the demonstration, and the guests who hadn't shown up. "You think H. B. Yang is behind that?"

"A friend of mine over there told me as much over an unofficial beer. There's still community opposition to East Point, you know. The mayor appointed H. B. Yang to smooth that over—that's what being the Mayor's Adviser is all about. Until the community's satisfied, the state won't throw in its share, and until it does the project won't move. And the NYLC's construction trade members have an interest in it moving."

"And H. B. Yang can stop it dead."

24

He shook his head. "He won't go that far. He wants the mayor to see him as a man who can deliver. But he can deliver faster or more slowly, easier or harder."

"So what do you mean, then?"

"Well, he *could* insist on concessions from the unions as the price of community peace. He could demand, for example, that the construction unions take on Chinese workers. Other communities demand that, and they get it. Or, on the other hand, he could tell Chinatown how fabulous this new commercial center will be, and to think how much money it will bring to our restaurants and stores, and to sit down and shut up. He seems to be going that route, but don't think there's not something in it for him."

"And that something is the NYLC abandoning your union?"

"It would make a big difference to him, and what does it cost them? They weren't so sure they wanted us anyway. It's not like we're real red-blooded Americans or anything."

"They don't really say that?"

"Oh, of course not, but you know they think it. Yerrow people, eat lice, talk funny, ah-so, math geniuses, go correge, their kids get better jobs than my kids, to hell with them."

He shrugged. I didn't have an answer, so I asked another question. "What you need from the NYLC—clout, Peter called it—can you get it somewhere else?"

"What we need," Warren Tan said, "is to be so visible we can't be ignored. And yes. If the NYLC won't help us, we'll do it ourselves."

"How?"

"Tomorrow night, for example." Pinning down the files in his lap with one arm, he rummaged on a desk, yanked out a red-paper flyer a lot like the one from the coffin demonstration. "We proved we could disrupt the dim sum business. Now we're going to show we can louse up dinner, too."

I read the flyer. It called, in English and Chinese, for a demonstration the next night, Friday, in front of Dragon Garden. "There might be banquets," I said. "Family dinners. Friday's a big night."

"That's the point. Every member we can get together will be

there. I called the media; this is our first night action, so they might even come.''

"Do you think you can get a big enough crowd to make a difference?''

"In H. B. Yang's pocketbook? No. In the restaurant owners' perception of us? Maybe. If not this time, next time. Or the time after. We have a lot of plans. A lot of actions coming up. But there's no next time without this time.''

I looked once more at the snowbanks of papers, the dusty, low-hanging overhead pipes, and thought about the difference between this place and the hushed halls of Yale. I asked Warren Tan what I'd asked Peter. "Doesn't it bother you to be going up against H. B. Yang?''

Warren Tan sat forward so abruptly that two of his files slipped to the floor. "No. We have to take Chinatown back from those guys. It's time.''

"Take it back?''

His eyes glittered as he said, "It's over, the way they used to run things. The ways they brought from China, where a few old men have all the power and that's okay with everyone as long as we're taken care of. Where Chinatown runs separately from the rest of the city, like Hong Kong used to run separately from China. It's time for Chinatown to reunite with America.''

The air was electric with his excitement. I couldn't help grinning. "Is that one of your recruiting speeches?''

"It's one of my best. Don't you think it's true? You must. You're still here.''

"Here, in Chinatown? I was born here.''

"You didn't have to stay here. Your brothers didn't, right? Jeremy moved out. Lots of people move out. But you're still here. Like Peter. You must feel it: it's our turn.''

"Our turn?''

"To take over. To run things. To actually bring these guys into the American dream''—he waved his arm around the room— "instead of throwing them crumbs and telling them how lucky they are and to work hard so their children can do well.''

"Is that why you're doing this?" I asked. "So you can run things? I don't believe that."

He shook his head impatiently. "Not me. Us. All of us, not a small crowd of old men. Look at us: educated, healthy, middle-class *Americans*. Our folks lived hard lives so we could be that. There's got to be more to it than a Rolex and a loft with a river view for all they gave up. My dad's gone. I can't pay him back for what he did any way but this: by fighting for these guys."

"Taking care of your ancestors," I said softly. "The ABC way."

Warren Tan looked at me, then picked up the fallen files and sat back in his chair. "You're right," he said. "Damn, but you're right. You see? You never stop being Chinese, no matter how American you are. Come on. Don't you want to be part of it? Bringing Chinatown into the USA?"

I met his gleaming eyes. "The only thing," I said slowly, "that I want to be part of right now is finding Chi-Chun Ho and his roommates. If that helps your cause, I won't object. But I have a job to do."

He was quiet for a moment. We both were, as heels clicked by the sidewalk-level window and water flowed in the overhead pipes. "Okay." He smiled. "It will help, even if that's not why you're doing it. From each according to his means. You have more questions for me?"

"Yes," I said. The electric moment passed. "Can you tell me anything about the men who disappeared? Anything at all might help."

Warren Tan ran a hand over his bristling hair, came back to the everyday. "The only ones I know are Ho and Song Chan. And I don't know much about them. They room together, but you know that."

My eyebrows went up. "You know Song Chan? Is he a union member? Peter didn't tell me that."

"No. A sympathizer, but he won't join. Peter probably doesn't even know. Chan comes around and does grunt work, stuffing envelopes, folding flyers, even makes contributions out of his two bucks an hour, but we can't get him to sign up."

"Isn't that peculiar?"

"Unfortunately not. We have a bunch like that. Mostly they're scared, though I don't get that vibe off Chan. But we don't push. Whatever they can do."

"And you don't know the others, Yuan Lee and Gai-Lo Lu?"

"No."

"Friends, co-workers, girlfriends?"

"No one I know. You might check around at Dragon Garden, if anyone will talk to you."

"They will. I'll find a way."

"That's what you do, huh?" he said.

"What?"

"Find a way. We're alike like that, that's why I recognize it. Yours is more private—maybe solitary's a better word—but that's what we both do: find a way. So now tell me: why do *you* do what you do?"

"Me?" I surprised myself by telling him the truth. "I have four older brothers. All my life I felt like no one would ever tell me what was going on. This way it's my job to find out."

That brought the grin back. "You like it?"

"A lot." I felt my cheeks redden. Well, gee, Lydia, I thought, just because you just told this almost-total stranger your deepest stuff is no reason to go getting embarrassed.

"Listen," I said. "If that's all you can tell me . . ."

"I could tell you all sorts of stuff," he said, still grinning. "But that's all I know about those four guys. You sure you don't want to join the revolution?"

"Not right now," I said. "Thanks." I stood to go.

"Invitation's open," he said. "Anytime."

Warren Tan walked me the three steps to the office door, still holding his armful of files. "Thanks," I said, and shook his hand. He grinned a final time and closed the steel door behind me.

I trotted up the stairs and back onto the streets of Chinatown. I paused on the sidewalk to look around as though I hadn't seen the place before. Then I headed home.

four

the next morning found me in Elmhurst, Queens. It was a bright, breezy, suburban sort of morning, and I walked along a peaceful grid of tree-lined streets between semidetached houses of red brick and beige brick and vinyl made to look like wood. Some of the trees had yellow-green leaves just unfurling, and some had gone further than that, waving big shady canopies over the sidewalks, practicing for when summer came.

The street didn't need their help to stay cool on this windy day, but I was grateful for it. The uniform jacket I'd wheedled out of my cousin Luke last night, with an absolute promise to claim I'd bought it at a yard sale if any trouble happened—and a promise to take him for drinks at the restaurant at the top of the World Trade Center, trouble or not—was made for colder days than this. "Well, I can't lend you the light one," he'd reasoned. "I have to actually work tomorrow." And the box I was lugging was full of flashlights and wrenches and pliers and things like that, which my mother had complained about my taking as I'd loaded them up the night before, even though she has never in recorded history held one of them in her hand.

"What if one of your brothers comes here to fix something? He can't if you have all those things out with you," she'd said as I'd clicked the box shut.

"Is anything broken, Ma?"

"No." She shook her head.

"Okay, well, I promise you nothing will break until I get back with the tools." I'd kissed her good-night and hauled the box into my bedroom as she squinted after me, probably thinking of the dire consequences to follow if the bathroom faucet, affronted by the arrogance of my guarantee, chose the next morning to begin to drip.

Anyway, maybe she was right. The toolbox was only insurance anyhow, just a costume accessory. I was the one beginning to drip, with sweat. The box was getting seriously heavy by the time I reached the house where, according to Peter, Chi-Chun Ho and three other workers from Dragon Garden lived in the basement.

The house was no different from others on the block: two small rectangles of treeless front lawn bisected by a straight cement walk led to the steps and the red-painted door. A driveway on the left ended in a garage. On the right, the house shared a wall with the house beside it. I stood for a moment, looking it over, then crossed the street and headed up the walk.

At the top of the steps I rang the bell. A few moments' wait, then the door half opened and a woman's face peered out. "Yes?"

That one word sounded Cantonese-accented to me, and she certainly looked Chinese. So, speaking English, I thickened my own accent, normally imperceptible, I'm told, to all but the most serious linguists among us. "Cable TV." I whipped out the ID I'd run off last night at the twenty-four-hour color-copy-and-laminating place.

She frowned, checked out the ID, my uniform jacket, my navy-blue pants, and my sensible shoes, and said again, "Yes?"

"Ah, problems in whole neighborhood. My partner, around the corner, with truck." I eyed her, switched languages. "Do you speak Chinese?" If I was right, "Chinese" would mean "Cantonese" to her, as it did to me.

She nodded. "Chinese," she said, Cantonese-fashion, sounding relieved. She continued in the ancestral tongue. "We aren't having trouble with the cable TV."

"No, the trouble is over on the Avenue." I gestured vaguely over my shoulder in the direction of the sounds of traffic. "But my partner has instructed me to check some houses where he thinks it might be coming from." I put down my toolbox—a welcome relief—and took a small notebook from my jacket pocket. I flipped it open and stepped back to check the number on her house, then closed it again. "Liu, is that right? May I please check your connections?"

She pursed her lips. "We aren't having trouble."

"Please," I said nervously. "I just got this job. My partner has a lot of seniority. I have to do what he tells me or I'll get fired."

I could see her soften. Being Chinese, she would have a hard time letting herself come between a worker and her boss's orders.

"Please," I said again. "It will just take a few minutes. Just a fast look at each TV." I flipped open the notebook again. "My records show you have cable on the first floor, upstairs, also in the basement. Very quick. No mess," I added.

Still she frowned.

"Oh." I let my eyes light up as though I'd caught on. "You have people living in the basement?"

Her face froze with suspicion.

"Don't worry about it." I grinned, lowering my voice conspiratorially, even though we were still speaking Chinese and even though there wasn't another human being on the street. "My mother has three people in our old garage in Flushing. After all, you have to make a living. Times are so hard."

She nodded in flint-faced agreement.

"That's why I need this job," I said. I almost added "To help out my mother," but I'd probably be struck by lightning if I used my mother in a lie. "I won't even *see* anything else down there except the TV," I told her. I looked over my shoulder anxiously, as though scanning the street for my partner's truck.

She frowned again, but then she nodded. I moved past her as

she held the door; she shut it behind me. She gestured me to the left, and I went that way, into a sky-blue-carpeted living room with brocade-slipcovered furniture and some really ugly three-dimensional landscapes made out of shells hanging on the walls. The TV wasn't hard to find; it was huge, filling the center of a wall of shelves, each of which held one or at most two showcased shell-encrusted items: statues or reliefs or bookends with no books between them.

"You have a lovely home," I told Mrs. Liu, setting down my box. "With times the way they are, you must be as skilled a home-maker as my mother, to keep things like this."

That was using my mother, but it wasn't a lie—at least, the part about my mother wasn't—so I didn't worry about the lightning.

"Everything is dusty," Mrs. Liu said, rejecting the compliment, which meant I had hit my target with it and she was flattered. "I wasn't expecting anyone."

"Of course not, with how busy you must be. I do appreciate your letting me in. I won't be long."

Mrs. Liu watched as I swiveled the TV on its revolving stand, poked at its wires, scribbled in my notebook. I opened my toolbox and took out a device I've seen my brother Elliot use. Elliot is responsible for electric repairs at our apartment; Ted does the plumbing and Andrew does anything that requires hammers and nails. Tim, of course, is totally useless.

Elliot uses this gadget to determine whether a circuit is live or not. I touched its ends to the place where the cable came into the box and to some other place, then turned on the TV and did it again, wondering whether I'd get electrocuted. I didn't, so I packed up the box and gave Mrs. Liu a reassuring smile. "This one's fine."

She took me up the stairs to the bedroom, past shell reliefs mounted on the walls. I was prepared for the bedroom to be Shell Central, even hoped for shell-covered nightstands and a shell-studded four-poster bed, but when we got there there wasn't a shell in sight, just the sky-blue carpet, simple gauzy drapes, and some family pho-tographs. I wondered what that meant in the lives of Mr. and Mrs. Liu, and decided never to ask. It took just a few minutes to go through the same rigamarole with the bedroom TV, and then we were ready for the apartment in the basement.

Mrs. Liu took me into the kitchen, down a few steps and out the side door onto the driveway, and immediately to another door right next to it. She knocked; nothing happened while we waited. She knocked again.

"Are your tenants home at this time of day?" I asked.

Mrs. Liu answered, "I don't know when they're here. We don't hear them coming or going. They probably left for work early today, as they usually do."

"Are they nice?" I asked. "The men who live in our garage seem to be nice, but they speak Fukienese, so nobody understands them."

"Nice?" She looked at me a little blankly. "I suppose. They pay their rent on time."

"They speak Cantonese?" I gave her a smile. "That makes it so much easier than it is for my mother."

"No," she corrected me, so I wouldn't think she had it any easier than anyone. "Three of them speak Fukienese, one also speaks Mandarin. My husband learned Mandarin during the war, so we can get by. Of course, they all speak some English, but mostly only the names of dishes at the restaurant they work in. All but one of them can read, also write, in Chinese."

The many dialects of the Chinese language are so different that they're mutually incomprehensible when spoken—not like British English and American English, but more like French and Spanish, where the structure is similar but all the words are different. But written Chinese characters have no phonetic content and always have the same meaning. That's how two Chinese people from the far ends of the country can communicate, and always have, provided they're both literate. Speaking the same sentence, they'll sound like gibbering idiots to each other; but if they write it down, they can smilingly agree and walk like brothers, arm in arm.

It didn't surprise me that three of these men could read and write and the fourth couldn't. Three waiters and a busboy.

I watched Mrs. Liu's face sidelong as she took out a key ring and put a key in the lock. Maybe she was blandly lying, and she knew all four of her tenants had hopped the night plane to San Francisco; maybe she knew they were sprawled in a pool of blood at the bottom of the basement steps. I thought back to her pursed-lip nervousness when I'd first proposed that she let me in, and to her decision to let me in anyway.

When she had the door opened Mrs. Liu knocked again and called downstairs. No answer came, so she switched on a light and we headed down.

The basement was different. No sky-blue carpet, no knick-knacks, no gauzy drapes. The glare of fluorescent lights totally defeated the daylight drifting dispiritedly through a row of small windows near the ceiling to reveal a large single room, smelling faintly of old garlic and oil and the mustiness of basements. The room was vinyl tiled and divided down the middle by the row of steel posts that held up the house. Blankets strung from clotheslines between the posts half hid the four beds on the other side. On this side, a rickety-looking bridge table and four folding chairs stood next to a sink and a hot plate. A line of open shelves on the wall held a mismatched collection of plates, mugs, and silver. Next to the shelves, pinned to the wall, was a four-color calendar from a Chinese grocery store in Flushing, plum blossoms framing a painted pagoda. Two shabby Naugahyde chairs and a broken-down sofa were arranged around a threadbare rug. They faced a TV.

I breathed the still, musty air, trying to feel what it would be like to live here. Maybe this was a place of optimism and excitement, a first new home in the new world, the first step up Gold Mountain for these men and so for their families back home. Maybe they sat around at night and laughed and talked about what they would do when their debts to those who'd brought them here were paid off, when they could bring over their wives and brothers and mothers from China, buy their own houses like this one, and send their kids to college. Maybe they got up early, eager for the new day, their fresh chance to make a new life.

Maybe; but this shabby room felt to me like a sad place, a

place no one would come to, no one would stay in, if he didn't think he had to.

Mrs. Liu, arms folded, nodded at the TV, in case I hadn't seen it. She pursed her lips, waiting for me to begin.

I set down my toolbox, wiggled the TV's wires, scribbled in my notebook. I took out Elliot's circuit tester, touched its ends to things, turned on the TV, touched things again.

I frowned. Around at the front of the TV, I switched cable channels, first with the remote, which I found on the bridge table, and then with the button on the TV. I went around behind again and poked things, and scribbled in my notebook some more.

I looked up at Mrs. Liu. "I think this may be it," I said with excitement in my voice. "How wonderful that would be, if I were the one to find the trouble! Me, so new on the job!" I turned back to the TV, trying to look as though it held my glorious future career in its electronic innards. "Can you help me?" I asked Mrs. Liu.

Her lips pursed again. "Help you to do what?"

I spoke a little breathlessly. "I need you to go upstairs, to turn on the other TVs, one at a time. You leave one on for a minute, turn it off for thirty seconds, then on again for another minute. Then you do the same for the other. Normally my partner would help me do this part," I added, to sidestep her hesitation, "but it would be so good for me if I found the trouble before I called him. Please, Big Sister? My family would be in your debt."

That wasn't exactly using my mother, I reasoned with myself. Besides, if Mrs. Liu helped me and I helped Peter and that helped my career as a P.I., it would sort of even be true.

Meeting my eyes, Mrs. Liu gave in. With a small smile of Chinese sisterhood she left the room.

That gave me a total of five minutes if she followed instructions. I began what I'd come to do.

Parting the blanket curtain, I moved to the beds. I pawed through the mismatched side tables—well, three side tables and a battered file cabinet—that separated them. I sorted through the meager possessions of men who'd come here with nothing and lived with no privacy, who had deliberately left behind on the other side of the globe exactly what the rest of us make sure we have with us when we leave home every morning: driver's licenses and passports, student IDs and library cards, the things that tie us into a family, a town, a place, a history.

Two of these men were illegals and couldn't afford any of that. The other two might have come here legally but left China illegally, might have gone through five other countries where they didn't have papers on their way here, might just be in the habit, as so many of the new immigrants were, of not leaving paper pieces of themselves where they could be found. I wasn't looking for that and didn't expect to find it. I didn't even know if Chi-Chun Ho was Peter's client's real name, but it didn't matter. What I was looking for was something that would lead me into the pattern of the lives they were living now—a name, a phone number, an address scrawled on a scrap of paper: anything that would take me beyond the opening move on the board Peter had laid out for me, the place where he'd gotten stuck, this small-windowed, musty room.

I sped through the shelves and drawers, finding socks, handkerchiefs, changes of underwear. There were occasional photos: smiling young women, somber older ones, cheerful skinny young men. I found an airmail envelope from China addressed to Song Chan. The letter was gone, if there had been one; maybe the envelope came holding only the photograph in it now, of a laughing woman sitting in the shadow of a pine tree, with a toddler by her side. I closed the drawer I'd found it in, feeling myself an intruder into a life this man didn't even really want to be living. The thought depressed me. Why couldn't this man, this Song Chan, be home with this woman and her child, laughing in the cool breeze from the pines, instead of in a damp and smelly basement in a strange land on the other side of the planet with their photograph in a drawer?

I shook myself mentally. Or not in that basement, Lydia, I pointed out. You've been hired—over the strenuous objections of your own client, I might add—to find out why he's *not* here, and three other men not here with him, not to ponder the inequities of the human condition as you observe it. Get back to work.

So I did. I couldn't tell if anything was missing, if what I was looking at was half these men's underwear supply or everything they owned. I looked around the sink and found soap but no toothbrushes. That was a good sign, at least indicating the men had gone away voluntarily; people who choose to go away, even in a great hurry, almost always take their toothbrushes.

Unless the Dragon Garden waiters and the busboy were so newly out of some seriously downtrodden backwater-type Chinese village that they didn't use toothbrushes.

I took a quick glance into the bathroom. It had no sink—the one in the main room was the only one—and the rust holes in the dinged metal stall shower matched the rust streaks in the toilet bowl. It smelled musty and damp, and the cracked linoleum floor was curling at the edges. I didn't want to think about what might be under it. Four towels hung from two old towel racks. I touched them; all dry.

Scurrying over to a makeshift hanging rack—a pipe, swinging on wires from a higher pipe—I started sticking my fingers in the pockets of the few pairs of pants and shirts there. My five minutes was almost up and I'd found nothing to help. Mrs. Liu would be back any moment. As I had that thought I heard her footsteps creak across the kitchen floor above me, heading for the side door. My heart pounded; I squeezed the clothes together like an accordion to stop the rack from swaying. I checked for my notebook and circuit tester, ready to give up the search for something to connect these men to the world outside and to turn back into Lydia Chin, Girl Cable TV Man.

Then I heard another sound, the ring of a doorbell. The footsteps above me stopped, then turned and went back the way they'd come.

Relief washed over me, and I wished a winning lottery ticket on whoever had rung the bell. I flipped rapidly through the garments on the rack, sticking my hand in more pockets, finding nothing, nothing, nothing. Then, something. A piece of paper. I pulled it out of the shirt it was tucked in and read it. An address, a few Chinese characters in a jaunty script across a scrap of paper bag. It might mean nothing to the man who'd scrawled it, only his dry cleaner, maybe his dentist. I didn't know if it was Chi-Chun Ho's shirt, or Song Chan's, or another man's. But it was something, a way to move into the game, past Peter's opening square. This was a place one of these men knew, and so maybe a place that knew one of them.

I tucked the scrap of paper in my pocket and kept searching. Nothing else came up in the hanging clothes. I started lifting bowls and mugs from the shelves and feeling around inside the pots and pans. It was unlikely I'd turn anything up that way, but I had the time, thanks to the sainted visitor who'd rung the doorbell. I was up to the plastic garbage pail with the fifty-pound burlap bag of rice safely tucked under its mouseproof cover when the footsteps overhead came back. Swiftly, I flipped the locking handles back on the pail's lid, snapped shut my own toolbox, and was standing by the bottom of the stairs radiating beatific patience when Mrs. Liu opened the door.

"Are you finished?" she said, starting down the stairs. "I was delayed. Someone rang the bell, a new neighbor with foolish questions. Where is the butcher, he asked, where is the dry cleaner, do any of the teenage boys here cut the grass or shovel the snow if you pay them. What will a teenage boy not do, if you pay him?" She shook her head at the inanity of her new neighbor. "Were you successful?" she asked me.

"Yes." I beamed. "Yes, I was. Big Sister Liu, you have no idea how much you helped me this morning. My partner will be so impressed with my skill. From this point this can be handled from the street, without troubling you any further. Thank you so much."

Smiling, she said it was nothing, but I could see in her eyes the pleasingly illicit satisfaction at helping another Chinese woman beat the odds. I said it was more than I could ever repay and she said again that it was nothing. We did that a few more times, and then I picked up my toolbox, climbed the stairs, and strolled down her driveway in the bright suburban sunshine. She went into the house by the kitchen door and was back among her shells before I rounded the corner.

five

Once out of sight of the Liu household, I headed down the block. In the leafy morning sun, my shoulders ached from the weight of the toolbox, and I was sweating in Luke's scratchy, heavy winter jacket. I wondered sourly whether lending me the winter jacket in May was really worth drinks at Windows on the World, and then, as I approached the end of the block, wondered in a different mood about the scrap of brown paper that had recently migrated from one of the waiters' pockets to mine. The picture of the woman and child under the pine trees came back to me, and with it the sense of sadness I'd felt in the air of the musty basement room.

I was absorbed in thought, about my next step, about next steps in general, and new lives, and shared fifty-pound bags of rice. I didn't see the gray car as it rolled up beside me, didn't hear the window noiselessly lowered. I plodded along, one foot in front of the other, as unaware as any civilian, as heedless as any person who hasn't spent years training her senses to notify her immediately of any unusual happenings in her vicinity. I didn't know he was even there until the low, insinuating voice slid through the soft spring air to reach me.

"Hey, beautiful," he called across from the driver's side through the open window. "Wanna come take a look at my cable?"

I spun around, stopped still on the sidewalk. Gripping the toolbox tightly, I took in his lazy grin, the curling smoke from his cigarette. He drifted the car to a stop beside me and reached to open the passenger side door.

I felt the hot blood rush to my face. "What are you doing?"

"Following you," he said with an easy shrug of his broad shoulders. His face was shadowed as he leaned across the car's front seats. "If you didn't want me to do that you shouldn't have been so gorgeous. Get in."

"You—" I resisted the urge to heave my toolbox through the open window at him. The street was silent and empty, no other pedestrians, not another car. I looked around and saw what there was to see.

Then I got in.

We took off before my door was even closed. "Why is it," I said to the driver, exhaling a sharp breath as the car rolled down the quiet, deserted street with me inside, "that you can't stick to the simplest plan?"

Bill Smith, my sometimes partner, who was supposed to be waiting for me in this very car at the end of the next block, grinned at me from the driver's seat. He switched his cigarette to his left hand so he could hold it out the window where I wouldn't have to breathe it.

"Just taking a little initiative, boss," he said. "I heard you liked employees who thought for themselves."

"Where'd you hear that?"

"Around the union hall."

"Rumors. Gossip. Not a word of it true."

"Uh-oh, my mistake. You going to fire me?"

"Immediately." Restrained by seat and shoulder belts, I struggled my arms out of the sleeves of Luke's winter jacket and tossed the thing in the back. "This is a very unpleasant item, by the way."

"But you look so fetching in it. How'd you do?"

I settled myself more comfortably into the seat, putting my feet up on the toolbox, which I'd thunked onto the floor in front of me.

"I'm not sure."

"That's good." He nodded sagely. "It always makes the next step easier if you don't know how this one turned out."

"How come you have a smart-guy answer for every question?"

"So you'll recognize me. Seriously, did you find anything?"

I sighed. "One thing. One dumb thing, and even it's probably not anything." I reached into my pocket and withdrew the scrap of brown paper bag. I held it up for Bill to see.

He glanced over, then returned his eyes to the street. "Looks like Greek to me."

"Hah. Shows how much you know."

"What does it say?"

"It's an address."

"Where?"

I frowned at the paper. "Brooklyn?"

"Are you asking me?"

"Only because of how much you know. Four-eleven Baltic Street. Is that Brooklyn?"

He nodded. "Probably. There is a Baltic Street in Brooklyn, anyway, and I don't know if there's one in any of the other boroughs."

"And you know so much. Of course, it could be in Kansas."

"What's it the address of?"

"I have no idea. Maybe it's a pizzeria, for when these guys get tired of eating Chinese."

"If I said that you'd kill me."

"That's absolutely true. The thing is, it's the only thing I found that ties these guys to someplace besides that apartment and Dragon Garden."

"Do you want to go there now?"

I considered that as the wind blowing in the car's open windows tossed my hair around. "Can we just drive by to see what it is? I have to think a little before I know how to go in."

"Sure, boss. Anything you say."

"You're certainly agreeable," I said suspiciously.

"I'm trying to learn from your remarkable instincts. I still don't know how you could be so sure these people were bound to have cable TV."

"Because there aren't nearly enough Chinese-language shows on standard broadcast TV, American cultural imperialism being what it is—"

"All right, all right. And they provide it to their tenants out of the goodness of their hearts?"

"Oh, you can bet those guys are paying for it. But if they're living four to a basement such a distance from work, they must be saving money as hard as they can to get out from under their debts to whoever paid for their passage. Cable TV is cheaper by far than any other source of entertainment they could find, especially gambling."

"That's what they'd be doing if they weren't watching cable?"

"Well, they can't go to the movies if they don't speak good English. And movies are expensive. They probably have wives or girlfriends back home, and even if they wanted to date, that's expensive, too. They work in a restaurant, so they don't have much incentive to go out to dinner. They probably gamble anyway, because it's such a big thing with, as you would say, us Chinese types, but having TV at home might keep them from getting carried away with it."

"You are a genius. I bow before your mighty brain. Where'd you find your scrap of paper?" Bill headed the car up the ramp for the expressway.

"I was lucky on that one," I said. "I'd looked through most of their stuff without turning anything up, and Mrs. Liu was on her way back down there when some neighbor rang her doorbell. He kept her occupied another couple of minutes with a bunch of dumb questions, and that gave me time to search their clothes."

Bill grinned as he eased the car into the whooshing traffic. "Yeah," he said. "I thought you'd like that."

I stared at him. "What—wait. You saw that?"

"Oh, from very close up."

"Close up—hey, that was you?"

"Just doing my job, boss."

I frowned. "What were you doing on that block?"

"Watching your back."

"I didn't need that."

"No one ever does."

He was looking casually ahead, and I knew why. I took the time he was giving me and felt the flush that had crept into my face recede. "You make me mad when you do that," I told him.

He looked over at me, eyebrows raised. "I seem to recall *you* popping up all over town trying to keep *me* out of trouble on innumerable previous occasions."

"And what a hopeless cause *that* is." I sighed. "Okay, draw. Drive on."

Which is how, in my own way, I said thank-you.

Bill drove us from Elmhurst, Queens, to Cobble Hill, Brooklyn, using a combination of the expressway and those back streets that only someone who grew up at least partially in Brooklyn could know.

"Is this near where you used to live?" I asked him as we turned a corner in a neighborhood of slightly shabby three-story row houses and down-at-the-heels two-story shops. A huge schoolyard ran all the way through the block, with brightly graffitied handball walls and basketball backboards with baskets that had no nets.

"No, that was further in. But I had a girl here when I was seventeen."

I waited for more, but there wasn't any; there never is. Bill doesn't talk much about the three years he lived in Brooklyn, between when his army family moved back from Amsterdam and when he joined the navy himself, at eighteen. He doesn't talk much about his childhood at all. It's none of my business, of course, and besides, there's no reason why I should really care about the parts of himself he doesn't want to share; so sometimes I ask a question, and if he won't elaborate then I just let it drop.

Or he cuts me off before I can ask the next question—supposing, of course, that I wanted to—which is what happened now.

"There," he said, nodding at a solid-looking brick building on the corner where a residential street met a commercial one. "That's the address."

I looked, but looking didn't tell me very much. The ground floor was taken up by a concern called Jayco Realty, which had propped corkboards in the windows and covered them with color photos of attractive properties for rent or sale in this convenient-and-still-affordable area. On the two upper floors were offices of one kind or another, dentists, I assumed, and lawyers, and CPAs, neighborhood folks making a living providing services to each other. Why any of these businesses here in Cobble Hill would have been the destination of an undocumented worker from Fukien Province by way of Elmhurst was not clear to me.

"I'm going in," I said to Bill, who'd parallel-parked us across the street from the place and was lighting a cigarette.

"Where?" he asked, shaking out his match.

"The upstairs businesses, then the realtor. Somehow for illegals living four to a room, they seem least likely."

"Although most needed. How are you going?" Which meant, what's the gag, the cover story?

I shrugged. "Nice Chinese girl looking for fill-in-the-blank. Got your name from a friend of a friend. I'll drop the names I know, Peter's client and the missing roommates, and see what happens."

"You want help?"

"I don't think it would help. Actually, you don't even have to wait. I could take the subway home. This could take a while, and it'll probably turn out to be boring and useless."

"Those are a few of my favorite things. . . . No, thanks, I think I'm getting into this chauffeur business. I'll get a cup of coffee and keep an eye on the building, in case someone tries to steal it with you inside.''

"I feel so secure having you around. Enjoy yourself.''

"You, too. Write if you get work.''

So Bill went to drink a double espresso at a window table at the Hill of Beans, while I went to see what manner of services were available on Baltic Street in Brooklyn.

As it turned out, they were many and varied. I was given prices and suggested appointment schedules for root canal, no-fault divorce, incorporating your small business—that one actually interested me—plus ballet classes for adult beginners, Lamaze lessons, and free introductory Weight Watchers sessions to get me ready for the summer swimsuit season, which would be here before I knew it.

It might be here already, I thought, arriving unnoticed while I was trooping, increasingly discouraged, through 411 Baltic Street. No one was responding to any of the names of the missing men. I forgot who'd sent me, I said over and over. Probably it was Chi-Chun Ho . . . or maybe Chan Song. . . . I'd used the other two names, too, Yuan Lee and Gai-Lo Lu, but all I'd gotten were polite blank stares. No smiles of recognition, no starts and quick cover-ups, not even a single pair of widened eyes. It wasn't fair, I found myself telling the universe: these men had come here alone, leaving their families, everything they knew, leaving a place where the machinery of daily life would have to rearrange itself to go on working without them. A place that missed them, where people thought about them, over and over, at little times, like when someone cooked a favorite food or the baby said his first word. They'd come from that to a place where they'd touched down so lightly that it hardly noticed they were here, a place they could disappear from as though they'd never existed. I thought back to the forlorn basement in Queens they'd tried to make into home.

I made my weary way downstairs from the last of the offices, a Lebanese immigration lawyer who specialized in his countrymen but was willing to give me the name of someone in Chinatown who specialized in mine. I took it, because some of the missing men were, after all, Chinese illegals, but the idea that they'd get to a Chinatown lawyer through a Lebanese in Brooklyn was far-fetched enough to make a visit to the ground-floor realtor seem like a hot trail to follow.

It wasn't, I was sure, but I had no other trails, hot or cold; if anyone in this building knew any of the vanished men, they were either superb actors or I hadn't met them yet.

I went back out into the late-morning sunshine and ran my eyes over the boards in the windows at Jayco Realty, checking out the apartments, homes, and business properties on offer. Some of them were appealing, but the prices seemed high to me. Cobble Hill, as the signboard said, is convenient to Manhattan, but it isn't Manhattan, and these were prices I might have raised my eyebrows at even on the other side of the river. I wondered as I entered the office just how out of touch with New York's real estate market I had become.

Three people sat at three desks in the neat but crowded office. The air gave off the faintly singed aroma of coffee whose useful life is over. A middle-aged white man with a bristling mustache looked up as I came in; a blond white woman was typing on a computer keyboard; and a youngish Asian man was on the phone in the back of the room. I felt a small electric charge sizzle up my spine. *Good grief, Lydia,* I mentally scoffed, *are you so desperate that a set of Asian features is enough to make you think you've cracked this case? He's probably Japanese, anyway, so just relax.*

But he wasn't.

The mustached man in the front of the room looked up when I walked in. "Can I help you, miss?" he asked, maybe a little more grudgingly than I would have liked. I therefore gave him my sweetest smile. The Asian man hung up the phone; he looked at me, too. The woman went on typing.

I said, "I'm looking for an apartment."

"Nothing right now," the other man grunted. "Market's real tight."

"Really? Chi-Chun Ho said you'd be able to help me out."

The mustached man looked at the Asian man and shrugged his shoulders. The Asian man smiled and came around his desk, extending his hand to me. "Joe Yee," he said. "Larry's right, we don't have much at the moment, but come on over and sit down."

Joe Yee was tall, a dark-skinned peasant like me but with a narrower nose and handsome, high cheekbones. His smile was engaging and his English unaccented, unless you counted a slight Midwest twang. Chicago, I guessed, or Madison, Wisconsin. As we shook hands he rolled his eyes in Larry's direction and gave me an ironic smile. His eyes, I noticed before I knew I was noticing, were that deep, intense brown that's as close to coal-black as eyes can get. Not all Asians have that eye color; my brothers don't. But my eyes are like that, too.

Joe Yee held my hand, and my eyes, a few seconds longer. As I sat, Larry turned back to his own paper-strewn desk as though he didn't much care whether I found an apartment or moved right in and lived in their office. I wondered whether Joe Yee got tired of doing damage control with the customers Larry spoke to first.

"Can I get you something, Miss . . . ?" Joe Yee gestured to the Mr. Coffee machine on the shelf behind him, the source of the air perfume.

"Ko," I said, in keeping with my principle of trying out a new identity whenever possible. "Marilyn Ko. No, thank you." The dark sludge in the pot looked like something even Bill might not drink. It reminded me, though, of the tea I wasn't having, and Joe Yee's smile and clear dark eyes notwithstanding, I determined to get my business with the realtors of Jayco over as fast as possible.

"Who did you say sent you to us?" Joe Yee asked me, pouring a mugful of the awful-looking coffee for himself.

"Well, I'm not sure. I thought it was Chi-Chun Ho, but there were a bunch of people at this party, you know? It could have been Chan Song, or Yuan Lee, or maybe Gai-Lo Lu. I'm sure it was one of them." I gave everyone's name its English order, not Chinese, since Joe Yee seemed like such an All-American boy.

Joe Yee's brow furrowed. "Those names mean anything to you, Larry? Maggie?" The other two shrugged. "I don't remember any of them," Joe Yee said. "The one who told you about us, he said we found him an apartment?"

"I don't know," I sidestepped. "They're actually roommates, those four guys. They live in Queens."

Now Joe Yee shrugged. "Well, we don't handle Queens, so I don't know what to tell you. But they sent you to us?"

I nodded.

He flashed me a grin. "Well, who knows? But as long as you're here, suppose you tell me what you're looking for."

So I made up some nonsense about two bedrooms and a good view, and Joe Yee wrote my nonsense on a three-by-five card. We chatted a little about walk-ups versus elevator buildings, and distance from transportation and shopping.

Once or twice Joe Yee's eyes caught mine, and I thought I saw in them a spark, something bright in their almost-black depths that said that this was more than just a business encounter and I was more than just a customer.

Or it might have been that Joe Yee was a salesman, and eye contact is a salesman's tool.

Not that Joe Yee had anything to sell me. He told me again there really wasn't anything but he'd call me when the market loosened up. "Listen, Marilyn, leave me a number. Things are bound to get better soon. Thanks for coming to us."

So I gave him a phony number and got up to go. Joe Yee held the wood-framed glass door for me, and we shook hands again as we said good-bye, another firm and friendly clasp. I crossed the street to the Hill of Beans, where Bill sat reading the *Times* in the front window, with dark strong tea the foremost thing on my mind.

six

"Useless!"

Bill folded his paper as I flopped into the spindly wire chair across the table from him at the Hill of Beans. As opposed to the sludge at Jayco Realty, the fresh-ground coffee scenting the air at the café smelled good enough to drink, even to me.

"Me?" Bill asked politely.

"Probably. But what I actually meant was spending the morning trawling among the petty bourgeoisie of Cobble Hill, looking for someone who knows four men I don't know myself."

"You came up empty?"

"Depends on your definition."

A thin young woman with a nose ring, an eyebrow ring, and a stud in her lower lip strolled up and asked if I'd like something.

I gave the blackboard tea list a quick scan. "A pot of English Breakfast?" Which was orange pekoe in the language of my people, not a subtle tea, but strong and dark, very revivifying.

"No problem."

"And I'll have another espresso," Bill said.

"I'll bet you will." She grinned at him and sauntered away.

"How many does that make?" I asked him.

"Five."

"Good God."

"They also serve who only stand and wait, but something has to keep them awake. So: no luck?"

"Well, as I say, it depends. You want to put on pink tights and learn the five classical ballet positions? You want to lose twenty pounds?"

"Which comes first?"

"Keep making wisecracks and I'll divorce you. Two hundred and fifty dollars, sixty days, no-fault. Although, come to think of it, that wouldn't work with you."

"Why not?"

"Because it's bound to be your fault."

"If you divorced me, you'd have to have married me," he pointed out, "and that would certainly have been your fault."

"Hmm," I said. "That's true."

The decorated waitress brought my tea in a round and comforting-looking white pot. She put another espresso in front of Bill and, with a smile, gave him a clean ashtray, too.

"They let you smoke in here?"

"They're enlightened in Brooklyn." He lit a cigarette to take advantage of the ashtray. "I'm sorry your scrap of paper was a bust."

"There's just one thing," I said. "I think it's likely I'm merely delirious, but let me ask you something. Don't real estate agents work on commission?"

"Yes."

"Then, if you walked into the office of one, wouldn't you expect to be snarfed up and jealously guarded by the first person who saw you?"

"Uh-huh. You mean the place on the ground floor?"

I nodded through that first, perfect sip of tea.

"Weren't you?" Bill asked.

"Just the opposite. 'Go away, little girl, you bother me.' 'No, you might as well come on over here and sit down.' One guy didn't want me, the woman totally ignored me, and they had nothing to offer me anyway.''

"Maybe they already knew how difficult you could be."

"You zipped across the street and told them?"

"Absolutely. It seemed only fair. What do you mean, they had nothing to offer you?"

"Zippo, zilch, nada. They say the market's tight but it's bound to loosen up soon. The prices in their window are high, so I upped the limit on what I said I could spend, but they still said they don't have anything. Is the market that tight?"

"I didn't think it was," Bill said. "Not in Cobble Hill."

I sipped some more tea, felt its warmth and enthusiasm encouraging my body back into a functioning state. "Can we have something to eat?" I asked.

"Always. You're hungry?"

"Always." I scanned the blackboard again and proposed a slice of carrot cake. Bill went to the counter and told them about it. A moment later the waitress, who was preparing to go off duty and had therefore just put a row of silver hoops in the five holes in her right ear—maybe she had a date—brought the cake to the table with two forks.

"Actually, there was something else," I said to Bill as I slid one of those forks through the moist brown crumbly wedge.

"What's that?"

"One of them's Chinese."

His eyebrows went up. "I thought they all were."

"Not the guys we're looking for, dingbat. One of the real estate agents. Joe Yee. ABC, obviously. By his accent I'd say he's from some state in the middle, one of those places I've never been to."

"Never mind, everyone all looks alike out there anyway."

The cake was dreamily spicy with nutmeg and cinnamon, and studded with chewy raisins and crunchy nuts. Its cream cheese frosting was cool and silky. I reached for another forkful and told Bill, "Maybe the other guy thought we'd look good together. That's why he passed me on to the Chinese guy."

Bill looked at me over his espresso. "Do I have to charge over there and defend your honor?"

"Thanks, but don't bother."

"Anyway, they didn't react to any of our missing guys' names," Bill said.

"How do you know that?"

"You'd have told me. You wouldn't have been able to keep it to yourself."

"Ah. But he did ask about them after I brought them up."

"What did he ask?"

"Whether they'd said Jayco had found them their apartment. But then he said they don't do Queens, so it's not something as simple as that."

"Not as simple as that," he repeated. "But you think this is the connection."

I looked up and met Bill's eyes. They're brown, too, not fathoms-deep, coal-black-brown, but plain, straightforward brown. "Until you said that," I said, "I wasn't sure I did. I'm still not sure. But they were weird, one of them trying to get rid of me, one totally ignoring me, one spending a little too much time with me for someone who has no apartments for rent. I think there's something peculiar about Jayco Realty. Or maybe I just hope so, because if there's not, this whole day has been a bust."

"What do you want to do?"

"I want to go home," I said, scraping up crumbs and raisins with the edge of my fork, "and look these guys up."

So we finished our carrot cake and our tea and espresso. I paid the check because this was my case. The waitress, who now had a delicate chain linking the ring in her nose to a stud in her left ear, waved to us as we left.

Bill dropped me at my office and drove away. He was off duty for the rest of the day, unless he thought of some path to follow that could move this case along. Because the case was mine, if that happened he was supposed to call and tell me what he had in mind; on

52

the other hand, we'd been working together for so long that if he couldn't get me he'd just go on ahead anyway. That would be all right with me, and he knew that, and I knew he knew that, although it was one of the many things we'd never discussed.

My plan was to settle in at the computer in my office and see what the state board that licenses real estate agents had to say about Jayco Realty of Baltic Street, Brooklyn.

My office is on the west end of Canal Street, in a part of Chinatown that wasn't Chinatown when I was born. As immigrants become citizens and sponsor their families; as Hong Kong money looks for a place to skeptically wait out the first years of one-country-two-systems; as threadbare and thin villagers choose cold, hungry, two-month trips in the lowest holds of cargo ships, all packed in the same windowless, rolling room, breathing stale air, never coming on deck, for their chance to work sixteen hours a day on the slopes of Gold Mountain because they think it's better than their chances back home; as all these things happen, Chinatown grows. People need places to live, money needs businesses to invest in, places to live need coats of paint and sheets and towels and pots for cooking in, businesses need lawyers and shopkeepers and pens and pencils. Everyone needs tea and chopsticks and fifty-pound bags of rice.

And Chinese people, those who've made it, need to go back home, bringing gifts for those who stayed, visiting the graves of those who never left. To do that, they go to travel agents, like the three ladies at Golden Adventure, on the ground floor at 127 Canal Street. And if traveling is not what they have in mind, if what they really need is someone followed, something looked into, some exploration carried out in secret—a private investigation—they can, once inside, continue past the door to Golden Adventure and come see me. My name's not on the street door; Lydia Chin Investigations is not on the buzzer. Not only would that not bring me business, it would probably cut down on the prosperity of Golden Adventure, as people would hesitate to go to them for fear of being suspected of coming to me. Chinese people don't like to admit they need to hire someone to help solve their personal problems.

Peter's not that way, of course, but Peter's a lawyer, and to him this problem wasn't personal, except in the way all his work is personal. Although, I reminded myself, he hadn't exactly been thrilled about the idea of my working on it, and that *was* personal. On the other hand, I hadn't gone very far toward solving it, either.

The street door was propped open, as it usually was during the day. I saluted Ava, Andi, and Mei-Lei, the three cheerful, bustling, middle-aged, and prosperous proprietors of Golden Adventure. They were always waving me inside, offering me a deal on a direct flight to Shanghai, a three-day shopping extravaganza in Hong Kong, a cruise package on the Yellow River. "Lydia, good bargain," Andi would say while Ava opened brochures one on top of the other. "Last minute, very low price." I kept thinking that one of these days I'd take them up on one.

At the end of the hall I unlocked the door to my own office, which was one room plus a bathroom that I sublet from Ava, Andi, and Mei-Lei. I was thinking about China, about the misty peaks of Guilin and the towers of Shanghai, about the mountain village in Guangdong both my parents were from, the frogs in the rice paddies and the dusty winding path leading away.

I wasn't thinking about my office, whether the door creaked in the usual way, whether the silence was the usual silence. I wasn't thinking, as I reached for the light switch, about the shadows.

Then: no shadows, just darkness. Cloth, rough, over my head, scratching my face, pulled tight around my throat, some kind of rope. An arm around me from behind, pinning my arms. My heart slamming wildly in my chest.

I kicked out, found nothing; I snapped my head back. That made contact—my skull, his nose. I heard a grunt behind me, and the grip loosened. I staggered forward, trying to keep my feet.

His hands on my shoulders spun me around. Then a blow, a tremendous, pounding, breath-exploding blow, crumpling my stomach. Through the rough cloth I gasped, choked, coughed for air. My whole body doubled up, contracted around my empty center. My desperation to breathe drove all thoughts from my head. I felt like I was drowning, struggling uselessly, helplessly, in a sea of dusty burlap.

54

A foot swept my legs out from under me, and I fell, crashing to the ocean floor. Pain flared in my knee. I lay still, forcing my chest to expand. I drew in a slow breath; flavored with dust and cloth, it was still the sweetest thing I'd ever tasted. I felt my arms yanked behind my back, my wrists tied together, and could do nothing about it.

Breathing took everything I had.

A booted foot pushed at my shoulder, rolling me onto my back. It planted itself, with weight, on my stomach. I drew the biggest breath I could, expecting the boot to suddenly stomp, expecting to drown again.

"Now," a voice came from above me, "stupid girl, stop make trouble. Shut up, listen me! You will? Say!"

English with a Chinese accent, Fukienese probably; a man's voice, young, a voice I didn't know. I had a cloth tied around my head, my hands fastened behind my back, and a boot on my stomach. I said hoarsely, "Yes, I will."

"Good. Not so stupid, maybe." The boot pushed in a little, just to remind me, then lifted away. "Now. You wondering, where gone, four men go away? You asking, here, there?"

I felt the boot toe my chin. It must be my turn to talk.

"Yes," I said, straining to make my breathing almost normal. "Do you know?"

"No! No one know! No one want know, you understand me?"

"Their families want to know." *Oh, God, Lydia,* my lungs cried, *could you possibly shut up?* But he was Chinese; the family thing might work.

It didn't. "No! No one! No one care, these four men. You don't care. Don't care now, anymore."

He knelt on my chest, squeezed a hand around my chin, forced my head back. The burlap scratched my neck under the grip of the rope, and his weight made my breath come short again. Something about the hand was repulsive, made my skin crawl; maybe it was the simple fact that it was around my neck. "Say," he demanded.

"I don't care." My voice was hard to force out of my constricted throat.

"Say again."

"I don't care."

"About what you don't care?"

"The four men," I rasped. "Who disappeared."

"Good." He released my head and patted my cheek like a big brother complimenting a child on a clever recitation. Through the burlap his hand felt large, but still somehow creepy. I coughed, and wondered how big he was, what he looked like. "Good. Now you don't care, you stop look. Look for something else, husband maybe."

He laughed. Then the weight was suddenly gone from my chest. I heard noises, rustling, clonking, not from the direction of the door but from the window. Then silence, and I was alone in my office.

My heart beat fast with leftover fear, and anger, and the effort to get up. When I was finally standing, I shook my head wildly, like a dog climbing out of a lake. The action did nothing for me except raise more dust inside my burlap hood to choke myself on.

Completely disoriented, I took two steps forward. On the third step my shin banged into something and I yelped. That must be the coffee table; the thing to do, then, would be to turn around and go the other way. One, two, three, four steps, and I'm at the door. Well, okay, the wall, but the wall next to the door. Move over, turn around, grab the handle behind my back, twist it—no, not that way, the other way, you're backward—and a click as the door opens. Turn around again and yell.

"Mei-Lei! Ava! Can you come help me a minute?"

"Lydia?" Mei-Lei called back.

"Can you help me?"

I heard the scraping sound of a chair being pushed back and footsteps down the hall.

"Don't scream," I said, just before Mei-Lei screamed.

"Lydia! Lydia, what happened? Oh, my God!" Mei-Lei, who was born and raised in Brooklyn, is the one of the three of them whose English is perfect.

56

"Mei-Lei, I'm okay," I said as another set of footsteps hurried toward us. I turned around. "Just untie my hands, will you?"

"Ah? Lydia? What you do?" That was Ava.

Mei-Lei said, "Look at her! Oh, my God! What happened?"

"Just untie me?" I asked again.

Ava said calmly, "We untie her, she tell us what happen." Hands reached for my wrists, poked and pulled, and the rope fell away.

My own hands reached for the rope holding the burlap around my head. I heard Mei-Lei drawing in sharp little breaths while I fumbled and found the knot. Before I could begin to figure it out, another pair of hands—Ava's, no doubt—moved mine away and poked some more. The rope came loose. I grabbed for the burlap and pulled it over my head.

Ava's placid, chubby face and Mei-Lei's thin and worried one filled my view. I shook my head, sneezed, and looked down at the cloth I was holding.

It was a burlap bag made for fifty pounds of rice.

It took me fifteen minutes to calm Mei-Lei down, to satisfy Ava and Andi that I would call the police, that I wasn't in any serious danger now that whoever it was had gone, that this kind of thing was all in a day's work for Lydia Chin, P.I. Most importantly, I had to assure them that none of this was their fault; they couldn't have heard the glass cutter slicing the window above the lock, shouldn't have been listening for the sound of evil people climbing in, were not responsible for the fact that the window had no bars.

It was about to, though. The first thing I did after bundling them back off to their own office with thank-yous for the tea Andi brought me from their ever-steeping pot, renewed promises to call the police, and a polite but heartfelt rejection of Mei-Lei's offer to call my mother, was to call the locksmith.

Then I called Bill.

"Don't get excited," I said when he answered.

"I'm long past getting excited just because you call," he told me in an elaborately bored-sounding voice. Behind him I could hear classical music, a piano and a violin. The piano played deep, quietly resonant chords, while the violin chattered nervously above it.

"You're not," I said. "But that's not what I meant. Listen calmly: I just had a visit in my office from someone who thought it would be a good idea to forget about Chi-Chun Ho and his room-mates."

"You did? Who?"

"I don't know. It wasn't a friendly visit." I told him how it had gone. My heart began to pound again as I spoke. My aching stomach muscles contracted; I concentrated on relaxing them as I glanced toward the window with the cardboard now taped over the hole in the glass.

"Jesus Christ." I'd given Bill an abbreviated, softened version, but he knew me too well to buy it; sharp anger and worry rang in his voice when I got through. "Are you all right? I'm coming over."

"No, don't. I'm fine. I just wanted to tell you to be careful. I don't know how he found out about me, but it may be that he knows about you, too."

"What do you mean, you're fine? I'm coming over." He completely ignored everything else I'd said.

"Don't. I have to go out, to see Peter. And I really am fine. He didn't hurt me. I guess he just wanted to scare me."

"Did he?"

"Me? I'm Lydia Chin. Nothing scares me."

I waited for the sarcastic answer, the joke response that shows he's playing along with my game, the return volley shot I always got from Bill. It didn't come. Through the phone, behind his silence, I could hear the violin start to soar, to connect its dissonant notes into lines that didn't sound like melodies, but still were heading some-place. The piano moved with it, changing key, helping without get-ting in the way. "We should talk," Bill finally said.

"Sure," I said, confused. "Of course. But I need to talk to Peter first. He's the one who hired me to look for these guys."

"Not exactly, according to you."

"Doesn't matter. But I'm worried that the guy who came to see me might go looking for him, too. Hang up so I can call him."

"You're sure you're all right?"

"Yes. Now get off my phone."

"You'll call me as soon as you've talked to him?"

"If that's the price of getting my phone line back."

As we hung up, I heard the violin approaching, once again, the deeper, calm rhythms the piano had never abandoned, although under the line of the violin the piano, it seemed to me, had changed key. I wasn't sure whether I liked that piece. I'd have to remember, I told myself, to ask Bill what it was.

Peter was in his office; he answered his own phone, the way he always did. He has a paralegal who comes in part-time, but generally, Peter likes to work alone.

"It's Lydia," I said. "Are you okay?"

"Me? Sure. Why shouldn't I be?"

"You should be. Is your door locked?"

"What do you mean?"

"Stay there, and don't let anyone in but me. I'll be right over."

I hung up and, leaving the door open so anything going on in my office would be heard by the travel ladies, I headed for Peter's. Mei-Lei, Ava, and Andi vowed to stay all night if necessary, waiting for the locksmith to come.

I picked up four scallion pancakes and some soy sauce chicken from one of the cooking carts that line Canal Street. This was not, I insisted to myself, the growling hunger I always feel after pounding fear has passed, after my heartbeat slows and my skin stops prickling danger warnings. The soy sauce chicken had nothing to do with the sweat I'd wiped away; the scallion pancakes were unrelated to the breathing I'd had to force back to normal in my office. It was just that it was lunchtime.

I buzzed at Peter's street door, and he let me in.

"Lydia, what's going on?" he asked when I got up to the office. "And what's that?"

"Lunch," I said. "You have tea?"

He put some water on to boil. I set the plastic lid from the scallion pancakes on his side of the desk as a plate and put two and a half pancakes on it. The aluminum bottom and the other pancake and a half stayed with me.

"Has anybody strange been to see you?" I asked as he took some chopsticks out of his pencil cup and handed me a pair.

"Besides you?"

"Don't be funny. Let me ask you another one: has Chi-Chun Ho turned up?"

"I would have called you if he had."

"That's what I thought." I bit into a piece of salty, crispy pancake. "Peter, someone just came to my office and suggested I forget about the waiters who disappeared. Who would he have been?"

"What do you mean, suggested?"

"He wasn't polite. And he didn't say why he cared."

"Wait. Is that what you meant, to lock my door?" His eyes, behind their thick glasses, drilled into me. "What happened? Did you get hurt?" He started to stand.

"Sit down. I'm fine. He just wanted to scare me—which, of course, is impossible."

"I know it is. Someday that's going to get you killed. Really, what happened?" He reached to the windowsill for the now-boiling water and poured it over tea leaves in a porcelain pot.

"Really," I answered, "he told me no one was interested anymore in those four men, especially not me. He told me to go look for a husband instead." I batted my eyelashes at him.

"He didn't hurt you?"

"No." Well, not much, I thought, and what's a little white lie between friends? "He hasn't been here?"

"No one's been here."

"Hmmm." I pushed some rice out of its take-out container onto my improvised plate and topped it with a darkly gleaming chicken wing.

"Who was he?" Peter asked. "You don't know?"

"He was Fukienese, I think. And big."

"You never saw him before?"

I never saw him, period, but I kept that to myself. "No. He hasn't been here?"

"You asked that twice already."

"Well, here's why: I'm only looking for those guys because I work for you. If someone scares me off, you can always get another P.I. The real thing to do would be to scare *you* off. How come he hasn't tried?"

"Because he doesn't know about me?" He poured tea into two mugs and handed one to me. I sniffed at it: a delicately smoky Assam.

"Then how does he know about me?"

"Did you do anything today he might have caught on to?"

"I did two things. I went to Elmhurst and got into those guys' apartment, and I—"

"Lydia! What? You broke in there?"

I sighed heavily. "Oh, Peter, of course not. I talked my way in using just another one of Lydia Chin's brilliant pretexts. What did you expect me to do when you hired me?"

"It wasn't quite like that, if you remember."

"Irrelevant. Anyway, I went there, and then I followed a trail I found there to Brooklyn."

"Brooklyn?"

"Cobble Hill. A commercial building on Baltic Street. Does Jayco Realty mean anything to you?"

He shook his head. "Who're they?"

"One of the businesses in the building. One of the realtors at Jayco is Chinese."

Peter's eyes lit. "Does he know our guys?"

"He says not. But they're weird. You have a minute to search some databases?"

So Peter and I did from his computer what I'd been planning to do from my office before my plans were disrupted by a burlap bag.

We found basically nothing. Jayco was a licensed real estate agency, owned by its three New York State–licensed agents: Joe Yee, Maggie Mason, and Larry Pontillo. All three agents' licenses were fairly recent—within the last three years—but that could just mean they'd all decided to go into business together, gotten licenses, and done it. We searched a few more databases that I, as a licensed P.I., have access to—Peter scowled and muttered something about the right to privacy once or twice—but nothing irregular turned up. Finally, we gave up. Clearing away the remains of lunch, I got up to go.

"I'll let you know how things turn out," Peter said.

"What?"

"If Ho turns up, I mean."

"What are you talking about?"

"Well, since you're off the case."

"I'm what?"

"Off, the, case," he articulated. "Isn't that what you came to tell me?"

"You have to be kidding."

"You're not resigning?"

"Of course not."

"Then you're fired."

"Forget it."

"You forget it, Lydia. I shouldn't have let you talk me into this in the first place. Now that you've been warned off and roughed up, you're over. Don't," he said, holding up his hand as I opened my mouth. "There's a scratch on your neck and you make a face every time you move your knee. You don't have to tell me what really happened, but I don't have to let you stay on this case, either."

I stared at him, taken aback. "You're really mad."

"Damn right I am. And Mary's going to be even madder if I let you go on with this."

"But, Peter." I sat down again, trying not to make a face as I bent my knee. "Look, the fact that that guy came to see me means there *is* something wrong. Somebody really has to find your waiters, now."

"Let the police do it."

"The police aren't interested."

"Did you ask them?"

"You did."

"Not since this guy threatened you. That may change their attitude. You didn't report it, did you?"

"No," I admitted. "What's the point? I can't identify him."

"And besides, they might tell you to leave it alone, just like I'm telling you."

I bit my lower lip in thought. "I'll make you a deal," I said.

"No deals."

"If the cops take it up I'll stop."

"You'll stop because you're fired."

"What if I don't?"

Peter stared at me, as I had at him. "You're serious," he said.

"Peter, someone doesn't want those men found. That means someone's *got* to keep looking. Maybe we never should have started, but now"—I searched for words—"now we're responsible. Now we're attached to them, connected. We can't just walk away."

The trouble with being a lawyer is that you can't deny logic, and the trouble with being a Chinese lawyer is that what I'd just said was, to Peter, logical.

He thought, my old friend, his eyes on mine. "All right," he said finally. "We'll call Mary."

"Why are we doing that?"

He picked up the phone. "Because she's a cop." He dialed, spoke, hung up again. "She's out. She'll call me later. Now that someone's threatened you, it can be a Fifth Precinct case. They'll take it up, and you're fired."

"If they do."

"Lydia—"

"And I'm sure they will," I said quickly. "Listen, I have to go." I grabbed my bag and headed for the exit. "I'll call you, to see what Mary says. Bye, Peter. Thanks for lunch."

I made a fast getaway down the stairs, waved to Peter's Uncle Lee Liang, standing in his shop door, as I sped past, and zipped around the corner before Peter could follow me out and fire me again.

seven

I called Mary from the phone on the corner, in case she'd come in in the last five minutes and I could head her off before she talked to Peter, but she was still out. Oh, well. It probably wouldn't do me much good anyway. Mary wasn't in any position to tell me I should do something dull and safe for a living, but as a cop and as Peter's girlfriend she was in a perfect position to order me off this particular case.

I was about to call Bill and invite myself up to his place to talk things over, but first I called my machine, just to see if anyone was interested in talking to me.

Someone was. The honking traffic filling my right ear had no chance against the dry, aged voice speaking into my left. "Miss Chin, this is H. B. Yang calling. I'd like to speak to you. You can reach me at these numbers." The Cantonese accent gave me a choice of two; one had the exchange the phone company reserves for cell phones.

My heart lurched. H. B. Yang would like to speak to me.

H. B. Yang was a legend in Chinatown. Seventy-nine, he'd

arrived sixty-five years ago, when Chinese exclusion was still a pillar of American immigration policy. He was a "paper son"—one of thousands who, for a price, had been given a detailed, intimate, and fictional account of his own growing up. The facts provided to paper sons included meticulous descriptions of the home village and family history of another man, the American citizen who, also for a price, claimed the son as his foreign-born own. Learning by heart the facts of a life he had never lived, each of these men destroyed the papers where those facts were found and recited their contents as though they were memories. Once inside the United States, they rarely met their sponsors, but they kept their sponsors' names. They sent money home to China for parents, brothers, sisters they would never see again. They supported aunts and uncles, nieces and nephews, but most didn't marry; Chinese women in America were scarce. They gave up their ancestors; they had no descendants. Breaking thousand-year chains of family, they became new and alone.

For some it was a tragedy. They were heartsick, bewailed their fate, did their duty, and died unhappy.

For others, it was freedom. They'd come to this country for a chance at a prosperity they'd never have known back home. If the price of that was loneliness, loneliness was a two-sided coin. For every festival day without a family banquet, without the games and the rituals and the laughter of children, there were risks that could now be taken, opportunities that could be seized because failure would reflect badly on no one but yourself; for every worry about who would tend your grave if you died childless, there were buildings to be bought and sold, businesses to build, money to be sent home to a muddy, unpaved village where you were considered a hero, a conqueror, a king.

H. B. Yang was one of the kings. Dragon Garden Restaurant was only one of his ventures. There were real estate deals; other restaurants, some still owned, some closed, some sold; import firms; business partnerships with suited men from Hong Kong to manufacture goods in Malaysia for sale in Europe. There was the Chinatown Businessmen's Association, which H. B. Yang had headed for years. Another man was now the association's president, but from political endorsements to the granting of college loans, H. B. Yang's voice was the one that still counted more than any other.

And now that voice was on my telephone, wanting to speak to me.

I gulped, put a quarter in the phone, and called Bill.

"You're fired," I told him.

"Me, your Employee of the Month?"

"Fired. Terminated. Excessed. Thank you for your years of devoted service, we're sure you'll find another excellent position, close the door as you go."

"You're replacing me with illegal aliens?"

"That's undocumented workers, you insensitive member of the ruling class. And no, I'm replacing you with a machine. It smokes, drinks coffee, and drives a car. What do I need you for?"

"Can it make bad jokes?"

"Yes, but I had to pay extra. Peter fired me, so I'm firing you."

"You're just continuing the cycle of abuse. They have programs for people like you."

"You want to hear what happened?"

"Only if I'm not fired. You know I only listen to you if you're paying me."

"Okay, you're rehired, but no benefits." I told him about my conversation with Peter.

"So it's possible we're not fired, if the Fifth Precinct doesn't want to bother with it," he said sensibly when I was through.

"They will. Mary will make sure. She'll make me go swear out a complaint against this guy I didn't even see, and then it'll be police business and Peter will fire us."

"You seem to be taking it pretty well." His voice was cautious.

"I could say, 'If the police really do take it up, then that's okay. If there's really something wrong here, they're in a better position to find it than we'd be.' "

"But you're not saying that because . . . ?"

"Because it would be complete and total hypocrisy and you know it. But we'll have to worry about that later. Right now I have something else to worry about. I called you for moral support."

"First you fire a guy and then you ask him for moral support? You're lucky I'm as dumb as I am. A lot of guys might not fall for that."

"What you fall for depends upon where you stand. Now, listen. H. B. Yang called me, and I have to call him back."

"I'm at a loss here. What's my line supposed to be?"

" 'You can do it, he's nothing to be afraid of.' "

Bill repeated back to me the words I'd given him.

"Thanks. I'm going to do it now, while I have my courage up."

"You understand I have no idea what's going on?"

"What else is new? I'll call you later."

"Mine not to reason, especially working with you. Just rub that bottle when you want me."

"Wrong ethnic imagery, but I get the idea. Bye."

"Lydia?"

"What?"

"Are you okay?" With that question, his voice was different: still light, but even so, with something softer behind it.

"You mean, from before?"

"Yes."

"I'm fine." Because of the way he'd asked the question, not clingy and disapproving the way my family would have been, I answered it truthfully. "I only got hurt a little, and I walked it off. Isn't that what you would have done?"

"I'm a hell of a role model."

"Yes, I've been meaning to talk to you about that. Put it on the list."

"Of my faults? There's no room on that list."

"Put that on the list, too. I'll call you later."

I hung up the street corner phone and stared at it. H. B. Yang. Maybe I should go back to my office, call him from where it was quiet, where I could concentrate . . . Yeah, and where I could put the whole thing off for the ten minutes it would take me to get there. Nuts to that, Lydia. Put the coin in the slot and call.

So I did. Ignoring the traffic and the pedestrians and the childhood memories of my father's courteous, correct, but distinctly distant bow to this leather-faced stranger every time they passed in the street, I dialed the first of the two numbers the voice on the phone had given me.

A young man, answering the first ring, told me in Cantonese that Yang Hao-Bing was not there. I left a message and called the other number. The ring was more high-tech and the answer not quite as immediate, but when it came it was the dry, quiet voice I'd heard on my machine.

"Yang Hao-Bing," it said, the name in the Chinese order, the tones the melodic Cantonese of my childhood. There was no English follow-up. Maybe everyone who had this number spoke Cantonese. Then what number did the mayor call on?

"This is Chin Ling Wan-ju," I said, automatically speaking Cantonese because he was. I wondered if I got any points as an ABC for speaking the ancient tongue.

"Ah," the voice responded. "Thank you for calling. Ling Wan-ju, an unusual name."

"My father had planned to call me Ling Wu, after his sister who stayed in China. But I have four older brothers. When they first saw me, this tiny baby, they thought I was a toy." Which is what Wan-ju means, and why I have one more name than most Chinese people, and why was I telling this to H. B. Yang?

"Yes, I knew your father," the voice said. "Not very well, but he once worked for me."

He did? Though why was I surprised? My father had been a cook. I was thirteen when he died, and though I'd played on the floor of many of the restaurants he'd worked in, it had never occurred to me to ask who owned them.

"I would like to speak with you on a matter of some importance," H. B. Yang continued, oblivious to my memories. "Is it convenient for you to come to my office?"

"Now?" I asked, and immediately kicked myself for not having come up with some elegant turn of phrase with which to request the same information.

"Yes," was the answer, proving H. B. Yang to be, when the situation required it, a man of as few words as I was.

I gave some quick thought to my clothes as I headed over the few blocks to the Bowery. I was still wearing the navy pants and flat shoes of the cable TV scam. Luckily, I'd switched my cousin's uniform jacket for one of my own in my office, and I supposed I looked decent enough, though if I'd known I was going to have an audience with H. B. Yang I'd probably have changed outfits three or four times and put on earrings or a necklace, some clinky jade bracelets. Maybe even a touch of lipstick. Just wait until my mother hears about this, I thought.

"Trousers," she would sniff. "For an appointment with Yang Hao-Bing! It's lucky he is a wise man, wise enough to know you are just a headstrong, foolish girl. Also lucky he has many more important things to concern him. Also perhaps, since you don't know how to dress, he will understand how little you do know. Then he will find you useless to him. That would not be completely unfortunate."

I know what you mean, Ma, I agreed as I reached Dragon Garden's big glass doors.

H. B. Yang's office occupied the third-floor front of the Bowery building that held Dragon Garden, a building he'd owned for years. On the first floor were a variety of glass-fronted stores that constituted a Hong Kong–style mall, though from what I've read the goods offered in Hong Kong as a rule are considerably more upscale than the polyester and plastic I'd browsed through on my visits here.

The huge space that was the restaurant took up the second floor. You got there up a polished glass-and-brass escalator, which, on weekends, was staffed at the top and bottom by hostesses with walkie-talkies. Parties of two or four or ten were chosen from among the milling, hungry crowds and dispatched upstairs as the waiters reported empty seats at the large round tables. If you came with fewer than the ten the tables seated, you ate your dim sum in the company of strangers, their chatter mixing with the din of dishes and the clatter of the rolling carts and the calls of the ladies trying to entice you to sample their chicken feet or boiled dumplings or sticky rice. No one seemed to mind the crowding or the noise. Chinese people like our restaurants like that; maybe they remind us of the teeming streets of home, even those of us who've never been to China except by way of family stories. And non-Chinese appeared to relish the exotic Chinese authenticity of it all, or at least be willing to put up with it for a chance at the clams with black bean sauce and the shrimp shiu mai.

This was a weekday, and it was toward the late side for lunch, so no one was guarding the entrance to the escalator when I walked through the glass doors that the Chinese Restaurant Workers' Union coffin had so recently rested against. As the escalator bore me steeply upward, the carved crimson dragon on the wall at the top of the stairs slowly grew, until it filled my entire view. This restaurant had become a favorite of my mother's since it opened five years ago, and the drama of the approach was one of the reasons.

"Beautiful dragon," she always said as we neared the top of the escalator. "So well done. Looks just like a real one."

I'd never asked my mother how she knew what a real dragon looked like, because I was afraid she'd tell me.

I stepped off the escalator and found myself face to face with a brick wall in a maître d's jacket. I inquired of him the way to H. B. Yang's office. "I'm Lydia Chin," I said. "I have an appointment."

He didn't consult a list or bat an eye. He looked me up and down, then he said, "Yeah?"

"With H. B. Yang," I elaborated, because he seemed to need a little more. "He asked me to come see him."

"Yeah," the brick wall said. "He told me." He spoke the same New York English as mine, and he didn't move.

"Well, then," I said, "maybe you could tell me how to get to his office. I don't think I should keep him waiting."

He scowled at that. "Keep Mr. Yang waiting? Don't ever do that." A few seconds later his brain, finished with his mouth, sent out a signal to his arm, and he pointed me through a door concealed in the pattern of the wallpaper. "Stairs," he said. "Or there's an elevator." But he didn't point at it; his arm stayed where it was, waiting to hear from his brain again. "Around back, the other side of the building."

His eyes narrowed slightly as he spoke, and I got the feeling that this might be some sort of test. But did you pass it by being a go-getter who'd choose the stairs any day because time was money, they were closer, and you were tough, or by being a lady who knew your own worth, never mind the sensible shoes, and headed without a backward glance for the two-ton piece of electrical equipment to carry you twelve vertical feet?

Clueless, I chose the stairs because they don't break down and trap you inside for hours waiting for a repairman. The maître d' tugged on the bottom of his black tuxedo jacket and went back to squinting vigilantly across the vast dining floor, on which absolutely nothing was happening.

The aromas of frying garlic and steaming broccoli and low-tide fish followed me through the wallpapered door, as though they were curious to see what was upstairs, too. Halfway up they fell away. Maybe they'd suddenly remembered that at the top was H. B. Yang.

The corridor was short and the door near the end of it open. I knocked anyway, peering into the room. A man had been standing, back to the door, looking out the window at the Bowery and the streaming traffic choking itself into two lanes to work its way over the Manhattan Bridge. He turned at my knock, and of course it was H. B. Yang. Though his hair was thinning, it was still black; his face was lined, leathery, and mobile. Smiling, he came around his wooden desk—more Midtown than Ming Dynasty—and extended his hand to me.

"Chin Ling Wan-ju," he said. "Thank you for coming. I am Yang Hao-Bing. Please, come in, sit down."

So we were going to speak Chinese, though we weren't going to bow to each other. I shook his hand, smiled also, and sat in the leather chair facing his desk. "I'm honored to meet you, Uncle," I said, wondering if that was laying it on a little thick. But something about this place—the heavy American desk and chairs resting on a maroon carpet figured with creamy plum blossoms in blue vases; the tall Chinese cabinet behind me, glowingly lacquered and displaying porcelain figures and bowls, bronze animals and incense burners; the walls hung with plaques and scrolls and photographs of H. B. Yang posing and smiling next to political figures of the last four decades, both New Yorkers and visiting Taiwanese; and the controlled silence, as though the scurrying traffic I could see outside and the restaurant bustle I could sense below were important parts of H. B. Yang's world, but still, had their places—made it feel right to me to speak to H. B. Yang in the old style, to refer to him as an honorary family member, one who was older and on that basis alone could expect my respect.

And it made him smile. "Yes, we have not met before," he said, sitting in the chair behind the desk only after I sat. "Have you eaten yet? You will have tea?"

That wasn't really a question, of course; it was a dance step, and I did my step, saying yes, I'd eaten, and no, I wouldn't think of putting him to any trouble, to which he replied that it wasn't any trouble. It wasn't, either; he moved to a sideboard where, on a hot plate, a small iron kettle was steaming. H. B. Yang poured the water from the kettle into a delicate blue-and-white teapot, which he covered and brought to a laquered tray already sitting on the edge of his desk, where I could reach it handily. On the tray were two covered tea bowls of the old-fashioned sort, two larger covered plates, and two small plates, all of them the same translucent porcelain as the teapot—not standard Dragon Garden tableware.

H. B. Yang sat behind his desk again while we waited for the tea to steep. "No, we have not met," he said, "although I have, naturally, followed your career with some interest."

"Mine? Uncle, I'm flattered," was what I said, managing to keep the sudden dryness of my mouth out of my words. Was this how bugs felt when, having thought all along they were just going about their own buggy business, they suddenly realized they were under a microscope?

"Yes, of course. I have been privileged to serve this community for many years.'' He gestured to the pictures on the walls. ''I am always pleased to see young people remaining here. So many of the best leave Chinatown; the ones to be commended are those like yourself, establishing your businesses here, using your talents in ways that make the community stronger.''

Chinatown boosterism could not be what this visit was about, I acknowledged to myself, though I also acknowledged that I sort of wished it were.

''This is my home,'' I said simply.

H. B. Yang nodded, looking gratified. ''Please,'' he said, ''help yourself,'' and he pointed to the covered blue-and-white dishes. I lifted the tops to find in one preserved plums, and in the other the little sesame-covered balls of fried dough my father used to make for us on his rare days off. Their warm, rich scent suddenly brought back to me our cramped kitchen and my father's voice. ''See how they smile when you cook them?'' he'd say as the balls split in the hot oil. And my mother would reply, ''It's a lucky thing the dough is smiling, because all the children in this house are quarrelsome.'' And my father's face would grow sad. ''Quarrelsome, ah? Such a shame. Quarrelsome children cannot eat Smiling Faces.'' And suddenly, the insurmountable difficulties between Ted and me, or Elliot and Andrew, or Tim and anybody, would vanish in the face of the crispy, chewy little pastries.

I reached for a Smiling Face from H. B. Yang's dish, wondering whether it would live up to my memories. Surprisingly, it did, or almost. The seeds were crunchy, the dough was soft and sweet. What was missing was the sense that came with the taste, of being surrounded by people who, confining, annoying, and dismissive as they were, nevertheless wanted the best for you.

''This is delicious,'' I told H. B. Yang.

''Yes, the chef who makes my sweets is quite good,'' he told me. ''He has been here some time. He's the son of an old friend from my village.''

H. B. Yang's face held a look of contentment as he poured tea, first for me, then for himself. I lifted the covered bowl, moved

73

the cover slightly back, and drank, finally grateful for my mother's nagging at us all to learn the ancient and difficult art of drinking gracefully from one of these.

"All your chefs are good, I think," I told H. B. Yang as I put my tea bowl down. "I've enjoyed all the meals I've had in your restaurant."

"I'm honored to hear you say so. That, in a way, is why I have asked you to come here."

Uh-oh, I thought, I was right; it's about the waiters. He knows I'm working for Peter, and he's playing divide and conquer.

"My staff is, as you say, quite good," he went on. "Some, like my sweets chef, have been in this country for many years. Some of the others were trained as restaurant workers in China. But most are peasants: farmers, laborers with no skills, when they come to me. I train them. I look after them. I am a stern but fair employer. They are, most of them, loyal men. They think of Dragon Garden as their home. I am proud that they do so."

Okay, I thought, probably the best answer to that is no answer, so I sipped some tea and smiled. H. B. Yang was serving me an aromatic black tea, deep-tasting with no bitterness. He sipped his tea also; I had a feeling he understood my silence and didn't mind at all. "Now," he said, "I must rely on your discretion, Chin Ling Wan-ju."

"Whatever I can do," I said ambiguously, trying to look help-ful.

He nodded and went on. "The laws governing immigration from China have changed since the time of my arrival. Even since the time your father came here, as you no doubt know," he said. "Still, as with any bureaucracy, the requirements of government can be arcane. Often they conflict with the needs of thousands desiring a better life." He smiled. "It was the Chinese people who invented bureaucracy as well as gunpowder, of course. Might the world have been better off, do you suppose, if we had created neither?"

"Probably," I answered. "But what's done is done."

"Yes, that's true. Sometimes the things that are done are re-grettable, but cannot be withdrawn. Instead they commit one to a course of action that must, then, be followed through. I need you, Chin Ling Wan-ju, to follow something through for me.''

I reached for a preserved plum to hide my confusion. I'd thought I was going to be told to follow my nose out the door and leave Dragon Garden and its union problems alone. And, I reflected, maybe that's what I was being told, just in a roundabout and very Chinese way.

But it turned out it wasn't. As I bit into the salty-tart plum, H. B. Yang continued. ''I've lost something,'' he said. ''In fact, someone. Four men, employees of mine. I would like you to find them for me.''

eight

back out on the Bowery, in what had turned out to be a sunny, breezy, and very complicated afternoon, I grabbed up the first phone I came to and called Bill.

"You're hired," I said. "Or fired, or rehired, or whatever we were up to. Can I come over?"

"You'd better," he said. "I don't think you're safe wandering the streets."

When I got to the Laight Street building Bill's lived in since before, as he points out, I got my first female undergarments, he was actually waiting outside, leaning on his own doorjamb and smoking a cigarette.

"What are you doing there?" I demanded, suspicious.

"It's a beautiful day. I thought I'd come down here and watch you stagger up the street."

"Don't be mean."

"I'm always mean," he said, moving aside and pushing open the street door for me. "It's at the top of my list of faults."

"No, it isn't." I started the steep two-story climb. "At the top is your tendency to be a smart-ass."

"Is that the same as my being always right?"

"They're related."

The upstairs door was open, so I walked right in and flopped on Bill's sofa.

I shut my eyes, just for a minute. Now that I was here, at Bill's, where no one was going to jump out of the shadows and jam a rice bag over my head and the scary figures of my youth weren't going to phone, I realized I was feeling my day. I heard the door click shut behind Bill as I let myself relax into the familiar soft wool of his sofa cushions. A breeze from the open front windows trailed gently across my face on its way through the apartment and out the back.

Even without the breeze I'd have known the windows were open. They always are. Bill was born in Kentucky, and his father, who had a desk job in the army, started moving the family from one subtropical Pacific base to another when Bill was nine. Bill claims to enjoy the heat, and he loves open windows. He even likes the hot air stirred up by fans much better than air-conditioning. I just put that on his list of faults. Although on a sweltering summer day, I have to admit, open windows and a ceiling fan have a certain amount to recommend them in the exoticism department; and on a warm spring day like this, the breeze from the windows moving through the room seems to tie this place to other places in the city in an offhand, intimate way, like the way something you see or hear during the day brings to mind an old friend. You might not call and tell them about it—you might even forget it the next minute—but the connection's been made.

"You okay?"

I opened one eye to see Bill standing above me, trying to look casual, not doing it so well.

"I'm perfect," I said.

"Uh-huh. But are you okay?"

I opened both eyes and straightened up. "I'm fine. Fine fine fine."

"Fine," said Bill. He might not have believed me, but he knows when not to press. "You want some tea, or something to eat? I have cookies. I bought them in case someday you showed up." He headed for the kitchen, an area separated from the living room by a counter he'd built, as he had everything in the place, walls included.

"Please, no. I haven't done anything but eat for the last two days."

"That's bad?"

"I didn't used to think so, but I'm beginning to wonder. Our new client fed me the foods of my childhood. That's not fair, is it?"

I turned my head to follow him as he came out of the kitchen with a mug of coffee. "You sure you don't want anything?" he asked.

"I'm sure. Answer my question."

He sat and took a thoughtful sip of coffee. "It's an interesting technique. Maybe I should feed you the foods of your adolescence. I wonder if the taste of them would bring back those hot, steamy nights of wild abandon—"

"That was *your* adolescence. We didn't have those kinds of nights in New York."

"You're kidding." His eyebrows went up in mock surprise. "I moved here for those."

"Twenty-five years ago? And you haven't figured it out?"

"Twenty-six, and so I'm slow. I didn't know we had a new client."

"H. B. Yang."

"The guy you were so afraid of?"

"Please. I don't think you can refer to H. B. Yang as a guy."

"He's a girl?"

I made a face. "He's a revered and respected elder member of the Chinatown community. He's an adviser to the mayor. If this were a Cantonese village he'd be the village leader by virtue of his age, his wisdom, his generosity, and his longtime survival."

"He sounds like the Wizard of Oz."

"There are certain similarities," I admitted. "Although Chinatown's not a Cantonese village anymore."

"Full of unwashed newcomers from the wrong side of the tracks, huh?"

"They're washed. But they're not from Guangdong so much, now. They're not hooked into the same networks. They don't slot right into the village associations and family name societies. They have their own power structure, different from the old one."

"So Yang's not the emperor of Chinatown anymore?"

"No, but he's still right up there. And there's another thing about him."

"And that thing is?"

"He owns Dragon Garden."

Bill lifted his eyebrows again, this time for real. "Where the waiters work?"

I nodded.

"Uh-oh. That sounds bad."

"That's what I thought at first. Now I'm just confused."

"So rare for you." I shot him a look. "What does he want?" he asked. "You to lay off and forget about it?"

"Just the opposite. He wants to find them."

Bill nodded slowly, drank some coffee, then put the mug down on the table beside him. "Why?"

"One, because he's a concerned elder. I think you have to think of it as a feudal kind of thing, like he's responsible for these men."

"Can I withhold judgment on that?"

"It's cynical of you, but okay."

"What's another reason?"

"They owe him money."

"And you called me cynical. His employees owe *him* money?"

I told Bill what H. B. Yang, over tea and sweets in the orderly peace of his office, had told me. "From before they were working for him. He paid for their passage over."

Bill picked up his coffee again. "And now they have to work it off, and if they've disappeared he's out what he laid out?"

"Right. But I don't think it's like you make it sound."

"How do I make it sound?"

"Bad."

"Bad like difficult, or bad like morally reprehensible?"

"Both."

He shook his head. "When my great-great-grandfather came here in the 1800s, they called it indentured servitude."

I cocked my head to look at him. "Did they think it was bad then?"

"Not him," he said. "He thought it was great. Life was hell for a few years after he got here, but it was hell back home anyway."

"Where was home?"

"England. Nottingham."

"Was he glad he came here?"

"Sure. After he paid off what he owed, he had the chance to make something of himself." Bill finished his coffee. "Of course, in his case, what he made was white trash, but that's not the fault of the system."

"So you don't think this is bad, either?"

He shrugged. "I don't see why your people shouldn't have the chance to be white trash, too."

"Do we have to eat Twinkies and Chef Boyardee?"

"It's one of the privileges."

I shuddered. "We'll never make it. But, Bill . . ."

"What?"

"I don't know. I just . . . those poor people, on those long trips. And they end up so far from home."

"So you're the one who thinks it's bad."

"I don't know," I repeated. "One of the Dragon Garden guys had a picture of a woman and a little boy on the table by his bed. I bet it's his wife and son. Why can't he stay home with them?"

"Because the world is a lousy place. If that's your point I can't argue with it. What do you want to do?"

I glared at him, because the world was a lousy place. "I want some tea." I got up and headed into the kitchen.

"I thought you were never going to eat again."

"A ridiculous notion." I put up the kettle and opened the cabinet where the tea I bring over gets put. Bill doesn't drink tea, but he's made room, over the last few years, for mine. I reached for the Yunnan, smoky and slightly perfumed. "H. B. Yang," I told Bill, "was sort of like the bogeyman of my childhood."

"What do you mean?"

"He was so important, so powerful, in Chinatown that some parents told their kids that they'd better behave or they'd tell H. B. Yang. It was all they had to say."

"Did your parents say that?"

"No. My father was always polite to him, but I got the feeling that really, he didn't like him very much. It made me even more afraid of him, actually."

"Of your father, or of Yang?"

I looked at him in surprise as the kettle started to sing. "Of H. B. Yang, of course. I was never afraid of my father." I spooned tea into a strainer and poured hot water over it. "That would be an awful thing, to be afraid of your father."

Bill said nothing, but the silence I heard was different from his usual silence. I turned around, looked at him curiously. "Were you afraid of your father?"

His eyes met mine; for a few seconds he didn't move or speak. Then he said, "Yes." He reached for the pack of cigarettes on the coffee table.

I asked, "Why?"

"Because he was a mean SOB." He put a match to a cigarette, tossed the match into an ashtray. "What does the H. B. in H. B. Yang stand for?"

That was about as definite a change of subject as I'd ever been pointed toward. I took the hint.

"Hao-Bing, which, as it happens, means 'great' and 'splendid.' "

"So he *is* the Wizard of Oz."

"It was part of his legend, how his parents gave him that name in China because they knew he'd have to go off to America from the day he was born, and whatever family name he got stuck with, at least he'd have his given name to see him through."

I carried my tea back over to the couch and sat.

"You know," Bill said, "we don't have to work for him."

"What?"

"He seems to still make you nervous. If you don't want to work for him we can say no."

I took a restorative sip of tea. "First of all, you can't say anything, because he doesn't know about you."

"He thinks you're working alone?"

"I just didn't see any reason to give everything away, even to H. B. Yang."

"Good instinct."

"Thank you. Second, I'm not sure I can turn down a direct request from H. B. Yang and keep up any reputation in Chinatown. And third"—I drank some more tea, trying to think of a way to put this to Bill—"I can't really say no. I sort of owe H. B. Yang myself."

"For what, all those childhood nightmares? Just because he was a big wheel in Chinatown doesn't mean he has any hold over you now."

"No, not that. And he's still a big wheel. But"—I gulped some more tea—"personally, I owe him. He brought my father over here, too."

"How do you know that?"

"My parents always told us. I think they thought it would make us less afraid of him, like he was a nice man or something. But really it just made him seem sort of all-powerful. I mean, someone who can move your parents around the globe?"

"I get your point; it took the U.S. Army to move mine. But I'm not sure why you owe him. Your father must have worked that passage off long ago."

"Of course. But still . . . it's a connection I have to him now. Does that make sense?"

"Maybe. You mean it's a connection your father would have, but he's gone, so his children inherit it?"

"I think you're beginning to think in Chinese."

"Hallelujah, it's a miracle." He stubbed the cigarette out. "Okay. Maybe I'd feel the same in your shoes, except my feet would hurt. But I can see you want to do this."

"Not exactly *want*. But I did tell him yes."

"Again, okay."

"But also," I pointed out, "it does keep us on the trail of the waiters."

"An extra added benefit."

"Well, it is. There's obviously something wrong here, and if Peter wasn't going to let us keep looking into it——"

"How's Peter going to feel about this?"

"Not so good. But he'll understand; you don't say no to H. B. Yang."

Bill's look was skeptical, as though he wasn't convinced. I wasn't either; but after all, Peter had fired us.

"What about the union guy's idea," Bill asked, "that they're on the run because they'd been threatened because of the union?"

"Warren Tan, you mean? That occurred to me, and not only that, it occurred to H. B. Yang. He said he was sure I was aware of the attempt to unionize Dragon Garden. He called it, quote, 'an unacceptable intrusion into my relations with those who work for me.' He said some people might think he'd dealt too harshly with the organizers he'd uncovered, firing them, but he couldn't allow so many people's livelihoods to be endangered this way."

"Harshly," Bill said, "and also illegally."

"About which I'm sure he's worried. But after the waiters disappeared, he thought maybe they were union men and were afraid he was threatening them with something more serious than firing—deportation, or something even worse. If that's why they disappeared he regrets it and considers it his fault, he says. He wants to make sure they know that as long as they forget about the union, they have a home with him."

"Or he wants to catch them so he *can* have them deported, or 'something even worse.' "

"I thought of that. But then I don't think he'd hire me. He'd get gang members or somebody. He came to me—I mean, brought me to him—because I'm semilegit."

"Semi? Is there something I don't know?"

"No, I mean, I'm completely legit, but it's still not going to the cops."

"And speaking of that, why didn't he go to the cops?"

"Well," I said, "I could tell you it was because the cops wouldn't do anything, because there's no crime. I mean, that's true; that's why Peter hired us in the first place. But that's not why."

"Why is, the waiters are illegals."

I nodded and finished my tea. "Not Chi-Chun Ho, Peter's guy. He's got a visa and he's working on his papers. Peter's in the middle of that for him, in fact. And not Song Chan, either. But two of them."

"So Yang can't ask the cops to find them, because if they did, he'd get in trouble for hiring illegals."

"And even if he got out of that, they'd turn them over to the INS, who'd send them back, and H. B. Yang would lose his sixty thousand dollars."

"Thirty thousand apiece? That's the going rate?"

"Yes."

"Jesus," Bill said. "For thirty thousand dollars you could get a suite on the *Queen Mary* to cross the ocean in."

"If you actually had thirty thousand dollars, instead of promising to work it off when you got here."

Bill lit another cigarette and leaned back in his chair. "And they think it's worth it. All those guaranteed hard years ahead, just for the chance to come here."

"Your great-great-grandfather did."

"Uh-huh. I just wonder if he was right, that's all. Okay, chief. So what do we do next?"

What we decided to do next was messy and a little bit confused, but it was better than the dead end we'd hit in the morning. It was also, at this point, all mine.

"H. B. Yang said if I want to go into the restaurant to ask around, just to tell him," I said. "Warren Tan suggested that, too. I don't want to go in straight—"

"You never do. I thought it was a matter of principle."

"Just good, modern P.I. practice. I mean, I don't think I'd get anywhere by asking the rest of the staff about these guys, saying 'H. B. Yang wants to know.' "

"I'll buy that. So what will you do?"

"The only women he hires are the dim sum ladies, so I'm going to go in as that, tomorrow." Tomorrow would be Saturday, and the dim sum crowds would descend on Dragon Garden. The Chinese would start crowding into the place at ten o'clock, the *lo faan* at eleven-thirty or so; and there would be Lydia Chin, pushing a stainless steel cart full of red bean buns.

Bill grinned. "You're not."

"Do I have a choice?"

"What do you mean, the only women?"

"It's traditional. The newer restaurants don't do it this way anymore, but it used to be women didn't work in them at all except as dim sum ladies. Not as waiters and not in the kitchen. That's the way it was when I was growing up, at all the places my father worked. H. B. Yang's too old to consider doing things differently."

"And you didn't take the opportunity to educate him in late-twentieth-century Chinese-American feminism?"

"How far do you think that would have gotten me?"

"Thrown out of his office. Then you wouldn't have had to work for him."

"Hmmm. I didn't think of it that way. Actually, I'm lucky he was willing to hire a female P.I. at all."

"Well, if he wanted a Chinatown P.I., you're sort of it."

"Thanks for the vote of confidence. Anyway, facts notwithstanding, I'm still lucky."

"If you call this lucky."

He had a point. The idea of working for H. B. Yang was giving me that bug-under-a-microscope feeling, which made me want to hide behind something. And though I, Lydia Chin, hated to admit it, any case brought with it the possibility of failure, this no less than any other. What if I couldn't find those guys after H. B. Yang had entrusted me with the job? The thought of the humiliation that would result, not only for me but for my mother and the rest of my family, made my stomach ache. I drank my tea and said nothing.

"So," Bill said. "I just wait until you need me?"

"I'm sure you can find something to do. There's also something else *I* have to do."

"What's that?"

"Well," I said reluctantly, "I have to see Mary. So Peter can finish firing us."

"What will you do if he doesn't? About having two clients who want the same thing."

"Oh, he will. And if there's a miracle and he doesn't, I guess I'll just ad-lib."

"Let me know if you want any coaching."

"You'd be the first guy I'd call."

"I have another question."

"Go ahead."

"What are you going to do about the guy who beat you up this morning?" He asked this casually, smoking his cigarette, just one partner reviewing the case with the other, and he carefully didn't look at me, because he knows me. Still, I felt my face redden.

"He did not beat me up," I huffed. "He threatened to beat me up, or something, if I didn't stop."

"If you didn't stop doing what now you have two clients wanting you to do."

"Well, you didn't expect me to actually do what a guy like that told me?"

"You don't even do what *I* tell you, so I guess not. But isn't he worth considering?"

I nodded slowly. "He is. For one thing, I sort of thought, in the back of my mind, he was working for H. B. Yang."

Bill stubbed out his cigarette. "So did I."

"But if that's not true and H. B. Yang wants the waiters found, then who else is interested in their not being found?"

"Any ideas?"

I shook my head. "No."

"Swell. And you wouldn't recognize this guy if you saw him?"

"Not unless he looked like the inside of a rice bag. You know," I said as a thought hit me, "there's something else I didn't tell you."

He looked at me. "You know the Marx Brothers routine on the ocean liner in *Night at the Opera*, where Groucho orders room service and keeps sticking his head out to yell to the steward, 'And one more hard-boiled egg'?"

"No," I said. "Why?"

"You remind me of it. Never mind. What else didn't you tell me?"

I gave him a confused look but continued. "Jayco Realty. I checked them out."

"And?"

"And absolutely nothing interesting. They're licensed real estate brokers. Newly licensed, and it's a new firm, but so what?"

Bill laced his fingers behind his head. "So what indeed?"

I shrugged. "I still think something was weird in that place. And that address was in one of those guys' pockets."

"The building's. Not necessarily theirs."

"True. Maybe I'm just suspicious of that Chinese guy."

"Probably a good idea. Very subtle, these Chinese."

I sighed. "Only to you big old galumphy white folks. Anyway, I'm going to head back to my office to see if the locksmith came yet to put on my bars, and then I have to see if I can find Mary." I pushed myself up off the sofa. "Can you stay out of trouble meanwhile?"

"Me? Nobody's come here to threaten *me* lately."

"It's only a matter of time." I rinsed my mug and put it in the drainer. Bill stood and walked me to the door.

"Seriously," I said. "Be careful? In case it is only a matter of time."

"Funny," he said. "I was just going to say that to you. You sure you don't need a big old galumphy white bodyguard?"

"I don't think I'd get very far in this case with you by my side," I said. "Though I'll invoke your name to Mary if it seems like it might help. But I'll be careful. The next thing I'm doing will only be inside H. B. Yang's restaurant anyway. If that rice bag guy wasn't his, he won't know I'm still on the case."

Bill frowned. "Okay," he said. "If you promise."

"Promise what?"

"I'm not sure."

"Okay, I promise."

I stood on tiptoe and kissed his cheek. He bent down and kissed my lips, but lightly. We left it at that. I felt his eyes on me from the doorway as I trotted down the two long flights, but I didn't look back.

nine

i walked back toward Canal Street and east, ambling slowly through what was now a soft late-spring afternoon. The air was clear and the sunlight still bright. It gleamed off the cars heading west to the tunnel to New Jersey as they inched past the cars heading east to the bridge to Brooklyn; they all honked at the cars trying to work their way south to Staten Island and the ones snailing north, uptown. All these people in this one spot, I thought as I stood at an intersection waiting for my brief chance to dash across, and none of them want to be here. Where they were headed for: I wondered how much they wanted to be *there,* how much thought people actually gave to where they were and whether it was the right place for them.

Oh, knock it off, Lydia, I commanded myself, you're standing around philosophizing like an old village lady. The spot you're headed for is your office, so call your mother now. I dutifully obeyed myself and did that, to find out if there was anything I should pick up before the shops closed. The merchants of Chinatown start and end their days early.

"You are calling me?" my mother said in answer to my ring.

"What amazing good fortune I have." Her sarcasm was every bit as clear in Chinese as it would have been in English.

"Amazing," I agreed. "Can I be fortunate enough to be allowed to bring something home for dinner?"

"You shouldn't speak to your mother that way, you disrespectful girl," she reprimanded me sharply. I was a little surprised; she usually just sighs and acts put upon when I'm not behaving like a good Chinese daughter should.

"I know, Ma," I said. "I'm sorry. Do you need anything?"

"Need anything? What could I need? I have four sons with prosperous, respectable positions. I have a daughter who, I've heard, takes tea with Yang Hao-Bing. How could I be greedy enough to ask for more?"

So that was what this was about. *I've heard.* A social coup of such magnitude—probably bigger than my mother ever expected from me, her unfeminine daughter with the embarrassing profession—and I didn't even let her know.

"I was just calling to tell you, Ma."

"You were calling to ask me if I wanted bok choy, or tofu. I also need wood ears."

"Bok choy, tofu, wood ears. I'll tell you about Yang Hao-Bing at dinner."

"Don't trouble yourself. Such an important personage must have a great deal on her mind."

"True. See you later." I hung up. There was no point in trying to get past this one now; my mother could go on like this for another half hour without a break. There also wasn't any point, when she was in this gear, to trying to find out how she knew about my tea party. And anyway, I needed a little time to figure out exactly what it was I was actually going to tell her about my talk with H. B. Yang.

I checked my watch: 4:45. Mary, according to Peter, was working the eight-to-four these days. I stuck another quarter in the phone and called the precinct.

"Detective Kee, please," I said to the tired voice that answered the phone in the squad room.

"Hold on. Kee!" the voice yelled. "Hey, Chester, you got any idea where Kee is? Hey, Kee! Uh, hold on," he told me again.

"My shift's been over for forty-five minutes," Mary said when, through the long waits and cop noises over the phone, she was finally found for me. "How'd you know I was still here?"

"Lucky for me, half a cop's job is paperwork. I figured you'd be there filling out forms."

She sighed. "If it was only half, I'd be grateful. I hear you're in trouble again."

"I am not!"

"Well, I didn't really hear that, either. But Peter says he hired you and fired you and that I won't like the whole thing. He's taking me out to dinner at that fancy Ethiopian place in Soho, so it must be pretty serious. You're calling because you want to take your shot first?"

"How'd you know?"

"The other half of a cop's job is brainwork."

"Where do the flat feet come in?"

"Through the door, ba-dump. Do you want to come up here?"

"Oh, yeah, right. What are you doing between now and dinner?"

"Nothing in particular, but dinner's early; Peter has some kind of meeting tonight. You want to get a cup of coffee?"

"I just had tea. How about a walk? Unless you really want coffee."

"No, I've been drinking this sludge they make here for so long that I wouldn't recognize real coffee anyway. Meet me by that weird fountain with all the little statues in it at Battery Park City. We can watch the sunset."

"Half an hour?"

"Sure. Can I bring my paperwork?"

"Only if it's cute and single. At least I could tell my mom it has a desk job."

I went another two blocks east to a vegetable stand on the fringes of Chinatown. I picked out two heads of crisp bok choy, deep green leaves fading to white on the top, light green again where they frilled out at the edges. The proprietor slipped two squares of silken tofu and a cup of brine into a container. I spent some time over the wood ears. Wood ears are just mushrooms that grow on trees instead of in the ground; my mother particularly likes their chewy texture. I carefully chose ones that weren't dried out, weren't broken, weren't soggy, ones pretty much the same size, ones I thought would look good cooked. My mother doesn't think I'm much of a shopper, but I did my best. Then, all my supplies together, I was ready to meet Mary.

But before I turned around and headed west again I dropped another quarter in a phone and called Golden Adventure. Andi and Ava were pleased to tell me—and they both did—that the locksmith had come and put bars on my window: "Very good ones, strong, also a good lock, three keys. We will wait for you, Lydia; until you come back tonight, we won't go home." They were so serious about this they were speaking Chinese.

"No, please don't put yourselves to any trouble," I said. This had to be handled delicately, because if I refused their help now, they'd think I was blaming them for the attack in the first place, because they were my landlords and therefore responsible for me. "You've done more than enough. I don't know whether I'll be back tonight." As I said that I realized it was true; I was tired, both physically weary and mentally slowing down. A nice walk in the sunset with Mary and dinner and a hot bath at home, followed closely by bedtime, sounded like a great sequence of events, even if it did involve fencing with my mother. "Just leave two keys in my desk. Keep the other in your office, so it'll be there if I need it." That should satisfy them that I trusted them and still looked forward to their help. "Thanks a lot," I added.

"All right," Andi said doubtfully, but they agreed, and I was once again on my way across town.

I hailed a cab and gave the African driver instructions to the north end of Battery Park City. Mary would be taking a cab, too, from the center of Chinatown to pretty much the same spot. Any other two people might have agreed to meet—for example, in front of Mary's place of employment, the Fifth Precinct—and go together, but Mary and I try not to be seen hanging around in Chinatown with each other. It wouldn't be good for business if we were generally known to be close buddies: mine, because people who come to me often do it specifically because they *don't* want the police involved in their affairs; and hers, because police brass distrust P.I.s, especially ones like me who were never cops, and any cop who hangs around with one had better, at the very least, be prepared to lean on that P.I. as a source if it's ever necessary.

I don't know if Mary would lean on me if someone told her to—Mary's a good cop, and being that is important to her—but ever since I went into this business, we've been getting together as often as we ever did, just in other places.

I paid off the cabdriver, strolled down the walk, and sat on a bench by the fountain where the strange little bronze statues are. Odd-shaped foot-high metal people peered into the mouths of dogs twice their sizes or grinned from the handrails of the steps leading down into the fountain area. I rubbed the head of the one that was peeking out from under my bench looking like he wanted to bite my toes.

The breeze that blew in across the Hudson carried the salty scent of the sea. It smelled distant and wide, calling up images of places it had come from, places I'd never been to but whose pictures drifted through my mind. I thought it was a marvelous, exciting smell. But then I began to wonder: what would I think of it if I were breathing that air day after day from the deck of a ship as it took me away, maybe forever, from every place I knew?

Familiar footsteps trotted up the path behind me. I turned, and there was Mary, her denim jacket buttoned against the breeze. She dropped onto the bench.

"Hi." She grinned.

"Hi." I grinned back.

"So," she said, "what bad thing happened that's Peter's fault?" She narrowed her eyes and gave me the once-over, looking for visible signs of trouble and injury.

Mary's no bigger than I am—well, okay, maybe she's an inch

taller, but barely—and she was even more of a tomboy when we were kids. Our mothers used to complain about it together, spitting out the shells of melon seeds on the sidewalk as they waited to walk us home after school, shaking their heads over our bruises and our skinned knees. Even today, while I Rollerblade and practice Tae Kwon Do, Mary lifts weights and plays soccer, outdoors in the summer, indoors in the winter. She was known to bungee-jump when that was hot, and last summer she took up rock climbing. Peter, Mr. Desk Job, who still thinks football has something to do with feet, adores her. He goes to her soccer games and cheers whenever it looks like something's happening; he massages her shoulders when she aches and takes her out to dinner when her team wins. At dinner they talk, and talk and talk; Mary says he's the first guy she's dated who isn't interested in either competing with her or changing her into the soft, gentle creature of his dreams.

"Especially cops," she'd told me once, a few years ago, as we were strolling through the lingerie department at Bloomingdale's looking for a shower gift for a cousin of hers. "Never date a cop. If you never listen to anything else I tell you, listen to that."

"You don't think I'm tough enough?"

"I think you get bored too easily," had been her answer. Then she'd asked a strange question: "This new partner of yours, was he ever a cop?"

"Bill? He's not really my partner, you know. But no, he's not a cop. But he used to live with his uncle, who was. Why? Does he act like one?"

"No." She'd looked at me and smiled a funny smile, and we'd gone back to sifting through the silk negligees.

Now, on the bench with the little bronze guy under it, she finished her scrutiny of my person. "Well, you look okay," she said grudgingly. "Does that just mean I can't see it?"

"No, I'm fine. It's not as bad as Peter probably made it sound."

"Oh, I'm sure it's not," she said, sounding sure of anything but. She stood; Mary doesn't like to sit for long. "Let's walk, okay? You probably need to walk off whatever H. B. Yang gave you for sweets, anyway." She took off down the path, her long braid swinging down her back.

"Wait!" I scrambled to my feet and caught up with her. "Is that all over Chinatown or something? How do you know about it?"

"It was on the news. You didn't see it?"

"Mary!"

She grinned again. "I talked to my mother this afternoon, who had gotten a call from your mother. Something about how unfortunate it was that H. B. Yang, who clearly had the rare wisdom to be able to spot quality where other people saw only willfulness and disobedience, nevertheless was—quite correctly for a man of his stature—too concerned with what was proper to consider having tea with a cop."

"She didn't."

"Of course she did. Do you think my mom could have resisted under the same circumstances?"

Mary's mom and my mom have been best friends for thirty years; offspring one-upmanship is their favorite game. "I guess not."

"You know not. So you'd better tell: what was it about? What's going on?"

So Mary and I walked down the path beside the river, and as the sun lowered and striped the sky and the water with lines of cerise and tangerine and gold, I told her about the case.

I started with Warren Tan and the revolution, then moved on to the waiters and the shell-loving landlady in Elmhurst. "Luke's jacket? Your mom's toolbox?" Mary's voice was shocked but she couldn't hide the laugh in her eyes. "You're nuts, Lydia! Also, as a cop, I have to say—"

"I didn't break and enter or anything. I was invited in."

Mary's look told me the official NYPD position on that.

I continued, describing the scene in my office, which I toned down just a little in the interests of not getting yelled at, and then went on to H. B. Yang and Peter—what one wanted and the other didn't, anymore.

When I was through we had reached South Cove, where a waterfall gurgles into a tiny pond with cattail rushes and lily pads.

We leaned on the rail looking out over the Hudson, now a dark blue with glints of yellow still riding the tops of the ripples.

Mary frowned. "I don't like the idea of you doing something you've been warned off of like this."

"But you can't possibly like the idea of me turning down H. B. Yang."

"No, I don't like that, either. But Peter's right. This is a police matter."

"Hey, come on. The police didn't want it just yesterday."

"Yesterday there was no crime."

"And today a punk threatens me and that changes things?"

She looked at me in surprise. "Sure. Someone's committed a crime—assault—to keep these guys from being found; that implies there's something to hide. You have to come in and swear out a complaint, then we can go looking."

"For the waiters?"

"No, for the guy who attacked you."

"What about the waiters?"

"I'll see if I can get the powers interested in them."

"What if you can't?"

"I'm pretty sure I can, now. And it'll be better for you if I do."

"Me? How? I have to keep looking no matter what."

"You told Peter if we take it up, you'd stop."

"That's *his* case. But H. B. Yang is something else. I can't just tell him, 'Forget it, the cops will take care of it for you.' "

Mary nodded; that was true. "Well, we might actually find them. And at least you won't be the only one looking, which might make you less of a target."

"The fact that I'm looking at the request of H. B. Yang might make me less of a target anyway."

"I thought of that. It's one reason I'm not yelling at you the way I just know Peter wants me to. Working for H. B. Yang should carry a certain amount of immunity with it."

"Peter doesn't know about H. B. Yang. Maybe if he did he wouldn't want you to yell at me."

"Lydia. Of course he'd want me to. Do you know how bad Peter would feel if something happened to you that was his fault?"

"Why would it be his fault?" My voice came out sharper than I meant it to be—after all, Mary wasn't actually yelling at me—so I tried to tone it down. "I don't understand this, how everybody feels that way. Like they were in charge of what I do and I don't even make my own mistakes. If something happens to me it's *my* fault."

She gave me a long look. "And you're just crazy enough to get in trouble to prove that. Is Bill working with you on this?"

"Yes. Does that make it better?"

"You know it does. Come on, Lydia, you know people only act this way because they care about you."

I sighed. "I know. But it drives me up the wall. Don't you get mad when people do that to you?"

Mary tried a frown, but a crooked grin elbowed it aside. "You bet I do." As I started to speak she added, "Of course, *I'm* backed up by the full strength and forces of the NYPD."

"Yeah, and all its paperwork."

This time she sighed. "You got that right. Listen, I have to go. If I tell you to be careful, will you bop me?"

"No, since it's you. But you better be careful, too, just on principle."

She laughed. "Yeah, okay, since it's you. Come by the station in the morning and we'll look at mug shots."

"Okay. Hey, Mary? Will you be mad at Peter that he hired me in the first place?"

She gave me a sideways look, then straightened up from the railing.

"No," she said, as we started walking out of the park, me to head back to Chinatown and my mother, Mary to Soho and dinner with Peter. "I know you too well. Once you got it in your head that this was something you were going to do, the poor guy didn't have a chance."

ten

i took the three flights of stairs to our apartment two steps at a time; it's good for the thigh muscles that way. At the top, I unlocked the two of the five locks we were using this week—my mother's formula for this keeps changing, but the principle behind it is that the bad guys trying to pick our locks will lock themselves out as they're letting themselves in—and slipped off my shoes in the tiny entry hall. I was pulling on my embroidered slippers when my mother hove into view.

"Look who has found the time to come here," she said in fake amazement. She picked up the plastic bag holding the groceries. "It's lucky we have no guests coming over for dinner. A guest might have starved to death before you brought the food."

I kissed her cheek and looked at my watch. "Hi, Ma. It's not late. Also, I'm sure you have enough food here to feed an army if one should happen to drop by. How are you?"

"At least I don't have to be worried about feeding *you* if *you* should happen to drop by. Last night, dinner with Lee Bi-Da, today, tea with Yang Hao-Bing." She marched the groceries into the kitchen.

"Yang Hao-Bing thought I was a very well brought up young lady," I said, following her and the food.

"He did?" She sniffed, but I could see she'd felt the compliment. Emptying the grocery bag, she said, "Perhaps, as wise as he is, he can see the great effort even when the results are poor."

I suddenly realized how I could make a gold mine out of this.

"What he wanted, Ma," I said while I dumped the tofu into the brine-filled container we keep for it in the fridge, "was to tell me he's been following my career. He wanted to express his satisfaction at how well I'm doing. He's very pleased at the fact that my work keeps me in Chinatown."

Her eyes widened involuntarily; otherwise, she kept her attention on the bok choy as she peeled off its outer leaves. "If Yang Hao-Bing has been following your activities, Ling Wan-ju, you have drawn too much attention to yourself."

"He said Chinatown's future was in young people like me. Also like Lee Bi-Da." I thought I'd haul Peter in under H. B. Yang's umbrella while I could. "Young people who stay here, who put our talents into helping the community. The way we would if this were our village in China."

"If this were our village in China your future would be with the husband from the next village I would have found for you by now. Did you bring the wood ears?"

I took the package of mushrooms out of the plastic bag and unwrapped them.

"Ling Wan-ju!" exclaimed my mother, peering at them. "They are so even in size, so perfectly colored. You must have paid far too much money for these. Broken ones are a better bargain, taste the same."

So my mother and I had dinner, adding steamed rice and sliced carrots and an assortment of spices and sauces to the food I'd brought. As opposed to her handling of my brothers and me, my mother has a very light hand with seasonings; as opposed to her personality, my mother's food is subtle and delicate. Except for special occasions like the Smiling Faces, my father, who had cooked for a living, had not cooked at home. And as much as I had always liked going to a restaurant he was working in and getting special treatment and the kind of fancy foods no one got to eat at home, I had, even when I was young, suspected my mother of being the better cook.

Dinner conversation consisted of praise of my brothers, gossip about neighbors and far-flung relatives, and me trying to reiterate the point that H. B. Yang thought private investigation was a perfectly admirable profession for a respectable Chinese daughter. My mother pointed out that H. B. Yang did not have a daughter who'd gone into it. He did have a niece, whom he had brought over from China many years ago. She was not a P.I., either. She had married and given him three grandnephews, all handsome young men now, one working in the restaurant and the other two in other H. B. Yang business enterprises. In fact, my mother mentioned casually, as though it had just occurred to her, the two younger ones worked so hard that they hadn't yet had time to consider taking wives.

I steered away from that, as I did from any in-depth discussion of what the rest of my conversation with H. B. Yang had been about. We finished our tea and did the dishes. I took the long bath I'd been craving, filling the bathroom with the steam from herbs for relaxation, for promoting healthy skin, and for healing bruises. I inspected my knee, which by now hurt only a little bit, and decided it would be fine by morning. After my bath I wrapped myself in my terry cloth robe and did a little home paperwork.

Since I'm the one who lives here, keeping an eye on my mother until she's ready to admit that climbing all those stairs and carrying home whichever groceries are too important for me to buy is getting to be too much for her—at which point my brothers and I have a plan that she'll move in with Ted and Ling-An, although she hasn't come around to anything more than disdain for this idea yet—I'm relieved of most of the responsibility for the bills and Medicare statements and any other paperwork it takes to keep my mother going. My brothers do all that. But since I am here, I have to at least inspect the mail and set aside whatever seems important for the attention of whichever brother is in charge of that particular aspect of my mother's life. That's what I did now, going through the pile on the table, throwing out ads in Chinese for AT&T calling cards and ads in English reminding Current Occupant that Nobody Beats the Wiz. When I was done I settled in with my mother to watch the news.

One of the cable channels in New York carries the ten o'clock news in Cantonese, and my mother watches every night. She's equally enthralled with what happened in Hong Kong and Taiwan as with the day's events in Chinatown and Flushing. The reporters on this channel can be less than objective and are at their most biased when reporting on events in China itself, which, until it reunites with Taiwan under the leadership of the current Taiwanese government, will continue to be considered by large segments of the overseas Chinese community to be a hostile foreign power. Reunification on these terms will happen at roughly the same time hell freezes over, so I try to get my news about China from the English-language papers; but I watch the Cantonese news with my mother to keep up with local events that could and sometimes do result in business for me.

Usually the top story on this channel is about some outrage perpetrated on the citizens of Hong Kong by their still-new Chinese rulers, or another installment in the long-running and gleefully reported story of the small but steady flow of student dissidents and political prisoners escaping their jail cells in China and vanishing only to reappear months later right here in the good old USA; or a solemnly portentous report on the rise of Chinese gangsters now that to be rich is glorious. The local stuff tends to come later, so I was surprised to see, as I started to organize myself on the sofa, that tonight they were opening with the local hard news correspondent, Moy Pang, in front of a scene swirling with red and white cop car lights and swarming with cops and with other reporters. I listened with interest to the start of her report. Then my blood froze.

". . . an explosion, caused, police say, by a bomb. The Chinese Restaurant Workers' Union, which had been holding a demonstration tonight in front of Dragon Garden restaurant, a few blocks away, is a relatively new player on the Chinatown scene. But some-one evidently has taken enough notice of them to want to send what was apparently intended to be a warning. The call that came in to the Fifth Precinct, however, was not in time for police to evacuate the union's office on the basement floor of this Mott Street building. The bomb exploded, perhaps prematurely, almost immediately after the call was made. One man is dead, one injured; the injured man is the union's attorney''—she consulted her notes—''Lee Bi-Da. The identity of the dead man is not yet known. Lee Bi-Da has been taken to Long Island College Hospital in Brooklyn Heights, where he is reported in serious condition. I'm here with Warren Tan, a union official. Mr. Tan, what can you tell us about the circumstances of this bombing?''

The camera pulled back to reveal Warren Tan, his bristling hair and rimless glasses emphasizing his ashen look. Moy Pang held the microphone toward him; he looked at her blankly for just a second, then rallied himself and spoke.

''I don't have any more facts than you do,'' he said. His voice seemed to catch in his throat, then it got stronger. ''The police investigation will have to give us those. But this criminal act proves that the antiunion forces are willing to go to any lengths to destroy us.'' He turned to look straight into the camera. ''That won't hap-pen. The CRWU will continue to grow. We won't be intimidated by pressure, threats, or violence. We welcome alliances with other labor groups, but if they're frightened off by this sort of thing, we'll fight alone. We say—''

I didn't wait to hear what they said. I didn't wait to hear what my mother said. I ran to my room, threw some clothes on, and headed for Long Island College Hospital in Brooklyn Heights. Just before I left, I tucked my .38 into its holster in the waistband of my pants.

Long Island College Hospital seems like an odd thing to put in Brook-lyn Heights, and I don't know why they did that. Brooklyn Heights might seem like an odd place to take someone hurt in a Chinatown explosion, but that actually makes sense. Brooklyn Heights is in a different borough, but it's right over the bridge from Chinatown, and depending on the traffic it can be an easier trip for an ambulance than trying to scream its way uptown or across town to a hospital in Manhattan.

Still. Still. The trip seemed to take forever, the eight minutes I spent in that cab some of the longest of my life. When we finally got there, the modern, redbrick building loomed huge and uninviting, as hospitals always do. I got directions from the reception desk to Emergency, which was around the corner, but that was as far as I got. They wouldn't let me in to see Peter and they wouldn't tell me anything more than I'd learned on TV about the condition he was in.

I was pacing, probably driving everybody in the waiting room crazy, when a squad car screeched up to the ambulance-only entrance. Before it had stopped rocking its doors flew open. Mary burst out from one and Peter's Uncle Lee Liang from the other.

Mary spotted me as soon as she'd yanked open the waiting room doors. We gave each other a quick hug, and she asked me, "Where is he?"

"I don't know."

"In surgery?"

"They won't tell me anything. I'm not family."

"We are," she said grimly. She grabbed Lee Liang's arm and pulled him over to the desk. "I'm Peter Lee's fiancée and this is his uncle," she snapped in her best I'm-a-cop-and-this-is-an-order voice. "We want to see him."

I didn't think that was going to work, but they were ushered right through the inner doors, leaving me to pace some more. I was trying to keep myself from kicking furniture and pounding the wall about ten minutes later when the inner doors swung again and Mary and Lee Liang emerged.

I rushed over and grabbed Mary's arms. Lee Liang headed for the pay phone at the end of the room; I heard him speaking rapid Cantonese to Peter's mother.

"A concussion," Mary said, "maybe a skull fracture. A broken arm, broken ribs. Abrasions, contusions. Some internal injuries, but they're not serious."

"Then why did they say 'serious'?"

"They always do with a head injury. They're still running tests, but he was sort of awake. I mean, I think he knew it was me."

She had, I saw, a smear of blood on her shirt and another across her cheek.

"That's good," I said. "That he was awake."

She shrugged. "It's better than if he wasn't."

The three of us sat down in an unoccupied row of waiting room chairs and started waiting. Lee Liang sprang up immediately and fed coins to a machine that produced three foul cups of instant tea for us. We drank that and did some more waiting. Mary got up and made a phone call. She came back and sat.

"I called the station," she said. "To find out what happened. The detective who caught the case, his name is Manny Patino. He says they don't know much yet. Someone set a bomb at the union office and it went off. They called in a warning but not in time. They haven't identified the dead man yet. Just the two of them were there, it looks like. Everyone else was at the Dragon Garden demonstration."

"Warren Tan told me about that. I thought that's where Peter was going to be."

"So did I." She shook her head. "How did you find out about the bomb?" she asked me.

"I was watching the news with my mother. Oh, my God! My mother! I'd better call her."

I went and did that and came back. "She was on the phone to your mother when I called. It's a good thing we have Call Waiting."

Mary smiled tiredly. "I tried that, but I couldn't get my mom to understand how it worked. How'd you do it?"

"Well, it was a problem, until I explained it would let her talk to two of my brothers at the same time. She caught on right away, then."

"How's my mom doing?"

104

"According to mine, she'd be doing much better if Peter's mom's only son took his responsibility to his mother seriously and stayed away from dangerous clients like the union. Then the mothers of women friends of his would also not have to worry in the middle of the night."

Mary considered. "On the Mom Scale, that's pretty good."

"Your mom and mine both offered to go over and stay with Peter's mom, but Peter's mom said no thanks. Lee Liang's wife is there, I guess."

I turned to Peter's uncle, who nodded.

We waited some more.

Finally a nurse came out, crooked a finger at Mary and Lee Liang, and took them back through the inner doors. I sat in my plastic molded chair and tried not to break its edges off with my grip.

I was wondering how much longer I could listen to the fluorescent light buzz over my head before I jumped up on my chair and smashed it to bits when Mary came back out. "No fracture," she said, dropping into the chair next to the one I'd just leaped out of. "No brain hematoma, or whatever that's called. They gave him something and he's asleep."

"Where's Uncle Liang?"

"Staying with him. They would only let one of us stay, and he's the one who's family."

I put my arm around Mary's shoulder and squeezed. "He'll be okay, then."

"I guess. God, Lydia! Peter's so . . . he's so . . ." She shrugged helplessly. "This is so . . ."

"I know," I said.

We sat silently for another little while, and then Mary said quietly, "H. B. Yang."

"What?"

"The bomb. I'll bet he's behind the goddamn bomb."

In all our tomboy years together, I've almost never heard Mary swear; she's legendary around the Fifth Precinct for her clean mouth. I looked at her; as I did, she got up and started to pace, but the

105

waiting room was too small for Mary. When she reached the ambulance bay doors she shoved them open and stood, hands on hips, breathing deep gulps of the clear night air.

I followed her out, put a hand on her shoulder. "I don't think so," I said.

"Why not?" She was clearly making an effort to control herself.

"He just hired me today to look for the waiters," I said.

"So?"

"Well, it doesn't seem——"

"Sure it does. You're looking for guys he doesn't want to lose his investment in and he's blowing up the place so the union can't hook any more of his guys. What's the problem?"

"It doesn't make sense. It's too attention-getting. And Peter said——" I was stopped by her look.

"Peter said what?"

I thought back to the breezy, bright morning on the street corner. "Peter said it wasn't done the old way anymore. That it was all done in court these days."

"Peter was wrong. He's wrong all the time." Her voice sounded bitter, an unnatural sound for Mary. She looked up at a sky full of stars it was clear enough to see even from Brooklyn. "Peter thinks if you work hard enough and add up enough of what he calls 'little victories,' good will eventually win over evil. That's what Peter thinks."

"You think he's wrong?"

"Of course he's wrong! You're as bad as he is! You two live in dreamland, saving the world all the time. Well, that's just great for you. Cops don't live there. Cops live——" She stopped, seeming to suddenly hear herself. She turned from the sky to me. "I'm sorry," she said. "I don't mean to be yelling at you. But Peter wouldn't be in this—he wouldn't be in here, if he just wasn't so . . . so . . ."

"And if he weren't, you wouldn't love him so much, would you?"

"That's not the point!"

"It's completely the point. You told them you were his fiancée." I couldn't help a little grin.

"I had to say something, didn't I?"

"You didn't have to say *that*. Is it true?"

"Of course not. Don't you think you'd be the first to know?"

"I think I am. Are you going to stay here?" I said, to head off the rest of that conversation.

She frowned, but said, "Yes, I guess. Lee Liang said he'd come out later so I could go in for a while."

"I'll stay with you until then."

"You don't have to. But, Lydia?"

"Yes?"

I heard her take a breath. "I don't want you working for H. B. Yang."

"Mary—"

"Don't. I don't know why I even thought about letting you do this. He hires illegals and has union organizers arrested and blows up buildings. He's a dangerous man and you'd better keep away from him."

I took a deep breath myself. "You're upset, and you're taking it out on H. B. Yang and me." She opened her mouth to object, but I didn't listen. "First, I really don't think he did this. Second, if he did, it might be a good idea not to let him know we think so and to stay close to him if we can."

"We?"

"Me, us, whatever." I waved that off. "Third, if I kept away from everyone in Chinatown who hired illegals I'd have no clients at all. And fourth—" I stopped, not wanting to say what I wanted to say.

"Fourth, what?"

"Nothing."

"What?" The way she said that, I knew she knew, so I went ahead.

"Fourth, you're not 'letting' me do this and you can't stop me."

Mary looked away and hissed out a sputtering breath. "You're so pigheaded—"

"I am not. But I'm going to do this the way I think it's right. I'm upset about Peter, too, but it was Peter who wanted me to find the waiters in the first place."

"That's not fair." Mary's voice sounded uneven. She wasn't looking at me, so I walked around in front of her to look at her. Tears brimmed in her eyes.

I hugged her, and she hugged me back, crying quietly.

"No," I said. "But it's true."

My mother was still awake when I got home from the hospital. I had called once more, to tell her I was going to stay with Mary for a while, and to tell her Peter was going to be all right, and to tell her to go to bed. But when I got to the top of the stairs I heard the high-pitched wavering of Cantonese opera leaking out from behind our door, and when I got inside I found my mother on the couch under the bright light of her sewing lamp, needle flashing in and out of the embroidered shirt she was working on for Elliot's daughter.

"How is Lee Bi-Da?" She looked up as I came in.

"He'll be fine, Ma. But he has to stay there a while. Mary and Lee Liang are with him."

My mother shook her head. "This union," she said. "I knew this was a bad idea. Now you can see I was right."

"The union didn't plant that bomb, Ma, their enemies did."

"If there were no union there would be no enemies." My mother's logic was, as usual, irrefutable, but I tried anyway.

"How could you not like it, Ma? All they want is to be treated decently, paid enough to live on. How can that be a bad thing?"

She gave me a pitying look. "Newcomers," she said with the eternal contempt of all those who've just stepped through the door for the ones still outside. "Troublemakers." Then the final insult: "Fukienese. They are too good for what was enough for your father. He worked hard, he was paid for his work. Your father didn't need a union. He provided well for his family."

108

"That's true, Ma," I said. Of course, my mother's twelve-hour days in Mr. Leng's sweatshop had helped some, too, but I didn't say that. It was the husband's job to provide, and my father had worked very hard at it. My mother's pride came from having chosen a husband who could do that—and from having raised four sons and a daughter who properly revered their father's memory. Pointing out her contribution to the family's prosperity would only, in her eyes, have meant I didn't appreciate his.

"But they will get what they deserve," she said smugly.

I was momentarily confused. "The Fukienese?"

"Of course. Lee Hai-Quoon"—Peter's mother—"has told me about unions, now I know. If they are successful, all the restaurant workers will have to join. They will all have to show their employment papers, their Social Security numbers, to get their wonderful union benefits."

I could see where she was going; it was a conversation Peter and I had had more than once. It was the flaw in the great union dream. "They're all supposed to have those now, to get jobs," I said.

She shook her head. "When your father and I came here, he had papers: a work visa, a promise of a job. The Fukienese, I understand, do not." She understood. She knew full well that many, many of the new immigrants came off of ships in the middle of the night, waded through cold, tugging waters off Long Island and New Jersey to be met by men they'd never seen, taken to rooms as crowded and dirty as the hold of the ship they'd come from, and told to report to their new place of employment first thing in the morning to begin paying off their debt to the men who'd arranged all this.

"Who will hire all these people without papers if the union wins?" asked my mother.

I didn't want to have that argument with her, not in the middle of the night with Peter in the hospital and a big day in front of me.

"Why didn't you go to bed?" I asked her.

She tied a knot, bit her thread off, and folded the cloth.

"Sometimes," she said, "the telephone does not tell the truth.

I wanted to see you say to me what you said to me on the telephone, that Lee Bi-Da was not badly hurt.'' She stood, put her sewing in her basket, and headed to her bedroom.

"Good night, Ma,'' I called after her. "Sleep well.''

"Good night, Ling Wan-ju.''

She closed her door.

I turned off the living room light and stood at the window, staring out over the city to the same stars we'd looked at from Brooklyn. Below the stars the asphalt roofs of Chinatown spread, sheltering the dreams of so many people. So many different dreams: good ones, bad ones, possible ones, ones that would never come true. It was very late; I thought about it twice, and then I called Bill.

"Smith.'' His voice was hoarse and sleepy; he coughed.

"I'm sorry,'' I said. "Did I wake you?''

"Yeah.'' He sounded more confused than anything else. "It's close to one. Are you okay?''

"Yes,'' I said. "But.''

"But what?'' I heard him strike a match. He'd once told me that the first cigarette after sleep is the best of a smoker's day.

"Did you watch the news tonight?'' I asked.

"No. Did I miss something?''

"Someone bombed the Restaurant Workers' Union office. Peter was hurt and another man was killed.''

"Jesus!'' He was fully awake now; I could hear that. "Were you there? Are you all right? How's Peter?''

"I wasn't there. Peter seems like he'll be okay, but he's kind of a mess.''

"Who was the other man?''

"They haven't identified him yet.''

"Peter doesn't know?''

"He's too out of it to talk yet. Maybe tomorrow.''

"One of ours?''

"You wonder, don't you?''

"Who planted the bomb?''

"They don't know that, either.''

"Big help they are. Are you okay? You want me to come over?"

"Yes. No. I mean, yes, I'm okay; no, don't come over. I'm home. If you came here at one in the morning my mother would probably shoot you."

"God Almighty, don't tell me your mother has a gun."

"For you, I'm sure she could dig one up."

"What do you want to do?"

"I just wanted to talk to you. Now I feel better." Those words came out before I could stop them. I held the phone out and stared at it. I was glad it didn't transmit heat across town so Bill couldn't feel my cheeks burn.

Bill's end of the phone was silent for a moment. Then his voice came gently. "Are you sure you're okay? I could come over, gun or no gun."

"No," I said firmly. "Stop asking. I'm fine. I'm sorry. I don't know what my problem is."

"Gee, I don't know, either. Could it be that one of your best friends just almost got killed?"

"Oh, you know me, things like that just roll off my back. Mary thinks H. B. Yang was responsible for the bomb."

"Hmm. Do you? Is this his sort of thing?"

"Honestly," I said, "I don't know. We Chinatown kids were always afraid of him, but I don't remember anything like this. More like he could tell everyone not to hire you or buy at your shop, and everyone would listen to him, and then you'd have to leave Chinatown in disgrace. We kids thought he could have us sent back to China for being bad."

"Did your folks tell you that?"

"No, it was something kids told each other. My mother got mad when she heard it. She said this was our home and nobody could make us leave it."

I watched the stars and the streetlights shine.

"But Mary still thinks it was him?" Bill asked.

"Chinatown logic is one thing; cop logic is another." I explained Mary's thinking.

"I say too obvious," Bill told me. "He's the only restaurant being picketed, isn't he?"

"Yes."

"So he'll be the first to be suspected. The cops are bound to haul him in and grill him. Especially when a cop's boyfriend was hurt."

"H. B. Yang is the mayor's pal. Doesn't that outrank a cop's boyfriend? And from what Warren Tan said, the union's not such a threat to H. B. Yang since he got the East Point thing."

"They'll go through the motions anyway. It would look too bad if they didn't. But assuming it wasn't Yang, you know what I wonder?"

"What?"

"Who he thinks it was."

"Good question. Maybe I'll ask him."

"Just like that?"

"Well, just like something. I'm going to work there tomorrow, you know."

"Good God, I'd forgotten that. Maybe I'll come for lunch."

"If you do, you'd better eat a lot of whatever I'm selling."

"Whatever you're selling," he said, "is just what I'm hungry for."

So that conversation ended the way so many of ours do: Bill hitting on me in a kidding-around way; me telling him to put a sock in it in an annoyed-sounding way. I didn't know about him, but my part seemed, this clear and starry evening, to be a little harder than it usually was.

eleven

I slept badly through what was left of that night, but I got up early, showered, and put on my frumpiest black pants and white shirt. Rummaging in my bottom drawer, where I keep junk that's already come in useful once and might someday again, I found a pair of really dorky black-framed glasses with clear glass lenses: about as much of a disguise as I could hope for today. I stuck the glasses in my pocket, kissed my mother, and didn't tell her where I was going. I hoped, as I clattered down the stairs, that none of my brothers was planning to swoop down to Chinatown and take my mother out for a surprise dim sum lunch.

I had to report to Dragon Garden at nine; before that, though, I had another task to get behind me.

The Fifth Precinct station house is one of the old New York police stations, a white building in the middle of the block with an elaborate green-bulbed lantern on each side of the stone staircase to the iron-studded double front doors. It was built in the early 1900s, and the inside looks as though it hasn't been painted since, although someone thought at some point that putting down vinyl tile over the original wood floors was a good idea. It's cramped and noisy and smells like yesterday's take-out food. It's also full of people who don't want to be there—a few of them cops. Usually when I'm inside, that's how I feel, too, because I'm generally trying to explain my way out of some situation that someone else, sometimes Mary, doesn't think I ought to be in.

That wasn't the case today, though. I met Mary in the Detective Squad Room, on the second floor, where she had already stacked the mug shot books on her desk for me to go through.

"You look terrible," I told her as she dipped a tea bag in and out of the cup of tea she was making for me. She had blue crescents under her eyes and her skin was dull and blotchy.

"Thanks," she said. "Same to you."

"Did you stay at the hospital all night?"

She nodded as she handed me the tea.

"How is he?" I asked.

"Stable. Not awake yet. Patino has a uniform over there for when he wakes up, in case he can tell them anything. Patino's already been to see H. B. Yang."

"Been there? Not picked him up to come here?"

Mary shook her head. "Not H. B. Yang," she said in a voice more dispirited than I'd heard from her before. "You don't ask him to come here."

I wanted to reach out and hug her and tell her Peter would be all right and we'd get whoever did it, but she was a detective and this was the Fifth Precinct, so I drank my tea and asked, "What did he say?"

"H. B. Yang? He said it was a terrible thing, but not surprising. He said people who have rice for brains and disrupt a wasps' nest are bound to get stung. Of course, he was shocked and saddened that anyone thought he might have had anything to do with this. He hoped the mayor didn't feel that way, too; he'd have to give him a call and find out. He understood, though, that the police had a job to do and offered to help any way he could. He commended Patino on his thoroughness."

114

"In other words, go bother somebody else or I'll swat you like a fly."

"I think that's a fair translation."

"But Detective Patino—he's not letting it drop, is he?"

"He's been told from above to tread very, very carefully."

"Above meaning the mayor's office?"

"In this department, 'above' can mean anything. One of the things above never wants you to know is who they are. But in this case if it turned out to be the mayor's office I wouldn't exactly fall over."

I said, "Well, I guess that's politics."

"There's something else," Mary said reluctantly. "Remember I said I would try to get the powers interested in the waiters?"

"Yes?"

"No. I put in a call yesterday after I left you. It was a little weird, but the result was: no."

"What do you mean, weird?"

"I talked to my lieutenant. He said upstairs knew about the disappearance of the men but they didn't see a crime and I'd better drop it and do some real work the way he told me to two days ago."

"Why is that weird? That sounds like what Peter told me."

"Except why did upstairs know? Two days ago my lieutenant said no crime, no cops. So why did he tell upstairs?"

I thought about this. "Is upstairs the same as above?"

"No. Upstairs is the department; above sends messages through upstairs to us down here."

"Because," I said, "this could just be more of keeping the NYPD's nose out of H. B. Yang's problems."

"Yeah," said Mary wearily, "I suppose it could."

I swore out a complaint, detailing the attack in my office. Mary called it as many crimes as she could think of: breaking and entering, assault, stalking—I thought that was stretching it, but she just glared at me—and intimidation, which is apparently, under some circumstances, illegal.

"*Attempted* intimidation," I corrected, but she just glared again.

We leafed through the mug shot books but gave up after I convinced her that really, really, I hadn't seen his face.

"Well," she said with a tired sigh, leaning back in her chair, "I'll see what I can do. There are a lot of gangsters running around looking for freelance work; we'll take some up and shake them. There's nothing else you remember at all?"

I thought hard. "There was something." I focused my eyes on a corner of Mary's desk, then stopped seeing it. I tried to bring back the scene in my office, to remember how it smelled, how it sounded. "He was revolting," I said.

"Oh, no kidding. A guy grabs you, ties you up, socks you, and you don't find him appealing? I guess that's healthy, at least."

"No, be serious. Something about him. About this particular guy."

"The way he smelled?" she asked dubiously. "The language he used?"

"No. Something—his hand! His fingers!"

"What?" Mary sat upright. "What about them?"

"There weren't enough of them! When he had his hand on my throat—something wasn't right, and that's what it was." I had my eyes closed, feeling the roughness of the burlap bag as it clamped around my neck. "Too big a space between his thumb and his fingers. And only three fingers squeezing. And the first one was—was pressing in a funny place. It wasn't long enough! That's what was re- volting—his hand was all wrong. What are you doing?"

Mary, with a grim smile, was flipping back through one of the mug books. She tapped her finger on a picture, a truculent-looking young man with broad shoulders, short hair, and a wispy goatee. "Three-finger Choi," she said. The man scowled into the camera, and then he scowled to the right for his profile shot. The lines painted on the wall behind him had him at just under six feet.

"I don't know," I said. "He's big enough. Who is he?"

"Three-finger Choi," she repeated. "Mutt-for-hire. He lost the first finger and part of the second finger on his left hand when a gun misfired. That turned out to be a lucky thing for a guy whose name I forget, who, they say, was trying to renege on a gambling debt to Duke Lo.''

"Duke Lo? One of the new guys, the one who owns Happy Pavilion?''

"Uh-huh. He came here three or four years ago. By now he's a big somebody in the Fukienese power structure. Fast rise, and it's too bad. He's a pretty unsavory type, but we've never been able to connect him up.''

I thought about the customers Peter's union had driven from Dragon Garden to Happy Pavilion Restaurant. "Connect him up with what?''

"Anything we can prove. Sending guys like Three-finger Choi around to beat up citizens, for example. General badness. The INS is hot to ship him back.''

"Can they do that?''

"Well, he's not naturalized yet, so they could, but they need a crime. The NYPD likes to help out those less gifted, so every now and then we do them a favor and go hunting for him. But it gets us nowhere.''

"Why not?''

"My theory,'' Mary said, "is that Duke Lo was very good in a past life, and the gods are looking out for him now.''

"If he was that good he wouldn't have had to come back as a person,'' I pointed out. "Or at least, not as a man.''

That got a smile out of Mary, the first I'd seen this morning.

"What do you mean, fast rise?'' I asked.

"Usually it takes longer for one of the new guys to build a power base. You have to get to know people. Kiss the right rings, pull some stuff that proves your worth so you can recruit your soldiers. Duke Lo rocketed to the top, behind guys like Three-finger Choi. He seems to have a loyal and dedicated following, bigger than you'd expect for someone still new.''

"Consisting of locals?''

She shook her head. "No, but mostly legals, newer than he is. He attracts the least appetizing of the FOBs. They seem to gravitate right to him.'' FOBs, in Chinatownese, are newcomers Fresh Off the Boat. ''Come to think of it, if the INS didn't go handing out visas and green cards to scum like Choi, they wouldn't need to be chewing their fingernails over Duke Lo. He has a record in China, you know.''

''Lo?''

''Choi.''

''So why did they let him in?''

''Because they're the Feds, in their infinite wisdom.''

''So,'' I said, watching cops come and go, ''what would be Lo's connection to the waiters?''

''No idea. Maybe they owe him something.''

''He's a money lender?''

''I told you, he's a general crook. No crime too big or small, as long as it's unproven.''

''What's his real name?''

''Lo Da-Qi.''

Roughly translatable as All in Readiness. ''Why does he call himself Duke?''

Mary shrugged. ''From what I hear, he sees Chinatown these days as the Old West. Wide open. Anybody's.''

''Wait,'' I said. ''And he's John Wayne?''

''The imagination of these guys amazes you, doesn't it? Chester!''

A bright-eyed young detective with a shaved head and a goatee looked up from a paper-covered desk. ''Yeah?''

''Want to come pick up Three-finger Choi with me?'' Mary stood.

''Hell, yes.'' Chester threw his pen down on his desk. ''Or here's an even better idea: I'll go do that and you stay and fill these out.''

''In your dreams, Chester. Come on.'' Mary stopped short and narrowed her eyes at me. ''And we can send someone over to your office to lift prints in case there's anything left. Why didn't you call us before you called the locksmith?''

"Because what were you going to do about it? When Golden Adventure was broken into last year, no one lifted any prints."

"No one put rice bags over their heads, either. Don't give me that innocent stuff, Lydia. This wasn't a B and E and we wouldn't have treated it that way. You were just afraid I'd find out and order you off the case. Yeah, I know, I can't order you off anything. Go away, I have work to do. Chester, come on, move it, let's go."

Mary and the other detective pulled on the jackets they wear to cover the guns they carry. They conferred briefly over at his desk. I opened and closed my mouth, but the right words didn't come. Mary didn't look over at me again, so I left her there and found my own way out of the Fifth Precinct.

I hustled through the sunny streets, crowded now with early-morning shoppers intent on scooping up the freshest piece of perch and the crispest cabbage to be had, for the family meal they'd be making at midday. The lo mein lady behind her metal cart was already dishing up steaming noodles to fortify those whose mission among the veg- etable stands had only just begun. I was hit by the scent of the soy sauce and sesame oil she used as I hurried by, and wondered what her clothes smelled like by the end of the day. Then I wondered what mine were going to smell like by the end of this day in and out of the kitchen at Dragon Garden.

I took a detour and went up Mott Street to the building that held the Chinese Restaurant Workers' Union office. I had come by last night on my way home from the hospital and found the bomb-sniffing dogs gone, the homicide investigators finished, the yellow POLICE LINE, DO NOT CROSS tape still up, evacuated residents milling around wearing blankets and worried looks, and the city inspectors just arriving to do their job of making sure the building was not structurally damaged and about to collapse into the street.

I didn't know what I expected to find now, but I went anyway, to make the explosion more real to me, to see for myself.

What I saw was the police tape down and the door at the

bottom of the areaway stairs standing ajar. Except for plywood over the areaway windows, the building showed no sign that a bomb had exploded there last night. Even the drugstore on street level was open for business.

I went down the stairs, stood in the open doorway, and knocked. Warren Tan knelt in the wreckage, a few wrinkled and torn pieces of paper in each hand. He looked over his shoulder and met my eyes. Saying nothing, he stood.

"I'm sorry," I told him.

He looked at me blankly for a moment, as if he'd forgotten who I was, but I didn't think that was it. Then he said, "It was only a small bomb. Something called C-4." He gave a short, humorless laugh. "An American military product. You only need a piece the size of a quarter." His voice was dull and his skin as ashen as it had appeared on TV the night before. "The cops said we could come back."

"They're through here?"

He nodded, looking around. The chaos of two nights ago, when I'd first come here, was nothing compared to the situation now. Chairs lay on their sides, file drawers gaped open. The bridge table Warren Tan and I had sat at tilted forward, two of its legs snapped in half. It looked like a camel kneeling in a paper oasis.

"It was under that desk," Warren Tan said, pointing to a file-covered patch of floor. Between the papers, envelopes, and yellow pads, I could see a shallow rubble crater in the concrete floor. I remembered a desk standing in that spot; nothing was there now.

"Blew the hell out of it," he said. "That's what killed the guy Peter was meeting with; a piece of it smashed his skull. The cops packed it up and carted it away; they're going to analyze it or something, I guess."

In the air I could smell something lingering and acrid, probably the explosive. "There wasn't a fire?" I asked.

He shook his head.

"That's lucky," I tried.

His look was one of disbelief. "Lucky? Peter's in the hospital,

120

another guy's dead—lucky?'' Unexpectedly he gave a small, tired smile. ''But maybe that proves what we said the other night—no matter how American you are, you can't stop being Chinese. Luck has to get in there somewhere, doesn't it? And maybe you're right. Guess who called already this morning?''

''Who?''

''The New York Labor Council.''

''They did? Why?''

''An unofficial call. My friend over there, sort of testing the waters. Apparently I said something last night on TV about other labor groups being scared off.''

''On the Cantonese cable channel. I saw it.''

''I don't remember what I said. But it seems the networks picked it up on the eleven o'clock news and the *Times* carried it this morning. The NYLC doesn't like to look scared.''

''So something good may come of this?'' It seemed a silly, Pollyanna-sounding thing to say, as both of us looked around the disaster of an office again.

''It had better,'' he finally said. ''Otherwise it's just . . . what a waste.''

''Did you know Peter and that other man were here?''

''Did I—God, no! Everyone was supposed to be at the Dragon Garden demonstration. This place should have been empty.'' He shook his head slowly, side to side. ''There's always someone here. But last night, it should have been empty.''

I glanced at my watch. Speaking of Dragon Garden, I needed to be on the move. ''Do you know who the other man was?''

''No. The cops asked me to identify him, but the head wound . . . I couldn't.''

Warren Tan and I stood looking at each other another moment or two in the rubble of his office.

''I have to go,'' I said.

He nodded and gave me another small smile. ''I guess this makes joining the revolution a little less attractive, huh?''

''No,'' I said, looking around once again before I turned to leave. ''More.''

The help at Dragon Garden didn't ride to work up the gleaming escalator, of course; they entered the building three doors down and climbed a steep staircase to a large room that served as both employees' break room and, it seemed, nonfoods storage spillover space. When I pushed open the room's door on this early Saturday morning a number of heads turned my way, a few welcoming, a few hostile, most indifferently curious. In restaurant work, people come and go all the time. Each new person or person newly gone makes the ground shift slightly, like a tug on a tablecloth, and the people who stay rearrange a little, like teacups that tip and then regain their balance.

I stopped just inside the door, smiled shyly, and bowed to my new coworkers, hoping my dorky glasses wouldn't slip off. Most of them tipped their heads to me with the automatic instinct people everywhere have to return a polite gesture.

"I am Chin Ling," I said softly, bobbing my head again, speaking Cantonese, giving them the truth, though not all of it. "This is my first day. First day," I said again in English, mindful of the fact that probably fewer than half these people spoke the language of the Chinatown of my childhood.

My new colleagues, most of them men, sat on the few available chairs—rejects from the dining room, with ripped seats or missing backs or uneven, shaky legs—or on cardboard cases of spare teapots, or on folded, string-tied piles of freshly laundered tablecloths. Some of them were smoking, the gray haze from their cigarettes sucked out through double swinging doors at the far end of the room by the powerful kitchen exhaust fans. One plump woman was knitting; she smiled as I came in, finishing her row, and starting the next without looking and without pause.

A sharp-nosed man with a long red scar slicing down his jaw-line from ear to chin sat swinging his legs on a drum of dish detergent. He checked his watch, stubbed his cigarette out, and said to me in Fukienese-accented English, "You almost don't make on time. Tomorrow, you come sooner."

I nodded quickly, apologetically. Without looking at me again he slipped off his perch and headed toward the kitchen doors. Everyone else finished their conversations and their cigarettes, stood, and followed.

The knitting lady hooked her arm in mine as I stood looking confused. She smiled at me. "Have you worked in restaurants before?"

She spoke in Cantonese, so I did, too. "At home," I said. "Hong Kong. But it was different. . . ."

She shook her head, still smiling. "The same. People are hungry, you have food. You offer it, they buy it. They are happy, you are happy. Come."

My benefactress introduced herself as Chen Pei-Hui. Arm in arm we made our way through the steamy, shout-filled kitchen, skirting the scowling chefs and their harried assistants. In the dining room, the waiters snapped tablecloths into the air and settled them on the large round tables, pinning them down with small, plump teacups, folded napkins, and chopsticks. The women chose rolling carts—Pei-Hui steered me away from my first choice, apparently well-known for a sticky wheel—from another side room and pushed them into the kitchen, where the chefs' assistants loaded us up with dumpling-filled bamboo steamers and plates of turnip cakes and upside-down glass bowls holding mounds of eight-treasure rice. As the new kid in town, I didn't get the premium dishes, the ones with the highest price tags; those went with seniority, though I suspected a nice smile at the right chef might not hurt, either.

By the time our carts were all full and our phalanx came rolling out the kitchen doors, customers were streaming off the escalator, being guided to their seats by black-clad maître d's, given their first pots of tea by maroon-jacketed waiters, and looking expectantly around for us.

I'd eaten enough meals here and at other dim sum palaces that I knew the drill, and though the work was tiring, it wasn't hard. I steered my cart among the tables, trying to catch diners' eyes, calling out in English and Cantonese the names of the food I was, literally, pushing. When someone stopped me and asked for a steamer basket of pork shiu mai I tried also to interest them in some shrimp-stuffed pepper or a nice plate of chicken feet. Whatever they took got them a stamp from the chop I wore on a cord around my neck onto the bill the maître d' had already placed on the table. Each chop told the price of the dishes the chop's wearer was selling, and the number of chops was, simply, the number of dishes the customer had taken. The function of the waiters in this system was to clear the empty plates and bring more tea, plus take orders for things people wanted from the regular menu. Non-Chinese don't usually take advantage of the menu when they're out for dim sum, but Chinese people like to end a dim sum feast the way we do any major meal, with a bowl of noodles.

The waiters sped around carrying pots of tea and plates of chow fun, adding up bills and resetting tables. The other dim sum ladies and I crisscrossed the dining room, calling out the names of our food, explaining it in halting English to the non-Chinese customers and plonking it down on the Chinese diners' tables. When our carts were depleted we rolled them back to the kitchen, where bad-tempered chefs with big metal cleavers barked orders at their helpers and new garlic or fish or black bean scented delicacies were piled up for us.

I was glad I'd eaten a bowl of cornflakes at home, glad for the tea Mary had made me at the station house, and glad for my crepe-soled shoes as I navigated past a rowdy tableful of Columbia fraternity boys who had just grabbed up the last of my spareribs and my lotus-leaf-wrapped sticky rice, though they wouldn't touch the chicken feet (my mother's favorite). The noise in the high-ceilinged room had just about hit the level where my head starts pounding, and my shoulders, which I stretch and lift weights with at least three times a week at the dojo so they'll be prepared for anything, were beginning to tell me they hadn't been prepared for this. I stopped briefly, straightened my aching back, and surveyed the room.

The escalators were removing customers and disgorging replacement ones at an undiminished rate, and the other dim sum ladies and the waiters were scurrying about attending to them. In the private room off to the side, tables were being set with the good dishes

124

and bowls H. B. Yang had used for tea with me. It had become something of a minor fad in New York for non-Chinese to hold wedding banquets in Chinese restaurants, and tonight was the banquet of a mayoral aide, Jo Ann Johnson. It wasn't quite the mayor, but it was still a political coup, and I found myself wondering how things like that sat with the new guys, who, after all, also ran restaurants. I was also a little surprised to find myself wondering, as cynically as Bill would, what special considerations—by which, of course, I meant what break in the price—H. B. Yang had extended to the bride to secure it.

I watched the pattern of everyone's comings and goings, spoonings and gobblings and clearings and dishings. It was all so intricate and so smooth it might have been a Detroit assembly line for the production of full people. The full-people factory sounds were clinking silverware, clacking chopsticks, loud calls, and rumbling conversation. A hive of industry, Dragon Garden, I thought. Everyone seemed to be single-mindedly and fruitfully engaged in production, except me.

Well, not quite everyone. As I looked around, I spotted the sharp-nosed, scarred waiter who had scolded me for being late. He glanced over the tables under his jurisdiction and spoke briefly to one of the other waiters, who nodded. He tossed his towel onto a passing busboy's tray and headed for the kitchen doors.

He moved like a man on a mission, with a look about him that I had seen on Bill. On Bill I knew what it meant; on this guy I hoped it meant the same.

I peered around the huge expanse of the dining room until I found Pei-Hui. I pointed my cart and homed in on her. She smiled as I approached but didn't stop moving, calling her wares.

"I need a few moments of a woman's privacy," I told her euphemistically as I paralleled my cart with hers. "Is there a time for that?"

"No break until lunchtime, half past three," she told me. "But if you need to before that, leave your cart in the kitchen. Go back to the room where you came in. What you need is on the left. Only, be quick."

"Oh, I will," I promised, and veered off from our parallel course to park my cart just inside the kitchen doors. The chefs who deigned to notice me at all glared at me as I made my way through their steamy kingdom toward the room in the back. I wondered as I went whether my father had snarled at the chefs' assistants and glared at the dim sum ladies where he'd worked.

I reached the end of the kitchen and pushed open the doors to the break room. The sharp-nosed waiter, as I had hoped, was there; and, even better, he wasn't alone. He was seated in a chair, legs outstretched, already halfway through the cigarette that had called him here. Straddling another chair with his arms resting across the back of it, one of the chef's assistants was just lighting a cigarette of his own.

I nodded, gave them a shy smile, and made my way to the bathroom. I spent the minimal amount of time there I could to be convincing, both because it was not by any definition a pleasant place and because I didn't want the men to escape. If the point of working here was to find out what I could about the missing waiters and not just to peddle dim sum, I needed to have conversations with my co-workers. These guys were my first chance at that.

When I came out they were both still sitting there, breathing tobacco smoke in and out.

I smiled again. The sharp-nosed guy didn't smile back, but the chef's assistant gave me a wide grin that displayed shockingly few teeth.

"This work, very hard," I said, putting as heavy a Cantonese accent as I thought I could pull off into my words. I didn't know about the chef's assistant, but the waiter and I didn't speak the same dialect, so if we were going to have any conversation at all, it was going to have to be in English. But if they knew my English was unaccented, they'd wonder what I was doing in this desperation-level job.

The waiter shrugged; the chef's assistant's grin turned into a smirk.

"Kitchen much worse," he told me with a Cantonese accent and the disdain of the strong for the weak.

"You work here long time?" I asked them, looking from one to the other.

The sharp-nosed waiter looked at me, pulling on his cigarette. There wasn't much of it left; I wondered how far down he intended to smoke it. The chef's assistant filled the silence. "Two year," he said.

"Ah," I said. "Work here longer, pay goes up?" I smiled apologetically. "I just start, pay very low. Hope can make more money, someday."

The waiter lifted his lip in a sneer. "You want make more money, come on time, don't stop for talk." What about stopping for a smoke, I thought, but the chef's assistant raised his arm in a grand, sweeping gesture.

"Or maybe, can join union. Yes, yes, union say, join with us, pay very big. You go find Ho Chi-Chun, big-deal organizer, you ask join big-deal union!" He took his cigarette from his lips and spat on the floor.

"Ho Chi-Chun? Cousin of my uncle's wife!" I made my eyes wide. "Working here?" I looked around as though I was expecting to find Chi-Chun Ho peering out from behind a case of chopsticks.

The waiter's eyes narrowed but he still said nothing. The look on the chef's assistant became one of complete disgust. "Ho Chi-Chun? Your cousin?" Contempt dripped from his voice. "Used to working here. Talk union, join, everybody together. Always talk, talk." He was waving his arms around, painting the scene in the air for me. "People listening, boss gets mad. Boss, Yang Hao-Bing, you know him? Big man, big face. Boss say, more talk, everybody lose job. Ho Chi-Chun keeps talk, everybody stay together, only way. Then Lee Yuan say, going to get rich, friends also, have big get-rich secret. Where Ho Chi-Chun now, big union guy?"

"Lee Yuan?" I asked.

At the same moment the waiter, tossing down his cigarette, said, "Chen Bao, you stop talk, start work, maybe you get rich."

But the chef's assistant only looked at me, cigarette dangling from his lips. "Roommate. Ho Chi-Chun, Lee Yuan, two more, live same place."

127

"Get rich?" I asked eagerly. "Ho Chi-Chun, cousin of uncle's wife, rich now?"

The waiter, rubbing the scar on his jawline, pushed to his feet and said sourly to me, "You want keep job, you go work. You, Chen Bao, also. Rich. No one rich. No one get rich. Big, stupid idea."

He walked past me and shoved open the swinging doors into the kitchen.

Chen Bao, the chef's assistant, rubbed his quarter inch of cigarette out against the detergent barrel and slowly got to his feet. "Ho Chi-Chun," he scoffed. "Big union guy. Everybody stick together. Now, everybody all here, still. Boss mad for union talk. Ho Chi-Chun, Lee Yuan, roommates, gone to get rich. Sure, you want make more money, you join union. Sure." He pushed through the kitchen doors also, and left me standing among the linens and the tableware, all alone.

twelve

the rest of the dim sum day was not very eventful. I got a few more people, including Pei-Hui, to talk to me about Chi-Chun Ho and Yuan Lee, and Song Chan and Gai-Lo Lu also. I also got a lot of narrowed eyes and shaken heads: Don't look at me; I hardly knew them; everyone knows the boss is mad; I have to get back to work now. Some of those eyes narrowed a little too slowly, some heads were just a touch too elaborately shaken; some people, I was sure, knew those men better than they were admitting. But I didn't push. Water wears down rock; rock has little effect on water.

The ones who would talk all knew about Chi-Chun Ho's union organizing, and some knew the four men roomed together. Most had heard Yuan Lee boasting about being on the road to riches, though few had taken him seriously.

"They always talk, don't they?" Pei-Hui had smiled indulgently as we'd waited in the kitchen for a cart refill. "The men. They're always getting rich. Tomorrow, they will all be rich."

"What did he mean, do you think?" I tried to look wistful,

as though I wished I'd been in on the deal. "What secret could he have had?"

"Oh, no secret, I'm sure." She shook her head. "He had been here only a month. Came from China with big ideas. Going to be a movie star, maybe. Or he thinks he has found a system to beat the casinos in Atlantic City."

"Do you think that's where they went?" I asked. "All of them, to Atlantic City?"

"Who knows where they went? Maybe to open their own restaurant in Brooklyn. Maybe home to China. Maybe they are in Hollywood, big movie stars. I know where I am going now. You also."

She smiled at me again and pushed her cart through the swinging kitchen doors, and there we were once more in the organized commotion of the restaurant floor.

By the time Dragon Garden closed at three-thirty the dim sum was down to the dregs. Actually, nothing new had been cooked in the kitchen since two, and the only late-afternoon customers were non-Chinese tourists who were enthralled by the exoticism of it all and probably thought Chinese food was supposed to be greasy, soggy, and cold, the way it was delivered from the lone Chinese take-out place in their hometowns. At three-forty-five, with the dining room cleared, the staff sat down to eat. The meal was plentiful, simple, and delicious: broad chow fun noodles with Chinese broccoli—a leggier, more bitter version than the bushy American vegetable— and deep-fried chicken with a hot pepper sauce. No one, I noticed, complimented the chefs, which was the polite approach, since a compliment would have required the chefs to assert that the food was unworthy of the company—something that was clearly the opposite of what they believed—but everyone shoveled it in, everyone took seconds, and the men and some of the women belched in appreciation.

For the waiters, this entire process was over in twenty minutes. They had stations and tables to prepare for the dinner crowd, and they finished their last cups of tea and stood up again in what seemed like one very fast motion. The dim sum ladies did not work dinner; what we did was clean up the staff tables before we went home, though by then we were on our own time. It was, Pei-Hui pointed out to me, generous of H. B. Yang to feed the ladies, since, unlike the waiters, our shifts were over when the restaurant closed, and he could have dismissed us. It was only fair that, in return, we should make the waiters' burdens a little lighter.

Before I left Dragon Garden I called the Fifth Precinct from the pay phone outside the bathroom, checking to make sure I was alone. I asked for Mary, but her shift had just ended, and for once she was gone. "Like a bat out of hell," the young detective she had called Chester told me. "I think she went to the hospital to see her boyfriend."

"Is he okay, do you know?"

"I guess. She talked to him just before she left."

Peter was talking on the phone? I felt like I was letting out the breath I'd been holding since I'd heard about the bomb. "That's great," I told Chester. "Hey, that guy you and she went out to pick up this morning, Three-finger Choi? Did you find him?"

"Nope. Vanished. Maybe he knows the heat is on. We did dig up an interesting fact, though. Kee said I should tell you if you called."

"What's that?"

"Word is he doesn't work freelance anymore, that he signed on full-time with Duke Lo. She said you'd know the rest."

The rest, I was sure, was "So be careful, Lydia." "What do you do now?" I asked Chester.

"We have the word out. Either he'll rise to the surface or someone'll point us toward his trail."

Someone should tell Chester his metaphors were a little confusing, but it wasn't going to be me. I thanked him and hung up.

As I walked down the steep stairs with Pei-Hui, I realized Bill hadn't come to Dragon Garden for dim sum the way he'd said he would. I was a little surprised; it wasn't like him to miss this kind of chance, to eat dumplings and watch me speak broken English and wheel a cart through a raucous crowd. Maybe he'd waited downstairs and run out of patience before he'd been seated; a non-Chinese customer eating alone isn't always a dim sum palace's highest priority. Or maybe he'd found something better to do. I decided to call and find out when I got to my office and my phone.

That, however, turned out not to be necessary. As soon as Pei-Hui and I stepped through the door at the bottom of the stairs I spotted Bill. He stood near the corner, just another guy browsing through a street vendor's tray of jade trinkets, but from a position where he could see the door the Dragon Garden staff came out of. Ignoring him as he ignored me, I spoke to Pei-Hui in Cantonese.

"Thank you for helping me," I said.

"One of the ladies helped me when I started." She smiled. "I'll see you tomorrow."

I answered, "Yes. Unless the boss fires me." I giggled to show I wasn't serious about that.

"He won't fire you if you do your work well, don't organize for the union." Pei-Hui smiled again and turned. I watched her walk south down the Bowery as, from the corner of my eye, I watched Bill watch me.

I headed in the opposite direction from Pei-Hui, toward Canal Street and my office. Bill trailed me but didn't make any effort to catch up; in fact, he fell behind, and when I got to my office he was a block and a half away.

I went inside, figuring either he'd eventually follow and tell me what was going on or he'd call, or I'd call his beeper and demand to know what he thought he was doing. I headed down the hall to my office, but first I had to pass the gantlet of Ava, Andi, and Mei-Lei, who were just winding down the business day at Golden Adventure. They all, as one, ushered me down the hall and pointed out proudly the reglazed, newly barred window in my office, showing me the huge lock on the bars and demonstrating how easily they opened once you had the key. Ava seized my arm and pulled me into the bathroom, where, in a fit of inspiration, they had ordered the locksmith to go ahead and install another set of bars, though the window in there was only twelve inches wide and had been painted shut ever since I'd moved into this office four years ago.

132

"Thank you for helping with this." I smiled at them all. "You're very kind."

"Lydia, no one comes here again, you don't know it," Ava declared.

"Thank you," I repeated. "Did the locksmith leave his bill?"

"We pay," Andi said defensively, her hands to her breast as though she were clutching the very bill to her.

"Oh, no," I said. "I won't allow it."

That continued for a while, but I had no chance against the combined Golden Adventure forces. Eventually I ushered them out, maintaining I was in their debt well into the next lifetime, and closed the door behind me. I sat down at my desk and lifted the receiver off the phone. At that moment the outside buzzer buzzed.

"Who is it?" I demanded, pressing the button to hear the answer, though I knew it was Bill.

"Me," the tinny speaker told me, and it was.

"What on earth are you doing?"

"Let me in and I'll tell you."

"Where were you at lunchtime?"

"Let me in and I'll tell you."

"What is—"

"Let me in and—"

"Oh, all right."

I buzzed the door-opening buzzer, and he was in.

"Are you suddenly turning into the kind of man who gets his kicks following women around?" I asked as he came down the hall to my office. "Because if you are, that's not a good thing."

"Only you." He kissed me on the cheek and moved past me into the room, strolling over to the window to examine the new bars. He moved easily, casually, but his voice held a tightness, a strain so slight maybe someone else wouldn't have noticed it. I did, because I've heard it before. My eyes narrowed as he said, "Nice. Good work."

"Chinese craftsmen," I told him, "displaying an ancient skill. What were you doing just now?"

"Watching your back, same as yesterday."

"Damn it!" I said, and his eyebrows went up. I never use that kind of language, but it seemed to me this situation needed to be nipped in the bud. "If you're getting to be like everyone else you're fired again. I don't need to be followed all over Chinatown just because some punk came in here yesterday—"

"Not yesterday. Not here. And not a punk. Will you just calm down?"

"Will I—" I blinked. "What do you mean, not a punk? What do you mean, anything?"

Bill plunked his large frame onto my small sofa. "I don't suppose a guy could get a cup of coffee around here?"

"He could get tea."

"He doesn't want tea."

Reaching into the under-the-counter fridge I have, Bill pulled out a bottle of grapefruit juice, which is in my fridge for the same reason Lapsang souchong is in his kitchen cabinets. "You smell like a Chinese restaurant," he said.

"You smell like a guy with a story to tell who isn't telling it." I sat on the desk chair and put my tired feet on the desk.

Bill uncapped the grapefruit juice and took a large swig. "Visitors," he said. "Similar to yours."

"What?" My heart lurched. I swung my legs down. "Three-finger Choi? Are you all right?"

"Three-finger Choi? What does that mean?"

"That's who was here."

"The rice bag guy? That's his name?"

"It's what they call him," I said impatiently. "He threatened you, too? How did he find you? Are you all right?"

"He didn't find me, or if he did, he's developed a subtle streak and now he's white, in a three-piece suit. I'm fine. No one laid a finger on me. What they threatened to do was pull my license."

"Your license? It was cops?" I frowned. "But the cops know we're working on this, at least Mary does, and her bosses. And besides, we're not in anybody's way. What's their problem?"

"Not cops. I mean, not normal cops. Supercops." He finished up the grapefruit juice and said, "Feds."

"Feds?" I heard the incredulity in my own voice. "You mean, like the INS?"

"No. The State Department."

"The State Department? I didn't know they even had cops."

"Everybody has cops. These jerks flashed badges, looked wimpy, and talked tough, so I figured they were probably authentic, but I checked them out anyway after they left."

That funny note was back in Bill's voice. I asked, "Did they check out?"

He nodded. "At least there are two guys in State Department Security with the names and badge numbers these guys gave me."

"What did they want?"

"They wanted to know what I knew about the disappearance of four Chinese waiters from Elmhurst, Queens."

My eyes widened. "How did they know you knew anything about it?"

"You know, I asked them that."

"What did they say?"

"That that was none of my business."

I watched him as he lit a cigarette. His movements were completely calm and controlled, his tone soft-voiced and offhand, except for the strain I had heard before, that small note that shows how hard someone's working. He dropped his shaken-out match carefully into the ashtray I keep there for him. "You're really steamed," I said.

He pulled in smoke from his cigarette and let it out in a stream. He looked into my eyes. "Damn right," he said, in a different, colder voice.

"Tell me."

He drew on the cigarette again. "It never occurred to them," he said, "just to ask. 'You know something we want to know, what do you say?' "

"Would that have worked?"

"No. I'm not alone on this, I'm working for you. I wouldn't have given them a pitcher of spit without asking you. But it might have gotten us off to a better start. Given me a warm, fuzzy feeling about them.''

I doubted the warm, fuzzy feeling part, but clearly the Feds could have used a better start. "But they didn't?" I asked.

"No. They thought pushing me around would work faster.''

Big mistake. They should have asked me.

"Did they call you?" I wanted to know.

"No. They showed up at the door and said, 'Let us in or else.' ''

That was bad. Living alone, for Bill, is a full-time thing. Not a lot of people get to go to his apartment, and never, if he can help it, people he doesn't like.

"Then what?"

"Then, while the little one told me how much they don't like P.I.s, guys who've done time, or anyone who messes in their business, the big one strolled around the goddamn place.''

From that thin outline, the picture filled itself out in my mind, color and shape and sound. Two well-groomed, business-suited intruders; Bill's jaw tightening, his hands curling at his sides; the air in the bright, solitary apartment ringing with angry words. A man who had not been invited walking smugly around as though the place were his. I could hear his soft footsteps, see each one land on Bill like a blow. I felt the knots in Bill's shoulders, smelled his sweat and the aftershave of the Feds.

"The little guy," Bill said, "finally worked around to what it was they wanted. The other one just kept walking. I asked them what their interest in the waiters was. They told me, 'We're the government; we can be interested in whatever we want.' ''

"They sound," I said, "pretty stupid."

"When the big one got to the piano," Bill said, "he picked up some music and asked the other one what kind of faggot plays Mozart in his spare time.''

"And?" I asked softly.

"I threw them out."

I looked at him, heard his dangerously quiet voice, saw the set of his shoulders and jaw as I'd seen them in my head. "Did you fight?" I asked, almost afraid to hear the answer.

"You mean, did I punch a Fed?" He lit a new cigarette off the old and stubbed the first one out. "No. They told me to tell them what I knew, including who'd hired me. I told them to go home and get a warrant and not come back without it."

"That was calm and rational of you."

"I'm editing it for you." He blew out smoke from the new cigarette and seemed, just a fraction, to settle into the sofa, to relax.

"I appreciate it. Bill?"

His eyes met mine. Wordlessly, he nodded. That answered the question I'd silently asked: his temper, hard to rouse and hard to calm, was back under control. He was all right. I let out a small, relieved breath and sat back in my chair.

"The State Department," I mused. "What kind of thing interests the State Department?"

"I'm not sure," Bill said, "but it's obviously the guys who don't make the grade as diplomats that they use in security."

"Do you suppose—?" I began.

But whether and what Bill supposed was not something I was destined to find out right then. The sharp ring of the phone cut off my sentence. I let the machine answer it, but when I heard it was Mary, I picked it up.

"Hi. I'm here."

"Hi. Listen, I'm at the hospital."

My legs propelled me out of my chair. "Is Peter okay?"

"Getting better. He's conscious. He told me to call you."

"To tell me to be careful?" The humor in that fell flat, but it was the best I could do.

"No," she snapped impatiently. "To tell you the man he was meeting with, the man who was killed in the explosion, was Chi-Chun Ho."

thirteen

Once again I found myself in a cab heading over the Manhattan Bridge toward Long Island College Hospital, this time with Bill.

"Peter wants to talk to you," Mary had said. "Can you come right away? He asked them to hold off on the pain medication until you get here because it makes him sleep, but . . ." She didn't finish.

"I'm leaving now." The thought of Peter in a hospital refusing to take a pain pill until I got there made me want to think about something else.

Bill and I locked up and grabbed the first cab we saw. Luckily, it was a weekend afternoon; heading toward Brooklyn, we were going out while everyone else was coming in.

"Why didn't he call me?" I growled uselessly at Bill as the bridge cables flashed past the taxi windows. "Before he went there, to tell me he'd heard from Chi-Chun Ho?"

"Maybe Ho asked him not to."

"Ho didn't know about me. Unless Peter told him. And so what if he asked him not to? He wasn't the client, he was the subject. I should have been there with Peter to meet with him."

"So you could have gotten blown up, too?"

"That's not the point."

"Yes, it is."

I blew out an angry breath and settled back in my seat. He was right, of course; that was exactly the point. If I'd been there maybe things would have worked out differently. *What things, Lydia? I demanded. You might have smelled the bomb? Your famous sixth sense might have told you it was there, and just before it exploded you might have flown everybody to safety like Supergirl?* I stared at the city beyond the bridge cables, mad at myself, mad at Bill for being right, mad at Peter for not taking his pain pill.

The cab dropped us at the entrance to Long Island College Hospital, and I led the way to the desk, where they would give us only one pass to go up and see Peter because Mary was already up there and he was only allowed two visitors at a time. I started to argue, but Bill shrugged, told me to take it, then wandered over to the water fountain. After that he kept wandering, reading bulletin boards, until he ended up standing next to me as I waited for the elevator. The reception desk people, busy with phone calls and anxious visitors, never looked up.

"What are you doing?" I asked him as the elevator doors opened and we both got in.

"Have you ever known them to check those things?" he asked, nodding at the flat plastic pass in my hand. "Save your energy for fights you need to have."

Oh, like you did with the Feds? I asked, but silently, because that might have started a fight we didn't need to have.

Peter was in a double room right near the elevator. He had the bed on the window side, overlooking Brooklyn Heights, but he didn't look as though he cared very much about the view. Thick white bandages wrapped his head, and little ones were plastered on his face. The parts of his face I could see were purple and swollen, with some stitches above his left eye. His left arm was in a cast that bent at the elbow, and I was sure that under the thin hospital blanket were more bandages and stitches and places that hurt a lot.

From a chair by the bed Mary stood up as Bill and I came

around the room's curtain divider. Peter turned his head slowly, but it was obviously hard for him. Walking around to the side Mary was on, I gave her a quick hug and asked Peter, "Is this okay?"

"Oh, sure," he said in a gravelly voice. "It's great."

"You don't look so bad," I observed, "for a guy who got blown up."

"You look lovely, too," he murmured weakly but politely. "Now listen."

"I didn't say you looked lovely. But I'm listening."

He took a few breaths, then said, "Mary told you? It was Chi-Chun Ho?"

"Yes. Why didn't you call me? To tell me he'd contacted you?"

"He didn't."

"I—"

Mary gave me a quick, sharp glance, so I shut up, and Peter went on. "Someone else called. Speaking bad English. He said his name was Jimmy Loo, wanted to join the union, but he was nervous. Afraid to lose his job." He paused to breathe again. "He asked me to meet him at the union office and talk about it."

"Who was he?"

"Nobody. Just after I got there, Chi-Chun showed up. He said he'd had the other guy, one of the other disappeared waiters, call so I wouldn't know it was him."

"Why not?"

"They're in trouble."

"Who? The waiters?"

"Yeah. The four of them. Some kind of trouble." Peter coughed, and a spasm of pain passed over his face. When he spoke again his voice was weaker. "They ran." He paused for breath. "When they didn't know what to do next, they decided Chi-Chun should come see me because I'm a lawyer."

"Why did he have the other guy call?"

Peter looked at me, and I got the feeling he'd have shrugged if he could have. "They were afraid if I knew they were in trouble before they had a chance to explain, I might not want to get involved.''

Very understandable, very Chinese. ''Does the trouble have to do with the union?''

''I don't know. He never told me. The explosion came too fast. Mary?''

''Yes?'' Mary rubbed the back of her fingers lightly over an unbandaged part of Peter's face.

''Can you get me that stupid pill now?''

She nodded. With a look at me I wasn't sure how to read, she left the room.

''Lydia?'' Peter's gravelly voice took on an urgency it hadn't had before. I leaned forward.

''What?''

''Find those guys.''

''Those guys, the three other waiters?''

''They're in trouble,'' he repeated. ''Bad enough they had to disappear.'' He closed his eyes, then opened them again. ''Mary'll be mad that I'm asking you. But Chi-Chun needed help. He came to me. Now I'm . . . here. And he's dead.''

''Do you know the other guys?''

''No. One of them is legal, Song Chan, I think. The other two, what are they going to do?'' A note sounded in Peter's voice, almost of panic. I felt a pang for him, lying helpless in a hospital bed while three scared men who had come to him for help hid somewhere in New York, worse off now than before because Chi-Chun Ho, their one link to the world of power, was dead.

''Peter?'' That was Bill, the first word he'd spoken since we'd walked into the room. Peter moved his eyes to him. ''Did you tell this to the cops?'' Bill asked.

''Yes. But they won't find them. They won't know how to look. No one will cooperate with them, especially if these guys are in trouble. And whoever they're in trouble with is going to be looking, too. Lydia? Please. You have to find them.''

''Peter?'' I said.

"What?"

"That's 'whomever.' "

"Lydia?"

"What?"

"Thanks for coming. Good-bye."

Peter's eyes closed again. The door opened, letting in Mary, followed by a nurse. Looking first at Peter, then at me, Mary said, "Wait outside. I want to talk to you."

I took another look at Peter, my old friend, Mr. Desk Job, lying wrapped in bandages in a place where the air smelled of eye-watering antiseptic and the tea, when he was finally able to drink it, would be Tetley's, brewed weak. With Bill beside me, I left the room.

The nurse stayed inside, but Mary was out in the hall again in half a minute.

"He looks good," I said encouragingly.

"Don't try to distract me," she ordered. "What was so important to say to you that he had to get me out of the room?"

I looked at her innocently. "I . . . he . . ."

"He wants us to find the other three waiters," Bill said calmly.

"Surprise, surprise." Mary stood with her hands on her hips. "What are you going to do?"

I looked at Bill, and then at Mary. "I want to do it," I said.

Mary nodded and said nothing.

I waited a few seconds. "Aren't you going to tell me no?"

She paced up the hall for a moment, then turned back to us. "As a cop," she said, "I have to. As your friend, I ought to. But Peter's really upset about those guys."

"It may not be dangerous," I said, seizing the opportunity. "I don't know what trouble they're in, but maybe it looks much worse to them than it really is."

"Uh-huh. That's why one of them is dead and Peter's here."

"Umm." I switched tactics. "Well, but who else can find them? Peter said the cops won't know how to look. I mean, nothing personal, but I think that's true."

"I think it is, too," Mary said. "Patino, who caught the case? He's good, but can you see him trying to get some undocumented busboy to talk to him?"

I didn't know Patino, but the idea didn't sound profitable to me. A thought struck me. "Do any of the non-Chinese cops at the Fifth even speak Chinese?" The Fifth had a full complement of seventy cops; 'non-Chinese' applied to all but ten.

"Actually, Patino speaks a little Cantonese. And Chester speaks Fukienese and Cantonese both. So do a few of the other detectives, some well, some just barely. But all it gets them is 'I don't know' in more than one language."

"They could give the case to you."

"They could. They won't, because of Peter. But even if they did, I'm still a cop. These guys, the missing guys, are probably like my father."

Bill looked questioningly at me.

"In China," I told him, "it's the authorities who give you trouble. Cops, soldiers, government officials, it's all the same: they make the threats, take the bribes, control your life. They're the enemy. People try to stay as far from them as possible. Mary's father was upset when she went into the department. He couldn't believe she wanted to be the enemy."

"I tried to tell him it wasn't like that here, that the bad guys in America are mostly civilians, but he doesn't buy it," Mary said. "If he was in trouble, he'd never go to a cop."

"Where would he go?" Bill asked.

Mary's brows knit together. "To his family association, or his merchants' organization, or someplace like that."

"And if a cop came to him, he'd stonewall?"

"Definitely. Even if he had no idea what it was about. The point is to avoid anything the authorities are interested in. That's why these guys didn't tell Peter what was going on over the phone. They were afraid he'd turn them down."

"Or in," I said.

"Right," she said. "Or in."

"But I'm not the authorities."

"I know," said Mary. "That's the only reason I'm even considering letting you do this."

"And," I said, forbearing to mention that no one had actually asked her to *let* me do anything, "there's another thing: H. B. Yang."

Mary gave me a long look, then nodded. "You mean the protection that comes with working for him."

"On the plus side. And on the minus side, whatever comes if I tell him I quit. After all, this is exactly what he asked me to do."

"He asked you to find four guys. Now one of them's dead."

"And I wonder," said Bill, "how he feels about that?"

Mary and I both looked at Bill, and we all said nothing for a minute. "You'll be involved in this?" Mary finally asked Bill.

"Yes, ma'am."

Mary scowled at the "ma'am," stuck her hands in the back pockets of her jeans, and paced the hall some more.

"Okay," she said, wheeling around. "You can look. But as soon as you come up with anything you have to let me know. And if anything even starts to look dangerous, you have to stop. Understood?"

Understood, used that way, is a cop word. As Mary stood looking seriously and severely at us from down the hospital hallway, I suddenly had a vision of her twenty years from now, in a blue uniform, speaking at a news conference as Chief of Detectives or Chief of Department or something, gold braid on her jacket and silver in the braid of her hair.

But right now she was in blue jeans and a jean jacket, and it was a good time for us to get out of here before she changed her mind. "Yes," I said. "Understood. You won't be sorry."

"I'd better not be, or you will be, too."

So with another quick hug and instructions to be sure she ate something and got some sleep tonight, I left, Bill beside me as we walked the short distance to the elevator. Mary turned back to Peter's room again.

Bill hailed a cab for us outside the hospital. I climbed in and

144

leaned back in the seat, letting Bill give the driver instructions. I also let him put his arm around me and pull me closer to him, and I leaned against him.

"Come on, I'll buy you dinner," he said.

I leaned my head back and looked up at him. "Didn't I just have lunch?"

"When did that ever stop you?"

"I see your point." I sighed. "I guess it's a good idea. I'm tired and confused and I don't have any idea what to do next. Like I'm out of gas or something."

Bill grinned. "Well, I know where we can go to get gas."

I punched him meaninglessly in the ribs and leaned against him again, which is where I stayed for the rest of the taxi ride.

The cab took us back over the Manhattan Bridge and turned north, but not very far. We rode up Chrystie Street, into the area that was once the heart of the Jewish Lower East Side, the place where Eastern European immigrants in head scarves and heavy woolen coats first came and pushed their pushcarts, baked their bread, built their synagogues, and raised their children. Some of the businesses the early immigrants established are still here, and a few of the original inhabitants, now elderly, still live in the tenements built for them. But the second generation, born here, didn't stay. They left for uptown, the Bronx, and the suburbs, making room for the Latinos who came after them, the blacks moving up from the South, and, now, Chinese people whose character-painted shop signs are as exotic and incomprehensible to most of the people of the city as the Hebrew lettering on the original shops was a century ago.

We U-turned and headed south for half a block, then stopped. I fumbled in my pocket for money, but by the time I found some Bill had already paid. I followed him out of the cab and onto the sidewalk. "Put it on your expense report," I said, looking around. "Where are we?"

"Sammy's." Bill crossed the sidewalk to a set of steps, went down them to a door, and held it open for me. The sign above the door did indeed say SAMMY's ROUMANIAN RESTAURANT.

"What do we eat here?" I asked as I went in past him. He

didn't need to answer me, though, because the air inside the small, low-ceilinged room was thick with the aromas of roasting meats with bay and rosemary, stews with garlic and onions, yeasty bread, potatoes. It was early for dinner, but the restaurant was half full, mostly older people working their quiet ways through huge platters of food.

Bill did answer me, though. "Boy food," he said as a waiter who must have been a hundred years old came and sat us at a white-tableclothed table. I looked around; all the waiters must have been a hundred years old. I said as much to Bill.

"It's the food," he answered. "It makes you live forever."

"What if I don't want to live forever?"

"Then this food will probably kill you."

I extracted a pickle from the bowl on the table. Next to the bowl was a seltzer squirter, the old-fashioned glass kind that you keep refilling. This one was full. I eyed it with interest. "The food knows what I want?"

"The food here knows everything," Bill said, running his eyes over the menu. "If you squirt me with that thing they fine you fifty dollars." Still looking at the menu, he pointed over his shoulder to a sign on the otherwise photograph-plastered wall that said as much.

"Me?" I protested. "Such a thing would never even cross my mind." I gave the squirter a regretful glance. "But isn't that what lawyers call an attractive nuisance?"

"No," he said. "You are what lawyers—"

"Oh, nuts to you." I looked over the menu myself. "Does the food here really know everything? And why didn't we tell Mary about the Feds who came to see you?"

"Is that a real question?"

"The first one or the second one?"

"The second one."

"No. How about the first?"

"Yes."

"Then what I'm hungry for should just come to me out of the kitchen." I closed the menu.

"It will." The waiter came shuffling over and Bill ordered: pot roast for me and a chopped liver sandwich for himself. He or-

146

dered himself a beer, too. I stuck to the seltzer; there wasn't any fine for squirting it into your glass.

"Okay," I said, chomping on another crisp pickle while we waited. "What are we going to do?"

"Well, I still want to know what I asked before," Bill said. "How does your man Yang feel about one of the guys he was looking for being dead?"

" 'My man Yang.' " I shuddered. "Well, I guess I can ask him, since he hired me to stick my nose into the case. Just to satisfy your curiosity, you understand."

"I appreciate it. Of course, you'll have to wait until the cops are through with him."

"They're through." I told Bill what Mary had told me that morning.

"Okay," Bill said. "Assuming for the sake of argument he didn't do it, that leaves another interesting possibility."

"And that is?"

The ancient waiter brought Bill's beer and poured it down the side of his glass for him. He peered at the seltzer bottle, either to see if it needed refilling or to see if it was safe in my hands. He didn't look convinced on either score, but he walked away.

"That someone wants it to look as though Yang did it," Bill said. "To make the mayor look bad."

I pondered that while I took in the photos covering the walls, tacked and taped-up Polaroids of customers eating, horsing around, having a good time. "I don't think I buy it," I said. "There must be easier ways to make the mayor look bad."

"Is that political commentary?"

"No. But it seems a little elaborate. Using an ox cleaver to kill a chicken."

"Now that *is* political commentary."

"No, it's something H. B. Yang would say. Or my mother. Besides, I don't think it would work."

"The ox cleaver? What *is* an ox cleaver?"

"You can't really think I know. No, embarrassing the mayor that way. He'd just cut H. B. Yang loose. You know, one of those speeches: I have complete faith in my good friend Mr. Yang and I can categorically state he would never be involved in any wrongdoing, but nevertheless Mr. Yang has generously offered to resign from his advisory post in order to keep the media focus on this incident from interfering with the ability of the government of this great city to operate smoothly . . ."

"You know," Bill said when I ran out of steam, "you're good at that."

I said, "I don't think that's a compliment."

"It's not. But you may be right about the mayor. So maybe *that* was the point."

"What was?"

"Getting him to cut H. B. Yang loose. If so, why?"

A little lightbulb went on over my head, like in the comics. I stared at him. "You're a genius."

His face assumed a worried look. "You must be light-headed from lack of food." He made a show of looking around for the waiter.

"No, you *are*. Listen." I gave Bill a quick rundown of the situation in Chinatown, the old guard and the new guys, the jockeying and the political games. He listened, sipping his beer, until I was done.

"So you think these new guys think if they dislodge Yang from the mayor's side they could get next to the mayor themselves?" he asked me.

"Sure. There's a lot of patronage power—in the East Point project, for example. A lot of money in jobs and contracts about to be floating around. H. B. Yang seemed like a permanent fixture when I was a kid, but he's teetering a little now. If I were the new guys, I might be thinking this was a great time for a shove."

"Hmm." Bill looked thoughtful. The ancient waiter pushed with more determination than strength through the swinging doors from the kitchen and headed over to our table. He brought with him, for Bill, a chopped liver sandwich that must have been six inches thick, with a pile of lettuce and raw onion slices on the plate beside it; and for me, what looked like half a pound of sliced meat covered in cooked tomatoes, onions, and carrots.

"This is too much food," I whispered to Bill when the waiter had gone.

Bill grinned. "I've never heard you say that before."

"You've never seen me eat half a cow at one sitting before, either."

"Well, do what you can. You can take home what's left."

"I'm not sure my mother would allow food like this in her refrigerator. She'd consider it a bad influence on the food she already has."

I cut into the first slice of pot roast, then put down my knife. The meat was so tender that it didn't need one. As I tasted it, savoring the sweet sting of the tomatoes and the salty richness of the well-herbed gravy, Bill asked, "So we have to find out who, among these new guys, would be most interested in pulling off something like this."

I swallowed and said, "We may already know."

He stopped his sandwich halfway to his mouth. "We do?"

"Remember the guy who came to my office? Three-finger Choi?"

"Oh, right," he nodded through a bite of chopped liver. "Good old Three-finger. Fine fellow. I remember him well."

I gave the seltzer bottle a considered look, wondering exactly where my bank account stood, whether I had fifty dollars to spare. I settled for saying, "He works for a guy called Duke Lo."

"And Duke Lo is . . . ?"

"One of the new guys. Mary says he's a rising star. She also says he's no good."

"How do you know this, that Choi works for Lo?"

"One of the Fifth Precinct detectives told me this afternoon," I said, thinking it actually felt like months ago. "I was going to tell you but I got distracted when you followed me."

"Many women do."

"They can't, you don't follow me that often."

"That you know of. Sometimes I hire people to do it for me."

"And then by your story about the Feds," I said, resolutely sticking to business. "And speaking of the Feds, what about them?"

"The Feds?" Bill finished the sandwich half he'd been working on, wiped his hands on his napkin, and waved to the waiter for another beer.

"Yes. If this theory is right, and Duke Lo's out to get H. B. Yang, then who invited the Feds?"

"And where are the waiters?" Bill asked, clearly not meaning the one scuffing over to our table right now.

"Oh, I don't know." I sighed, suddenly deflated. "But that's what we're supposed to be finding out, isn't it? Not all this other stuff?"

"No," Bill said.

"No, I'm wrong, or no, I'm right?"

"No, you're right. Unless we have to get to the bottom of this other stuff to find the waiters."

I bit on a piece of potato while I thought. "Look at this," I said to Bill. "Suppose Duke Lo heard that the waiters had disappeared. He doesn't know where they went or why, but it's good luck for him. It's a chance to get H. B. Yang in trouble, because one of the disappeared guys is a union organizer. That's why he sent Three-finger Choi to stop me from looking for them—as long as they're gone H. B. Yang looks bad, as people get suspicious."

"Which could be another reason Yang wanted you to find them. Besides the money they owe him and his warm, paternal feelings for them."

I shot him a look, but he ignored it, and I was too caught up in the possibility that we'd found a way to untangle this case to get involved in trying to defeat Bill's cynical approach to things.

Not that I believe for a minute that he's anywhere near as cynical as he wants everyone to think, but it's not my business to unmask the Lone Ranger.

"Okay," I said, as the waiter finally reached us and poured Bill's second beer. He raised his eyebrows at the seltzer bottle and me before he started to meander away. He was probably as impressed

150

with my self-restraint as I was. "Then Lo blows up the union office," I went on, to Bill. "And all eyes fall on H. B. Yang."

Bill nodded, sampling the beer. "Could be. So the union wasn't really the target, and Ho and Peter were just unlucky?"

"In the wrong place at the wrong time," I said. "It happens. But look how great it is for Lo: the dead man was one of the disappeared waiters!"

"Convenient," Bill agreed. "And the Feds?"

I devoured some carrots and onions to help me think. "Mary says the INS is dying to ship Duke Lo out. Maybe the State Department's helping, trying to dig something up on him to do with the waiters."

"Why?"

"Maybe they owe the INS a favor. Can't we figure that out later?"

"Obviously we can't figure it out now. But here's another thought: maybe they aren't just blindly hoping Lo had something to do with the waiters' disappearing. Maybe they know."

"Oh," I said. "You mean, like he paid them to disappear? To start this off?"

"Could be."

"But that's not what Chi-Chun Ho told Peter," I objected.

"All he told him was they were in trouble," Bill said. "Maybe they realized being pawns in this game wasn't safe."

"And they don't know how to get out of it," I said slowly, turning this idea over in my head. "That could be trouble, by anyone's definition."

"You know what this means?" Bill asked, wiping his fingers on his napkin again, the other half of his sandwich having totally disappeared.

"You outate me," I complained, pointing to his empty plate and then to the two slices of meat and the odd potato left on mine.

He settled back in his chair and lifted the last of his beer. "I always do."

"Don't be smug. Pound for pound, we both know I'm better. I demand a rematch."

"Right now?"

"Absolutely not. At a time of my choosing. And I do know what this means. It means Duke Lo probably knows where the waiters are."

That was what it meant. Bill agreed, "At least, it makes him worth asking."

So we paid the bill at Sammy's, very maturely leaving the seltzer bottle still half full in the center of the food wreckage on our table. We took the remains of my meal with us to give to the first homeless person we saw, and went out to ask.

fourteen

the first thing we needed to ask was where to find Duke Lo. I wasn't sure whom to approach with this question, but I knew better than to try Mary.

"Or," Bill said, "on the other hand, we could tell her we think Lo did the bombing and may have hidden the waiters, and let the cops take it from here."

I gave him a quick look as we walked back down Chrystie Street toward Chinatown. The spring air felt sharp against my skin now that the sun had gone down. The same dusk that put into the air an edge you could feel also blurred the outlines of cars and buildings and people, things you could see. Making some things sharper, others more obscure; like the setting of the sun, each event in this case seemed to have the ability to do that.

"We can't tell the cops that," I said. "It would be the same problem as before; Lo's much less likely to talk to the cops than he is to talk to me."

"Why is he so likely to talk to you?"

"Because I'm not a cop."

"Your logic is circular, but I get it."

"Seriously, if we're right, the guy's not out to get into trouble, just to get H. B. Yang into trouble. If I can hint in a roundabout and elegantly euphemism-filled way that someone suspects that, and that things will only get more difficult for him unless the waiters turn up and everything goes back to relatively normal, maybe he'll buy it."

"You can do that?"

"What?"

"That elegant euphemism thing."

I shrugged. "I'm Chinese."

His "Uh-huh" was noncommittal. "And what are you going to do about the fact that a bomb we think he planted killed one of the waiters?" he asked.

"I'm not going to bring it up unless he does. If that happens I'll make it sound like I'm sure he had nothing to do with it but the cops are so much dumber than I am that they might be very irritating if they come to think he might have been involved."

I felt Bill's eyes on me but I didn't look at him, just kept walking toward Chinatown, my home.

"Okay," Bill said, "but I'm coming with you."

"*No.*" I heard the irritation in my own voice. "You can't. The whole problem is, is a Chinese-white thing—"

"The hell it is. It's a cop-noncop thing. I'll buy that you're more likely to get somewhere than the cops are, but this is a guy they have on the bad guy list. He sent some creep to beat you up, and he might have killed Ho. You can say I'm your bodyguard, you can do the whole thing in Chinese, you can say I'm deaf and dumb and do it in English, but I'm going to be there."

"We can't do it in Chinese. He's Fukienese. I won't be able to understand a word he says."

"Then think of something else. This is nonnegotiable."

"Nonnegotiable?" I stopped walking. "You're working for me. You can't give me ultimatums like that."

"I can and I will. There's no one I'd work with that I'd let go into something like this without backup."

"Let?" I felt my face flush hot. "You sound just like Mary! And Peter! You don't get to *let* me do things——"

"Goddammit, Lydia!" Bill's shout silenced me. I stared at him, my mouth open, as we stood, not moving now, on the darkening sidewalk. "Who the hell do you think I am, one of your goddamn brothers?" His voice echoed off the old brick buildings around us. "This isn't about who lets who do what! It's not about who's boss and it's not about proving how goddamn tough you are. Jesus Christ!"

We stared at each other wordlessly for a moment. Bill rubbed his palm on the back of his neck and peered up into the sky as though searching for words. I tried to find some myself, but the ones he'd just yelled were ringing in my ears.

Bill spoke again, his voice lower. "When I have work, and I call you," he said, "it's because I know I can depend on your instincts and your training and your guts. Because I know I can trust you. Why the hell can't you give me that, too?"

I looked at him, his face obscured by the failing light. Stars now glowed in pale pinpricks through the dusty blue sky behind him. I thought about the Feds stomping through his place that afternoon, about the worry in his voice when I told him about Three-finger Choi, about how he'd wanted to come see if I was all right but he didn't because I told him not to. I tried to see his eyes, but they were hidden in shadow.

"I . . ." I said. "I . . ." I lifted my hands, let them fall to my sides helplessly. "I know you're not one of my brothers."

He bent his head, looking down at the sidewalk, and then looked up again, as if to see me in a different way. I could see his eyes then, and I met them with mine. We held each other that way for a few moments, trying to let our eyes tell each other things our words couldn't manage. Then a smile started slowly at the corners of Bill's mouth. It spread to cover his whole face. "And a damn good thing, too," he said, and he leaned down and kissed me.

That took a while, that kiss. I only know that because the stars were sharp and the color had gone out of the sky by the time I stepped away from the warmth of his arms.

"Not now," I said, trying to make my voice normal, not quavery the way it felt to me. "Not in the middle of all this."

"The street?" he asked. "The traffic?"

"No." I shook my head. "The case. Peter in the hospital, that poor man dead, those other men somewhere they don't want to be. That. In the middle of that."

His look was long and still. Then he nodded. "Okay," he said. "I know."

I knew he did. I squeezed his hand, then let it go. We walked on into Chinatown, to go see Duke Lo, together.

On the way I had an inspiration. I had a feeling I'd pay for it later, but right now it seemed like the shortest distance between two points.

I called Chester, the young detective at the Fifth Precinct.

"Nah, he's gone," another cop told me, answering the squad room phone. "Can I help you out?"

"No, I'd like to speak to him. Is there somewhere I could reach him?"

"Doubt it."

"It's important."

"Gotta be Chester?"

"Yes."

He sighed. "Awright. Give me your number, I'll see if I can find him, tell him you want him."

I gave him my beeper number and my office number, telling him to tell Chester to try the office first. I hoped he wouldn't leave my numbers lying around for Mary to see. Then we hightailed it over to my office to wait for Chester's call.

Our wait wasn't long. We'd barely made it down the hall, unlocked my office door, and turned on the light when the phone rang.

"Lydia Chin Investigations," I told it, and then as an after-thought repeated that in Chinese, in case the caller wasn't Chester. But it was.

"You were looking for me?" he asked cheerfully, his rambunctious voice almost masked by the sounds of loud jukebox rock and roll and the laughter of semisober people.

"Yes," I said. "What if I asked you where I could find Duke Lo?"

"Hmm," he said as someone yelled to someone else in the background. "I think I'd ask why."

"I'd say I wanted to talk to him."

"Oh-ho, no shit. C'mon, you gotta give me more than that."

I had a sudden thought. "Did you ask him where Three-finger Choi was, when you were looking for Choi?"

"That what you want to ask him?"

"No. But did you?"

"Nope. Didn't get the chance. Kee and I went over to the restaurant but he wasn't around. We left word to call us, though."

"Did he?"

"Not yet."

"Will he?"

"Oh, sure. He likes to show how cooperative he is. But he won't give us shit."

"Is that where I'd find him now?"

"Where, the restaurant? Sometimes, sometimes not. What do you want him for?"

"Some questions. About these waiters. Mary knows I'm looking for the waiters," I added. "She doesn't have a problem with it."

"Lo does," Chester pointed out. "That's why he sent Choi to beat the crap out of you."

"Choi did not beat the crap out of me," I said, impolitely but accurately. "He was supposed to warn me off. In a way, I want to tell Duke Lo that it worked."

"If it worked, why do you want to tell him? You stop looking, he'll know."

"It didn't work. I just want to tell him it did."

"And you expect him to believe you? Shit, you're killing me. You know, Kee may be right about you."

"Right about what?"

157

"Never mind. Listen, I don't think this is a good idea."

"Chester, I can find him anyway. It will just take longer if you don't help."

"So let it take longer. Kee outranks me. She gets pissed off, she'll hand me my butt on a plate."

Bill had been watching and listening to my side of this frustrating conversation. I rolled my eyes at him as I tried to think up something to say that would change Chester's mind. Before I could, Bill leaned over and pushed the speaker button on my phone. "Chester, this is Bill Smith, Lydia's partner."

"Hey! How you doing?" Chester responded jovially, his voice now echoing out of the speaker phone. I took the receiver from my ear. "Kee's told me about you," Chester said to Bill. "You used to be a cop, right?"

"No, but it's in the family. Dave Maguire was my uncle."

I stared at Bill, eyes wide, as Chester said, "Oh, yeah, hey, that's right. She told me that. I was just out of the academy when that happened. That sucked, man, that really sucked."

"That," I knew, was the death of Bill's Uncle Dave. Dave Maguire had been a tough, popular police captain, an instructor at the academy, a Precinct Commander. He was the one Bill had lived with when, at fifteen, he'd moved out of his own family's place. I didn't know that whole story, but I knew it wasn't a good one. I did know this: Dave Maguire had died six years ago in an ambush set up by a rogue cop in the pocket of the drug dealers Maguire had been closing in on. And Bill had been there. Shot and badly hurt, he'd managed to kill one of the hit men, but he hadn't managed to stop the other from killing Dave Maguire.

I'd learned most of this from people who know Bill, not from Bill himself, because it's one of the things in his life he never, ever talks about.

And from Mary I'd also learned this: that Dave Maguire's name was still magic around the NYPD.

"Yeah," Bill said now, in answer to Chester. "Listen, Chester, I'm going in with Lydia on this."

"Yeah?" Chester asked dubiously. "I don't know. What's the point here?"

"We think we can smoke out the waiters. We think Lo may know where they are."

"How come?"

"A hunch. But Mary Kee agrees we have a better chance of finding them than you guys do. We'll try not to spook this guy Lo. And if it turns bad, we'll get out fast."

"I don't know," Chester said again, but he sounded like he was wavering. "You're gonna be there?"

"Uh-huh. And we want to find him somewhere where it's public. Just for the insurance."

Chester, on his end, was silent. The music behind him changed, from one screaming-guitar seventies song I couldn't recognize to another. "Well, yeah, okay," he finally said. "I guess she's right, you could probably find him sooner or later anyway."

"Probably."

"All right. Check out the Zhen Rong Association. Lo hangs there. It's like his club. But you're going in with her?"

"Yes."

"Because if anything happens to her, Kee's gonna tear me a new—"

"Yeah," Bill said quickly. "Thanks, Chester. We owe you one." He pressed the button that cut the connection.

I had been holding the receiver uselessly in my hand the whole time that conversation was going on. I replaced it now, still staring at Bill. He perched on my desk and lit a cigarette and didn't meet my eyes.

"Bill," I started.

"I know," he said. "You don't need that kind of help. You especially don't need one big white guy telling another big white guy that he's going to be looking after you. I know."

"No. That's not it. I . . . you didn't have to do that."

"Uh-huh," he said. He took a drag from the cigarette, threw out the match. "This is important to you." He stood up from my

159

desk, still not looking at me. "You know where to find this Zen place he was talking about?"

"Zhen," I corrected automatically. "Zhen Rong. Roughly, 'to cause oneself to grow in honor.' Yes, it's on East Broadway."

"Good. Let's go."

"Bill—"

"No." He shook his head. "Let's go."

So we went. We locked up my office and headed for East Broadway, through a spring night that had now grown chilly. It would have been dark, too, if not for the streetlights, charged with power born in roaring forest waterfalls a thousand miles from here.

I did know where the Zhen Rong Association was, though I'd never been inside. I've never been inside any of the family or village association places in Chinatown except my own, Chin Family Association, and Mary's. Chin Family Association was upstairs in a building on Bayard Street with, of course, a restaurant at street level. As kids my brothers and I played on the linoleum of the curtained front room on the second floor while Ba—my father—drank tea and debated politics with the other men, from the world's to that of whatever restaurant they were working in at the time. The restaurant debates always drew the most heated opinions. Sometimes, surrounded by cigarette smoke, the clink of teacups, and the rising and falling tones of Cantonese talk, Andrew and I would sit at one of the folding card tables and, bamboo brushes in our clumsy fists, clunkily copy the graceful strokes of the calligraphy—one of the Five Arts of ancient China—that an old, white-haired man patiently showed us. When we did well, he would smile and give us sweets, and I remembered his glittering rimless glasses, the almond chewiness of the sweets, and my determination to practice my calligraphy harder, though I was never anywhere near as good as Andrew.

As we inked the paper or did our homework or chased each other around the place, a steady stream of people came and went from the room in the back. These were newly arrived Chin clan immigrants looking for somewhere to stay, who would be put up for

160

a few days in the quietly illegal bedrooms on the third floor until more permanent places were found for them; or they were garment workers, like my mother, hoping for justice in a dispute with a sweatshop owner; or parents needing a loan to send their most promising child to college. They waited their turns and went in with little gifts, a bag of oranges or a new fountain pen; most came out satisfied that, at worst, they had been heard and, at best, they might get what they wanted because someone with power was taking them seriously.

That someone was the man—it was always a man—who, back home, would have been the village chief, the headman—the mayor, if you wanted to do it in English. Every family name and village association had a headman. Only these men weren't elected. It was obvious to everyone who they were, and they held their power because they could. They were men who had money, successful men, men with connections and a personal presence that inspired fear as much as confidence in the people who were perfectly happy to look up to them. The ones who weren't happy could challenge them— not overtly, of course, but by taking over some of their functions, by lending money or settling disputes—until it became clear where the power really lay.

Chin Family Association ran that way. I was sure Zhen Rong did, too, and I was willing to bet I knew who the headman was.

The Zhen Rong Association was housed on the first floor of a residential building on the piece of East Broadway right near the Manhattan Bridge. The building's brick front had only two small first-floor windows, and they were curtained; but keeping track of the outside world was never the point of a family or village association, after all.

"Is Zhen Lo's family name, then?" Bill asked me as we approached the place. "Or Rong? Or is it the village back home?"

"None of those, I don't think. Zhen Rong is a made-up name." I waited for the complicated traffic light at the Bowery to figure out when to let us through. "Village ties aren't as strong in China now as they were when the last generation came over," I told him. "Some of these people are coming from cities, or they were internal migrant workers before they left. And the new guys come from a wider area than my father's people did, or H. B. Yang's. I bet any Fukienese can belong to Zhen Rong as long as he's willing to accept Duke Lo as his fearless leader.''

"Or hers," Bill added in an admonitory tone.

"Don't get smug with your display of feminist sensitivity," I advised him, "because you're wrong. At least in the old places, only the men belong. Widows of members get looked after, sort of, but these aren't the kinds of places women hang around and gossip and gamble. We do that at each other's homes."

"Chinese women gamble at home?"

"Just being married to most men is a gamble." We reached Zhen Rong's door. "Maybe this place is different, though," I added just before we went in.

But it wasn't.

As soon as I pushed open the door into Zhen Rong I could see I was the only woman in the place. So could everyone else there. And they could also see that Bill was the only non-Chinese. I don't know which confused them more, but the potential for irritation was strong and already showing itself on some of the faces that were turned to us.

I bowed that Chinese bow that doesn't exactly bend from the waist but isn't just a nod of the head, either. Bill stood a little behind me, unmoving and silent. I knew he'd be running his eyes around the room, mapping and cataloging it as he always does in a new place, but I also knew he'd be trying to do it without making eye contact with any of the men, because I'd asked him not to.

For their part, the dozen or so men seated at the scattered tables, the two sofas, and the overstuffed armchairs had fallen silent as they looked at us, teacups and Chinese newspapers and fan-tan buttons temporarily abandoned. The room wasn't as large as the front room at Chin Family Association, but it was similarly decked out: chairs and tables, sofas and coffee tables, cigarette smoke draping the air. On the walls, where Chin Family Association had hung scrolls promising good fortune and prosperity, Zhen Rong displayed photos of Fukienese leaders in the smiling company of New York politicians.

Like the ones in H. B. Yang's office, I thought, only not going back so far.

I bowed again to the watchful, silent men. "I'm very sorry to disturb you," I said. "I am Chin Ling Wan-ju. I would be very grateful for a few moments with Lo Da-Qi."

Even though I spoke in English, I gave our names in the Chinese order, because it was polite, and politeness seemed like a minimum requirement with this crew. I got no response except a few shuffled feet and changed seating positions, mostly enabling the men who moved to see us better.

"I won't take up much of his time," I promised them. "It's a matter of some importance, and only a powerful man can help me."

I'd thought that might work, but still no one spoke in answer. I looked around the room at the unsmiling faces, young and old, and realized they were waiting for something else. I did what they wanted.

"This is Bill Smith," I said, standing aside so they could see Bill clearly. "My husband."

Beside me, I felt Bill nod to the group, a careful greeting.

The expressions on the faces of the men before us softened into a mixture of recognition and contempt. A few of the younger ones smiled knowing, mocking smiles. There weren't a lot of reasons these men would consider legitimate for a non-Chinese to penetrate their sanctuary. The point of a place like this, after all, was to let these men, amid asphalt and English, thousands of miles from where they were born, feel safe and at home. An important politician could probably come here, or a fire inspector, though he wouldn't be welcome; and after that, almost no one's presence was acceptable unless he was Chinese.

But the white husband of a Chinese woman was something they understood. This would be a man smart enough to get himself a real wife, not one of those loud, demanding, sexless women of his own race; and as for me, though they resented me for it, they could see the sense in my latching on to a man much closer to the possibilities of power and wealth by the fact of his birth than they would ever be no matter how hard and long they worked.

So, as I cast my eyes down as was proper to do when introducing my husband to a group of men, these men, their faces either derisive or carefully blank, relaxed and waited for me to ask again what I'd asked when we'd first walked in.

"We need help on a matter," I said, raising my eyes to them. "We would be grateful for a few minutes of Lo Da-Qi's counsel."

Another few moments of silence. Then one of the older men rose, scraping back his chair. He said nothing, but he walked to and through a door in the rear wall. None of the other men moved, and Bill and I didn't either, standing where we'd stood since we walked into the room.

The silence and the stares were getting just a little on my nerves, making me want to do things like check that my hair was all lying flat and my socks matched, by the time the door in the back opened again and the old man gestured us through. We walked the length of the room, me with eyes once again properly downcast, Bill not looking left or right. We went through the door, and the old man, walking out, closed it behind himself, leaving us alone with the room's occupant.

The man before us sat on a leather easy chair in a grouping of three chairs and a coffee table on one side of the room that balanced the desk and side chairs on the other. I ran my eyes over the furniture, a mixture of department store English men's club and department store French Provincial: maroon leather with brass studs alongside distressed white wood with curvy legs and gilding where you least expected it. The room's single window, which faced the building's rear courtyard and probably didn't have any better view than the one in my office, was covered with heavy blue velvet drapes that matched the blue lattice-patterned carpet. The picture frames were curvy and gilded and eclipsed the glass-framed brush paintings in soft blues and grays that they contained.

The man in the easy chair smiled slightly behind his tortoise-shell glasses. He was, I judged, around fifty, his skin lined as much with the deep creases that smiles bring as with age, his hair still full and black. He wore a well-made three-piece blue suit, a glisteningly white shirt, and a navy tie. Without rising he gestured us to sit. There wasn't a lot of room to maneuver around the furniture, but we managed it. As we did, and before I could open my mouth, one of the younger men from the other room came in with a pot of tea and a plate of coconut squares. The rising steam of the tea mingled with the heavy, dead scent of stale tobacco left behind in a room where there's too much upholstered furniture and the air doesn't move.

The young man put the tea and sweets on the coffee table, smirked at me, sneered at Bill, bowed to the other man, and left.

The suited man waited until the door had clicked shut. Then he turned to me with the broad smile his lined face had promised. "Chin Ling Wan-ju," he said. "Lydia Chin! Please, have some tea, please."

His English was accented but clear. I answered, then, also in English. "You are Lo Da-Qi?"

"Duke Lo," he said, his smile growing even broader. "Duke Lo. I certainly am. It's a pleasure to finally meet you. Lydia Chin! Also, your husband! I didn't know; forgive me. Sir." He leaned forward in his chair to shake Bill's hand. Bill shook with him, returned his smile, gave Lo his name, and was otherwise carefully silent.

"There's nothing to forgive," I said, pouring the tea into three Western-style cups with saucers and handles. The first I handed to Duke Lo, the second to Bill. "You couldn't have been expected to know. In fact," I said, looking straight into his eyes with a frankness I knew would be considered unacceptably forward by the men in the other room, "I don't see why you should have been expected to know anything about me at all."

Duke Lo, however, didn't seem to take my forthrightness, or my words, as an affront. He just smiled again, sipped his tea, and spoke to Bill. "Oh, I find I must keep up with many things. Important to my business. Only sometimes I don't know why, but that doesn't matter, I always find out." He turned to me. "Certainly, I wish someone had told me how pretty you are! I would have kept up with you sooner.''

He winked at Bill and went back to his tea.

Bill just sat, his hand wrapped around his teacup.

''If you'd wanted to meet me''—I spoke into the silence, putting aside my own tea, an unremarkable pekoe—''you could have invited me over, instead of sending Three-finger Choi to try and scare me.'' I emphasized the ''try'' maybe a little more than I had to, and kept my eyes on Duke Lo.

''Oh, no no no!'' Duke Lo protested, putting his teacup down, erasing the air with both hands. He looked from me to Bill. ''Choi completely misunderstood my instructions! He is a very stupid man. I am extremely sorry for any unhappiness he caused you. Ah, the worry he must have caused you, also, Mr. Smith! No, it's unforgivable. But Choi is a very stupid man.''

I noticed he didn't say, *And I've fired him.* I asked, ''Really? What were his instructions?''

Lo looked at Bill again, but Bill said nothing. Lo turned and answered me. ''I'd requested,'' he said, ''*requested,* that he suggest you not trouble yourself with the tedious search for four useless men, ungrateful menial workers worth no more than the dung they wallowed in in the villages at home where they should have stayed. That was all. Yes, believe me, that was all.''

Believe me. Trust me on this. Uh-huh.

''That wasn't the message as it was delivered,'' I said.

Duke Lo nodded sadly. ''Choi is eager and loyal, but he is stupid. He often, yes, often goes beyond his instructions in his desire to accomplish what he believes to be my goal. But an admirable motive!'' His eyes lit up. ''You cannot reprimand such a man, you cannot punish such loyalty, such devotion! I am lucky enough to have a number of such devoted employees, but it is rare in this world, Lydia Chin, rare.''

Rare indeed. I dropped the subject of Three-finger Choi and returned to the disappeared waiters.

''You speak of these men, these waiters,'' I said, ''as though you know them, and dislike them.''

"I? No. No no. But why would I need to know them? It's clear from their behavior that they are nothing. The kind of men who would run out on their jobs, their responsibilities; the lowest of worms, the dust the worms crawl through."

"And you wanted me to stop looking for what reason?"

"Just to save you trouble! Yes, to keep you from wasting time, when you have so many important things to do!"

Yeah, sure. "Perhaps these men are, as you say, useless and ungrateful," I said. "Although their families may not think so. They may be living on the money the men send home. They may be waiting right now for money that won't come anymore unless the men return to their jobs."

"I suppose that's possible," Duke Lo agreed. "Although one of them won't be returning, I fear." He let his face grow appropriately solemn. "I understand he was killed last night. By a bomb." He dropped his eyes to the floor with the sadness of it all; then he glanced up at me again. His face still wore the soft, sad expression, but his eyes, for the brief second they met mine, were icy and hard.

"Yes, I'd heard," I said noncommittally.

"Not a surprising end for a man of his kind." Duke Lo sounded detached and philosophical. He glanced at Bill, then he rested his eyes on mine. They were frank and friendly again, looking like eyes that fit with the smile crinkles around them, the way they'd looked when we'd come in.

"Maybe not suprising," I said. "But unfortunate."

"For him, yes." Lo shrugged. "But what could he have expected?"

"No, not just for him. For a good many people involved with him."

Lo cocked his head and smiled again. He shifted in his chair, recrossed his legs so that he was facing me fully now, and Bill was on the sidelines. "What do you mean?"

"In New York," I said, "as I'm sure an influential man like yourself must know, the police are required to investigate violent deaths. Whether the dead were useless in life or not doesn't seem to matter."

"Yes, of course. An investigation will inconvenience some people, certainly." Like H. B. Yang, I thought to myself as Duke Lo lifted his teacup and covered his smile with it.

"The New York police," I went on, "don't think in a way that's . . . straightforward. They expect things to be complicated. Twisted. Those men may have been useless as far as you're concerned, but they weren't useless to their employer."

"Useless to their employer?" Lo said. "No worker is. How would he have a job in that case? But also, few are irreplaceable."

"No, that's true," I agreed. "But when a man's employees disappear, the New York police tend to look to his enemies for an answer."

Duke Lo cocked his head at me in a thoughtful sort of way. "That's interesting, what you say."

"Yes," I pressed on, "it's often what happens."

"But one of those men—the one who was killed—was an irritation to his employer, if what I hear is true. Is this incorrect?"

"No," I said. "I'd heard that, too. But this employer had had other irritating workers, and they'd been fired. Not killed, and they didn't disappear."

I bit into a creamy-sweet coconut square and listened to the silence. The thing practically melted its way down my throat. I said, "Do you want to know what I think happened?"

"Certainly, very much." Duke Lo nodded politely. I noticed his teacup was empty and filled it for him, and topped off Bill's, too.

"Well," I said, "I think perhaps someone—some enemy of the men's employer—asked the men to disappear. Possibly even paid them to. Just to embarrass the employer. Because, as you say, one of them was an irritation to him, and it looks bad." I poured myself some fresh tea, too, now that the men had been served. "Maybe the death of the man yesterday was accidental and unrelated. But it will get the police all excited. They've probably started thinking all kinds of strange thoughts already, and looking for people to ask questions of."

I carefully didn't mention Mary's and Chester's earlier visit to Happy Pavilion, although Duke Lo's thoughtful face told me he knew

168

about it, and he knew I knew, and he knew that it, among other things, was what I meant.

"The police may have strange ideas, which lead them along strange pathways," he said conversationally. "But if so, what can anyone do?"

"The police like to solve cases," I said. "If they're solved, they're over. If, for example, the remaining missing men were to reappear and tell the police that neither their employer nor their employer's enemies had anything to do with their disappearing in the first place, I think the police would be satisfied with that."

"You do?" Lo asked. "But what about the man who died?"

"If the employer and his enemies had nothing to do with the men disappearing, there's no reason to think they had anything to do with killing one of them, either," I said logically. "The police will probably put that down to the antiunion forces."

Duke Lo knew that the antiunion forces were most publicly identified with H. B. Yang, so this idea could not have been unappealing to him, but he didn't say anything about that, and I just sipped my tea.

"Well," he finally said, "this is certainly very interesting, everything you say. But I cannot, no, I cannot imagine just why you have come here to say these things to me." He smiled broadly, the benevolent headman pleased to spend some time on a lazy spring evening chatting with a villager—even from a different village—although the visit was purely social, with nothing in it for him.

"I thought," I answered mildly, "since you'd sent Three-finger Choi to . . . suggest I not waste my time on these men, that you might have some interest in them."

His smile grew almost abashed, as though he were a child caught playing a practical joke he was rather proud of. "No," he said. "No. I have no interest. Men like that? Turtle's eggs, as we say at home. Here I think you would call them little pieces of shit." I almost flinched as he spat those words, sharp and poisonous, into the air. His mischievous smile, though, did not change, and his voice, when he spoke again, was pleasant once more. "Who could be interested in them? I must admit, yes, it amused me, the trouble their disappearance caused. I would enjoy seeing that continue, for my amusement.''

I wondered if Duke Lo found it amusing that Peter was lying in a hospital room in Brooklyn. I looked at him, his smile lines and good blue suit, his English men's club chair in his Chinese men's club. I suddenly wanted to leave, to be out in the evening where there were no heavy velvet drapes or overstuffed furniture or patterned carpets, where whatever the city smelled like, it wasn't old, stale smoke and motionless, imprisoned air.

Before I could make a move, though, Duke Lo asked, as though it had just occurred to him to wonder, ''Miss Chin—or perhaps I should say Mrs. Smith—''

''Miss Chin will do just fine.'' I cut that off at the pass.

''Miss Chin,'' he said again, nodding pleasantly, ''in your search for these missing men, who is *your* employer?''

There was no way he was getting the whole truth to that one. In fact, since he had to ask, let him keep guessing.

''I can't tell you that,'' I answered, equally amicably. ''I'm sure you understand. But it's someone with a friendly interest in the men's well-being.''

''Yes.'' He smiled. ''Of course. Although . . .''

''Although?''

''Although. A friendly interest, you say. Perhaps. Perhaps not. In any case, *your* interest, Lydia Chin, may, it may, be different than your client's.''

''Do you think so? In what way?''

''You were born and raised in Chinatown. Though you are now married''—a smile and a nod to Bill—''you retain an office here, am I right about that?''

''Yes, you're right.''

''You retain, then, an interest in Chinatown. An interest in the future here.''

''I do.''

''Well, then, well, then, it might be worth your consideration: Chinatown is changing. Your client—could it be your client is part of the old Chinatown? You should think, Lydia Chin, about that. You

170

should think about where *your* loyalties lie. There is the future; there is the past. Chinatown will move forward, but not everyone will move with it. Will you move forward, Lydia Chin?"

Move, I thought. The first good idea I've heard since I got here.

"I'll consider that question," I said, swallowing what I wanted to say. "I don't know how to answer you, but I'll think about it. In any case"—I stood—"we came here because I thought you had some interest in the situation of the vanished waiters. I can see, however, that I was mistaken."

"I'm afraid so." Duke Lo's words were gently apologetic, as though the mistake were his, not mine. His eyes twinkled. "Although I certainly don't regret the error, because it gave me the chance to meet you. You also, Mr. Smith," he said to Bill, who had stood when I had. Duke Lo, remaining seated, said, "I hope to see you both soon again."

Neither Bill nor I answered that. We just shook Duke Lo's hand and walked out of his club.

fifteen

Can we go for a walk?'' I asked Bill as we hit the night air. Never before had East Broadway seemed so sweet, so breezy, so easygoing and full of possibility. Exhausted and achy as I was from my dim sum day, I was also too wired to want to do anything except keep moving.

"Sure," Bill answered, shaking out the match to the cigarette he'd pulled out the minute we hit the sidewalk. "Where?"

"It doesn't matter. I'll walk you home."

"That's backward."

"You want to make something of it?"

"No. Although," he ruminated as we started west, "that's the second time you've married me without telling me about it. I wonder what your shrink would say about that?"

"I don't have a shrink."

"Go get one, and find out what he'd say."

"*She* would say I'm very quick, clever, and able to think on my feet."

"That's not your shrink, it's your fortune cookie."

"It's probably just as accurate. You were great in there, by the way."

"Me?" He sounded surprised. "I said absolutely nothing."

"That's what I mean. You ought to do that more often."

"You hurt me to the quick."

"No, I don't, because you know I don't mean it. But in this particular case it was perfect, because it made Duke Lo talk to me. If you'd opened your manly mouth just once he would have ignored me completely and spoken only to you. He kept trying to do that anyway."

"I saw that. That's why I shut up. So you think my mouth is manly?"

"The same as the rest of you, sahib."

"Too many compliments and I'm going to think you really do want to marry me."

"That's just like a man."

"I am a man."

"That's your problem. But let me ask you something: why didn't you have a cigarette in there? You usually do when you're just sitting around, and that room's obviously not a no-smoking zone. I kept waiting for you to light up."

He shook his head as he took a deep drag on the cigarette he was having now. "It was a power thing. He's a smoker—and it's a good thing, by the way, or he would've blinded us with all those toothy smiles. It would have been a mistake for me to light up before he did."

"Really?"

"Absolutely. It would have meant I was less able to control my craving. Weaker than he was."

"Cigarettes work that way?"

"Everything works that way."

I considered that for a block or two. As we waited for a light I said, "I wonder if you are."

"If I'm what?"

"Less able to control it. I wonder what Duke Lo craves."

Bill looked over at me. "What are you thinking?"

"Did you believe him?"

"About what?"

"When he said he only wanted to see the men stay disappeared because he thought it was funny. In other words, because it made trouble for H. B. Yang."

"Isn't that our theory? That his power grows as your friend Yang's shrinks, and the point of this was to embarrass Yang?"

"My friend Yang. My mother would keel over if she heard you say that. And that was our theory, yes. But I don't know," I said. "Did you hear what he called them? And the way he said it?" I frowned at the memory of Duke Lo's voice. " 'Turtle's eggs.' That's a *really* bad thing where I come from. And 'little pieces of shit.' " Bill raised his eyebrows to hear that word come out of me. I pushed right on. "Do you talk that way about people who aren't anything to you, just pawns in your game? Pawns who, actually, are doing just what you told them to do?"

"Maybe you do. Maybe you despise weak people at the same time as you're using them."

"Maybe. Or maybe he's the reason they disappeared. Ho told Peter they were in trouble. Maybe he's the one they're in trouble with."

"Could be." Bill nodded, pulling smoke from his cigarette. "And what's the trouble?"

"How do I know? This is a brand-new theory. It needs to ripen. And something else."

But I didn't get the chance to tell Bill what else I was thinking. Putting a hand on my arm, he stopped on the sidewalk. I stopped, too, wondering why; then two doors opened simultaneously in a Ford parked in the yellow zone in front of his building. Two men stepped out. My hand snaked to the .38 clipped to my waist, but I didn't close my fingers on it, because Bill stood calmly, not moving as the men approached us.

"Well," he said, eyes on them. "Look, Lydia, it's Mickey Mouse and his dog Pluto."

The big man's jaw tightened at that, but the little one actually smiled, though it wasn't a nice smile.

"Smith," he said. "And this must be Lydia Chin."

"Who are you?" I demanded.

"Oh, I beg your pardon," the small man said with sarcastic politeness. "I'm Ed Deluca, and this is Jim March." He reached his hand into his coat as his partner did the same. That automatically made my hand want to fly back to the gun on my belt, but I forced myself to stand still the way Bill was doing. Deluca and March both came out with gold badges in little leather cases. The badges identified them as State Department Security.

"You guys go to finishing school since this afternoon?" Bill asked.

Deluca shook his head. "We've been feeling bad about that, Smith. Maybe we did come on a little strong. Let's go on up and discuss it." He made a move in the direction of Bill's apartment door.

"No," Bill said.

March said, "Listen, Smith," and stepped forward. Bill turned, just slightly, to face him, and I knew from Bill's eyes what his shoulders felt like, how the backs of his hands tingled. I wanted to put a hand on his arm, to try to bring him back to where we were and who these people were, but that would make it worse.

Deluca watched for a moment, then he smiled and shrugged.

"Okay," he said in the mock-generous voice of the guy who's got everything going his way, the guy who amuses himself giving you a crumb because he's got the keys to the kitchen. "How about we buy you a drink?" He cocked his head toward Shorty's, the bar downstairs from Bill's apartment.

"No."

"Don't make this hard, Smith."

Bill held the smaller man's eyes. "Coffee," he finally said. "You can buy us coffee." He looked at me as if to ask whether that was all right. Now I did lightly touch his arm, feeling the wire-tightness. He nodded once and stepped off the curb, leaving Deluca and March to follow him up the block or not. They did.

There are two coffee shops on that block, one Bill likes and one he doesn't. The one he held the door at was the one he doesn't. I figured that was for the same reason he wouldn't let Deluca and March back up into his place and wouldn't drink with them at Shorty's, which is as much his home as the apartment upstairs.

We settled in a booth and ordered three coffees and a tea. I wondered, not for the first time, how drinking bad coffee had gotten to be part of the American macho image.

After the waitress left, Deluca took four quarters from March and fed the jukebox. Gloria Gaynor came on, singing "I Will Survive."

"Background noise." Deluca smiled. "Always a good idea." He turned to me. "I'm glad you're here. Saves us the trouble of looking for you."

"I'm here," I said.

"This afternoon," he said, "your buddy here told us to get lost. We just had a few questions, but he wasn't very friendly."

"I'm not friendly, either," I said.

"I'm sorry to hear that."

"What I told you," Bill said quietly, "was to come back when you got a warrant. You have one?"

"It's not like that," Deluca said.

"What is it like?" I asked.

Deluca sipped his coffee. "We had some questions," he repeated, speaking to me. "We just want a little help."

"Questions about what?"

"See?" Deluca said to Bill. "Already she's nicer than you." He smiled again at me. "About four Chinese waiters who disappeared."

"I'll tell you one thing," I said. "One of them's dead."

Deluca and March looked at each other. "Bomb at the union office," Deluca agreed. "Saw it on the news. We want to know where the other three are."

"A lot of people do," I said.

"And?"

"What makes you think Bill or I have any idea?"

"When we came to visit Smith today," Deluca said, putting down his coffee cup, leaning forward with the sour smile, "we didn't know about you. That you're his partner. Now, you can't tell me that a guy is tied up with these Chinese guys, and has a Chinese girl for a partner, and they don't know anything."

"Where did you get the idea Bill's tied up with the Chinese guys?" asked the Chinese girl partner, congratulating herself on not flinging her tea into his little ferret face.

Bill sat silently drinking his coffee, but I detected a grin behind his coffee cup.

Deluca shrugged. "Okay, we'll trade. Our people saw his car where it shouldn't have been. We traced the car."

"Where?"

He looked into my eyes, then said deliberately, "Brooklyn."

"Who are your people," I asked, "who saw the car?"

"You know," Deluca said, "the point of this isn't for you to ask questions."

"You know," I said, "you obviously don't have a warrant, because you're the type who'd flash it if you did. So if I help you out, it'll be because I'm a good citizen. I'm still deciding."

Deluca looked at March, then at Bill. "How come you're letting her do all the talking?"

Bill shrugged. "How come *he's* letting *you* do all the talking?"

"Shit." Deluca turned back to me. "All right, listen," he said. "I'm going to lay this out for you, just once. The government has some interest in certain shipments of goods coming into this country. A serious interest. We've recently come to believe our shipments also contain goods we didn't order and don't want. We want to know who's bringing those in and we think these waiters can help us."

"What goods?"

Deluca grinned and shook his head. "You go," he said.

I considered, finishing my tea. At this place, it wasn't even Tetley's; it was something so no-name the only way to make it drinkable was to brew it really weak and put milk in it. "We're looking for them, too," I finally said. "We haven't gotten anywhere. Everyone says they don't know where to find them."

"Who are you working for?"

"The lawyer for the union. The man who was killed was a union organizer. His lawyer was worried their disappearance had something to do with the union."

"Like what?"

"Like they'd been threatened by the restaurant owner for organizing, or something."

"Is that what happened?"

"The restaurant owner says no."

"What brought you to Brooklyn?"

"You mean Jayco Realty?"

"I mean Brooklyn."

I was tempted to be as cute as he was being, but why? "One of the men had that address on a scrap of paper he'd left behind."

"What did you find out?"

"Nothing."

"Which man?"

"We just found the paper. I don't know whose it was."

"Can I have it?"

"I threw it away."

"I don't believe you."

"If you get a warrant," I said, "you can look for it."

"You know," Deluca said, "you're right. You're not very friendly."

I shrugged.

"Look," he said. "Jimmy and me, we got a job to do here: keep this little project going."

"What's the project?"

"What's the difference? It's our job and we're going to do it. I was a Marine, sister. I'm still Marine Reserves, eighteen years later. I've been a cop, and now I'm this. I don't back off. I bring it home. There's never been an assignment I haven't completed, and this isn't about to be the first."

"Meaning?"

"Don't get in our way, Ms. Chin."

I didn't think that needed much of an answer, so I didn't give it one.

Deluca got to his feet. "C'mon, Jimmy. Let's go find a judge and get a warrant."

March stood also. Deluca smiled, March's face didn't move, and they walked out, leaving Bill and me to pay for the bad coffee and worse tea.

Bill and I sat for a while, until we were sure they'd had time to get into their car and drive away.

"Gee," I said, "I can see why you weren't crazy about those guys."

"You want another cup?"

"Of this stuff? Are you kidding?"

"I don't get it," he said.

"What?"

"Why did it take them this long to find out about you? How can they have seen my car and not seen you?"

"That's a really good question," I said, because it was.

"Let's go," he said, standing. As we stepped out the coffee shop door he lit a cigarette and drew deeply.

"What goods?" I wondered out loud as we started to walk.

"And what goods don't they want?"

"And why didn't they have a warrant?"

"And," Bill said, "why are they interested in the three remaining waiters but they don't seem to be concerned about who killed Ho?"

A truck rattled past us on its way to a night delivery.

"I'm so confused," I complained. "I can't think."

Bill looked down at me. His face and voice softened. "You look exhausted."

"Me?" I protested. "I'm fresh as a daisy. Perky and ebullient."

He smiled. He had a much better smile than Ed Deluca. "I think you're pronouncing that wrong."

"How do you say it?"

He pronounced *ebullient* for me.

"Well, I don't care how you say it. I am it."

"Uh-huh. You need to go home and go to bed."

I waited, but he didn't say anything else.

"I don't believe it," I told him. "Those guys must have really gotten to you."

"How so?"

"You said 'bed' and me in the same sentence, and you're not going to say anything lewd?"

"No, it's just that I'm tired of rejection. Besides, now that we're married I've lost all interest in you."

"I guess that's good."

"Good or bad, it's inevitable. So go home. You want me to walk you?"

"You're kidding."

"No, but I knew you'd say no. Just be careful, then."

"I thought you'd lost interest."

"Only romantically. You still owe me money on this case."

We'd reached his building, for the second time that night. He smiled, put his hands on my shoulders, and kissed my forehead. In a jingle of keys he unlocked the street door, stooped to collect his mail from the mat, and waved me good night. He started up the stairs as the door closed behind him, and I stood on the sidewalk, thinking about rejection.

I did walk home, and I was careful, looking out for Fords as I ambled my way east again in the cool night air. Bill was right: I was tired, and getting home, taking a long, quiet bath, and going straight to bed seemed like a perfect plan. Maybe, by morning, everything would have become clear to me.

Like how pigs managed to fly.

It was an hour since we'd left Duke Lo's, and it took me twenty minutes to get home from Bill's. Still, it was early, not quite nine o'clock, when I pulled open the heavy front door and began the climb to our fourth-floor walk-up.

My brothers—even Elliot, the fitness freak—had all been glad to move out of here into buildings with elevators or, in the case of Ted, a house; but I liked this creaky climb. It gave me time to think, to let the day recede and settle into its place, until the things that had happened today shrank in size and softened in color and began fitting in among the rest of the things in my life. These stairs and hallways weren't like the streets, public and available to anybody to walk along and share with you, people whose paths would never cross yours again; but they weren't like your own home, either, where no one came unless you knew who they were and what they wanted. They were for the people whose lives, by virtue of the heavy street door and these very stairs and hallways, were intertwined with yours. On these scuffed stairs and in these narrow hallways the aromas of other people's dinners and the sounds of their music, the welcome mats they used or didn't use, and the laughter and greetings as they came in and out, reminded me that lives I knew nothing about were going on ten inches below my feet or six inches on the other side of the kitchen wall. I found that idea comforting. It made me feel like even if I screwed up, maybe someone else wouldn't. Like we were all in this together, living so close and so separate.

I reached our apartment, the door I'd been coming home to for all of my twenty-eight years. I unlocked the locks and called, "Hi, Ma," to the back of my mother's head where she sat on the living room couch. I started to slip off my shoes, letting the door close behind me. In the middle of the first shoe I stopped as the scene in the living room registered on me. My mother wasn't alone.

Seated on the easy chair with the flowered upholstery, sipping tea from the red-and-yellow special-occasion china and holding a scrapbook of family photographs on his lap, was that paragon of salesmanship from Jayco Realty, Joe Yee.

My mother's smile was proprietary and broad. Joe Yee's was

quick, but his almost-black eyes, while they smiled, seemed to be adding things up, appraising, calculating. He looked ready to step this way or that, to adjust to whatever the situation turned out to be. That adrenaline edge, that dancing without a net, was what accounted, I was sure, for the sparkle in Joe Yee's bottomless eyes.

My mother, though, obviously thought it was the sight of me.

I realized I was perching on one foot in the vestibule like an ambushed crane. Quickly, I yanked my slippers on and strode into the living room. Joe Yee rose and stood, photo album still in hand, as my mother said, in Cantonese, of course, "It's good you came. I was going to call you on that foolish device to tell you your friend was here."

That foolish device was my beeper, which my mother loves in concept because it can let her get a hold of me at any time and place, except that in reality she's never used it because she doesn't believe an object that tiny could really contain all the words she wants to say.

In this case, though, with a handsome, well-spoken Chinese man who claimed to know me sitting in her living room, I was willing to bet my mother would have galloped hell-bent for leather on the Pony Express if that were the only way to find me.

But it wasn't. I was here, Joe Yee was smiling, and my mother was beaming, and I pushed down my hot-cheeked anger, my bad-tempered confusion, at this invasion of my living room and evening and the meaning of it. I didn't smile, though. I just said, "Hello," and waited.

Still smiling the easy smile, Joe Yee said in English, "Relax. I know this is a surprise, but don't worry. Everything's fine."

Fine, my fine Irish foot, you nervy creep, I thought, but I didn't get a chance to say anything, as Joe Yee switched to Cantonese and continued, "I just took a chance on dropping by. Your mother's been showing me some great pictures. You were a cute kid, Ling Wan-ju. Of course, I expected that. She's been serving me some excellent tea, also."

My mother blushed and denied that her tea was at all tasty, as it would have been if she'd had any idea that Yee Ji-You would be coming over so she could have properly shopped and prepared. This was accompanied by an accusatory glance at me and a reassuringly fond smile for Joe Yee.

I had no idea, either, Ma, believe me. I still said nothing as I processed what this visit meant. It meant I'd been right about Jayco. It meant Joe Yee, whoever he was, knew where to find me. He knew my real name. He even knew my Chinese name, though he could have learned that from my mother in the first thirty seconds he was here. I didn't know who he was or what he wanted, but I knew one thing: I had to get him out of here, away from my mother and her home, as fast as I possibly could.

I smiled then. "What a surprise to see you here!" I said, also in Cantonese, so my mother wouldn't be left out. "Ma, I would have told you, except I didn't think Joe was coming here. I thought I was going to meet you at the club," I said to him with a quizzical look.

"Well, I got through early at work, so I thought I'd come pick you up," Joe Yee answered smoothly, taking my lead.

As I'd suspected, this idea—that I not only knew this good-looking Chinese man but actually had a date with him—sent my mother over the moon.

"Well! Then you must be going," she said, seizing Joe Yee's teacup, rapidly arranging the tea things on the tray to carry them back to the kitchen. "But Ling Wan-ju"—she stopped and frowned at me—"you're not going out dressed like that?"

"No, Ma." I sighed. I gave Joe Yee a sweet smile and said, "I'll just be a minute." I ducked into my bedroom, clicked the door shut behind me, and thought, *Thank you, Ma,* as I grabbed up the phone. Bill's number was on the speed dial button. I punched it and waited, chewing on my lip, but all I got was his service. That figured; he'd been home half an hour by now, enough time to have gotten comfortable and settled at the piano. He turns the phone off when he's practicing, and though I'd never tried to beep him in a situation like that, I felt a sinking certainty he turned the beeper off, too.

I left it a message, anyway, as I had his service, in case he checked when he was through. I wasn't sure what good calling me back would do by the time he got around to it, but I was taking my beeper anyway—and my .22: smaller and more easy to hide than the .38, but just as useful in certain situations.

I peeled off my shirt and slacks, clipped beeper and gun onto the waistband of a pair of deep green velvet evening trousers, which I chose because the shirt that goes best with them is a flowing white tunic that's really good at hiding stuff. I jammed a big jade brooch onto the tunic, slipped on a pair of gold earrings, ran a comb through my hair, and, though my mother wouldn't approve, pulled on a pair of black suede flats, because there was no way I was going to leave this apartment with Joe Yee in shoes I couldn't run in.

I was back out in the living room in less time than it took Joe Yee to carry the tray of tea things into the kitchen for my mother and to admire my father's collection of mud figurines in their glass-fronted cabinet.

"You look great," Joe Yee said when he saw me. My mother beamed, not at me but at him.

"Thank you." I smiled, meaning, *Who the hell asked you?*

I took my black, tent-shaped coat from the closet—all the better to hide the tunic that was hiding the gun—and said, "Bye, Ma. Don't wait up." I knew she would, though, to pretend she wasn't interested in all the details she would be trying to pry out of me about my date with this handsome man.

Joe Yee and I descended the stairs in silence. When we reached the front door he held it open for me; when we reached the street he said, "That outfit is too good to waste. Let me take you someplace nice."

"You have to be crazy!" I spun to face him. I spoke in angry English; we had dropped the Cantonese facade. "You expect me to actually go someplace with you?"

"We can't stand here on the sidewalk."

"We can't—" I sputtered. "We can do any damn thing I want to do! Who the hell *are* you, anyway?"

"Joe Yee," he said with a smile. "Which is truer than what you told me, Marilyn."

"So what?" I demanded. "And how did you find me, any-way?"

"Really, can't we go have a drink?"

I tried to calm down and be rational. "All right," I conceded after a few moments' thought, not because I wanted to go anyplace with Joe Yee but because, Chinatown being what it was, if we stood here arguing for another thirty seconds my mother would be sure to hear about it from at least a dozen people.

Chinatown being what it was, though, the place I chose was outside Chinatown. I had criteria: it had to be within walking distance—I wasn't about to get into a cab with this man—and it had to be big, lots of people to keep an eye on me. I stalked out ahead of him, taking us the longer but more crowded way over to Canal Street, then west. In the beginning we strode along silently, Joe Yee's long legs easily keeping up with my angry, determined, but shorter ones. After a few blocks on Canal, though, he ventured a comment: "Your mother's a lovely lady."

"My mother is none of your business!" I snapped. I sped up and cut around a group of teenage boys, who didn't even notice me passing. Joe Yee didn't move out of their path. For him, they parted and came back together again, like water around a stone.

"Hey, okay, I'm sorry," he said as he caught up to me. "I didn't mean to upset you, but I need to talk to you."

"Sorry!" I snorted. "If you'd just wanted to talk and not prove how smart you are you could have called me instead of busting into my house in the middle of the night. Since you know so much about me, I'm sure you have my office number."

"If I'd called, would you have been willing to meet me alone? Like this?"

"Are you kidding? Why should I? The only reason I'm on the same sidewalk with you right now is that I didn't want to up-set my mother, like by throwing you out!" Which was not true. If Jayco was just a bunch of realtors, that was one thing; but if they were, Joe Yee wouldn't have hunted me up. And the Feds, Deluca and March, wouldn't have had any interest in 411 Baltic

Street where they'd spotted Bill's car. If Joe Yee insisted on presenting himself to me on a silver platter, I certainly wouldn't have let him get away.

But I would have chosen the time and place, to control the encounter better. Thinking about that made something Joe Yee had said finally register.

"What do you mean, alone?" I waved my hand at the crowded sidewalks around us. "We're not alone. And you came to my house, where we were most definitely not alone."

"This is New York," he answered. "Isn't this the place where people come to be alone in a crowd? No, come on, just kidding. I meant without your partner."

"I don't have a partner."

"Well, whatever you call him. Smith, I mean. Bill Smith."

So Joe Yee not only knew I wasn't Marilyn Ko, he knew about Bill. Who, I demanded of myself, is this guy? And what the hell is going on?

I found myself without an answer, except to point out in passing that I was using language with Joe Yee and myself that I normally resist employing. Great, I told myself. Thanks for the tip. I'll take that up with you later.

Joe Yee and I reached the bar I'd been heading us for, Lightning Rod's, toward the western end of Canal Street. It's a huge, hopping place in an old first-floor warehouse where everything, including the floor, is made of metal: the tables are zinc, the ceiling's the old-fashioned stamped tin you find all over New York, and on the floor, welded together, are the steel plates they use to cover really big holes in the street.

Metal is good at bouncing back sound, and the noise that came roaring out as Joe Yee pulled open the door for us was enough to knock you flat onto the sidewalk. I happened to know, though, that all the action here was concentrated toward the back, where the sinuous bar and the restaurant tables were, and that at the drink tables along the front wall you could actually hear your companion speak, provided you were willing to lean toward him. These tables had the extra added advantage of being visible from the street through the big front windows, just in case your companion had anything nefarious in mind.

"Let me get you a drink," Joe Yee said as I slipped into a shiny steel chair, the kind that belongs in the garden, at one of those front tables. "Unless you're going to sneak away while I'm gone?"

"I don't sneak," I said, nastily and inaccurately. "That's you. Besides, you'd just show up on my doorstep again."

"That's right, I would. What would you like?"

I sent him to get me a seltzer with lime and watched him walk away. He blended in just fine here, a hip young Asian man in an up-to-the-minute four-button charcoal suit over a black T-shirt, with confident shoulders and a fluid walk. As soon as he was swallowed up by the crush at the bar I whipped my beeper off my hip and checked it.

Someone had called. A number I didn't recognize marched by in little red lights, along with the symbol that shows you there's also a verbal message and you should call and pick it up.

Well, not right now, I thought. Whoever you are, you'll have to wait.

I left the sound turned off and stuck the thing back onto my pants just in time, right before I spotted Joe Yee working his way across the floor with my seltzer in one hand and a slender glass of dark beer in the other.

"So," he said as he put the drinks on the table and scraped back a chair for himself, "are you ready to listen to what I have to say?"

"I'm ready to break your nose, if you must know," I said, leaning forward so we could hear each other. We were both speaking in voices that would have been audible two blocks away if they weren't being smothered by the sounds of a New York hot spot Saturday night. "For someone I have no idea who he is, you have some damn nerve. Who are you?"

"Joe Yee," Joe Yee answered. "Please," he said as I opened my mouth. "That's all I can tell you. I shouldn't even be here talking to you."

"Shouldn't according to who?"

"The people I work for."

"Who are . . . ?"

"I need to find those waiters, Lydia."

I hadn't said he could call me Lydia, but that didn't seem like the biggest issue in front of us right now, so I let it pass.

"Waiters?" I asked casually, pulling on the straw stuck in my seltzer. "What waiters?"

"Oh, God, Lydia." Joe Yee sighed. "Things will go a lot faster if you don't try to blow smoke."

If *I* don't? I swallowed my indignation on the principle of giving Joe Yee rope.

He went on: "You're a private investigator looking for four men who used to work at Dragon Garden Restaurant. One way or another you're working with another investigator, Bill Smith. Probably you're working for him, because he needed someone Chinese to get him inside."

I thought about pitching my drink across the table at him, the way I'd contemplated flinging my tea at Ed Deluca. Lydia Chin, Menace to Café Society. But Bill had once told me that being underestimated is the best thing that can happen to a P.I., so I tried to view this idiocy as a strategic mistake on Joe Yee's part. Trying to seem innocent and even a little dumb, I asked, "Where did you get that idea?"

"That you're a P.I.? Will it help if I tell you?"

"It might."

"Smith's car," he said. "After you left the office, I watched you. When you drove away in that car, I had it traced. I found him, checked him out, found out about you, and here I am."

That car. Bill was going to have to do something about that car.

"Traced the car," I said. "Checked us out. You're a P.I., too?"

"Forget it," he said. "That's off-limits. And it doesn't matter what your relationship with Smith is."

Not to you, maybe, I thought as he went on: "What's important is who *he's* working for."

"Oh?" Gee, if you only knew. "Who's that important to?"

"Me."

I would have asked him again who he was, but I didn't want to hear that he was Joe Yee, so instead I said, "Why?"

He shook his head. "Lydia, you must know that one of those waiters is dead."

And a friend of mine's hurt, I thought, but Joe Yee might not know about Peter, so I didn't bring it up. "Funny, I do know that."

"Then you must have figured out that the others are in danger."

"The thought had crossed my mind."

"I need to find them before anything happens to them."

The music, which had been a pounding thump under the roar of conversation, changed to a techno-shriek above it. I thought for a minute, and said, "Assuming that any of this is true, and I even know what waiters you're talking about, how do I know it isn't your job to make things happen to them?"

He helped himself to more of his beer. "Who are you and Smith working for?"

"Why don't I feel like that answers my question?"

Joe Yee gave an exasperated sigh. *My sentiments exactly, fella.* He rubbed his forehead and stared at me. The din swirled around us like dirt in a dust storm.

"I told you," Joe Yee said, "I'm not even supposed to be talking to you. This thing is too big for someone like you and I'm taking a chance. But you seem like you might care about these men. Their only chance is if I find them."

Too big for someone like me? I hoped it was dark enough that he couldn't see the angry color flood my face. "Their only chance for what?" I demanded. "And how do you know what I seem like?"

Joe Yee drank from his beer and put it down again. He caught my eyes with his. I returned his look steadily and waited for what he had to say.

It was, "Lydia, we're both Chinese. We're looking for three Chinese men who need help."

Chinese, I thought. Duke Lo's Chinese. Three-finger Choi's Chinese. And H. B. Yang, and Mary, and my mother, and the mail-man.

"I've never heard this you-all-look-alike stuff from a Chinese person before," I told him.

"That's not what I meant. I'm trying to help."

"Is this why you came to me instead of Bill? You thought I might help you just because you're Chinese?"

Joe Yee shook his head. "Not me. The missing men."

"The missing men." I thought for a minute. "What kind of trouble are they in?"

"I don't know."

"You're the only one who can help them but you don't know what the problem is?"

"I shouldn't be telling you that, but it's true. I was hoping you did."

I shook my head.

"But," he said, "whatever it is, I know no one else can get them out of it."

I finished my drink and settled back in my chair. Let him lean across the table to hear me for a while.

"You know," I said, "you keep saying you shouldn't be telling me things I didn't ask to hear. But you're not telling me anything I did ask. Like who you are and why you care about these men. And what's so big about you that you're their only hope."

"Do you know where they are?" Joe Yee asked, his voice about as soft as it could be and still be heard in here.

"No," I said. "And if I did, you'd probably be the last person on earth I'd tell about it."

"That would be a mistake."

"Maybe." I shrugged and finished my soda.

"What if I ask Smith?"

I looked at him, his handsome face, his coal-black eyes. We

190

were both Chinese, he'd said, and that, at least, was true. And Bill wasn't.

"He doesn't know any more than I do," I said, feeling suddenly the same way about Joe Yee asking Bill anything as I'd felt seeing him in my mother's living room. "But I will tell you one thing. I'll tell you who he's working for."

Joe Yee sat up a little straighter. "Who?"

"Me."

The swirling noise around us kept Joe Yee's response from being actual silence, but it was speechlessness.

"I'm the investigator in charge of this case," I said. "He works for me. Legwork. Driving. Muscle. That sort of thing." That was underplaying Bill's part maybe just a tad, but it should serve to keep Joe Yee away from him.

Joe Yee smiled. "Oh. Uh, sorry."

"Sure you are. Anyway, that's how it is. Not only can't he tell you anything, but if he could, he wouldn't, unless I told him to."

"So he works for you. Then who do you work for?"

I stared at him in disbelief. "You know, if I didn't already dislike you, I might start."

He shook his head. "I really can't afford to worry about your feelings right now."

"Who's Ed Deluca?"

He stared at me blankly. "Who's who?"

"Ed Deluca. A nasty little guy who also knows I was visiting your place in Brooklyn."

"I never heard of him. Who is he? He knows you came to see me?"

"He's a federal cop."

Joe Yee missed a beat. "A what?"

"State Department Security. He wanted to know what Bill and I knew about the waiters, too."

"He told you he was with State Department Security?"

"I saw his badge."

"When?"

"Just about an hour ago."

He paused. "What did you tell him?"

"Pretty much what I've told you."

"Did he ask you anything about me?"

"No. Would you have expected him to?"

He shook his head. "I don't even know who the hell he is. But don't you see this makes it even more important that I find the waiters?"

"No, I don't see that. He's the government; the government is supposed to be the good guys. Maybe I should have told him everything I know."

"What do you know?"

"Nothing."

Joe Yee pressed his lips together. He stared at me, not looking at all pleased. Standing, he took out a business card and dropped it on the table in front of me. JAYCO REALTY, it read. "Call me if you change your mind."

Yeah, I thought, sure, but I said nothing as Joe Yee turned and walked away.

He reached the big steel door without looking back, but I sat still just in case. When he yanked the door open I jumped up from our table and pushed through the crowd after him. I was in time to see him slam the door shut in a cab heading east. I'd been hoping to be able to follow him, but on Canal Street on a Saturday night the chance of a cab is fifty-fifty. Joe Yee's luck had been good, and mine had run out.

Well, not completely. I found a pay phone and picked up my beeper message. The number had been unfamiliar, but the call, it turned out, was from Bill. "Call me here," it said, so I did.

"Yeah, hold on," said the voice that answered, sounding slurred and uninterested. "Smith!" he yelled. "Hey! Your call. And keep it short."

"Thanks," I heard Bill say, then, "Lydia?"

"Hi," I said.

192

"Hey. I got your message. You okay?" Bill's words came quickly, the way they do when someone's worried.

"Sure," I told him. "What can happen to a woman in a crowded bar on a Saturday night?"

"You have no imagination. Is he still with you, Joe Yee?"

"No, he's gone."

"What did he want?"

"The waiters."

Bill was silent for a moment. Through the phone pressed to my ear I could hear the background fuzz of TV sportscasting. He said, "A hot commodity, those guys. Who the hell is he?"

"I don't know."

"How did he find you?"

"He traced your car."

"My car. Jesus, I'm going to have to do something about that car. Then why you and not me?"

"I'm Chinese."

"And . . . ?"

"That means we have some sort of mystical bond. I don't know. The guy gave me a big pain. But you'd have been proud of me."

"I'm always proud of you. Why this time?"

"Because I acted cute and stupid to see if he'd make some dumb mistake and spill his guts."

"Did he?"

"No. Maybe it doesn't work."

"You probably just can't convince anyone you're stupid, though I'm sure you were cute. What are you doing right now?"

"Right now? What do you mean? I'm standing on a street corner wishing I were home in bed."

"Put it off. There's someone I want you to meet."

"Now?"

"It's important."

"The last time I heard that word it was from Joe Yee."

"This time it's true."

"It might have been from him, too. Who?"

"A guy I know. Can you come here?"

"Where are you?"

"At a bar," he said. He gave me a Lower East Side address.

Great, I thought. *Another New York hot spot. Lydia Chin, Queen of the Night*. I took a look at my watch: ten-thirty. "All right. My mother would be heartbroken if I came home so soon, anyway. She'd think things weren't going well between me and Joe Yee."

"As opposed to the truth. See you in a few minutes."

As I said good-bye I heard the other voice telling Bill in a bad tempered growl to get off his damn phone.

sixteen

i had to walk three blocks north to get a cab, and when I finally did the cabbie had to maneuver us east along twisting one-way streets through the heart of New York's late-night neighborhoods. I rolled down the window on the soft night and watched as the overcoated older crowd left their white-tablecloth restaurants to mingle on the sidewalk with leather-jacketed, pierced-lipped post-punks. Young bridge-and-tunnelers from the outer boroughs romped across the streets on their way from one hot club to another as though there were no cars at all. It was slow going until we made it into the East Village, where the clubs are cooler than cool but a little more thinly spread out. Then we were east of even that.

The cab stopped on Third not far from Avenue C, a narrow street where in another lifetime the arched windows and lacy fire escapes might have combined with the trees' swaying shadows to convince me life here was lived with a certain elegance, a grace that took for granted the soft spring breeze and the clear white moon rising over the rooftops. But it never was: these buildings were built as tenements, jamming in as many new immigrants as was legal then, and that's who lives here now, too. Once, the buildings were new, and in those days even the rich didn't have elevators or air-conditioning, so maybe it didn't seem so bad, so different from where you wanted to be, not an unreasonable stop on the road from where you'd started to where you wanted to end up. Now, the buildings were a century older and shabbier; now, everyone understood the difference between this and the America of their dreams.

Still, this was where you began. And for some, this was as far as you got. But the same spring breeze that wafted past the balconies of uptown high rises moved the tree branches here, and the moon still shone.

I paid the cabdriver and descended a few steps to a bar with a dingy, paint-peeling sign nailed above the door: Parnell's. A Bud Light sign reddened the window. Everything else was dark: dirty brick, cracked concrete, the steel door painted some muddy shade of green. I pulled the door open and went in.

For a Saturday night in New York, Parnell's was hardly hopping. The skinny, bushy-haired bartender—maybe Parnell himself—leaned on his forearms on the bar, ignoring his half dozen customers, all of them men. Only two of them seemed to know anyone else was there anyway, as they argued in a dull and bad-tempered way about the stock car race glowing from the TV over the bar. The others stared into their drinks or into space. Two turned to the door when I came in, one swiveling right back to his drink, the other moving his red-rimmed eyes slowly over me in my flowing coat and velvet trousers.

I was wondering if he was planning to put the moves on me, and whether his liquor-soaked limbs would be too rubbery to get him off his bar stool, when I saw Bill stand up from a table in the back and head smoothly in my direction. He kissed my cheek when he reached me, and put his hand gently on my back as he moved me along, gestures I assumed were as much for the other guys as they were for me.

The air at Parnell's was stale with the smells of old cigarettes, old whiskey, old sweat: tired odors without the energy to get up and leave. The vinyl tile floor was sticky and scratchy. I was glad for

196

the dim light as Bill and I headed for the back, where tables scattered the area between the bar and two blinking video games. One screen, looking to lure players, repeated over and over a drive down a highway where the scenery constantly changed, desert to mountains to glass-towered city by the ocean, to desert again.

Only one of the back tables was occupied, by a young, scraggly-haired kid hunched over a bottle of Budweiser. He watched us approach, surrounding his beer as though he suspected we might want to seize it from him. Bill pulled a chair over for me and sat down himself opposite the kid where another Bud waited patiently. Three other bottles, now empty, stood on the table like one-armed cacti.

Bill raised his eyebrows at me as he picked up his beer. "I didn't ask if you wanted anything." The look I gave him wasn't calculated to make him grin, but it did anyway.

"This is Henry," Bill said, lighting a cigarette. He offered one to the kid, who jerked out a hand to take it and went through two matches before he could make one work. "Henry, Lydia."

I nodded to Henry. His eyes skittered from me to Bill, and he said, "You sure she's cool?"

Bill nodded. "Don't worry, Henry, you're safe with me."

Henry's twitchy hand shoved his cigarette between his lips. "Yeah." The cigarette jiggled as he spoke. "I always feel just great when you're around."

"Just tell Lydia what you told me before," Bill said, "and then we're out of here."

We waited a few moments; then, "Come on, Henry," Bill prompted. "I haven't been sitting here nursing beers all night with you because I like you."

Henry scowled at that, in no one's particular direction. He said, "Yeah, okay," but he didn't say anything else.

Bill spoke. "Henry's a junkie," he said, talking to me, looking at Henry. "He spends his days hunting up a fix, and then floating on it, and then hunting up another one."

"Screw you, Smith." Henry made an effort to sound belligerent. "I don't have to—"

"Yes, you do," Bill said. That stopped Henry again, so Bill went on. "Henry lives down here, in a squat with a bunch of other junkies. Henry's father lives in Scarsdale. He won't come down here himself. Considers it dangerous and, even worse, distasteful. But he hired me twice to bring Henry home. I did it, but Henry doesn't like Scarsdale, so he came back here."

Henry pulled sullenly on his beer.

"Henry's father doesn't try to bring him home anymore. But every now and then he gives me a little money to give Henry, make sure the kid is eating, that kind of thing. Henry spends it on junk."

I looked at Henry, his bad skin, his bony wrists sticking out of a long-sleeved flannel shirt. He was jabbing his cigarette butt in the ashtray, over and over. "Hey, I'm doing you a fucking favor, Smith—"

"No, you're not. You're talking to me because if I tell your father I'm through, you lose that Scarsdale lifeline. And I'm fed up with both of you, so that could happen any time. So."

Bill stopped, drank some beer, and waited.

Henry turned his watery eyes to me and glowered, but Bill continued to say nothing. Henry finally spoke.

"I don't see what the goddamn big deal is," he said. "My connection didn't come through, so I hadda go somewhere else. So fucking what?"

"Your connection?" I said, more to get into this conversation than anything else.

"Yeah. Cupboard was bare. But so what? I got fixed up."

"Lydia doesn't give a damn whether you got your junk or not, Henry," Bill said. "She wants to know why you had to scramble."

"Because," Henry said, with the exaggerated patience of a chipped-plaster saint, "my connection, he came up dry because *his* connection got shorted."

"Got shorted how?" I asked, still mystified about what I was doing in this unappealing bar talking to this unattractive boy.

Henry shrugged. "Word is, someone boosted a piece of his shipment."

"Who?"

"Oh, man, I don't know. Don't even think that." Fear sprang into Henry's eyes.

"Why not?" Bill asked.

"Because they say he's pissed the hell off. He's gonna blow away whoever took his shit. No way I want him thinking I had anything—" A light went on in Henry's eyes, making them bounce wildly from me to Bill. "Jesus Christ!" He clambered to his feet, shoving his chair back. "She's with him! Oh, man, you set me up—"

Bill leaned forward in his chair, put a hand on Henry's arm, and spoke more gently than I might have expected. "No, Henry. She's not with him and I didn't set you up. You can go in a minute. But tell Lydia why you thought she might be with him."

"With the fucking Duke? Why the hell do you think?" Henry bounced lightly on the balls of his feet as though he were about to break into a sprint. "Because she's goddamn Chinese."

I turned to Bill; the light had gone on for me, too. "The Duke?" I said. "Duke Lo?"

"Seems that way. Sit down, Henry."

"No, man. No." Henry shook his head. "I got to go."

"The Duke," I said to Henry. "His name is Lo? He's the guy who supplies your heroin connection?"

Henry stared, then dropped sharply onto his chair. "Jesus Christ, don't talk so loud."

I looked around. No one in the bar seemed to have moved since I walked in.

"Yeah," whispered Henry almost frantically, in what was probably an attempt to head off anything more from me. "My man, he gets his from this guy, the Duke. I don't know his last name. I don't know anything else, I swear it." He gave me the look of a cornered puppy about to get swatted.

"And the Duke's Chinese?"

He nodded.

"When did this happen?" I asked. "That someone took some of his junk?"

"A month," Henry said. "I don't know, something like that.

Look, can I go now? I mean, that's what you wanted, right?'' He rubbed his mouth with a dirty hand and turned to Bill. ''I got to go.''

''Okay, Henry,'' Bill said before I could ask anything else. He took out his wallet and pulled two fifties from it. ''One from your father, one from me. Try to eat something.''

''Yeah, man, sure.'' Henry grabbed the bills and stuffed them into his pocket as he jerked to his feet. ''Yeah. See you. Uh, nice meeting you,'' he said to me, and he was gone.

I turned to Bill. ''Nice meeting me?''

''A well-brought-up boy,'' Bill said. He took his cigarette from his lips. ''A tenor sax player. Damn good. His father wanted him to be a lawyer.''

''So he left home and came down here?''

''No. He tried it his father's way. NYU, prelaw. He hated it. Started to play, late nights, around the Village, while he was still in school. He was sitting in with some of the best inside of a few months. He's good,'' he repeated.

''But his father didn't like it?''

''He said, 'Forget that, spend your time studying.' Henry didn't stop. So his father said, 'Either give up that damn thing or go out and make a living with it.' He cut him off, told him not to come home until he was ready to stop playing.''

''My God,'' I said. ''So that's what he does now?''

Bill shook his head. ''He tried, but talent's not enough. He was too young, too soft for that life, the places you hang in, the people you meet. For Christ's sake, he was raised in Scarsdale.'' Bill jammed his cigarette butt into the ashtray. ''Lately he was playing less and less. Six months ago he pawned the sax to buy junk.''

I stared down the length of the bar to the front door, where Henry had gone. ''Does his father know?''

''Of course he knows. That's why he brought him home, to put him in rehab.''

''But it didn't work?''

''Programs work for some junkies, not for others. He was in two, but they didn't work for him.''

"What do you think will?"

"For Henry?" Bill finished off his beer and, eyes on the bottle as he carefully placed it on the table, said, "Nothing."

Bill and I left Parnell's in silence. Third Street, when we came out onto it, was silent and peaceful, watched over by a silver moon. As if by agreement, we walked west for a few blocks without a word. The avenues were clogged with honking traffic and each block west collected more and more people, scurrying from one place to another, determined to have a good time on a Saturday night.

When we reached Broadway, I stood on the corner feeling as though the things I knew now, the things I still didn't understand, the traffic and the crowds, were spinning my head around.

Bill said, "Come on back to my place. I'll make you a cup of tea."

The thought of Bill's spare, quiet apartment, familiar and empty, was like the call of the oasis to a desert traveler. I thought about the cactus beer bottles on the tables at Parnell's and nodded. Bill hailed a cab and we were on our way.

"Turtle's eggs," I finally said, after a few silent blocks of watching the city slip by.

"What?"

"Duke Lo called them 'turtle's eggs.' The waiters. He did have a reason to hate them, after all."

"So you're thinking what I am? That one of them was a courier, and stole the package he was supposed to deliver?"

I nodded. "It explains Three-finger Choi. And that nasty waiter at Dragon Garden said one of the roommates had a get-rich secret."

Bill said, "You think this could be what Deluca meant by goods the government doesn't want?"

I looked over at him. "Mind reader. But if these are the goods they're getting that they don't want, where are they getting them and what are the goods they do want?"

"Or, to rephrase, which one of these guys is the courier and how did he get here?"

"Is that the same question?" I turned to watch through the window as three laughing high-heeled teenagers jaywalked in front of our cab. "Duke Lo." I sighed. "Running drugs."

"Is it surprising?"

"Not to me, especially since we met him. And Mary said, 'No crime too big or small.' She'll love this. It could make her career."

"If she could prove it."

I frowned. He had a point: all we had was hearsay from a strung-out kid.

"Do you know who Henry's connection is?"

"He won't tell me."

"If Mary arrested him and then cut him a deal, a lighter sentence or something, he might tell her."

"No." Bill spoke calmly but his voice was like a stone. "No."

"Jail would get him off the street—" I started.

"Jail would kill him," Bill cut me off. "No."

"To get at Duke Lo—"

"Duke Lo's not my problem."

"He sent someone to beat me up!"

"And I'll personally break his legs for that if you want. But he's not the only drug dealer in town. Getting him would make us feel good and get Mary a promotion, but not much more. I won't sell Henry out for that."

I stared at him. "You don't even like Henry."

"That's true. But I started with him and I'm stuck with him."

I put my hand softly over Bill's. "That's how I feel about the waiters," I said.

He threaded his fingers through mine. "Then we'll find them. And if they stole Duke Lo's dope, that'll give Mary what she needs. Henry showed us the problem, but I don't see that anything else changed. You're still more likely to find these guys than the cops are, even if they know why they're looking."

He was right. I squeezed his hand and leaned back against the seat of the cab. "Speaking of looking," I said, "how did you find him?" I looked out the window, still seeing a skinny kid slipping out of a dim bar with two fifty-dollar bills burning a hole in his pocket.

"Henry? He's not hard to find. His friends know I usually mean money, so they steer me to him."

"No, I mean, what made you go looking for him?"

"Those damn SOBs—Deluca and March—they made me too edgy to sit still. I wasn't looking for Henry in particular; he was just a lucky hit. While you were dealing delicately with your countrymen, I thought I'd poke around a little, on the off chance that someone involved in this case wasn't Chinese."

I turned from the window to him. "You think I've been handling this case wrong?"

His forehead creased. "No. I didn't say that."

"I can't help it," I said, "that everyone involved is Chinese."

"But they're not," Bill said. "Deluca and March aren't. Henry and his connection aren't. I didn't think it would hurt to widen our net a little, and I made a lucky catch. What's wrong? Did you not want me striking out on my own?"

"It's not that. You always do when we work together."

"Isn't that good?"

"Of course, it is. It's just . . . it's . . ." I leaned back against the seat again. "I don't know what it is."

Bill was silent for a while as the city blocks swept by. Then he said, "It's that you're afraid there's something going on you think I won't understand. Something Chinese that I'll screw up."

"No," I said. Then, after a while, "Yes. Well, not exactly that. But . . ." I searched out the window, trying to find the words. "These people—I mean, H. B. Yang brought my father over here. I used to dream about him." I looked at Bill, who didn't look at me. "Does that make sense?"

He nodded, but said nothing for the rest of the ride.

At Bill's place, we climbed the stairs still in silence. He unlocked the door, switched on the light, and threw his jacket over a chair. I hung my coat in the closet while he filled the kettle in the kitchen.

"Do you want me out?" he said.

"What?" I listened to the rush of water, to the clink of the kettle onto the range.

"Of the case. Do you want me out?"

"You're crazy."

"What you said in the cab—"

"I said this is more complicated than other cases. That's all I said."

"You could be right. I could mess it up."

"I didn't say that, you did."

"Still."

"No." I walked toward him, over to the counter separating where I was from where he was. I leaned on it, watching him.

"What kind of tea do you want?" he asked.

"Chamomile."

"I have that?"

"Uh-huh. Second shelf, on the left. Bill?"

He turned to me as he rummaged through his cabinet.

"You won't mess it up. I don't even think you will. I'm just afraid."

He found the tea I knew was there and put the box down on the counter. "Afraid of what?"

I looked at the tea box, not at him. "Afraid we won't find those men. Afraid Peter won't be all right. Afraid I'll screw something up with H. B. Yang and that will humiliate my mother. I'm afraid *I'll* mess it up."

Bill's eyes found mine. I blinked and looked away.

"I've never heard you talk that way before," he said.

"Maybe I've never felt this way before."

"Funny," Bill said, as he came around the counter and wrapped me in his arms. "I feel that way all the time."

We stood, just holding each other in this big silent room where there was no one but us, until the kettle started to sing. Then Bill pulled away and went to take care of the tea.

"Nice shirt," I said.

"What?"

"Your shirt. It feels good against my cheek."

He grinned from the kitchen. "You don't mind if I don't follow that line of thinking?"

"In fact I'd prefer it." I smiled back, it was Bill and me again, and he got busy with the tea.

He made my chamomile in a mug and poured boiling water into one of those press-down coffeemakers for himself. Bringing everything into the living room, he said, "Okay. Since I'm still on the case, you want to talk about it?"

"Joe Yee," I said. "He said he came to me because we're both Chinese. If what this is about is a bunch of idiots stealing dope from Duke Lo, where does he fit in?"

"Maybe he works for Duke Lo."

"He could. But he doesn't seem Lo's type. Although," I said, thinking back to the Fifth Precinct squad room, "Mary said Lo climbed up fast, backed by more loyal soldiers than you'd expect a new guy to have."

"You don't sound convinced."

"Are you?"

"No."

I sipped my tea, trying to think.

"Just tell me," Bill said.

"What?"

"Just tell me what happened. Maybe something will come out."

I nodded; that was how we usually did it. So I did that now, filling Bill in on my evening with Joe Yee. My tea disappeared as the story went on, and Bill, listening, got up and made me another cup.

"Well," he said, sitting again, lighting another cigarette, "what do you think he's up to?"

I tried, against the call of exhaustion, to think logically. "I believe he doesn't know what the problem is, because if he did, he'd have told me he knew but he wasn't going to tell me. But you know what was weird?"

"What?"

"His reaction when I asked him about Deluca."

"How?"

"I think he really didn't know who Deluca was. But when I said State Department Security he seemed to get spooked. He left pretty soon after that."

"That would make sense, if that's where the Feds saw my car."

"So he has something to do with the dope?"

"Or with the shipments the government does want."

I sighed. "Okay," I said. "That's our work for the morning. I can't think anymore tonight. God, I'm tired."

I put my tea mug down and leaned back into the sofa cushions. I thought about the steamy, herb-filled bath I'd looked forward to steeping in, and the cool sheets I'd been hoping to slip into, before Joe Yee and the metallic clangor of Lightning Rod's, Henry and the disconsolate filth of Parnell's, had filled my evening. The tension in my shoulders began to melt; the fresh, sweet scent of chamomile lingered in the air. I closed my eyes.

"You can stay," Bill said.

My eyes flew open and my forehead creased into a frown. I looked at him; he was smiling softly.

"It's not a proposition," he said. "I have a spare room; I'll behave. Or I can get you a blanket and you can stay where you are. It's just that you look like someone who doesn't want to move."

"I don't," I agreed, sighing. My eyes wandered over the room again: the white walls hung here and there with charcoal drawings or black-and-white photographs; the figured Persian carpet under the piano—"to soften the edges," he'd once told me, and that had surprised me; I hadn't known Bill was interested in softened edges—the shelves of books, the desk, the neat kitchen. It was more than the physical effort of getting up, which was becoming harder to contemplate by the minute; it was going out, after I got up, into a street where you have to keep your eyes open, to a cab where you have to study the cabbie's name and license number, to a home where I'd have to watch every word I said to my mother. All those things, as opposed to the sofa cushions and chamomile tea in Bill's apartment.

And, of course, Bill.

I mustered all my strength and pushed myself to my feet. "I have to go."

"You're sure?"

"Uh-huh," I said, and even I heard the regret in my voice.

I took my mug into the kitchen as Bill headed for the closet where I'd hung my coat. The sight of the stainless steel sink, the rush of the hot water, brought a thought that jolted me awake. "My God, I have to work tomorrow!"

"And every day," Bill said, holding my coat for me. "Until this case is solved."

"No, I mean, like, *work*," I said. "At Dragon Garden. I have to be behind the wheel of a dim sum cart by nine-thirty!"

"You're going back there?"

"Don't you think so?" I said. "It's still not a bad bet for finding the waiters. At least someone there might know how they got here, which would tell us how the dope comes in. And if I don't go, H. B. Yang will want to know why."

"That sounds right," he said.

"If you think of something better before morning, call me. Otherwise I'll talk to you tomorrow afternoon. And," I said, "thanks."

"For . . . ?"

"Finding Henry. Helping me."

"It's what you pay me for."

"Um-hmm. And I know that's why you do it."

"It is," he said. "It definitely is."

Bill walked me downstairs, waited with me for a cab, kissed me gently good night beside the curb. I studied the cabbie's hack license as I told him where to take me. The rattling vehicle screeched into the New York traffic, and I hurtled through the streets toward my mother's apartment while Bill slowly walked back up the stairs to his.

seventeen

It's a good thing I'm a morning person. Worn out, weary, and lost as I had been the night before, I bounced out of bed at seven anyway, early enough to take a hot, pounding shower, do a long series of stretching exercises, have breakfast—congee with pickled vegetables, which I found my mother making when I came out of my room wrapped in my yellow silk robe—and call the hospital to find out how Peter was. His condition had been upgraded to good, they told me, and they offered to switch me to his room, but I thought it was too early to talk to him. I might be waking him up; besides, what was there I had to say, besides to tell him what the trouble was his waiters were in, and who with? If I were lying in a hospital bed and someone called to give me that news, I'd only get high blood pressure and heart palpitations from not being able to do anything about it. I left him alone.

I didn't call Bill, either. No point in waking him up—he's *not* a morning person—especially when I had nothing to tell him, one way or the other, except hi, and thanks for the tea.

I did call Mary, though. It was Sunday, her day off, so she

was home, in the Lower East Side loft she shares with two other women: a Korean dancer and a divinity student from Mississippi.

"If I told you Duke Lo was dealing dope," I asked her, "would you be flabbergasted and amazed?"

She was silent for a moment. "Tell me you have proof. Please, please, say you have proof."

"No. But I'm working on it."

"Lydia—"

"We think the waiters ran off with a package that was his. One of them may have been a courier. There's a federal connection, too, we think." I told her about Deluca, Joe Yee, the sharp-nosed waiter at Dragon Garden, and the roommate who was going to get rich.

"You have to give me one of these guys," she said. "Your snitch, the waiter, someone. You have to."

"I can't. But I have an idea."

"No. You'll get killed, Duke Lo will get away, something bad will happen. I'll take it from here."

"You'll take it where? None of these people was particularly excited about talking to me. My snitch"—Bill's really, but I didn't tell her that—"will run. The waiter may not know anything more than he told me already. But someone up there might."

"Up where?"

"Dragon Garden. I'm going back today, and it'll be my last chance, because there's no dim sum tomorrow. Let me see if I can come up with anything else. Maybe we can bring the waiters in before you guys start up with Duke Lo. They'd be safer that way," I added, then shut up and let her think.

"You win," she finally said. "God, I hate it when you're right. Go ahead and see if you can get a lead on them. But after today it's all mine."

"Whatever I get, it's yours," I said, and hung up. Which wasn't exactly the same as "After today it's all mine." It meant I didn't plan to be shut out of the grand climax here, the gift wrapping of Duke Lo, drug dealer and employer of vicious thugs.

I hadn't pointed out to Mary that this theory made H. B. Yang

Most Likely Suspect on the union headquarters bomb for the original, boring reason: to intimidate the union. She'd figure it out, but by then I'd be out of the house and on my way to work at H. B. Yang's restaurant.

So I put on my white shirt, dark slacks, and sensible shoes, and headed on over to Dragon Garden.

The Chinatown morning was fresh-scrubbed, blue and bright and sharp and shiny. I found myself lingering on the short walk over, looking at inkstands and porcelain fish gleaming in store windows, watching the teenage crews eyeing each other on street corners and the bent-over grandmothers eyeing eggplants and oranges in sidewalk stalls. The sweet, spicy scent of red bean buns came wafting from the corner bakery, and I was tempted, but I reminded myself I'd be spending the morning surrounded by food of such high quality and huge quantity as to make a red bean bun completely redundant.

I took a few seconds to get into character at the bottom of the stairs; then, with an eager, ambitious smile and the pair of dorky glasses fitted onto my face, I trotted up to the stock-and-break room of Dragon Garden.

As I pushed open the door, I found the aromas of steaming pork and shrimp and the hiss of sizzling oil already hanging in the break room air. They were getting ready for work, too, no doubt, just waiting to be called upon to assault the senses of the diners soon to flood the carpeted room beyond.

Today I was early, as befitted the new person who'd been reprimanded by the sharp-faced waiter on her first day at work. A few of my fellow cart pushers and waiters were early, too, not including him. They lounged around smoking and talking; two of the busboys rolled dice on a case of toilet paper. I looked for Pei-Hui and found her knitting calmly on a broken-legged chair held parallel to the floor by the upturned soup bowl under it. She smiled as she saw me, and I crossed the room to sit by her. Luckily there was a pile of table linens next to her chair for me to sit on; a lot of the new immigrants, like I was pretending to be, can go easily into that Asian squat where you balance on the soles of your feet and your bottom doesn't touch the floor, but I'd have fallen flat on my face and given the game away.

"Good morning, Chin Ling," Pei-Hui said.

"Good morning," I returned. "What are you knitting?"

"A sweater." She held it up for me to see. "For my second granddaughter."

"Grandchildren! You are so lucky!"

She smiled again, agreeing with me—though not out loud, to keep any jealous ghosts that might be hovering in the stockroom from noticing she was happy. To me, Pei-Hui didn't look old enough to have grandchildren, but that's only a compliment in English, not in Chinese, so I didn't say it.

Pei-Hui and I made small talk for a while, about China and Hong Kong and Chinatown. I invented a past to tell her about, other jobs I'd had and how and why I'd come here, and she told me about other restaurants she'd worked in, about her grandchildren, and about how to get along here at Dragon Garden. I already knew the part about not organizing for the union, but she mentioned it again; and she told me the boss liked people who were reliable, who didn't call in sick, and who got along with the other workers.

"There was a dim sum lady working here," she told me, "who could not say a polite word to Cao Zhi. They argued constantly. Soon she was asked to leave."

"Cao Zhi?" I asked. "Who is that?"

"The waiter with the sharp nose and chin." With true Chinese discretion, she didn't mention the long red scar puckering his jawline. "Sharp eyes also. He is difficult, but a very good worker. Yang Hao-Bing thinks well of him."

Ah, I thought, a classically Chinese indirect approach. Don't fight with this guy, Chin Ling, or you'll find yourself out on the street.

"He works hard," she repeated, blissfully ignorant, I guessed, of yesterday's cigarette break. "He has been given extra responsibilities, to see that these items are always readily available to the dining room, so that no one, during the day, needs to run to the basement for them." She nodded at the teapots and linens waiting their turn to serve, and at the door across the room, to the basement they would have, without Cao Zhi, otherwise have had to wait in. "It is a measure of Yang Hao-Bing's respect."

Her eyes met mine. I smiled and nodded to show I understood, and nothing more was said on the subject.

Pei-Hui and I continued to chat while the room filled with waiters and ladies. Eventually, the subject of her cautionary tale himself came up the stairs. Cao Zhi pushed open the door, stood in the doorway, and surveyed the room as though it were his personal kingdom. Maybe it was. He spotted me, curled his lip in a sneer, and went over to sit with the dice-playing busboys.

Pei-Hui saw me following him with my eyes and reminded me, "Yang Hao-Bing thinks well of him."

"Does he think well of anyone?"

She smiled again as she rolled up the soon-to-be sweater and buttoned it into her knitting bag. "Not that I have noticed."

The workday soon began, as hectic as the one before it. I pushed my cart and emptied it onto tables of ravenous uptown couples, college students, and extended families both Chinese and non. I went back to the kitchen for more. Then I pushed my cart again. All my attempts at conversation openers with my fellow employees came to naught. On a fine Sunday at Dragon Garden, time was money, work was all, and chitchat was in everyone's way.

The din of talk, laughter, clinking chopsticks, and clattering dishes flew around the room, bouncing off the walls and slicing the air next to my head until I felt like I needed to duck as the noise flew by. My shoulders ached, my feet started to hurt, and I began to wonder what I was doing there.

I started to contemplate the idea of giving myself a break, no matter what the sharp-nosed Cao Zhi might say. Surrendering three bowls of sticky rice and my last plate of turnip cakes as I went, I wheeled my cart across the room to an alcove between a crimson-painted column and a steam table mounded with shellfish of every possible variety, including some so ugly you'd have to eat them with your eyes closed. There, temporarily out of traffic, I put my hands

212

on the small of my back and bent backward, feeling the little hot needles of muscles stretching in a direction they'd given up hope of ever going again. I bent forward and felt the same thing in other muscles. Then, standing straight, I felt the needles again, this time in my chest, from the flood of adrenaline released by the sight of Joe Yee riding up the escalator into Dragon Garden.

All right, Lydia, I told myself, *just calm down. Maybe the guy's only looking for lunch.* But that theory was quashed immediately by Joe Yee himself, who, after a brief conversation with the maître d', was ushered through the wallpapered door I had used myself two days ago, when I'd been summoned to speak to H. B. Yang.

Ah! I said to myself, not to mention, Ha! Joe I'm-the-only-man-who-can-help-the-waiters Yee on his way to see H. B. I-only-want-the-waiters-to-be-safe-and-happy Yang. Tell-me-everything-you-know-for-no-good-reason having tea with tell-them-if-they-quit-the-union-they-always-have-a-home-here. We're-all-Chinese-in-this versus we're-all-Chinese-in-this.

Fascinating.

And what could it mean?

Obviously, I had to know. Ideas flew through my head, visions of various ways I could find out what Joe Yee and H. B. Yang had to talk about. I could, of course, go charging up the stairs and, as employee of record on this case, demand to know what was going on, but that approach seemed, simply, doomed. If H. B. Yang had thought Joe Yee was any of my business he'd have told me about him.

Or maybe H. B. Yang didn't know Joe Yee had anything to do with the waiters. In that case my duty as a loyal employee was to tell him—later, after I followed Joe Yee out of there and saw where he led me and what that told me. But, I pointed out to myself, I'd failed at following him last night. And there was the possibility that he might not go out the way he'd come in, and I'd miss him.

I thought of a couple of other ideas, none of them really any good, including the Spiderwoman one of clinging to the wall outside H. B. Yang's office window with my ear pressed to the glass. The only thing left, then, was the simplest, lowest-tech method: listening at the figurative keyhole. I would amble casually upstairs, stand nonchalantly in the hallway outside the office door that, to my recollection, H. B. Yang kept open whether he had visitors or not. I'd hear what I could hear—and think up some really clever excuse for being there if anyone should happen to spot me.

I didn't love it, but what was the worst thing that could happen? If I did get caught and my clever excuse wasn't good enough, H. B. Yang would fire me. My mother would be ashamed of that, but I could at least tell her it was a disagreement over methodology, not my failure to do the job, that caused it. If I got caught, Joe Yee would know I was involved with H. B. Yang, but that was okay, too: it might make him approach me differently, and, in his rush to rearrange, I might find out what his interest really was. The question might have been, how to get upstairs? But there, I was in luck.

The broad-shouldered fellow who'd been maître d' when I'd come during the slow time the day before yesterday was not maître d' today, but he was there at the top of the escalator, just sort of looking things over. Probably maître d'-ing and guarding the realm were jobs that had to be divided up on busy days.

I left my cart where it was, bothering nobody, and strode purposefully across the floor to where he stood looking like a mobile brick wall. His eyes narrowed in recognition and suspicion as I approached. He took in my glasses and my dim sum lady garb with a frown as I stepped up close to him and spoke in lowered, conspiratorial tones.

"I'm Lydia Chin, remember I was here Friday? I'm a private investigator"—figuring he already knew that—"doing some undercover work for Mr. Yang, something about a couple of the waiters he wanted to know. He told me to report to him *immediately* whenever I had something." I started to move past him to the wallpapered door.

"Mr. Yang's with someone," the brick wall told me, putting himself between me and the door and not looking happy.

"I know," I said, making myself sound surprised but patient. "Mr. Yee. He's right on time. I was supposed to hold off until he got here, but I don't think Mr. Yang will be happy if I don't come up now.''

"Maybe I'd better go upstairs and check,'' he said, scowling at me for making him confused. A lot of people must see that scowl in the course of a day, I thought.

"Well, okay,'' I said, surprised again, "but I thought you were supposed to stay down here at all times. That's what Mr. Yang said, that everyone was safe here because you were always here. I mean, I've counted on that, and I'm sure the others do, too.''

"The others?'' The brick wall squinted at me, thinking maybe his problem was that he wasn't seeing me clearly enough.

"Well, of course, I don't know how many other investigators he's got out there. He has us all working independently, you know.'' I gave him lifted eyebrows, as though I wasn't sure why he was having me tell him things he already knew.

"Oh,'' he said, squaring his shoulders and slowly surveying the crowded dining floor. "The others.'' He nodded. "You're right. I'd better stay down here. You sure they're expecting you?''

"Absolutely. My orders''—I emphasized the word—"were to come up when Mr. Yee got here, if I had anything to report. And, oh boy, do I,'' I added with the grin you'd give your accomplice in a delicious scheme.

He nodded again, slowly, without smiling. In fact, he scowled again. He was clearly more experienced in the ways of the world than I, not so given to finding fun in what was, after all, important and serious work. He fixed on me a patronizing, superior look, stepped aside, and let me at the wallpapered door.

I clicked the door shut behind me before I started up the stairs, mostly so the brick wall wouldn't see me tiptoeing. I kept as close to the wall as I could to keep the stairs from squeaking, although the fifth, seventh, and ninth steps couldn't resist trying to give me away. After the little creak each of them made I stopped, worried that there might be another human brick wall at the top guarding the summit meeting going on up there. Well, if so, my clever excuse would just have to start sooner.

There wasn't, though. The hallway was empty, and it was silent, except for the quiet murmur of male voices and the clink of teacups from the open door near the end. Ah, I thought, they're up to the have-some-tea-I-wouldn't-trouble-you-it's-no-trouble part. I wonder if this means H. B. Yang knew Joe Yee was coming, or just that he's a good host, always prepared?

I worked my way silently and slowly down the hall, intent on trying to make words out of the soft, conversational sounds coming out of the doorway. I was almost there, too, almost close enough to hear, almost near enough that I could stop and listen and find out what was going on. One more cautious step, maybe two, and that would be enough.

But I didn't get to take them.

Behind and below me I heard a soft click. I froze and listened. In a moment, a tiny creak; silence, creak, silence, creak.

Someone else was creeping up the stairs.

I had surveyed and recorded in my head the layout of the place as I came up the stairs, the way I always do—I learned that from Bill—though there wasn't much to it: a hallway with doors. I retreated fast to the door that seemed the most likely, grabbed its knob, and was rewarded as I deserved. It was unlocked; but it was a damp and ammonia-smelly janitor's closet.

I left the door a little ajar and peered out, in time to see the other guy who was trying to infiltrate this little tête-à-tête. He did what I'd been doing: slinking down the hall, pausing before he reached H. B. Yang's office, flattening himself against the wall.

I silently pushed open the door I was lurking behind, noiselessly walked up to him, and without a sound pressed the barrel of my .22 into the small of his back. He was taller than I, but I managed to pull up my Cantonese accent and the bad grammar that went with it and whisper in his ear, "You make some noise, they know you here. You want that? No? Then come with me."

He must have not wanted that, because he let me pull him backward into my concrete-floored den. I steered him toward the slop sink end, shut the door, and flipped on the light. Under the single bulb screwed into the ceiling I examined my prize: Cao Zhi, the sharp-faced waiter who at that moment should have been endlessly plonking teapots onto tables on the floor below. As I should have been pushing a cart.

"You surprise, see me?" he asked, giving me the curled-lip sneer again, maybe so I would recognize him. "Want shoot me, go ahead." He pulled a cigarette from the pocket of his maroon waiter's jacket and lit it up. The smoke mingled harmoniously with the scents of ammonia and mold.

"No," I said, slipping the gun back into the holster on my ankle. "I know was you: smell cigarette smoke."

He watched the gun disappear. "Oh," he said. "You so smart, know so much." With narrowed eyes, he looked at me past his cigarette. "So now you tell me, why you up here, instead do your job? Want learn more things to know?"

"Why you up here, Cao Zhi?" I snapped. "I think you knew everything already. I come for ask boss for raise. Hear you sneaking behind me, wonder, what great Cao Zhi need with sneaking?"

He tapped ash onto the floor without looking. "You think I believing stupid story like that?"

"So what, what you believing? This your job, decide whether believing dim sum ladies?"

"My job?" Cao Zhi shook his head. "No, my job carry plates, tea, watch people eat, carry more tea. Big Brother Yang Hao-Bing pay, I shut up, carry plates. Someday, in great America, have own restaurant, pay other people carry plates." He dropped his cigarette on the floor and squashed it with his foot.

"Then why you spying on Yang Hao-Bing?"

"Not spying on Yang Hao-Bing. Spying on you."

"On me?"

"Not so easy, shut up, carry plates, get pay. Other people making trouble. Like, dim sum ladies sneaking up stairs, could be trouble. Better check, why sneaking." He folded his arms across his chest. "So: why you up here? Don't telling me, ask for raise. Why you have gun: Yang Hao-Bing doesn't give raise, you shoot him?"

I shrugged. "You know lies, must know truth, also."

"Know more than you," he said, unperturbed. "Know you

not dim sum lady, not FOB from Hong Kong. Know you have meeting with boss, Big Brother Yang Hao-Bing, have tea with him. Know you Chin Ling Wan-ju, born in Chinatown, New York. Police. Know enough?''

Cao Zhi and I looked at each other, him leaning his thin body against the slop sink, arms folded, me standing by the door.

''Not police,'' I finally said. ''I'm a private investigator. I work for Yang Hao-Bing. There were some things he wanted to know so he hired me.''

He nodded, as though this information was no more surprising to him than the abrupt change in my accent.

''What things Yang Hao-Bing want know?''

''I can't tell you that.''

''So. You sneaking up here for spying on boss who hires you?''

''Not everyone tells the truth all the time,'' I said, ''not even the boss. Sometimes I have to find out things my own way.''

''Like by listening, what boss says to visitor?''

''Maybe.''

''What Yang Hao-Bing want to know, hire you for finding out?'' Cao Zhi said, fingering the scar on the side of his face. ''About waiters disappear?''

The shadows from the bulb glowing in the ceiling made it difficult to make out his expression, but it seemed to me that though it wasn't friendly, the sneer was temporarily gone.

''What do you know about the waiters?'' I asked.

The sneer came back. ''Know they stupid men. Have job, place to live, food to eat. Not enough, for stupid men. Have big plan, cheat gangsters, make lots of money. Now look.'' He spread his arms wide. ''Disappear.''

I kept my voice steady. ''You know where they are, don't you?''

''Me? Just Cao Zhi, only waiter.''

''Don't give me that. How do you know who I am?''

''I ask Li Rong.''

''Who's he?''

218

"Big man, top of escalator. Used to waiter. Too important now, doesn't carrying plates. Guard Yang Hao-Bing against bad people."

"And why did you ask him? Do you ask him about all the new people who come to work here?"

"Only, they come day before, go upstairs, see big boss."

"You saw me do that?"

"Shut up, carry plates, see a lot."

I nodded. "Okay. You knew who I was. Why didn't you call me on it as soon as I got here?"

"I want knowing why you come."

"Why? Unless you're involved in something that you think might be the reason. Cao Zhi, I know why the men are hiding. I know about the heroin they stole."

Cao Zhi held up both hands and shook his head. "You know, don't say. Already too much knowing. Cao Zhi never involves in something. Carry plates, get pay."

I looked at him steadily. "Yang Hao-Bing isn't the only person I work for. I'm looking for the waiters because I want to help them. Before Yang Hao-Bing hired me I was already looking for them, working for Lee Bi-Da. You know, the lawyer who was hurt in the explosion, when Ho Chi-Chun was killed."

In the dingy room Cao Zhi's eyes seemed to take on an expression of weighing and balancing. "Working for Lee Bi-Da? Why Lee Bi-Da looking for waiters?"

"Ho Chi-Chun was a client of his before he disappeared," I said, and then, afraid Cao Zhi might not know the word *client,* I restated it: "Ho Chi-Chun had already asked Lee Bi-Da for help, on other things."

"Other things." He gave a snort. "Stupid union, get him killed anyway. Get everyone excited, thinking can making more money, find some good, easy way." He narrowed his eyes at me and said, "Lee Bi-Da, lawyer, can help them?"

"I don't know," I said. "But I know he wants to try. And whatever, it might be safer for the ones still alive if they let him try.

They don't want to end up like Ho Chi-Chun." I didn't mention that it was going to be a couple of weeks at the least before Peter was in any position to help anyone.

Cao Zhi wasn't budging yet. "Suppose you finding them. Tell Yang Hao-Bing?"

"Before he hired me," I said carefully, "I was working for Lee Bi-Da."

Cao Zhi thought about this while I waited. If I had just come out and said *No, I won't tell Yang Hao-Bing,* he wouldn't have believed me; I had, after all, taken the job, and Yang Hao-Bing was a powerful man. It would take more than two seconds' thought to decide to ignore what he wanted.

But first loyalties were important. Peter's interests might win out over Yang Hao-Bing's if I gave the situation the consideration it deserved, and I let Cao Zhi mull over that possibility.

"I bring you," he said at last. "They telling you about trouble, you help them. Better help," he warned.

"I'll try," I said. "I really will. Where are they?"

With a sneer, he said, "Home."

eighteen

home?'' I stared at Cao Zhi in the rancid dampness of the janitor's closet. "Home, China? Where?"

"China?" Cao Zhi spread his arms expansively. "Home, Chinatown, New York, America. Wonderful place, everything here, everyone happy. Stupid men have place for sleep, no rain, food to eat, no work to do. Ah? Maybe not so stupid.''

I was trying to think up an answer to that when the soft slap of footsteps in the hallway silenced us both. We stared at each other as the steps went by. They quickened into the trot of a person descending a staircase. A sudden surge of restaurant hubbub and its equally sudden muffling let us know the door below had opened and closed, and with it my chance to find out what had brought Joe Yee here to see H. B. Yang.

But maybe now it didn't matter. Maybe I'd made an end run around these guys, unearthed the Rosetta stone of missing waiters, found the golden key that fits the silver lock. Whatever the cliché was that fit the situation, maybe I'd done it.

"Okay," I said when we were surrounded by silence again. "Can we go to the waiters now?"

"No." Before I could object he said, "I ask them. Maybe want seeing you, maybe don't."

"You said you'd take me to them."

"I ask them. You give me number for call you, maybe tomorrow. Now, finish work. Push cart. Carry plates." With the sneer I was growing to feel I'd known since childhood, he shoved himself off the slop sink and stood before me.

I gave him some more argument; he gave me some more stonewalling. Finally, I gave him my number.

Then, with the caution of people trying to sneak away from where they weren't supposed to be in the first place, Cao Zhi and I inched open the janitor's closet door, tiptoed down the hall, crept down the stairs, and successfully reemerged into the chaos and din of the dining room floor. I grabbed my cart, he lifted a teapot, and we found ourselves very much in demand for people who didn't seem to have been missed.

By three-thirty, quitting time, I was bursting with impatience, which distracted me from my aching shoulders. Cao Zhi, however, gave me a sneer even broader than his regular one, and as we all sat down to lunch together he made some rude remark addressed to no one in particular about new people who didn't know what they were doing and so made everyone else's work harder.

I sighed and reached for the platter in the middle of the table to pick out some pieces of pork with ginger. Turning my chopsticks around to use the end I hadn't eaten from, I served some also to Pei-Hui, who smiled at me.

"Don't be upset," she said. Although Cantonese could be heard in scattered conversations from the other tables, at our table Pei-Hui and I were the only ones speaking it. "You're learning very well."

"Why is he so difficult?" I asked. "Why can't he be nice?"

"In China," she said quietly, "I have heard, he was different. A political organizer, a student. He was arrested for his writings about

222

government corruption. The police wanted him to tell them things about some of the other students, but he would not. He had . . . a difficult time. Finally, he was released, ill. It was months before he was well again.'' She spooned shrimp fried rice onto my plate, then onto hers. ''He was arrested a year later, a second time.''

My chopsticks hovered above my plate as I asked, ''What happened?''

''He was sentenced to twenty years in prison. But he escaped.''

''Escaped?''

Pei-Hui nodded. ''Escaped somehow, came to America. Changed his name, now he's Cao Zhi. Now, he is always angry. He wants only to work, then go home to sleep.''

I looked curiously across the table at Cao Zhi. *Carry plates, get pay,* he had said to me upstairs, among the cleansers and the mops. *But not so easy. Other people making trouble.*

Like coworkers with big get-rich dreams. And private eyes sneaking around. I wondered what it was like to be a man who'd had big dreams once, of changing his world, and had seen what they'd brought him—a difficult time—and now only wanted to be left alone. I wondered, then, what had gotten Cao Zhi involved with the waiters, this man who had told me *Cao Zhi never involves in something.* I watched him across the table, reaching his long arms to the platters, stabbing his chopsticks into the food as he exchanged curt, crabby-sounding comments in Fukienese with the waiters on either side of him. Rubbing his jawline scar, Cao Zhi glanced up and caught my eye. He curled his lip and muttered something to the man on his right. The man looked at me, snickered, and muttered something back. They both smiled unpleasantly. I went back to my lunch, thinking about China.

After we'd finished, the dim sum ladies once again cleared the tables as the waiters and busboys, dishwashers and chefs swallowed their last cups of tea and hurried back to work. I did my share, carrying plates to the kitchen and napkins to the laundry cart, and we made, as we had yesterday, short work of it. Finally, there was nothing for me to do but leave. Cao Zhi, of course, had to stay and work the evening before he could even propose to the waiters that I come and see them.

As I pulled on my jacket and headed down the stairs to the outside I realized Bill hadn't come to lunch today, either. Well, too bad; he might have missed his chance to order dim sum from me and my stainless steel cart. If Cao Zhi really took me to the waiters tomorrow, this case might be over; and not a moment too soon, if you asked me.

Outside, I stood for a few moments, just breathing in the late-spring air and watching people come and go, people in a hurry to do this or that and people only strolling, people going home, leaving home, buying food for their families, people with no families to buy food for. I ambled around the corner from Dragon Garden, and there, where no one from the restaurant would see me, I took off the glasses and checked my beeper to see if Bill had called. He hadn't, so I continued on to the corner and called him. My eyes followed the antics of a four-year-old who giggled as his grandmother chased him down the sidewalk while I listened to Bill's phone ring a few times before his service picked up and asked if they could help me. I just said to tell him I'd called. I hung up as the grandmother caught up to the laughing little boy and swung him in her arms. Well, I could hardly expect Bill to be sitting around waiting for me to call. I'd talk to him later; right now I was going home.

But I wasn't. The human brick wall from the top of Dragon Garden's escalator appeared on the corner I had just come around and, as I watched, stood looking bewildered, peering up and down the crowded blocks. Then he spotted me, and his face filled with a mixture of contempt and relief.

"Hey!" he yelled, pointing, as though he'd caught me red-handed at something.

"Me?" I asked, looking around, then back at him, just for his benefit.

"Yeah, you. The boss wants to see you."

"Mr. Yang wants to see me?"

224

"What are you, stupid or deaf or something? He wants to see you *now*. Come on, let's go."

He looked ready to charge on over and tuck me under his arm like a football, and as much as part of me just wanted to see him try it, my better, smarter self won out.

"Okay, sure," I said with a syrupy smile. "Of course, why not?"

He escorted—more like surrounded—me along the sidewalk, up the stairs, and back through the break room. Not until we hit the wallpapered door on the far side of the dining room did he step away, seeming satisfied now I wouldn't break and run—or anyway, wouldn't succeed if I did.

"Thank you, Li Rong." I smiled again as I turned the doorknob, entered the stairway, and left him standing, arms folded, mission accomplished. He was looking very pleased with himself, not wondering for a minute how it was that I knew his name.

I, of course, was not nearly as cheerful and relaxed about this turn of events as I appeared to be. If I hadn't been sneaking around up here, having urgent conversations with a waiter in the janitor's closet just a few hours ago, I might have felt some of Li Rong's self-confidence as I mounted the stairs, listening to the fifth, seventh, and ninth ones squeak. As it was, I was worried I was about to get my head handed to me on a noodle platter.

"Chin Ling Wan-ju," H. B. Yang greeted me in Cantonese, standing up from his desk as I knocked on his open office door. He was smiling, but I wasn't sure that meant anything. "Come in, please, sit down."

I did those things. I couldn't help noticing that the iron tea kettle sat idle on a cold-looking burner and the blue-and-white teapot was nowhere in sight.

Nevertheless, H. B. Yang's leathery face beamed at me. "How have you been getting along with my staff?" he inquired.

"Very well, Uncle."

"Excellent. How do you find the work? For a new employee I understand your progress has been quite good." He looked amused, as though he'd found my cart-pushing abilities were an extra added bonus he'd gotten for hiring me.

"I haven't had a problem with it," I reported, trying not to bristle at his amusement, though my shoulders protested that I was not being entirely truthful.

"That's fine," H. B. Yang said. "I imagined a fine young woman like yourself would be quite capable of handling such work. Now, tell me, please, what progress have you made on the project for which I employed you?"

"I have made some progress, I believe," I said in what I hoped was a noncommittal way.

"Ah," he said. "You have found what I seek?"

"No," I said. "But I believe I'm getting closer."

"Very good," he said. "Please tell me what you have found thus far."

The little hairs on the back of my neck, short as they were, rose. *Not everyone tells the truth all the time, not even the boss,* I heard myself telling Cao Zhi not ten feet from here, not four hours ago.

"Uncle," I said carefully, "I have found only paths to follow. I have gone some way down some of them, but taken none to its end. I believe one of these paths may lead to what you seek. However, I do not yet know which. I have no wish to mislead you with false direction. You have asked me to accomplish this task for you. I will try faithfully to do what you ask."

After all, I reminded us both silently, I was talking to the man who might well be responsible for the bomb that cut the number of what he was seeking from four to three. The man who not long ago was sitting here with Joe Yee.

"I appreciate your delicacy in this matter, Chin Ling Wan-ju," H. B. Yang replied. "It is a characteristic your father would have taken pride in."

I get it, I thought. My father, who owes you one. Who is now with his ancestors and thus unable to pay his debt. A debt that therefore belongs to his children, specifically the child sitting in your office right now.

"Nevertheless," H. B. Yang went on placidly, knowing the

unspoken was understood by us both, "I would be extremely interested in knowing what the paths are that you have found, regardless of whether you have explored them yet or not."

I considered how to answer this. A cup of tea would have helped me think, I reflected grumpily. "I don't want to raise false hopes in you, Uncle," I said, "or false angers, either. The methods of my profession often bring me to paths which, in the end, lead nowhere. It is unavoidable, something I have become accustomed to, yet following these incorrect paths can cause someone inexperienced in these matters to take his enemies for friends—or worse, his friends for enemies. I would not have that happen to you."

H. B. Yang waited a moment before he spoke. "Do you consider, Chin Ling Wan-ju, that I am unable to distinguish my friends from my enemies?"

"Given full information, I have no doubt you can," I told him. "Given partial facts, even false ones, how can any man?"

This Chinese fencing was driving me crazy, and he didn't look convinced, but I didn't see any other way out.

H. B. Yang, however, did.

"So: you will not share with me your progress to this point?"

He was no longer smiling, but his voice was still calm and friendly.

I said, "I don't want to give you incomplete information. When I have followed these paths to their ends—which I do believe will happen soon, as I said—I will have a full picture. Then I will paint it for you."

"If you do not follow these paths?"

"Why would I not?"

"Because you no longer work for me."

I had come up here expecting something like this, but it was still a stunner. I was temporarily wordless, which gave him a chance to go on.

"It saddens me, Chin Ling Wan-ju, to remove you from this project before you have had the opportunity to prove to me you are capable of satisfactorily concluding it. I have no choice, however, if you fail to trust me."

"I didn't say I didn't trust you."

It was, however, what I'd meant. My heart pounded as H. B. Yang's unsmiling face directed its dark eyes at me. "No. But you will not tell me things I have paid you to learn."

"It's not the way of my profession, Uncle."

"I have paid you," he repeated.

And that means you own me? "Uncle, I will return your money."

That was the wrong answer. "Money!" H. B. Yang's eyes flashed. "American children—hollow bamboo!" He slammed his palms down on the desk. "You think the money is all that matters!"

Hollow bamboo: Chinese on the outside, nothing on the inside. Distractingly, irrelevantly, I was hit by a memory: many years ago, our crowded apartment kitchen. My mother's elder sister, who came from China already an old woman, shelling peas. Me, a young child, helping, but squirming to get away and join Tim and Andrew at Monopoly, because I knew I could clobber them both. My aunt had also called me "hollow bamboo"; I thought it was a Chinese term of affection. When one of my brothers explained to me its real meaning that day in the kitchen I started to cry, thinking my aunt despised me. Seeing my tears, my father took me on his lap and handed me two of the mud figurines from his collection, small sculptures of a scholar and a fisherman.

"Ling Wan-ju, which of these men is Chinese?" he asked me.

"Both are." I sniffled, confused, looking up at him.

"How can that be?" he asked. "They are so different. One walks along smiling, with his fishing pole; the other sits in deep contemplation of a delicate scroll. But you say they are the same?"

"Not the same," I said. "They lead different lives, so they dress differently, they act differently. But aren't they both Chinese?"

"Chinese people can be different, then, one from another?"

I nodded. He wiped my teary face with his handkerchief.

"And which of these figures is hollow?" my father asked me.

I turned them both over and around, but I knew the answer. "Both are solid clay."

He pointed to the glass-fronted cabinet that held three dozen similar statues, large and small. "Are any of those figures hollow?"

I shook my head.

"The children of this family are not hollow, either," he said. He stood me firmly on my feet. "Now, go help your aunt with preparations for dinner. Later, you will teach me this silly game with houses on boardwalks. Your brothers will play on one side. You will play with me on the other. They, I think, will lose."

I met H. B. Yang's dark eyes. My aunt had been wrong. H. B. Yang, though he was H. B. Yang, was wrong also.

I spoke to him. "I am very sorry, Uncle, to have been so poor at expressing myself as to give you that impression. The way I feel is quite the opposite. Your money means little to me. Your trust means a great deal. I would regret losing it, but to go against what I believe is right is something I cannot do."

H. B. Yang regarded me coldly, without moving. Out the window behind him I could see cars and trucks inching through the archway onto the Manhattan Bridge, up over the crest of the roadway, and out of sight.

"You may leave," H. B. Yang said.

It wasn't permission so much as an order, and I got up to obey; but it was permission, too, of a kind. I wasn't sure H. B. Yang had the power, and I knew he didn't have the right, to keep me here if he'd wanted to, but it was clear that he fully thought he had both. I didn't argue. Turning from this quiet room with the streams of traffic moving in never-repeated but organized patterns outside and the intricate assembly line of waiters and diners below, I just left.

n i n e t e e n

God, Lydia, I thought as I stood on the Bowery in the gleaming afternoon sun. You just told H. B. Yang, one of the most powerful men in Chinatown and the bogeyman of your childhood, to go jump in the lake. Boy, that's terrific; and what's your next trick?

The traffic straining at the crosswalk for the light to change offered no advice. Not content to spew impatient fumes, as red flashed to green and the car at the head of the line didn't move fast enough everyone started to honk, everyone annoyed at everyone else for being here, in this place, at this time. The sound was loud, messy, and uncontrollable. I just stood planted where I was, until I was hit by the not totally unpleasant realization that I was hearing something no one—not H. B. Yang, not Duke Lo, not the State Department, or even the NYPD—could do anything about.

I checked my beeper, silenced during my ejection from H. B. Yang's retinue, to see if Bill had called, but he still hadn't. I looked around me at Chinatown both wearily and warily, and headed for home.

I had a few ideas for how to spend the evening, but I wanted to give Bill more time to turn up first. I also wanted to take a quick shower and get out of these sesame-oil-and-sweat-scented duds into something that reminded me more of me.

The problem with that plan was my mother.

My mother had been difficult to head off last night, late as it was when I got home. I'd told her I was tired; I'd told her I didn't think Joe Yee and I really had that much in common, a concept she scorned as overrated: "If you have less in common, you will always be able to surprise each other." I'd told her I wasn't sure if he'd call me again: "But you also have his number?" she'd asked, looking ready to box my ears—something she'd never done when we were children—if I'd failed to think of that. Another assault when I got home today was unavoidable, though I'd told her I was going to be working during the day and therefore not likely to experience much action in my personal life. That had carried about as much weight with her as I'd expected.

Heading up the stairs to our apartment, I found myself dreading both my mother's driving enthusiasm at the thought of Joe Yee and her tight-lipped disappointment when I told her H. B. Yang no longer thought quite so much of me as he'd seemed to when we met. I'd never actually told her that he'd hired me, but the fact that he'd fired me was likely enough to get back to her one way or another that I had no option but to give her a sanitized version of events myself first.

I unlocked our multilocked door, pulled on my slippers in the tiny vestibule, and found my mother sitting peacefully on the couch in the living room, her embroidery needle flashing in and out of the blouse she'd been working on the night before last, the one for Elliot's daughter. The diffuse light of a spring afternoon fell softly on the glass-fronted cabinet where my father's mud figurines sat. From the living room I could hear, faintly, as I'd heard it all my life, traffic funneling itself over the Manhattan Bridge, the same cars and trucks you could see so clearly through the window in H. B. Yang's office.

My mother looked up briefly from her work, then returned to it with a frown of concentration. "Ling Wan-ju," she said. "How was your day?" Finishing the difficult stitch at the center of a plum blossom, she tied off a knot and looked up again, smiling this time. "Did you see anyone interesting?"

We both knew who that meant.

Looking for a way to deflect that conversation, I was suddenly struck with inspiration. I realized I might, after all, have something to offer her.

"Not today, Ma," I said from the kitchen, pulling a bottle of seltzer from the fridge. "But guess who I ran into yesterday? Tan Wei-Lian,"—Warren Tan—"remember him? From Clinton Street."

There you go, Ma, I thought as I carried my seltzer with lime slices into the living room, a good-looking single Chinese male for us to discuss.

But as usual, my mother threw me a curve.

"Tan Wei-Lian," she said. "Pah. With that family there is always trouble."

"The Tans?" Surprised, I perched on the arm of the over-stuffed chair. "I thought they were nice people."

"The parents, yes, of course. Very hardworking, very diligent. But without any luck in their children."

"Both sons went to college," I protested. "Jian-Min"—Jeremy—"even went to graduate school. They're both handsome, smart," I had to swallow some seltzer to stop myself from adding, single, "both attentive to their parents. You don't like them?"

"College." My mother snorted. "Some people learn nothing from education. Wei-Lian thinks and plans for that union. You think I don't know this, Ling Wan-ju, but I do. He is a troublemaker. Like Jian-Min, his brother, making that stinking mess in your classroom, you had to clean it up."

"Chem lab," I said. "I had to clean it up with him because I helped him make it."

"He should have known better. He is older than you."

"By three weeks, Ma."

"Three weeks, three years, what's the difference? He is older, he was responsible."

232

"That was more than ten years ago. Anyway, we're not talking about Jian-Min."

"At least Jian-Min has a respectable position now. Not like Wei-Lian, sitting in a basement finding ways to get other people into trouble. Worrying his parents, also, not taking care of his heart."

How did this conversation get away from me like this, I wondered, finishing my seltzer. My mother went on, delivering her final dismissive remark: "Besides, Ling Wan-ju, he is much too young for you."

Well, I thought, so much for my attempt, not even to beat my mother at her own game, but just to try to play it.

"Now," she said, with a small smile of satisfaction, "Yee Ji-You, that nice man you saw last night. Well-spoken, a man with a future, I think. Have you heard from him today, or were you too busy at your business?"

My business. Probably it was something about the light, or how tired I was, but my mother, smiling up from the couch, suddenly looked old to me. Old, and smaller than the last time I'd seen her, before H. B. Yang had told me he didn't like my way of doing business.

"No, I haven't heard from him," I said, moving around to sit on the couch beside her. "But I ran into a little problem today."

"Ah?" She threaded blue silk through the needle where red had been before.

"I had another talk with Yang Hao-Bing."

My mother raised her eyebrows but said nothing.

"The truth is, Ma, when I talked to him on Friday he asked me to do a . . . small job for him. Today, he decided that had been . . . unnecessary."

Three stitches; then, "You have been fired?"

I sighed and flopped back on the cushions. So much for spin doctoring. "Yes."

Three more stitches. "Why?"

"Why? Because we don't do things the same way."

"Yang Hao-Bing did not like your way?"

"No, he didn't."

"What is your way, Ling Wan-ju?"

That was, I guessed, a fair question. "He asked me to tell him things it would have been . . . unprofessional . . . for me to tell him." As well as possibly dangerous for any number of people, but I didn't see a reason to go quite that far with my mother.

"Unprofessional?"

"Not the way things are done in my profession, Ma. We have certain standards. Rules. It wouldn't have been right."

"So you decided what was right, rather than doing what Yang Hao-Bing asked you to do?"

"Yes." I turned my head to look at her; she kept her needle moving through the embroidery frame, above, below, above, below.

"Could you have done this thing another way, Ling Wan-ju?"

"I've been thinking about that, Ma. I'm sure there were all sorts of ways that someone smarter than I am could have thought of. Or someone more experienced, maybe. But it was only me. No was the only answer I thought wouldn't be wrong, the only answer I could find to give him. Politely," I added hurriedly. "I was very polite."

My mother stitched some more. The wing of a swallow began to appear on the cloth. "Then," she said, "what you have done is right."

My eyes widened. I sat upright and turned to face her. "It is?"

Now she looked at me, stilling her hands, one above her fabric, one below. "If agreeing to Yang Hao-Bing's request would have forced you to act in a way your profession considers wrong, you have done well to refuse."

Her hands began to move again, and she focused her attention back on her needle.

"You hate my profession, Ma," I said.

She nodded. "I consider it unsuitable for you. It brings you into the company of people no mother could approve of her daughter knowing. It puts you in danger. Men who might otherwise become attracted to you dislike the way you dress, the way you walk, the way you talk, which are required by your profession.''

That was going a little far, I thought, but it was hardly the point. "But you think what I did was right?''

"If you insist on engaging in this profession, Ling Wan-ju, I would expect you to behave in a professional manner, with proper conduct, just as I expect your brothers to do in their professions.''

Oh, I thought. Oh. Oh, my.

"You're not mad?'' I said. "Yang Hao-Bing?''

She looked sharply at me. "A public disagreement with Yang Hao-Bing is not something to be proud of.'' Turning back to her work, she said, "However, there are many people in Chinatown who over the years have found it unavoidable.''

"Even after what this family owes him?''

"Except for the respect due a man of his age, with his accomplishments, what does this family owe him?''

I stared at her in astonishment. "He brought Ba over here,'' I said. "While you waited with my brothers''—Ted and Elliot, the oldest of the four—"in Hong Kong. You always told us that.''

"Brought him over, yes. But what of it? Your father paid Yang Hao-Bing for his passage, many years ago.''

"Well, he worked it off, sure, but—''

"No, Ling Wan-ju, what are you talking about? Your father worked very hard for a long time, sometimes two jobs at once in Hong Kong, to earn the money for his passage to America.'' She started the long stitches of the swallow's wing.

"But then, what does it mean, Yang Hao-Bing brought him over?''

My mother looked at me as if I were seriously missing a piece. "On his ship,'' she said. "Yang Hao-Bing sold your father passage on his ship, the ship that brought him here.''

She waited another moment, watching to make sure that that registered. Then, apparently satisfied that my lights, however dim, were on, she went back to her needle and thread.

I sat motionless, watching her hands move over the cotton

fabric of Elliot's daughter's blouse. The ship. H. B. Yang owned the ship my father came here on. H. B. Yang, octopus-armed entrepreneur. Why should he not be in shipping? And how dumb was I?

As if I were not the only one who wanted the answer to that question, the phone in my room that rings through from my office started to shrill. I jumped up to answer it.

"Hi," Bill said in my ear. "It's me."

"The damn ship!" I shouted. "H. B. Yang owns the damn ship!"

He paused. "What damn ship?"

My words tumbled out, tripping over one another. "When my father came here, legitimate passenger ships. Now, I'll bet anything, immigrant-smugglers. The ship the courier came on!"

Bill was briefly silent. "The one who stole the dope?"

"From Duke Lo. Who ships his dope via H. B. Yang!"

"Working together?" Bill asked. "You think they work together and the rivalry's a front? How do you know about this?"

"It's a long story. Damn!"

Bill's voice was cautious. "Lydia? Are you okay?"

"Why? Just because I'm swearing like a sailor?"

"I used to be a sailor," he reminded me. "You have a long way to go. But you sound upset."

"Well . . ." I took the phone over to my bed and plunked down on it. "H. B. Yang. Smuggling dope."

"That's bad?"

"Of course it's bad!"

"I didn't mean for society as a whole," he said dryly.

"I didn't, either. I meant for me, for Peter, for us Chinatown kids."

"Why?"

I thought. "Because that was never him. He was scary and powerful, but he was the boss. The guy you went to instead of the police, who were corrupt, or your own boss, who was unfair, or the protection racket gangs. He was the good guys. You might not get what you wanted from him, but you could trust him."

Bill said, "I guess not."

236

"I guess not. But I don't want to know this!"

"I'm sorry," Bill said, sounding like he really was. Then he said, "And how do you know this?"

"It's complicated. Can we get together and I'll tell you? Where are you?"

"We can, but it'll take me a little while to get in, and that might not be what you want me to do. That's why I'm calling. I'm in Cobble Hill."

"Cobble Hill?" I frowned. "At Jayco?"

"Across the street," he said. "At the coffee place. I thought I'd come out and look around."

"Your—"

"I rented one. So I've been sitting here looking through their front window, and it's been a boring afternoon until now."

"What changed?"

"Well, if I have the right guy: tall, very pointy nose and chin, scar down the right side of his jaw? Is that the waiter you told me about from Dragon Garden?"

"Yes," I said, propelling myself to my feet. "Cao Zhi, what about him?"

"He's sitting with your pal Joe Yee right now."

"Cao Zhi?" I yelped, then quieted down, as I heard my mother rustle in the living room. "He's supposed to be at work!" I hissed at Bill.

"Well, he's not. He got here a minute or two ago. Joe Yee wasn't here when I got here, but he's been back about two hours. This other guy went straight to the back, Joe Yee's desk. They're leaning forward, lots of hand jive, like old buddies working something out."

"Working?" I felt my hand clenching into a fist. "Selling! He's selling out the waiters, Bill."

"Isn't that a stretch?" Bill asked cautiously. "How do you know he knows anything about the waiters? He could be looking for an apartment. I just thought it was interesting, something to tie your buddy Yang to Joe Yee, if Yang's employees come here."

"No," I said, trying to curb my impatience. "There's no time to tell you the whole thing now, but believe me, those guys are tied together already. Joe Yee came to the restaurant today. And Cao Zhi knows where the waiters are!''

"You know that for a fact?"

"He told me he did!"

"Okay," Bill said calmly, taking this in. "Tell me the whole thing later. What do you want me to do?"

"Stay there. Follow them if they leave—maybe they'll go to them. God, I wish I were there!"

"Well, you're not, and there's no point in your coming out. I'll keep in touch if anything happens."

I spoke into the growing afternoon shadows in my room: "I have to find them."

"What?"

"The waiters. I have to find them before Joe Yee and Cao Zhi get to them! Cao Zhi, that lying sneak, acting like he wanted to help them! You stay there and follow those guys. I'm going to go find the waiters."

"How?"

Maybe it was the shadows in the room I'd always lived in, maybe it was the sounds of the unseen traffic or the glow of the light from the living room, where my mother sat sewing, but I had, not one of those ideas that hits you like a bolt of lightning, but one of the ones that rises like the sun, beginning so faintly you can't really pinpoint the moment when it starts or the moment when you realize that you are seeing things totally differently now from the way you were just a short time ago.

"I know where they are," I said quietly to Bill, over the phone to Brooklyn. "I'm going to go find them."

Because, of course, they were at the restaurant; they were at Dragon Garden.

Home, Cao Zhi had told me, gesturing sardonically around the janitor's closet beside H. B. Yang's office. Hurrying through the dusk-covered streets, I thought of his sneer when I'd asked if "home"

238

was China. And *home,* H. B. Yang had told me, was what he offered his employees, a home they always had with him as long as they worked hard, obeyed his rules, and didn't ask for anything more by right than he was willing to give them by his magnanimity. Four men, unsafe in their basement in Elmhurst, unsafe on the streets of Chinatown, four men whose only connection with one another was that they worked at Dragon Garden—where would they go but home?

Getting into Dragon Garden up the employees' back stairs was no problem; it was dinnertime, the restaurant still open. I could hear, through the door at the top of the stairs, no sound but the faint clanging of woks and pots from the kitchen beyond. I pushed the door open slowly; the break room was empty. Scuttling across it, I reached my goal: the basement door on the other side of the room.

Cao Zhi was the man who made frequent trips to the basement, two flights down, to check his all-important nonfoods supplies, to make sure the waiting stock of linens and chopsticks was adequate for the demands of the diners. He was, Pei-Hui had told me, very assiduous about it.

I pulled the door, slipped through it, and closed it silently after me. I crept down the concrete stairs, concentrating on silence. My shadow started out behind me, then swung around ahead as I passed the single fluorescent light in the ceiling of the narrow stairwell. At a landing, the stairs reversed direction, and there was another light, more shadows. Then I was through a door and in the underground warren that was Dragon Garden's basement.

The space was low-ceilinged but huge, extending the width and length of the building above. There was a sort of a hallway, and off it rooms with locked doors; but it turned and twisted and was piled with boxes and crates, lit with naked lightbulbs that mixed my shadow up with weird-shaped other ones. I could smell spices and onions and dampness; I could hear the humming whine of the motors that kept the freezers and walk-in coolers cold.

Brushing past sagging cardboard boxes, maneuvering around tubs of who knew what, I worked my way along the basement passageway, doubling back, turning left, right, wherever it took me. My heart was pounding, but I was patient, and I was rewarded: I saw the light.

The light was what I had been looking for. If the waiters were here, hiding in the basement under Dragon Garden, in some storeroom not made for the storage of people, it had to be, as this whole space was, a place with no windows. So I crept along the passageway, peering into the dusty dimness for a telltale line of light under a door, illumination that dish detergent or cabbages wouldn't need.

When I found it I stopped, stood near, and listened. First, nothing; then, voices, in the tones of Mandarin.

I took a breath, stepped to the door, and knocked. Instantly the voices stopped and the light went out.

"I'm Lydia Chin," I called softly in English. "A friend of Peter Lee. Lee Bi-Da," I added, giving them a chance to recognize Peter's name any way they could.

No response but silence.

"Please," I said. "Cao Zhi told me you were here. I've come to help you."

Rapid, hushed voices rose inside, quick-fire Mandarin and, I thought, also Fukienese; this time, an obvious argument. The light came back on, I heard sounds of movement, and then the door was opened for me.

I stood face-to-face with a stocky young man with muscled arms. Briefly, we met each other's eyes in silence.

In English, he said, "I am Chan Song."

Yahoo! I wanted to shout, but I didn't. Calmly, I said, "Maybe I'd better come in?"

twenty

Song Chan stood aside for me to enter his kingdom, and he shut the kingdom's gate—a dinged wood door—behind me. I stood just inside, staring around.

Steel shelves piled with cardboard crates of paper goods bordered the walls of this small sovereign state, leaving a cramped town square in the center. Overhead a single circular fluorescent tube shone palely like the moon among clouds. Sweat and the faint sweet odor of mold scented the air.

On the floor three or four different, mismatched carpet remnants overlapped one another—one I recognized as the dining room pattern—and a few battered chairs held cups and dishes and were draped with clothes. Next to the chairs were three tidy blanket rolls, and next to them stood two more men.

"Lee Yuan?" I asked, looking from one to the other. "Lu Gai-Lo?" I gave their names in the Chinese order, as Song Chan had given me his, although we were speaking English. As new immigrants, the men would not yet be used to the strange western custom of waiting until the end of your name to find out where you belonged.

Song Chan, my guide through this foreign land, pointed first at one of the standing men, then at the other. They regarded me through narrowed eyes.

In Chinese tradition, you travel after death to the vast caves of the netherworld, where you wait for the decision to be made by immortal higher-ups about what your next life will be. This can take days or centuries; the immortal bureaucracy is like any other. If your relatives have provided you with a sufficiency of spirit food, clothing, and money—made of paper and burned at your funeral, and then again on the annual, at a minimum, visits to your grave—your stay won't be too bad, because you'll be able to keep warm, eat well, and, most important, bribe the demons whose job it is to make the dead miserable in punishment for the misdeeds of their earthly lives. If, on the other hand, you're sent into the next life without any of the still-living taking ample precautions to insure your needs, you're likely to have a pretty unpleasant time, both because you won't have what it takes and because the demons especially despise those who leave behind no one who cares enough to look after them once they're gone.

Those caves, I'd thought as a child, were probably dim and damp places, crowded and uncomfortable, with nowhere to sit or to sleep and nothing good to eat unless the still-alive people had remembered about you. I used to worry about how to make sure that happened, but I could never figure out a way.

My eyes wandered slowly over this cramped, dank room once again, and then I spoke.

"I've come to help you," I told the men, repeating what had, evidently, gotten me through the door.

They were not totally sold, however.

"Cao Zhi sent you to us?" Song Chan asked. "Why?" His English, though accented, was clear and businesslike.

I spoke carefully. "He told me you were here. I've come to get you away. You're in danger."

The man identified to me as Gai-Lo Lu whispered in rapid

242

Fukienese to the one I'd been told was Yuan Lee. Yuan Lee nodded but didn't say anything. They both stood silently, waiting, apparently, for Song Chan to speak.

He did. "Where is Cao Zhi?"

I hesitated, while Lu whispered to Lee again. He must be translating, I realized. "I don't know where he is," I told Song Chan, which was technically true. I didn't go any further; if I told them that last I heard their protector was in Brooklyn selling them out, they would distrust me for giving them such an unbelievable story before they'd distrust Cao Zhi on my say-so. "But I know you're in danger if you stay here," I told them. "We have to leave immediately."

"Cao Zhi said he would bring you here," Song Chan said, unbudging. "He never said he would tell you where to find us or that we were to leave with you when you came."

So Cao Zhi had actually spoken to them about me. Why, I wondered? "I'm here, aren't I?" I said. "How else would I have gotten here? If the danger weren't so near," I went on, inspired, "I would have waited for Cao Zhi. I knew you wouldn't want to trust me on my own. But there isn't time. You must leave with me now."

Yuan Lee and Gai-Lo Lu were carrying on a furiously sotto voce Fukienese conversation, Yuan Lee frowning, his tones sounding hostile and dismissive, even though I couldn't understand him. Gai-Lo Lu turned and addressed me. "Where supposed to taking us? What place can be more safe than here?"

"This place is only safe as long as no one knows about it," I said. "There are people who know now, people who know what you did and are your enemies." At "what you did," Gai-Lo Lu turned and glared at Yuan Lee, who scowled and kicked the carpet. Song Chan remained unperturbed. "I'm working for Lee Bi-Da," I went on. "The lawyer who was injured trying to help Ho Chi-Chun. I want to take you somewhere else."

Lee whispered to Lu while Song Chan asked me, "Where?"

I hadn't until that moment thought much about that question, I realized; but I also realized that was because there was only one answer.

"Chin Family Association," I said.

Among the Chinese people—roughly one and a quarter billion of us—there are only about three hundred family names in common use, some much more common than others. When you meet someone whose name is the same as yours, written with the same character, you have met a relative. The relation may go back eighteen or twenty generations, and you might never establish exactly whose triple-great-grandfather was the brother of whose great-great-uncle; but a relative is a relative, and taken very seriously. Family name associations were set up by the earliest immigrants as self-help groups, and you don't need any more credentials than your last name when you present yourself at the door.

If my father had needed to help waiters being hunted by Duke Lo, he would have taken them to Chin Family Association. These men had not been here long enough to connect up with their own family name associations, or else as Fukienese they didn't feel welcome in the established places, which were Cantonese; I knew this because if they had felt they could, they would have gone there, not to Cao Zhi, for help. But I was my father's daughter, and the men of Chin Family Association would not turn me down.

It took a little more, but I persuaded Chan and Lu and Lee. Partly it was my insistence that the danger was imminent; partly it might have been their lack of desire to spend very much more time in this constricted underground kingdom; and mostly it was that Cao Zhi, bless his duplicitous heart, had actually told them about me and apparently suggested that I be allowed to help. Why, I wondered? If he was intending to betray them, why mention me at all? And if he was intending to betray them, why wait until now to do it? Maybe he'd been waiting to negotiate a good price. I thought about Cao Zhi, the way he'd been described to me by Pei-Hui, and as the three no-longer-missing men got their few things together for the trip through the streets, I thought about how and why people change.

We ran into a brief snag when Yuan Lee, in addition to his extra shirt, his underwear, and his toothbrush, hefted and hugged under his arm a rectangular plastic-wrapped package the size of a concrete block.

My first reaction was, "No way that comes with us," which was translated for Yuan Lee and occasioned a certain amount of sharp-toned dispute in English, Mandarin, and Fukienese, Gai-Lo Lu working very hard to bring my words and Song Chan's to Yuan Lee and his to us. Yuan Lee, contempt clear in his eyes, seemed ready to plant himself and his package where he was, never moving again. We had no time for this, I realized; and I was just being squeamish. The package was evidence, the only thing we had. It would be safer with us than it would be if it remained behind, no matter how carefully hidden; and the waiters would be safer with it, because it still retained its value as a bargaining chip.

"Can't hide it anyway," Gai-Lo Lu told me as we prepared our exit from their hideaway. "On ship, was hidden, Lee Yuan finds it."

"He found it?" I said. "He wasn't bringing it here?"

"Bringing?"

"He wasn't working for Duke Lo? Lo Da-Qi?"

"Working for Lo Da-Qi, stupid man like this?" Gai-Lo Lu gave me a wide-eyed look while Yuan Lee gave him another scowl. "So stupid, goes to man who does working for Lo Da-Qi, says, I have package, maybe your boss wants. Don't even know belongs to Lo Da-Qi until try selling it. Find out fast, then."

"You found out how?"

"He finds out." Gai-Lo Lu jerked a thumb at Yuan Lee. "Chan, Ho, I don't know about it. Lee comes home one day, tells that Lo Da-Qi is chasing all of us, no one will buy what he has, all must disappear. Before this, know nothing."

Hmmm, I thought as we crept along the subterranean passageway toward the cellar steps. So Yuan Lee wasn't a courier, he was just a lucky guy who stumbled onto something that was going to make him rich. Better he should have bought a lottery ticket. And did this mean the human cargo on H. B. Yang's smuggling ships didn't know about the other kind of goods they were sharing transit with? Well, maybe that figured. If you had people to pack it on board in foreign ports and unpack it on this end, maybe you didn't need anyone to keep an eye on it during the journey. Or thought you didn't. Where had it come on board? I wondered. Did the ship stop in Thailand, Sri Lanka, Cambodia before or after it anchored silently off some hidden, night-shielded cove in Guangdong, running lights dark, engine off, taking on men and women who arrived from shore in rowboats? Or was the heroin transported overland to China, to be piled on board at the same time as the hull was filling with people who clambered up rope ladders and down metal ones?

I didn't know, and, I supposed, except to satisfy Lydia Chin's need to know everything, the answers to those questions didn't matter. The thing that mattered most right now was to manage the four short blocks to Chin Family Association in the company of three fugitive waiters without running into anyone who didn't like us.

Fortunately, those blocks took us from the Bowery, Chinatown's old border, to Mott Street, deep in Chinatown's historic heart. We didn't have to go anywhere near Duke Lo's newer Division Street territory, and by now it was dusk.

Exiting the Dragon Garden building made my heart pound faster, as we inched up the stairway to the ground floor landing and then, rather than continuing to the staff break room on the second floor, we followed a short twisty hall to a likely-looking service door. Slipping through it, we found ourselves back on bustling Canal Street, among people going about their urgent daily business, getting their last Sunday afternoon tasks accomplished before Sunday night fell. They paid no attention to the four of us, returning to their world from our sojourn in the anti–Shangri La downstairs.

The urge to scurry like rats was strong, but we had decided we would draw less attention to ourselves by walking calmly and casually toward our destination. Gai-Lo Lu and Yuan Lee followed behind Song Chan and me. As we walked I spoke to him.

"Lu Gai-Lo seems angry with Lee Yuan for trying to cheat a gangster this way," I said quietly, not using Duke Lo's name out loud, even if this wasn't his turf.

"Of course. We all were. It was a very stupid thing to do."

"If the rest of you thought it was stupid, why did you all run? Wasn't there something else you could have done?"

I'd meant, go to the police, or give the dope back, or something, but he answered the question the way he'd heard it: "The man who owns this package thinks we are all partners in this. The only way to be safe from him would be to betray Lee Yuan. Lee Yuan is a stupid man, but by the time we found out what he had done we had been sharing a home together for one month."

I thought about that home, another basement, in Elmhurst, and the photo of the young woman and toddler in the envelope addressed to Song Chan.

"That was why we sent Ho Chi-Chun to see his lawyer," Song Chan went on. "To find a way for us to correct this stupid mistake, for all to be safe."

We turned the corner from Bayard onto Mott. "I must ask you something," I said. "About a theory of mine. The ship you and the others came here on: did it belong to Yang Hao-Bing? Did he arrange for your passage?"

He gave me a sideways glance. "Is this your theory?"

"Yes."

"In China, I was a student of biology," he said. "In science, a theory is usually formulated based on data—evidence—which that theory will explain. Questions are only asked in order to confirm what one already suspects."

I nodded. That was Chinese for "Yes, but you didn't hear it here."

"Your English is very good," I said. "Did you study a long time?"

"Many years, in Shanghai."

"Oh," I said. "And that's why you speak to these men in Mandarin—you're not Fukienese. Cao Zhi also?"

"Yes. Lee Yuan speaks no English—or Mandarin, either—but Cao Zhi speaks both equally well. And for Gai-lo Lu, his Mandarin is poor, but it is better than his English."

Unexpectedly, Song Chan flashed me a quick, sharp smile, which lit up his round and somber face. A well-educated Shanghai- nese, I thought, a biology student from the fastest-growing and most prosperous city in China, and now a waiter in Chinatown, New York, America. "Why did you come here?" I asked him.

He gave me another sideways glance. "For opportunity. Is this not the land of opportunity?" He gestured at the crowded sidewalk, reminding me of Cao Zhi waving his arms in the janitor's closet.

"For someone as educated as you are, there must be better opportunities than pouring tea at Dragon Garden."

Song Chan looked away and said nothing else. A minute later we arrived at the building that housed Chin Family Association.

I looked up at the old brick front for a moment, then pulled open the door and led our expedition up the stairwell. I hadn't been inside for probably two years, and sparingly in the years before that since my father died when I was thirteen. In that time, the old man who had taught calligraphy to Andrew and me had also died. The leadership of the association had passed to different men. Most of the children I had played with on the vinyl floor had moved away, out of Chinatown, including my own brothers.

But as I opened the second-floor door to the room where the men sat drinking tea, nothing, at first, seemed changed. General Gung still stood above his pyramid of oranges on his altar high in the corner, and the incense burning in front of him smelled the same as it always had. The scroll paintings still hung on the walls, which had been freshly painted in the same ivory color I remembered, and on the floor here and there children scribbled in coloring books or did their homework, looked after by fathers and uncles so that their mothers could cook or shop or visit their sisters. Men still sat drinking tea, talking, playing cards; but, I realized, it was they who had changed. Half of the men—there were perhaps twenty—were familiar to me; the others, mostly the younger ones, were not.

As I had been at Zhen Rong, I was the only woman in the room; as they had done at Zhen Rong, the men looked up when we came in, to assess the new arrivals. I had a feeling we were surveyed with considerably less hostility than at Zhen Rong, maybe even welcomed with interested curiosity, but, it occurred to me, that might have been because that was what I expected to feel here. Song Chan and the others stood warily just inside the door; perhaps they were experiencing the feeling I had had at Zhen Rong, the sense of being where others belonged and you didn't.

One of a pair of men playing Chinese chess at a table by the window rose and smiled broadly. The skin hung looser on his pudgy face than I remembered, and he was almost completely bald, but the wide smile before me was the same as in my memory.

"Chin Ling Wan-ju!" He grasped my shoulders and beamed as he looked me over. "How rare the sight of you here has become!"

"The loss is mine, Uncle." I smiled back. This was Chin Zhuang Si, a laundry supplies dealer called in English, for reasons known only to himself, Webster. He preferred his English name to his Chinese one, and everyone always used it, whether speaking in English or, as now, in Cantonese. Uncle Webster had been a great friend of my father's and, as a bachelor, a frequent dinner guest at our home. He was one of a number of men who had taken on the job of overseeing my brothers' and my own growing up after our father died. "I have been too concerned with the small demands of daily living to have the sense to come here and ask for the counsel of my wise uncles."

"You mean you've been solving your own problems, avoiding the meddlesome interference of a pack of old men." He winked. "But of course I have been keeping an eye on you, Ling Wan-ju. If my meddlesome interference had ever been required, you can be assured I would have provided it."

The idea that Webster Chin had been keeping an eye on me filled me with an entirely different sensation than the one I'd gotten when H. B. Yang had told me the same thing. "Uncle, you are too generous, as always."

"Not as generous as you are polite, to say such a thing," he replied. "Now, tell me, why have you come here this evening, after such a long time? Have you eaten yet? Who are your friends?"

"My friends are in trouble," I told him. "Yes, thank you, we've eaten, but I've come to ask for help for them."

"Trouble?" Uncle Webster, dropping his voice, eyed the three men standing uneasily by the door. "What kind of trouble?"

"None of them speaks Cantonese," I told him. The men's uneasiness was probably increased by the fact that my conversation with Uncle Webster was in a language they couldn't follow, but

Cantonese was the language in which Uncle Webster was most comfortable, and using it was also a way for me to ask for his honest response to the situation without his having to worry about offending the strangers.

"The trouble is serious," I said. "I don't want to mislead you. They've stolen something that belongs to Lo Da-Qi." At this name the three men responded each in his own way, Song Chan with cocked head, Yuan Lee with narrowed eyes, Gai-Lo Lu with widened ones. "Do you know him, Uncle?"

"The owner of Happy Pavilion Restaurant." Uncle Webster nodded. "We have met on one or two occasions." He glanced again at the men. "These men are thieves, Ling Wan-ju?"

"No, Uncle. One of them made a foolish mistake, a poor man's attempt to become a rich man. The man in the middle there, he did the stealing. His friends, caught up in his error, have not deserted him."

Uncle Webster didn't ask me what it was the men had stolen. It was obvious I'd had the chance to tell him and hadn't taken it. I thought he was better off not knowing; and he apparently understood that and was willing to trust my assessment.

He asked, "What is the help you want for them?"

"I'm going to try to solve this problem," I said. "I need a safe place for them to stay until I do."

"You are asking if they may stay here?"

"In one of the rooms upstairs. Maybe for a day, maybe for just a few hours. I'll be responsible for the rent, of course." The room rates at Chin Family Association were minimal, more a matter of saving face for the guest by giving him the opportunity to pay for what he received rather than accept charity.

Uncle Webster looked at the men solemnly. "Who else knows you have brought these men here?"

"No one. There are people right now looking for them, but I don't believe they'll think to look here."

Uncle Webster gave me a long look. "In your attempt to solve this problem," he asked, "what will you do?"

"I'm going to talk to some people," I said. "Just talk. I'll be very careful, Uncle, I promise."

He smiled. "That, of course, is what I was asking. Very well, Ling Wan-ju. I'll arrange this. You go do your work. When your task is completed, perhaps you'll return to take tea with an old man?"

"Uncle, I can think of nothing I'd rather do," I said, and meant it.

I introduced Uncle Webster to Song Chan, Gai-Lo Lu, and Yuan Lee, and explained briefly in English what the situation was.

"It won't be for long," I said. "I'm going to see if I can fix things up."

"How?" Song Chan asked. "Will you find Cao Zhi?"

I sure will, I thought, but not the way you mean. "I'll try," I told him. "I'll let you know what's happening."

All three of them seemed less than thrilled about the circumstances they found themselves in, but I imagined they'd been feeling that way since Yuan Lee revealed his illicit prize and its unintended consequences to his new roommates. They acquiesced to the deal, and, leaving them in the care of my father's old friend, I trotted back down the stairs and set about my next errand.

I hit the pay phone on the corner and called Bill's beeper and then his service to make sure he knew what I had done and what I was planning to do. Then I called Mary. Not at the precinct, this being her day off, and not at home: I called the hospital and asked for Peter's room.

"I found them," I told her when she answered Peter's phone.

"*What?* She says she found them!" she said, not to me, then spoke to me again. "The waiters? Lydia, you're a genius! Are you okay? Are they okay?"

"Everyone's okay," I said. "How's Peter?"

"Better than he was two seconds ago. Can't you hear him? He's practically jumping up and down. They're okay," she said to

Peter, then to me: "Where were they? Were you right about the package?"

The vision of Peter jumping up and down in his hospital bed was almost funny. I giggled. A very funny car drove by and turned the corner. I giggled harder. A really silly-looking man jumped back onto the curb. I laughed. A horn honked with a sound so comic it cracked me up. "Wait," I told Mary. I took a deep breath, closed my eyes, and counted to ten, breathing in, out, in, out, until the urge to chortle and guffaw and cry was gone. The hysteria of relief wasn't something I had time to give in to right now.

"What's going on?" Mary asked in my ear.

"Traffic," I said. "Nothing. Yes, I was almost right about the package. They have it, but sort of by accident. The one who came here last month, he stumbled across it on the ship and stole it."

"Just an innocent opportunist?"

"Seems that way."

"If he's all that innocent how did he recognize it?"

"I—that's a good question." Not many Americans, where heroin is much more widespread than in China, could identify the stuff if they'd never been mixed up with it; how had a semiliterate Fukienese illegal had any idea the package was worth lifting?

For that matter, what made him approach Duke Lo's man with it once he got it here?

"Where are they now?" Mary asked impatiently.

"Chin Family Association. But it's more complicated than that."

"Than what?"

"Than you think."

"Not true. When you're involved I always think it's very complicated." To Peter: "They're at Chin Family Association." Back to me: "That was a sneaky place to put them, Lydia. Where did you find them?"

"Dragon Garden."

"Seriously? Peter, they were at Dragon Garden! The whole time? Where?" she asked me.

"In the basement. Listen, Mary—"

"I know. You want to tell me the complication, why I shouldn't just come down to Chin Family Association and pick them up and take over from here."

"Well—" I was taken slightly aback. I regrouped and said, "Well, yes. Because, see, what do you have if you do?"

"A couple of kilos of heroin that belong to Duke Lo?"

"That's the point: you can't prove that. We only know that because of Bill's—because of my snitch, who'll deny he ever met me if you squeeze him."

"I'm going to pass over the issue of whose snitch the guy was," Mary said, "although I have to tell you, the point interests me. But the waiters must know whose stuff they had, otherwise why did they run?"

"No, you're right. The one guy tried to sell it and heard on the street that it was Duke Lo's missing piece and no one else would touch it. If you take these guys up now, maybe they'll tell you that. But Duke Lo will tell you he never heard of it."

Mary was silent on the other end of the phone; maybe it was her turn to count to ten.

"All right," she said. "What's your brilliant plan?"

"I want to try to sell it back to Duke Lo."

"What?" I waited for her to repeat this bit of idiocy to Peter, but she didn't. That, I thought, was a good sign: if she were going to let me do something really crazy, she might not want him to know about it.

"I won't take it with me," I said. "So you can use it as evidence later, and so I still have a bargaining chip once I'm in. I'll wear a wire. Just to get him on tape admitting he knows what I'm talking about."

There were no words from Mary's end of the phone, though I could swear I heard the faint sound of her grinding her teeth.

"Where?" she said.

"Zhen Rong."

"With Bill? Like last time?"

"You know about last time?"

"You didn't get killed, so Chester felt like it was okay to tell me. So: with Bill, right?"

I didn't bother to get indignant. "If he turns up in time. There's another complication." I told her about Cao Zhi and Joe Yee, about my theory about H. B. Yang and Duke Lo. "So the heat's on," I said. "I don't want H. B. Yang or Duke Lo to know these guys have been found and lost again. I don't know who this Joe Yee really is, but he knows H. B. Yang and that's not a good sign."

"Lydia, I can't arrange a wire and a listening post and all that in a hurry."

"You don't have to. I have a tape recorder. I can go in on my own, and then I'll testify in court where the tape was made and who's on it. I know it's not great, Mary, but it's better than you'll have if you guys go in right now or if you wait to get all set up."

Cars turned the corner one after another, some of them heading from Chinatown, where I was, to Brooklyn, where Mary was. Silent phone to my ear, I waited for her to speak.

"I'm coming in," she said. "And I'm calling Chester. It'll give him a chance to make up for telling you where to find Duke Lo in the first place. We'll be close. If anyone at Zhen Rong sneezes loud, we'll be there. And I want you to take Bill with you."

"I want to take him," I said. "I called him before I called you. I'll call him again after you hang up." Which, I didn't point out, probably wouldn't do me any good; if Bill were in a position to talk to me my beeper would have gone off already.

"Lydia, this is so crazy—" Mary began.

"No, it's not. Duke Lo thinks he's smarter than everybody. He knows you guys have never been able to touch him. I'll be careful to make him think I'm not a threat, just a dumb opportunist like the other guy. I'll let him scare me into promising to return his dope, and then I'll beat it out of there."

She sighed, and I knew I had her. "I think it's nuts," she said. "There must be another way."

"There must be. But if you want these guys, it's the only way I can think of."

254

We didn't talk much longer. She was in a hurry to get back to Chinatown, I was in a hurry to run over to my office and grab my tape recorder, and Duke Lo, I hoped as I hung up the phone and scuttled off down the street, was in a hurry to get the comeuppance he would never see coming.

twenty-one

bill was nowhere to be found. I guessed that meant he was still keeping an eye on Joe Yee and Cao Zhi, and it probably meant they were on the move, because he'd have gotten my beeper message by now and he'd have called me from the coffee place if he could have. I wondered if it also meant that when this case was over I should reopen the cell phone discussion, which Bill is against because they aren't secure but I'm sort of for because you spend less time gritting your teeth and wondering where your partner is.

Oh, well. Time was a-wasting. If Joe Yee and Cao Zhi discovered the missing men were missing, and with them the missing kilos, they might go to Joe Yee's pal H. B. Yang, who'd go to Duke Lo, all of which might spoil my attempt to get Duke Lo's voice on tape saying "Yes, that dope is mine." Mary, I was sure, would understand and approve of my decision not to wait for Bill, which I would tell her about as soon as all this was over and she'd gotten so many NYPD points for hauling in a fish the size of Duke Lo that she couldn't possibly yell at me.

So I zipped over to my office, waved at the Golden Adventure ladies, stuck my palm recorder in my pocket, and dashed across Chinatown from my office way beyond the old western border to Zhen Rong, way beyond the eastern one.

When I reached the building on East Broadway I stood for a moment, just looking. It seemed, in the almost-faded light, a little droopy, worn out perhaps from the crowded, noisy, immigrant life going on in the apartments upstairs, cooking and TV, children doing their homework at the kitchen table, bachelors living eight to a room, families working toward the dream of moving out to a better place, and families moving in for whom this was a better place.

I took a breath and went in.

The front room was more sparsely populated than it had been yesterday, but otherwise it was the same: men drinking tea and whiskey, playing cards, smoking cigarettes. Some of the men were the same, and obviously recognized me; some were not, and stared. My heart was pounding harder than it had yesterday, and I was alone, but otherwise I was the same, too.

I bowed the bow I had used the first time, glancing around quickly to see who was there. Finding the face I had hoped to find, I spoke to the man in the easy chair, the older man who had silently guided Bill and me into Duke Lo's inner sanctum.

"I'm Chin Ling Wan-ju," I said in English, reminding him. "I was here yesterday, to see Lo Da-Qi."

His eyes fixed on mine, the man didn't respond at first, then he nodded.

"I would like to see him again," I said. "I have something of interest to discuss with him."

A few of the other men whispered to one another, and I heard a snicker from the corner. The eyes of the man I was speaking to flashed over there, and the snicker stopped. Silently, he stood and walked to the back, opening the door in the wall and then closing it behind him, as he had done yesterday. I waited under the watchful eyes of a dozen Fukienese men, not looking at any of them. When the door in the wall opened again and the silent man beckoned me in, I was more than ready to go.

Duke Lo sat this time not in the easy chair, but behind his

hefty desk. The drapes once again hung closed across the window and the air was overfull of the scents of old cigarette smoke, tea, and leather upholstery. The silent man closed the door and left us. Duke Lo smiled a smile that crinkled the skin around his eyes. He waved me to a seat opposite him. He did not stand.

"Lydia Chin, to see you again so soon," he said brightly, speaking in English as we had the first time. "Certainly, I am a fortunate man!"

I took the chair across the desk. "Perhaps," I said, "we are both fortunate."

"I hope so, I hope so." Duke Lo rubbed his hands together, then settled them both on the desk. "But where is your husband?"

"He's busy," I told him. "He sends his regrets. He's sorry he wasn't able to join me in this visit." I was sure that once Bill found out where I was that would be true, and it gave Duke Lo the idea that Bill knew I was here.

"I'm sorry also." Duke Lo took a cigarette from a gold case, lit it without offering one to me. "I would like to know him better." He dropped his match almost gleefully into a brown glass ashtray. "The husband of Lydia Chin, what an interesting man he must be!"

If you lay it on any thicker I'll need a shovel, I thought. Well, time to get down to business.

"Actually," I said, "I've met a lot of interesting men recently."

"Have you?" Duke Lo's eyes behind his glasses were pleasantly open and expectant. "Really, have you?"

"Oh, yes. I met three men just today, for example. Living in such a strange place. And with such fascinating possessions."

Before Duke Lo could answer me the door opened and a young man came in carrying a teapot and cups on a lacquered tray. There were no sweets this time. Duke Lo watched the young man set the tray down and leave. He turned to me. "Please," he said. He reached for the pot, poured two cups of tea, and handed one to me. "Please, have some tea while you tell me about these interesting men. What is the strange place they live in?"

"Oh," I answered, sipping my tea, which was as flat and

unexceptional as the tea yesterday had been, "it was strange but foolish. Nothing worth the attention of such a busy and distinguished man as yourself." Gosh, Lydia, I thought, you're throwing it around here with the greatest of ease yourself. "But their possessions are a different matter. Fascinating." I put my cup back in the saucer in my palm. "Sadly," I said, looking into Duke Lo's eyes, "I think they've fallen on hard times. They seem very interested in selling some of their things."

"Selling some things?" Duke Lo's eyes twinkled, but not, it seemed to me, in the way of Christmas lights. "That could be sad, certainly. Or"—his face became thoughtful—"or it could mean better fortune for them than they might have expected."

Good. That was the first hurdle overcome; he was willing to talk about it, anyway.

"It's hard to tell the outcome at the start," I agreed. I put my half-empty teacup back on the tray. Duke Lo made no effort to pour me a new cup of tea, so I picked up the pot and did it for myself. When I was done I put the pot down, settled back in my chair, and sipped. "These men," I said, "they have one item in particular that they're anxious to see once again in the hands of its former owner."

"Is that true? What is this item?" Duke Lo sipped at his own tea, cigarette still going in his other hand.

"It came here on a ship," I said. "One of these interesting men was on the same ship. But it isn't clear to them who the thing belongs to."

"Isn't it?"

"No. They've been told, I have to tell you, that it's yours. That such . . . turtle's eggs . . . would be in possession of an item that was once yours," I said, sipping my new cup of the dull tea—how far you do go for your art, Lydia, I patted myself on the back mentally—"is something I find hard to believe. I told them it's more likely to belong to the man who owned the ship."

Duke Lo laughed, sharp and loud. "The man who owned the ship? They would certainly be fools to believe that."

"That's what one of them told me. He said he thought it was

a business arrangement, that the man who owned the ship was paid to transport goods—for you—the same way he was paid to transport people. That you paid for its crossing but the item is yours. I said, however, that you and the ship owner must be partners in this importing enterprise."

Duke Lo laughed again. As quickly as his laugh had started, it stopped. "Partners! The ship owner is a fool."

"Well," I said, "but people sometimes go into partnerships with fools. If he's useful to you—"

"A man stupid enough to be useful without even knowing it, why would I make a man like that my partner?"

This is H. B. Yang we're talking about here, I thought, but I focused on a different problem. "Without knowing it? I don't understand."

"The fox borrowing the tiger's might," Duke Lo said with a smug little smile.

I almost spit my tea across the room, but in a supreme display of professionalism I maintained my control. My mother would have been proud.

"Please," I said, swallowing, "I still don't understand."

"Oh, Lydia Chin, showing your lack of traditional knowledge!" Duke Lo wagged his finger at me. "The fox and the tiger went through the forest together. All the other creatures fled, yes, they fled. The fox had the way cleared for him by his association with the tiger. The tiger, formidable but never smart, did not understand what a service he had done for the fox. But why would the fox explain?"

That wasn't how I'd heard it, I thought, but okay.

"Lydia Chin," Duke Lo said briskly, "enough games. Tell me where to find this item."

"Maybe it isn't yours," I said. "Shouldn't we make clear what it is, to make sure we're both talking about the same thing?"

He paused, and smiled. "Maybe it is not mine," he said, relaxing back into his chair. "No, maybe not. But perhaps I want to be generous. Perhaps I'd like to help these men, men you say are in a bad position—although if they are, I'm sure it's a result of their own disloyalty and stupidity. Ah, but this is America." Duke Lo smiled again, in a way that made me want to pull my jacket more tightly around myself. "And a hound that bites his master, though he cannot be trusted, can be useful in other ways."

"In what ways?" I couldn't help asking.

His eyes became ice above his smile. "He can be cooked for food."

Oh, I thought. Maybe I'd better mention that to the truculent Yuan Lee.

Duke Lo went on. "So, whether the item is mine or not, yes, yes, I'd like to help. As to what exactly it is, let me be surprised! I like surprises very much, very much—as long as they are pleasant ones."

Duke Lo waited, his eyes glittering behind his glasses.

So much for getting someone in this room to say "heroin." He wasn't going to mention the word, and he'd be suspicious if I tried to bring it up again.

"That's kind of you," I said. "I'm sure the men will be pleased. But they do have one fear."

"Have they? What is their fear?"

"They are superstitious men," I said apologetically, "and they have strange beliefs. They think that this item is protecting them. They're worried that if they give it up—if, for example, you obtain it—then they will be in danger."

"Ah. No, I think they are quite wrong. I feel sure, in fact, that giving up this item is the only safe path for these men. Although it certainly matters who they give it to."

"And giving it to you will guarantee their safety?"

"Yes." He nodded slowly. "I think so."

"I'm very glad to hear that," I said. I wasn't sure I personally would take Duke Lo's guarantee to the bank, especially in view of the idea of cooking the hounds, but we both knew what I meant. "When you say 'help,' " I asked him, "what exactly did you have in mind?"

Duke Lo appeared to think about it. "Where is this item?"

"Actually," I said, lying through my teeth, "I don't know.

They've moved it. They were worried about its security, you understand.''

"Its security?''

"The authorities,'' I said portentously, "would also be interested in it, if they found it.''

"Would they?'' he asked, as if this idea were new to him. "In that case, please satisfy my curiosity: why haven't you, Lydia Chin, gone to the authorities? Doing that would no doubt put them in your debt. Given your profession, that might be valuable. Yes''—he nodded,—"it might.''

"Given my profession,'' I said, "it's hard to make a decent living. That kind of debt is, you'll pardon me, worthless. A sound business relationship with Lo Da-Qi, on the other hand, could be something quite valuable. Especially''—my teacup rattled as I put it on the desk—"in view of the current, shall I say, changing situation here in Chinatown.''

He smiled again. "I understand. I do understand. Lydia Chin: remarkable!'' He rolled his cigarette out in the brown ashtray. "About the item: you don't know where it is?''

"Not now, no. In fact, I don't know where the men are, either.'' I continued to lie like a rug. "They got tired of the interesting place they were living in, you see. But,'' I ad-libbed, thinking furiously, "we discussed this situation. If you're interested in regaining the item, perhaps you would be good enough to offer a reward for their trouble in preserving it for you. Out of your generosity, of course. I might find a way to convey your offer to them.''

"Of course.'' His smile said he'd been expecting this. "Do they have a figure in mind?''

"Fifty thousand dollars,'' I said without blinking. "They understand the item is worth far more than that, but they aren't greedy. They will be pleased to see it back in your hands.''

He didn't blink either. "Thirty,'' he said.

I pursed my lips as if in thought. "Thirty is very low,'' I said. "The men might not believe that the rightful owner of the item would treat it so casually, to offer so little. They might begin to worry that it wasn't really yours.''

"Ah. Well, I wouldn't want them to worry, no, I wouldn't. Perhaps, then, yes, perhaps forty. Ten thousand each for the men for returning the item to me. Ten thousand for you, Lydia Chin, for your trouble." His glittering eyes rested on mine. Twenty-five percent. Quite a go-between's fee. I had a rug merchant's urge to negotiate, to try to force him up just to see if I could, but, I reminded myself, the money wasn't actually the point here.

"All right," I said, trying to seem a little greedy, a little intimidated. "I'm sure the men will agree."

At that point an inspiration hit me. I was helpless, powerless to resist it, even though I knew as I spoke that Mary would surely kill me. "The men," I said, "will give the item to me and I'll bring it to you. Not here, of course."

He looked around his inner sanctum and smiled. "Not here?"

"No. Bill would never permit it." I gave him a shamefaced smile and wished I had the ability to blush becomingly on cue. "He feels East Broadway is a dangerous street to cross if you're carrying a package. Also," I went on, tossing my head, "if we're going to do business together, I would insist that you allow me to honor you with a feast on the occasion of our first transaction. Not at Happy Pavilion, of course; I wouldn't dream of making you feel responsible in any way for this event."

Duke Lo, still smiling, nodded at this delicacy of feeling on my part. "Where, then?"

"At No. 8 Pell Street," I said.

His smile grew broader. He poured himself a cup of tea and held the pot out, offering to top off mine. Pouring for himself before his guest was so rude that I was tempted to match his rudeness by refusing his offer, but I held myself in check, smiled sweetly, and put my cup under the spout.

Duke Lo would understand why I was unwilling to make the exchange at Happy Pavilion, his territory. He also knew the standing of No. 8 Pell Street, as did everyone in Chinatown who needed to know these things.

"This is not necessary," he said, offering the standard demurral. Under most circumstances this would indicate a becoming modesty on his part, though now there was also a reassurance involved I wasn't sure I was quite ready to buy.

"Oh," I said, "but I insist."

"Very well," Duke Lo answered. "This is most generous of you. Will I have the honor of meeting your three interesting friends at this feast?"

"They, unfortunately, won't be there. Bill will, though; he will absolutely insist on coming." I knew how deeply that was true. "And please invite any of your associates you like, to make up our party." That was to let him know I was not about to front-load this feast with bodyguards or henchmen of my own; that I was inviting his people to be the majority of our party would imply to him that I really did want to just do business.

Duke Lo smiled some more, his eyes glinting, and told me again how unnecessary and hospitable this was. I smiled also, and repeated that I insisted. He asked me, as the host, what day and hour I had in mind. I wanted to say "Breakfast!" but restrained myself and suggested lunch the following day, twelve o'clock.

"Ah!" Duke Lo said, smiling a last, dazzling smile of delight. "High noon!"

So that was how we set it up. Things all fine and dandy between us, Duke Lo and I parted company, he remaining in his curtained, carpeted hideaway and me stepping gratefully back out to the traffic-swept, pedestrian-choked, breezy nighttime streets of Chinatown.

Blocks away, back near home, I took myself to a little tea shop I know and got a cup of tea, drinkable tea, jasmine tea. I wondered, as I selected a red bean bun to go with it, and then a couple of almond cookies to go with that, what was wrong with Duke Lo that he drank such lousy tea. Then it occurred to me that his usual visitors were probably men, and like men everywhere trying to outmacho one another, he probably served them whiskey or rice wine. Tea was most likely reserved for older men who appreciated the propriety of it, and for the occasional upstart woman like me.

264

Well, I'll show you who's an upstart, your dukeship, I thought as I felt my jasmine tea flowing directly into my veins. It jolted my tired body into a sense of alert readiness, though I knew that wouldn't last long. And speaking of alert readiness and outmachoing each other, I bit into the red bean bun and while I was enjoying the warm, sweet chewiness I checked my beeper.

Bill had called, from home.

I moved my operation from the front to the back, to the phone booth there. It's the old-fashioned kind of phone booth, with a door that closes and a little shelf for your tea and cookies and the pile of extra quarters you'd just gotten with your change. I moved in, shut the door, sipped my tea, and weighed my quarters in my hand. Bill or Mary? Mary or Bill?

I called, Bill answered.

"Duke Lo?" he demanded as soon as he knew it was me. "Did you really go see that guy again?"

"I tried to find you," I protested, to head him off. "I left a message so you'd know where I was. It had to be quick, that's all. And I told him you knew I was there. He seemed to be very impressed with you."

"Oh, yeah, I'm sure he was. We'll work this out another time: obviously, you survived. What happened?"

I took another bite of my red bean bun and told him about my meeting and what Duke Lo and I had arranged.

"And he'll just go there, making an exchange like this in a public restaurant? He's not worried you're setting him up?" Bill's incredulity came out in his voice.

"Not at No. 8 Pell Street. It's like shooting the guy with the white flag."

"That's been known to happen."

"Well, this won't. Anyone who used No. 8 Pell Street like that would lose all face in Chinatown, all credibility. No one would ever do business with them again. The tongs might even get together to wipe them out, to eliminate the lying sneaks and make a statement about the sanctity of neutral territory."

"That's the tongs. You could be working with the cops."

"The cops know about the neutral places. They have enough trouble getting anyone in Chinatown to trust them. They would never in a million years make a mistake like that."

"Not even to reel in Duke Lo?"

"No fish is big enough."

"You're telling me in Chinatown there's honor among thieves?"

"No," I said. "But there's enlightened self-interest."

"And what happens when you testify to all this in court? Don't you become the one who used No. 8 Pell Street that way?"

"If I did, I would, but I won't, so I won't," I said. "Mary will pick up Duke Lo and his crowd blocks away. She and Chester have already been looking for him and everyone knows it, so they can make it seem like coincidence that they happened to finally find him when he's got a few kilos of dope in his back pocket."

"All right," Bill said. "I'm not sure I buy this, but as long as there's a good Chinese lunch in it for me. . . . Now, explain why you were in such a goddamn hurry to get to Duke Lo that you couldn't wait for me."

I frowned, but he couldn't see me. "I was afraid that when Cao Zhi and Joe Yee found out the waiters had split they'd go to H. B. Yang. Then H. B. Yang might go to his partner Duke Lo, and everybody would get too confused and suspicious for my scheme to work."

"I'm confused and suspicious already, and I'm *your* partner. But anyway, they didn't."

"They, Cao Zhi and Joe Yee? Didn't go to H. B. Yang?"

"Right."

"But did they go to Dragon Garden like I thought they would?"

"Yes, genius. You were right about that, and I guess you were right about the waiters' being there in the first place?"

"That's where I found them." I gave Bill a very brief rundown on the waiters, where they'd been and where they were now. "And if I'd thought about that anywhere near the first place then I'd be a genius. So what happened?"

"Cao and Yee? They went in, I waited, they came out looking mad. It was quick, three or four minutes, so I doubt if they had time to go upstairs to see your buddy Yang."

"Good. I was afraid they'd think he was the one who found them and moved them, so they'd want to confront him."

"That would be a reasonable theory on their part. So why didn't they?"

I thought, swallowing some red bean filling. "I guess because they didn't want *him* to know *they* knew where they were, especially that Cao Zhi had hidden them right under his nose. Then what happened?"

"They had some words," Bill said. "Mad at each other. I heard 'imbecile' from one, 'idiotic' from the other, not much else. Then they split up, Cao Zhi on foot, Joe Yee back to his car. I figured a guy like me wouldn't get far following Cao through Chinatown, so I stuck with Yee. He headed for Brooklyn. Somewhere along the line he caught on that he had a tail."

The phone demanded, through a bored electronic voice, another nickel. "Rats," I said. "Wait." I fed the slot a whole quarter to keep it quiet, thinking about cell phones, and asked Bill, "Joe Yee made you?"

"Not that it was me, in the rented car," he said. "I wore shades, I was a few cars back, I'd muddied up the license plate."

"I think that's illegal."

"I'll have to remember that. Anyway, I don't think he knew who it was, but he knew I was there. He did some evasive stuff. I hung with him for a while, but he wasn't about to go anywhere interesting with me there, and I didn't want him to get too involved in trying to figure out who I was. So I pulled over, made a few calls, didn't get you, and came back here."

"I think it shows great strength of character that you didn't come charging on over to Zhen Rong." I dipped an almond cookie in my tea, which was cool by now but still better than Duke Lo's.

"It would have served you right if I'd wrecked whatever you had going."

"Aren't we on the same side?"

"Sometimes I wonder."

"You don't mean that."

He sighed. "No."

"Good, because there's something else."

"What?"

"Well, this partner business."

"I know, I know," he said. "I shouldn't have said that. We're not partners, we're just—"

"No," I said. "Not you and me. Call me whatever you want. I mean H. B. Yang and Duke Lo."

"What about them? And can I really call you whatever I want?"

"I think they might actually not be partners. And no."

"Damn. What do you mean?"

So I told Bill about the fox and the tiger.

"Hmmm," he said. "I'm supposed to take that seriously? And if I did, what would it mean?"

"That Duke Lo's dope-running operation piggybacks on H. B. Yang's people-running one and H. B. Yang doesn't know anything about it?"

Bill was silent for a minute; I could hear him pulling on a cigarette. "Sounds risky for Lo."

"Well, he trades one risk for another. Suppose he loads up H. B. Yang's smuggling ships with hidden dope. If the ship gets stopped, he loses his dope. That's the bad news. But he's not connected to it. And H. B. Yang, circumstantially, is. That's the good news."

"I guess it could be done," Bill said slowly. "If you knew when the ships were leaving and when they were getting in."

"That can't be hard to find out, on either end. You just have to bribe the right people."

"If you're right about this," Bill said, "I wonder why Lo chose Yang? He can't be the only immigrant runner around."

"For sure he isn't. Maybe Mary will let us ask Duke Lo tomorrow after lunch."

"So we're planning to go through with this?" Bill asked.

"You have to be kidding. Could we resist?"

"Not me."

"Me either."

I felt a charge zing through the phone line, an anticipatory adrenaline sizzle tying me to Bill the way an electric current ties together the two poles it jumps between. It was, I realized, something I'd felt between us before. I'd just never noticed it.

Or I'd never admitted it.

Well, forget that. Too much to do. Places to go, people to call. No. 8 Pell Street, for one. Chin Family Association, for another.

And Mary.

Before I could speak, though, Bill said, "I have something else."

"Something else?"

"I told you I made a few calls. Just because you weren't around doesn't mean I had no one to talk to."

"Come on," I said, "who?"

"I have a friend at state motor vehicles. I wanted to run Joe Yee's plate, which turns out to be registered to Jayco Realty on Baltic Street—"

"You call this news?"

"—*and* I asked him, while he was at it, to see if he could find out who ordered the checks on my plate yesterday."

"Well?"

"There's a code they use when the request comes from a federal agency, and that's what was there. But," he said, before I could ask him why he was telling me things we already knew, "there was only one."

"Only one what?"

"Only one request to run my plate."

I felt again that sizzle of adrenaline in the silence between us as the meaning of this hit me. "What about Joe Yee?"

"What about Joe Yee? If the Feds are the only ones who ran my plate, who told Joe Yee the results?"

There was one obvious possibility: "He's a Fed?"

"Working separately from Deluca and March?"

"Wouldn't you?"

"Good point. But not too separately, or they wouldn't be sharing information."

"Maybe they're not. Maybe the right hand just doesn't know what the left hand's doing."

"Who's right, who's left?"

"I don't know. But look: If Joe Yee was the one who ran your plate, that explains why Deluca and March didn't know about me. They weren't in Brooklyn. They never saw the car."

"Joe Yee just gave them the information?"

"Gave them, or they just took it."

Through a few more of my quarters and the crumbs of my cookies we talked some more, taking apart what we had, putting it together again, throwing around our data, concocting a theory to fit it.

"Wow," I said, at the end. "I'm going to go check this out."

"Does it change the plan for tomorrow?"

"I don't think so. Duke Lo still imports dope, we still can lock him up. Let's do it."

"We could mess up something else."

"They'll find a way," I said. "They always do."

"Okay," Bill said. "I'm with you."

"I'll call you when I get home."

"You're going to go risk your life again without me?"

"No, I'm going to talk to those guys, then I'm going home to my mother."

"Aha, risking *my* life."

"Good-bye."

"I'm off duty?"

"Sure," I said. "Everyone knows I'm good to my employees."

"Uh-huh. But you drive your partners nuts."

"Good thing I don't have any. Talk to you in the morning."

That was the end of that, and of my tea, my red bean bun, and my almond cookies. I had more quarters, but I didn't want to sit there any longer. I wanted to be up and moving around. I left the tea shop and went about my business.

270

The first piece of business was to stop by No. 8 Pell Street and arrange a minor banquet for lunch. The short notice caused Mr. Shen to raise his eyebrows at me, as did the identity of my guest, but he hadn't gotten to be the Switzerland of Chinatown by asking questions.

We got down to business. I chose only six courses, including the cold platter at the beginning and the fried banana with sweet sauce at the end. Partly this was to avoid ostentation, partly it was because although the NYPD was going to be the largest beneficiary of this event, I doubted if they would pick up the tab. Technically, the only client I had left was Peter, who was not a rich man. Chances were that Peter and I, with maybe a small kick-in from the NYPD petty cash fund, would be footing the bill for this party.

To me it was worth it. I was sure Peter would feel the same. Still, six courses was enough.

After I'd gotten things settled with Mr. Shen, I found a quiet corner phone booth. It wasn't that I didn't trust my new business partner, Duke Lo, or that I was convinced he could really work this fast, but it seemed to me there were certain calls I just might not want to make from my own phone.

First I called Chin Family Association. The man who answered the phone had to ask me to wait while he got Uncle Webster for me. I did, watching the cars roll by as the stoplight changed.

"Ling Wan-ju," Uncle Webster's voice finally came smiling at me over the phone. "How did your plans work out?"

"They're working out well, Uncle. I need to come up and talk to my friends. Is everything all right with them?"

"They are fine. They have bathed, which everyone appreciated," he said dryly, "and they have eaten. Chan Song in particular is a well-spoken, educated young man. We've been playing Chinese chess."

"Who's been winning?"

"He has."

"I'm sorry, Uncle. Next time I'll bring you opponents you can beat."

"As you very well know, Ling Wan-ju, there is nobody I can beat at this game."

"You could probably beat me. You used to beat my father."

"Your father used to let me win because I was older. But when you come for tea, let us play. You'll be here soon to talk to them?"

I told Uncle Webster I would, and hung up.

Now it was time to call Mary. Mary wasn't going to be happy about any of this, especially the plan for tomorrow. Talking her into it would take a little work on my part, but I had a feeling she'd buy it. There wasn't, after all, any real danger involved. Duke Lo was going to get what he wanted, pay peanuts for it, and walk out of the restaurant. He'd be surrounded by men he'd planted there, of course—Mr. Shen was going to have a good day—so he'd feel comfortable and safe. Bill and I would be long gone by the time Mary and as many other cops as she wanted around stepped out of the woodwork to arrest him, nowhere near No. 8 Pell Street.

I called the hospital, in case Mary was there, but she wasn't. Peter, not surprisingly, was.

"How did it go?" he asked.

"You sound better," I said.

"Don't try to distract me. And I feel, for your information, lousy. Are you at a pay phone?"

"Good instinct, asking that. Yes, I am."

"My life isn't as dull as you seem to think. A lot of my clients call from pay phones."

"They do? Why, they think the INS has all immigrants' phones bugged just in case?"

"They think a government is a government. Even when it's working for the ultimate good of the people, individuals are bound to get screwed."

Behind him I heard another voice offer what sounded like a weary agreement.

272

"Peter, I'm shocked to hear such stuff from you. Who's there with you?"

"Warren. He brought me some decent tea."

"Tell him I said hi. How's the rebuilding going?"

"Slowly. But there's good news: the New York Labor Council is going to take on the union. They're letting them in as a full-fledged member."

"Peter, that's wonderful. Why are they doing that?"

"The bomb. 'We cannot stand idly by while the enemies of labor use vicious intimidation tactics to brutalize the working man.' Especially they can't after what Warren said about them on network TV."

More background words, then Peter said, "He says he didn't plan that, he was just too dazed and angry to know what he was saying after the bomb. Sure, Warren," he said to the union strategist. "Nothing ever happened to you that you didn't plan within an inch of its life. But if that's your story, I'm your lawyer."

"Well, I think it's just great," I said to Peter. "Is Warren okay? He looked pretty rotten last time I saw him."

"Well, you know," Peter said vaguely, which I took to mean that Warren Tan probably still looked rotten but Peter wasn't going to discuss it with him in the room.

"Peter—" I started.

"Lydia, I'm glad you're happy for the union, because it shows that your politics are in the right place. But," Peter said, "but, you're avoiding telling me what I want to know, which is how it went."

I said, "I'm surprised that Mary even told you what I was up to."

"It was an interesting reversal," he admitted. "But she wasn't happy."

"I know. And it went okay. But I have something else set up for tomorrow that'll be even better. I need to talk to her; did she go home?"

She had. Peter spent a little more energy trying to get me to tell him my plan, but I wouldn't, on the spoken basis that the fewer people who knew, the better, and on the unspoken one that worrying wasn't good for people in hospitals. Finally, I sent greetings to Warren Tan and said I had to go; finally, Peter said I'd better be careful or somehow, whatever happened, Mary would blame him.

"Nothing," I said, "is going to happen."

Mary was harder to convince. She yelled at me, she said it wasn't possible, she said it wasn't safe, she said it couldn't get set up in time.

"There's nothing to set up," I said. "It's just lunch. At No. 8 Pell Street." Mary knew as well as anyone what that meant. "He'll put people at all the other tables and I won't. He'll decide I'm on the level. He'll give me a gift; I'll give him a gift. He'll leave. You'll just have to think up some clever reason to pick him up, like his taillights are out or something, and then, *quel sorprise*, find the kilos on him."

"He won't be carrying it himself; you know he won't."

"Then you hold them all and turn the guy who *is* carrying it, or tell one of the other guys you did, or something. Come on, Mary, you people do this kind of thing all the time. The only thing is you have to make sure it looks like a coincidence, to keep No. 8 out of it. You can do that because you've already been looking for him for a few days and he knows it."

She hated it, but I pulled my trump card: dumb as I might have been to set it up, there was no way I could now not go through with it. Duke Lo wanted his package back and he knew I could get my hands on it. It was costing him little enough that if he really got it I was willing to bet ("Yeah, bet your life!" Mary growled) that he'd probably just walk away with it rather than risk teaching me any kind of lesson once we all left the neutral territory of No. 8, especially since I wasn't the one who'd stolen it in the first place. On the other hand, if I didn't go through with this, I was toast. Therefore, one way or another, Duke Lo was going to get his missing kilos tomorrow at lunch, from me.

"If you want in," I told her, "you're in. In fact, you'd better come in, or else you're letting a drug deal you know about go down without doing anything about it."

Mary's voice was appalled. "Is that *blackmail*?"

"Not technically. But it's something pretty bad," I admitted.

"You're totally crazy."

"He's a bad guy, Mary. This will wrap him up."

In the end, I was right—in more ways than one. It was safer for me to do this than not to do it. It was safer for me to do it under the watchful eyes of the NYPD than to do it without them. And it would net Duke Lo, and net him for Mary Kee, Detective Second Grade.

"I'll set it up," she said grimly. "And when it's over, we'll talk."

"Sure," I said. "Thanks."

"Sure," she said. "You're welcome."

Phone calls at an end, I stood a little dazed on the street corner. Then I gathered myself together and headed for Chin Family Association.

twenty-two

Uncle Webster was drinking tea and arguing politics with a small group of other men when I arrived. His position, as I stood respect-fully listening, seemed to be that no government could be trusted—a statement with which, I noticed, no one disagreed, and in which he included the government of the host country, America—but that the current Chinese government was probably no less trustworthy than any other. This got him some cigarette-waving, teacup-clanking ob-jections, and his final point, that therefore improved trade and po-litical relations between China and America could only be helpful to the Chinese people, was received with a certain amount of con-temptuous slurping.

I hated to interrupt a man as much in his element as Uncle Webster talking politics, but I stepped forward and smiled.

"I'm glad to see that you're settling this difficult problem in this august assembly, Uncle," I told him in Cantonese.

"Pah." Uncle Webster stood to greet me. "Wisdom is said to come with age, yet I hear from these decrepit specimens the same hotheaded nonsense spouted by your young friend upstairs."

The other tea drinkers made disparaging sounds directed at Uncle Webster and nodded or smiled in greeting to me.

"You've been talking politics with the men I brought here?"

"Only Chan Song. The others have no politics, just a desire to get rich. Chan Song, with the absolute confidence of youth, opposes the current government of China. He is positive that a large movement of the people can change it."

"Well, it's happened before. Uncle, I need to see the men."

"Of course. I believe they've been waiting for you."

With Uncle Webster, I went upstairs to the third floor and knocked on the door he pointed me toward. Song Chan cracked it open, and, seeing who it was, pulled it wide and stepped aside.

"Thank you, Uncle," I said to Uncle Webster, who caught his cue.

"I will be downstairs," he said to me, "trying to instruct certain empty-headed fools in the ways of governments."

I smiled as he went off to battle.

"Did you find Cao Zhi?" Gai-Lo Lu began anxiously in English as I stepped inside the room. It was small but clean, furnished with four beds, a few chairs, two bureaus. Mismatched though it all was, it was comfortable and cozy, with floor lamps casting soft pools of light on the scattered rugs. I was willing to bet it was hands down the most pleasant place these men had spent the night in since they'd left their homes in China.

China. In a way, exactly what I had come to talk about. Before I began, though, Song Chan shot Gai-Lo Lu a look and said to me, "We're grateful for your help, Lydia Chin. Before any other discussion we must thank you for that."

Lu nodded vigorously and apologetically, translating for Yuan Lee, who just scowled and looked away. I noticed he wasn't able to resist a glance under one of the beds, where I assumed the missing kilos rested.

"You're welcome," I said. "I'm happy that I was able, finally, to do the job I was hired for. Now we have something further to discuss, the plan I have; but first, I'd like to ask you some questions, if I may."

Song Chan nodded and gestured me to a chair. He settled his stocky form on one of the other chairs, and Gai-Lo Lu and Yuan Lee positioned themselves on the nearest bed.

"I haven't found Cao Zhi"—or looked for him, but I didn't tell them that—"but I have a question about him." I spoke to Song Chan. "How well did you know him in China?"

"In China?" He raised his eyebrows. "I didn't know him. I met him only at Dragon Garden, when I came to work there."

"Then when you four got into this trouble, why did he help you out? He told me he never gets involved in anything. I assumed he did this because he was an old friend of yours."

Gai-Lo Lu spoke up. "He did not want to. He was angry at us. But he said he has no choice."

Song Chan shot him a look but didn't say anything.

"No choice?" I asked. "Why?"

Gai-Lo Lu looked puzzled. "Because we are workers. All together. Ask for his help, he cannot refuse."

Oh, right. I held him with my eyes a moment longer, then asked Song Chan, "And when you speak with him, it's in English or Mandarin, because he speaks both well?"

"Reasonably well."

"Because he was a university student in China?"

Song Chan crossed his legs. "A student? I suppose he was."

"Oh, he was. He was arrested in Beijing for antigovernment activities. He spent some time in jail because he wouldn't rat on other students, friends of his. He'd still be there except that somehow he escaped and came here."

"If that's true he is a lucky man."

"It's true."

Through this conversation my every remark, and Song Chan's, was shadowed by Gai-Lo Lu's whispered translation to Yuan Lee. Listening to Lu's voice, I thought about the basement hideaway where I'd met these men, and the other basement, where only their few, poor belongings remained.

"Chan Song," I said, giving his name in its Chinese order as a sign of respect, "you're a fit, well-educated young man with a wife and child. A biology student, you said. I suppose it's possible that you decided there was more opportunity for you here than in China. But that a man with your advantages should willingly leave his family behind and start his American career as a waiter at Dragon Garden is too much for me to buy.''

I stopped, meeting Song Chan's eyes, which were fixed on mine. Gai-Lo Lu and Yuan Lee were frowning in confusion, one presumably because he didn't understand the language, one even though he did.

Song Chan spoke; to my surprise, he spoke in accented but clear Cantonese. "How do you know about Cao Zhi's past?"

The confusion on Lu's and Lee's faces grew.

"I'm a detective, Chan Song," I answered, also in Cantonese. "I know Cao Zhi's story. Part of yours, also."

"I have no wife," he said. "No child."

I smiled gently. "If you could see your face as you said that, you would understand why I don't believe you."

"What are you doing?" Gai-Lo Lu demanded in English, sounding a little panicked.

"Speaking about private matters," Song Chan responded, in English also. "None of this concerns you, Lu Gai-Lo, or Lee Yuan, either."

"We are all—"

"No, we are not," Song Chan said. "I said I would not betray you over this theft, the problems it created. I will not. But other things aren't your concern. I will talk privately with Lydia Chin. You will not interfere."

"We must—"

"No."

The look Song Chan gave him, the steady look of a man who will not be persuaded no matter the circumstance or the argument, silenced Gai-Lo Lu. Except for the translation he offered Yuan Lee of that brief discussion, he spoke no more.

"Are they well?" Song Chan asked me, in Cantonese again. Under his steady voice were the clashing notes of hope and fear. "My wife? My son?"

"I'm sorry," I told him. "I don't know. I'm not a government official—of either government. I'm an investigator, an American, hired to find you by another American."

His brows knit together, and it was clear he had a lot of questions. "How do you know about my family?" he asked, choosing first the most important.

"I know nothing about your family in China," I told him, "except that they exist."

Song Chan's voice softened. "My marriage, made three years ago in my village, is secret," he said. "We told no one, to insure my family would be safe."

"No one will learn from me," I assured him. "But I'm not sure you can trust all those you think you can."

"I trust very few," he said. "But some have taken risks for my safety, for the safety of those like me. It is for their sake that I did not abandon this fool. Or his friend." He gestured toward the other two men, one following our incomprehensible words with an anxious look, the other scowling at the floor.

"I know nothing about your family," I repeated, watching his face, "but I know that you are a student dissident, like Cao Zhi." I didn't actually know that, but it seemed like a very safe bet.

"Cao Zhi," he said, not reacting at all to my statement, which confirmed it. "Cao Zhi didn't send you to us?"

"From Cao Zhi I learned you were at Dragon Garden," I said carefully. "But I was looking for you before that."

"Why?" asked Song Chan.

A fair question. "When you four disappeared, Lee Bi-Da felt a responsibility. He thought your disappearance might have to do with the union, with Yang Hao-Bing. But your relationship with Yang Hao-Bing is quite different, isn't it?"

"We work for him," he said simply.

"Why? As a dissident exile I'm sure there were other paths open to you in America."

"In China," he said slowly, "I dedicated my life to working for democracy. When I had to leave China, I thought, This is a tragedy, but at least I'm going to America, where there is opportunity, where everyone is equal. I arrived, and many people said, 'Come to our university, become a doctor, get rich.' But I see men like these''—he gestured at the confused men in the room with us—''I see how they work, how they live. This cannot be, I think, in America. I spoke often, late into the night, with Ho Chi-Chun, with Cao Zhi. If there must be justice in China, we said, there must also be justice in America.''

''So you work for the union.''

''To leave China, to leave my family—this must be for a reason, Lydia Chin. Otherwise, it is too hard.''

''But you won't join.''

''The antiunion forces claim that the union does not represent the restaurant workers but only the ambitions of outsiders. Members of my reputation—forged in China—would only, according to them, prove their point.'' He gave me an ironic smile.

I smiled back at him, this stolid, steady man whose heart was thousands of miles away. ''I have a Chinese name,'' I said, and told him what it was.

''Ling Wan-ju,'' he said. ''A name full of hope, full of joy. Your parents must have been very glad when you were born.''

''I was the youngest, a daughter born after four sons. My father said four sons made him tired. In any case, sons could only grow up to be like him, irascible, foolish, nothing to aspire to. He wanted a daughter, he said, who could grow up to be like my mother: a worthy goal.''

''I think you are lucky, Chin Ling Wan-ju, to have such parents.''

''I agree,'' I told him, and I did. ''Chan Song, I must ask you something else. Cao Zhi—why did he help you? He seems so bitter, so determined to stay uninvolved.''

Song Chan nodded. ''He will not join the union. But he despises those who come to America, get rich, buy, buy, buy. He chooses to stay with those who have least.''

''Why won't he join the union? For the same reason as you?''

''No. He is afraid.''

''Of getting into trouble, the way he did in China?''

"He is afraid," Song Chan said, "that this time, he will not be able to withhold information, the way he did in China."

My stomach tightened a little as I realized what that meant.

"We don't do things that way here," I said.

Song Chan nodded and said, "Ho Chi-Chun always said that also, that things are different here."

There was no answer I could make to that, so I asked another question. "Did you also escape from jail to come to America?"

He smiled again, but with no joy. "I was luckier than Cao Zhi. I was never jailed. I found the way to America, the ship others like me came here on—Cao Zhi was one—before the People's Liberation Army found me."

"Yang Hao-Bing's ship?"

He nodded.

"The way to America," I said, "was paved by the American government? By our State Department?"

Song Chan tilted his head, his look one of cautious interest, but he didn't answer.

"You have a visa that allows you to work," I said. "Ho Chi-Chun had one also. Lee Bi-Da was working on Ho's citizenship papers, but he had nothing to do with yours. Yours came from our State Department." I said this as though it were a fact I knew as well as any other, not another piece of the theory that Bill and I had worked out. "I'll bet Cao Zhi's did also. Your State Department contact is Yee Ji-You."

Dropping Joe Yee's Chinese name like that was really fishing, checking out the theory. I wasn't sure what would happen, but as it turned out, two interesting things did.

Song Chan, with a long look at me, nodded.

And Yuan Lee, with an "Ah?" that when pronounced emphatically is understood to mean "Say what?" in all Chinese dialects, began a fierce arm-waving diatribe at Gai-Lo Lu.

Gai-Lo Lu, after what seemed like an unsuccessful attempt to shush Yuan Lee, spoke reluctantly. "Lee says," he told us, sounding apologetic, "he says, please, he asks you protecting him from the anger of Lo Da-Qi."

Yuan Lee didn't look as though he was saying please or asking for anything, but that wasn't what I was interested in. "Lo Da-Qi?" I asked. "Why is he suddenly concerned about Lo Da-Qi? Because of the dope?"

Gai-Lo Lu and Yuan Lee had a quick exchange, and Lu asked, "What are you discuss with Chan Song?"

"Nothing that concerns either of you," Song Chan said, as he'd said before.

Lu and Lee spoke again, and Lu, looking even more apologetic than before, said, "He doesn't believes you."

"Doesn't believe us?" I shot a look at Song Chan to keep him quiet. "About what?"

"Lee Yuan says, if doesn't concerning Lee Yuan, why talking about Yee Ji-You?"

Looking at Yuan Lee, I asked Gai-Lo Lu, "Does he know Yee Ji-You?"

A quick translation, then: "Of course, knowing him. Why else you discussing him?"

"How does he know him?"

"Contact person here for Lee Yuan. Supposed find Yee Ji-You, get orders. Before Lee Yuan finds package, of course."

"Lee Yuan's a dissident, too?" I looked from Lu to Lee to Song Chan. Song Chan shook his head; he seemed as confused as I was.

Lu translated for Lee, who frowned and spoke scornfully. Lu turned back to Song Chan and me. "Dissident? Lee Yuan says politics for fools only. Lee Yuan come to America for opportunity, for working for Lo Da-Qi. Lee Yuan big-time gangster."

twenty-three

gangster?" I stared at Yuan Lee, who smirked back proudly. "What do you mean?"

"In China," Gai-Lo Lu answered, while Yuan Lee continued to smirk. "Big lieutenant, working for big boss. Lo Da-Qi say, 'Come to America, working for me.' "

"He knew Lo Da-Qi before he came?"

Gai-Lo Lu shook his head. "Not knowing. Lee Yuan is—" He shook his head some more, searching for the word. His face lit with inspiration. "Like union. 'Come join with us.' " He smiled from me to Song Chan, looking hopeful.

"Recruited?" I asked. "Lo Da-Qi recruited him?"

Gai-Lo Lu nodded eagerly. "Recruited. 'Join with us.' "

I sat silently in the cozy room, taking in the meaning of this.

Fast rise, Mary had said about Duke Lo. Usually it takes more time, kissing the right rings, recruiting your soldiers. But Duke Lo had shot straight to the top, behind men like Three-finger Choi.

Duke Lo was importing his own gangsters.

Like Three-finger Choi, about whom Mary had said that if the INS hadn't been so willing to give him papers, making him hard to ship back, the NYPD's life would be a lot simpler.

Duke Lo was importing gangsters with valid United States papers.

"Does he have papers?" I asked Gai-Lo Lu about Yuan Lee.

Another hurried consultation, and then Lu nodded. "Papers," he said.

"Forged?"

"No," Lu said. "Real."

I nodded, too. "Provided by Yee Ji-You?"

This was translated again for Yuan Lee, and again the answer was yes.

"The other cargo," I breathed, mostly to myself. "Not the dope. Gangsters."

"Cargo?" asked Song Chan.

"How does it work?" I turned to him but ignored his question. "For the dissidents who come over?"

"How does—"

"Answer me!"

His eyes widened, then he said, in English, because with Gai-Lo Lu in the conversation, that's what we were speaking now, "There is a network. People who help. If you are hiding, they help you, get you to the ship. If you are in jail, sometimes they can bribe the right people, you can get out."

"And when you get to the ship?"

"There is a man you speak to. He knows who you are. He has been told by the man in America to look for you."

"The man in America is Yee Ji-You? Joe Yee?"

He nodded.

"Who pays the passage?"

"The people who help. Everyone knows it is really the American government, but no one says."

The United States government—specifically, the State Department, unless I missed my guess—smuggling out dissidents on H. B. Yang's illegal alien ship. Deluca's and March's little project, the one it was their job to protect.

"What if the ship gets stopped?" I asked Song Chan. "All that work, and then they lose you?"

Gai-Lo Lu had been watching this exchange with an eager but confused look. It wasn't the language this time, but the content, that was beyond him. Now he smiled; he had something to add. With a helpful look, he offered, "It is lucky ship."

"Lucky ship?" I asked.

He nodded. "*Bright Morning*. Name of ship," he explained. "Everyone coming to America wants coming on *Bright Morning*. Nine times across ocean, never stopped by INS."

Well, of course. If the United States government was slipping its own immigrants in among the illegals on the *Bright Morning,* why wouldn't the word have gotten to the INS that this was a ship to leave alone?

I wondered in passing what the State Department owed the INS for this favor. That thought was immediately replaced by another.

"The fox," I said. "Borrowing the tiger's might."

All three men, the two who spoke English and the one who didn't, gave me identical blank looks.

"Duke Lo. Lo Da-Qi," I translated myself. "He has his people, his gangsters, carrying his dope. H. B. Yang doesn't know anything about it."

Lu and Lee whispered again. Lu confirmed what I'd said, while Lee smiled, looking superior. "Ship owner knows nothing about packages. Knows nothing about gangsters, work his restaurant. Lee Yuan says, old man, stupid man. Soon, Lo Da-Qi be big boss, Yang Hao-Bing working for Lo Da-Qi."

That's some bragging on Duke Lo, I thought, coming from the dog who bites his master.

But the important question remained. "The man in America who arranges the gangsters' passage," I said to Gai-Lo Lu. "Pays for them, provides their papers. It's Yee Ji-You also?"

The consultation and the answer: "Yes."

286

"Joe Yee," Bill said from his kitchen, pouring boiling water into a one-cup teapot for me and into the glass coffee press thing for himself.

"Joe Yee," I said. "Working both sides of the street. Why not? The State Department already has this underground railroad thing all set up. All Joe Yee has to do is take the money Duke Lo gives him and funnel it into the system, tell the guys in China, 'Bring me this guy and that guy.' The guys in China don't know the difference between the dissidents the State Department actually wants and the gangsters Duke Lo wants."

I answered him from his desk, where I was trying my best to do a creditable job of wrapping a concrete-block-size package in shiny red paper. I had left Chin Family Association with it—to the obvious relief of Song Chan and Gai-Lo Lu, and to the clear but impotent dismay of Yuan Lee—going out the basement door, scurrying across the rear yard and through the building behind. Not that I thought my new business associate, Duke Lo, was having me followed or anything treacherous like that. Still, the back exit route was there, developed to be employed in the occasional Chin Family Association emergency, so why not use it?

The paper ripped, for the second time. I sighed, balled it up, smashed it into the wastebasket, and cut a new sheet.

"And when they get here," Bill said, "they become Duke Lo's soldiers."

"Working off their passage," I said. "The same as anybody else." I pulled tangled Scotch tape from my fingers.

"Except when a guy like Lee gets ambitious and steals the package he was supposed to deliver."

I shook my head. "He wasn't the courier. There were two of them, Duke Lo's guys, on that ship. Yuan Lee didn't know whose dope it was when he found it. He just thought it would make a nice nest egg to start his new life with." I folded the new piece of paper around the package, but it was a half inch short. "When he got here, the only criminal he knew to offer it to was his new boss."

287

"Some joke, eh, boss?" Bill came into the living room.

"What?"

"The Marx Brothers. You're driving me nuts. Here. You pour, I'll wrap the damn thing." He took wrapping paper and Scotch tape from me. "Gift-wrapped kilos. This is important?"

"It's an elegant touch," I said. "He'll be impressed. I bet the money he brings will be in a red envelope." I went into the kitchen and poured the tea and coffee into mugs while Bill maneuvered paper, package, and tape.

"You sure you don't want to call Deluca and March, tell them we found the source of the cargo they don't want?" he asked.

"We will. After we get Duke Lo. They can wait."

"Good," Bill said. "Just checking. Okay, there." He stepped back, through rustling and folding. "How's that?"

"So it's not my strength, gift-wrapping," I said defensively, looking at his rather beautiful package. "I'm not so used to it. My people don't have all the centuries of Christmas practice your people have." I brought the mugs into the living room.

"All right," Bill said as we sat, him in the easy chair and me on the couch, to drink our tea and coffee. "Are you ready for this?"

"For what?"

"For lunch tomorrow."

"Oh, that," I said breezily. "Oh, sure."

"Good. Just checking."

"How about you?"

"Always prepared. I was a Boy Scout."

"You weren't."

"That's true. But I thought like one."

"Don't tell me what that means."

"Okay, then, distract me."

"Why, is that my job?"

"You're the boss."

"Oh." I sipped my tea. "I don't know about this boss stuff. Employees seem like dangerous things to have."

"No question."

"I mean, they get you all messed up with things, dogs and foxes and tigers and who knows what."

"Undeniable, if a little obscure."

"Maybe partners are better."

"Well," said Bill, after a long sip of coffee, "I wouldn't know. I've never had one."

"Me, either."

He said nothing.

Me, either.

Finally, someone had to make a sound in this very quiet place. I said, "Everything changes."

twenty-four

a Chinese banquet never starts on time.

A guest invited to a twelve o'clock feast who actually appeared at noon would be considered pushy and obnoxious, maybe even offensive, implying that he thought if he'd come later there wouldn't be enough food. The more formal and grand the party, the more tardy the guests are expected to be.

This little luncheon of ours was small—just the one table—and modest—just the six courses. So by my Chinese calculations I expected Duke Lo and his entourage at No. 8 Pell Street at twenty past twelve.

For the host it's a different matter, of course. As the party giver, it was my responsibility not to arrive too early, thereby insulting the restaurant manager and the chefs, who did this sort of thing every day and didn't need anyone hovering, thank you; but not too late, in case the crab for the corn-and-crab soup was unavailable but the restaurant owner had snagged a small supply of shark's fin, excellent and well worth the slight increase in price, didn't I think?

Which is why the breezy, bright, late morning saw Bill and

me strolling along Canal Street from his place to Chinatown. I had gone for a long, early walk after eating the rice porridge my mother had made me for breakfast, plus an orange and a big pot of tea; then to the dojo, where I'd worked out hard, staying halfway through the class after the one I'd gone to take, until it was time to shower and go pick up Bill and the gift-wrapped five kilos.

As we walked, Bill carried the kilos in a shopping bag, as though a hundred thousand dollars worth of dope—"Probably worth five times that, stepped on for the street," Bill told me—was just another kind of baggage. Well, maybe it was.

The sky was blue and cloudless, and despite the wind the sun was strong. I unzipped my jacket and watched the cars and trucks rolling, honking, shouldering their way east with us or west against us. They seemed boisterous and excited, impatient to get to their destinations and get things done.

I was on the point of telling Bill that I'd never realized the walk from Tribeca to Chinatown was so *long,* when we crossed Lafayette Street and entered my home ground, the territory I'd been raised in.

The noise, the smells and chaos of crowds trying to push past street vendors, of street vendors trying to outcry one another as scallion pancakes bubbled in sizzling oil, of wind-up plastic frogs kicking their legs in shallow tubs of water between trays of knockoff Rolex watches and boxes of glistening fish lined up on shaved ice, of gawking tourists staring and pointing, trying to take in all this exotic action, made me instantly calm. I was home. I knew every inch and corner of this place, understood who was here, what they did, and what to expect, even when I didn't like it.

Duke Lo, ha. I could take him. Me and Bill, with Mary in the background—Duke Lo and his criminal empire didn't have a chance.

I was still feeling that way when we got to No. 8 Pell Street, where Mr. Shen greeted us with a smile, had someone take our coats, and showed us to our table. Semisheltered in its own private alcove, it was set with crisp linen and the restaurant's best soup bowls and teacups. Mr. Shen went over the menu with me, a formality that had to be pursued, but only because propriety called for it, not because there was anything I could do now about any changes he or his chefs had seen fit to make. He assured me everything was in order, and told me how fortunate it was that I'd ordered the sea bass, since the bass at this morning's market was the freshest, and the largest, he'd seen this spring.

I liked the menu. I looked over our table, and I liked it, and I liked the restaurant. This was going to work. Duke Lo, maybe even Three-finger Choi. I felt powerful. I felt clever. I felt unstoppable.

I felt that way until I heard the shots.

If you didn't know, you'd think you were hearing a car backfire. If you didn't know, if you hadn't heard it before, if you weren't in a business where shots get fired and people get killed and things you didn't plan for happen all the time. Bill and I burst through No. 8's front door together, Bill yanking me back so I stayed in the doorway, sheltered some, while, guns drawn, we took in the scene on the street.

It wasn't hard to figure out. At the end of the block, Duke Lo on the ground, not moving, his chest gleaming sickly crimson. Two men with drawn guns, one crouching over him to protect him from more shots, the other—tall, with a deformed left hand—standing in the middle of Pell Street, firing at the rooftop of the building next to No. 8. People screaming and running for cover. Over the shrieks, shots, and footsteps, I heard Chester, the bright-eyed NYPD detective, shouting, ''Up there!''

A shooter, on the roof. Duke Lo ambushed on the way to lunch with me. In a spectacular athletic display, Chester holstered his gun and leapt for the fire escape ladder on the front of No. 8. He yanked it down and swarmed up it, heading for the roof.

But the shots had come, if Three-finger Choi in the middle of the street was right, from the building next door. Taller than No. 8, it had no fire escapes, on the street front or on the back, either. And no way to it from the roof of No. 8. Chester didn't know that. But I had grown up here, and I did.

I dashed out past Bill, who turned and followed. As we raced past the tall building, old Mr. Sun, the building's super, charged into the street, calling me. "Chin Ling Wan-ju! Wait! No! *Lo faan! Lo faan!*" he yelled in Cantonese, waving his arms. A foreigner. "On the roof!"

I stopped, grabbed him, held on to one of his arms as the other kept windmilling. "How do you know?"

"Big man! Paid me, this morning, to let him on the roof! Big! I would not have, but he talked about taxes . . ." Old Mr. Sun looked abashed, and I understood: the *lo faan* had been taken for a tax official, and old Mr. Sun must be a tax cheat. "He said, tell no one, but now . . ." He peered at me anxiously.

Bill, beside me, looked at me for a translation, but there was no time.

"Is the door open?" I asked Mr. Sun.

"No! He locked it!" Old Mr. Sun appeared both appalled and affronted by this behavior on the part of the *lo faan*.

"Go back inside!" I ordered him, and he ran with relief to obey.

I sped on and pushed open the door of the next building, the one on the other side of the tall one. The tiled lobby and glaring fluorescent lights raced by in a flash as I pounded up the stairs past the offices of dentists and accountants, acupuncturists and employment agencies. Bill's footsteps clattered after mine.

This building, six stories, was also shorter than the building the shots had come from. But I knew, from being a kid around here, from spending long summer afternoons with Mary exploring our neighborhood as though it were the ever-thrilling, untouched surface of the moon, that this building had a ladder to the roof of the taller one. It had been bolted there forty years ago by two old men, one from each building, who liked to bring their birds in their cages to visit each other in the good weather mornings.

I was breathing deeply, evenly, focusing on it the way I do at the dojo, by the time I reached the roof door. Behind me I could hear Bill's more ragged panting. We stopped, and met each other's eyes. I threw the door open.

A man was on the roof, and someone was vanishing over the parapet onto the fire escape in the back.

Ed Deluca turned his ferret face to Bill and me and swore. He shouted, ''Get the hell out of here!'' and raced after the disappearing figure. Jamming his gun into his belt, he swung over the parapet.

Bill and I charged across the roof and looked over. Two floors below Deluca was his partner, March, racing down the shaking steel fire escape, chasing Joe Yee.

March, on the run, fired down at Joe Yee. Joe spun around and shot back up, wildly. I dived behind the parapet, scraping my hand on the tar paper roof. I looked for Bill; he was behind a chimney, peering down into the building's yard. Another shot screamed through the air and feet pounded on steel. Bill hoisted himself over the parapet and onto the fire escape. I did the same.

I was just in time to see Joe Yee, not bothering with the ladder, leap from the lowest fire escape to the ground. He lost his footing when he landed, rolled into a pile of old appliances and kitchen garbage. He scrambled wildly to his feet.

But by that time Mary had stepped out from behind a garbage pail and was holding her new shiny NYPD 9mm automatic pointed at his heart.

Jim March leaned over the railing, his weapon trained not on Joe Yee but on Mary. ''Drop the gun!'' he yelled at her, while Deluca ran past him and swung over onto the ladder. It lowered under his weight and deposited him on the ground.

''March!'' shouted Bill, from two stories above him, racing down. Echoing him, charging down also, I yelled, ''March! Drop yours!''

''NYPD!'' Mary barked, waving her automatic to include March and Deluca in its range. ''Drop all the goddamn guns!''

Deluca, stopped on the ground a few steps behind Joe Yee, smiled at Mary. ''Okay,'' he said, patting the air with his hands as though reassuring a child about to throw a tantrum. ''Okay, everything's cool. We're Federal.'' He flashed Mary his gold badge.

294

"Calm down. This here's your shooter, but you can't have him."

Mary didn't answer. March straightened up, holstered his gun, and climbed down the ladder.

Then Bill, then me.

"I don't care who the hell you are," Mary said, not moving. *Two curse words in two sentences,* I thought irrelevantly as I watched them all, *a record for Mary.* "I want all the guns and I'm taking you all in. You can sort out whatever the hell you want to at the station."

Three.

Deluca seemed to think this over. "Sure, why not?" He smiled. "I'll end up with my man, and we'll all get points for interagency cooperation."

"He's not your man," I said.

Mary flashed me a look, saying both *What the hell are you doing here?* and *Go on.*

"He shot the gent lying in the street," Deluca explained patiently to me. One child on the verge of a tantrum, one not very bright. "That makes him my man."

"Jesus Christ, I didn't shoot him!" That was Joe Yee. "He did! And then he tried to shoot *me*! Who the hell are you guys?"

"I told you about these guys, Joe," I said. "Deluca and March, State Department Security."

"Oh," Joe Yee said more quietly, after a beat. "Oh. Shit."

"What do you mean, you told him about us?" Deluca growled. "I warned you once about getting in our way. It's not a good idea."

"I know," I said. "It could get a person killed. It just got Duke Lo killed."

"Listen—"

"Shove it," I said. If Mary could curse, I could talk dirty. "I have a witness. March was on the roof. I just wonder how you knew this was going down."

March took a step toward me while Deluca said, "You can't—"

"I want everyone"—Mary broke in commandingly—"Lydia, Bill, that's you, too—to put your guns on the ground. Then we're going to wait for my backup, and we're all going to the station, and you people can argue there about what happened here.''

"I—" Deluca began.

"Now!" Mary snapped. "This gun's new and it's heavy. My hands could start to shake any minute now." She moved the muzzle of her weapon to point right at Deluca's belt buckle.

He smiled. "No," he said. "I can't do that."

No one else did, either, but no one made a move toward a gun, all of which were holstered away. That left Mary still in charge, barely.

"Deluca shot Duke Lo," I said to Mary, "to keep him out of your hands." Blocked by the wall of buildings around us, the faint scream of an ambulance ribboned on the air. "They were afraid he'd spill how his dope and his soldiers get here. Joe arranges for the soldiers, sort of a sideline while he's working on Deluca's project: smuggling dissidents by way of H. B. Yang. Right?" I turned to Deluca but went on before he opened his mouth. "This way you eliminate Duke Lo and frame Joe at the same time. Then you take him away from the NYPD because you're Feds, and the project goes on."

Mary's face was still cop-tough, but her eyes, which I know so well, told me she had no idea what I was talking about.

"Damn right," Joe Yee said. "Thanks, Lydia. Of course, I didn't shoot Lo. And that other thing, I know what you think, but what that is—"

"Save it," I said.

Deluca looked around at all of us. He found his voice, and spoke to Mary. "I bet you have a great future," he said, smiling. "Everyone looking forward to your rising to the top. First Chinese woman at a really high level in your department, stuff like that."

"At a high level," Mary said. "Where every move the department plans related to guys like Duke Lo is relayed to the Feds out of professional courtesy."

My eyes widened. "It is?"

"There's a list," Mary said. "Guys the INS is interested in, or the FBI. Or these guys."

296

"That answers my question, then."

"It also suggests," said Deluca, "that you think hard about what you want to do here."

"Are you threatening me?" Mary's voice was hard.

Deluca shrugged. "Lo was a worm, and you people are better off without him. Yee here's a bum, and we'll deal with him internally. You'll get some kind of credit in your department, I promise you. Even you two"—indicating Bill and me—"we'll find some way to make you look good." He spread his hands and grinned. "Everyone wins."

"The trouble with that plan," I said, "is that Joe's a little more than a bum."

"We'll send them all back," Deluca said, "the guys he brought over. He's finished, Joe is."

"And the dope the guys he brought over brought over?"

"Oh, Jesus, Miss Chin, don't get all holy on me. It's not the only dope in New York. Lo's not even a big player yet. And now"—he grinned his little ferret grin again—"it looks like he's not going to be. Being as you're Chinese, I would think you'd even want to thank us."

"Well, and I might," I said, "if one of you hadn't planted a bomb that killed a man—not a 'worm,' Deluca, an innocent man in the wrong place—and put a friend of mine in the hospital."

"They did that?" Mary spoke very quietly.

"They must have," I said. "One of them. To keep the union from messing with H. B. Yang. If the union won and he had no use for illegals anymore, he'd stop smuggling them. Then whoever gives Deluca his orders would have to start all over. And Deluca would have failed. He hates that."

"Now you're crazy," Deluca said. "We had nothing to do with that."

I turned to Joe Yee. "Joe?"

"What, me? Why the hell would I take a risk like that? Detailed planning, careful execution, that's all you ever need," Joe Yee answered. "Listen, folks, I think we all should recognize we're on the same side here and that working together is the way to go."

He said that so reasonably that all I did was open my mouth to respond. Bill, Mary, and the State Department Twins were caught as off guard as I was when Joe Yee suddenly dived sideways, tackling me to the ground.

We thumped heavily to the broken backyard concrete and pain screeched in my bruised knee. I slammed Joe Yee with my elbow. Everyone else pulled a gun on him, but when his gun pressed against my head I stopped moving, and so did they.

Keeping me in front, he brought us to our feet. He said, as reasonably as before, "Now I'm leaving. Lydia's coming with me. She'll be all right as long as no one forces me to shoot her right now, which I'd probably get away with."

"Where can you go?" Bill asked quietly, calmly, defusing the situation, buying time. "Everyone will be looking for you."

Pressed up against Joe Yee, I could smell his sweat, feel his heart pound, hear his confident smile. "You don't think I thought this would last forever? I have a dozen ways out, a hundred places to go. I'm just making this easier for everybody."

I didn't agree, but I moved with him as he took me along, slowly, toward the building's rear door. I was patient, waiting for my chance; but in the end, it wasn't me who took it.

It was Chester, leaping with a snowboarder's howl of glee from a second-floor fire escape directly onto Joe Yee and me.

twenty-five

"You know what I hate most about this case?" I said to Mary in the relative peace of the Fifth Precinct Squad Room, after two hours of interviews, questions, answers, more questions, and the same answers in the wake of the arrest of Deluca, March, and Joe Yee. The phones were ringing and detectives came and went, but at Mary's desk, our own little island, Mary and I drank tea and ignored them all.

"I can think of a lot of things," she said, leaning back in her rickety wooden chair.

"Yes, but *most*. Besides Peter being in the hospital and the discovery of how sleazy the human race turns out to be."

"Well, it's not like *that's* news. Okay, what?"

"I hate most the way every man I met tried to get me to do what *he* wanted by telling me I should because I'm Chinese. Joe Yee wanted me to tell him where the waiters were. Warren Tan wanted me to join the revolution. H. B. Yang wanted me to tell *him* where the waiters were, and Duke Lo wanted me to help him take over Chinatown. Even Deluca, wanting me to thank them for killing Duke

Lo! Every one of them thought I should do what he wanted just because I'm Chinese. Every one."

"Not Bill," Mary said.

I looked at her, my tea stopped on its way to my mouth. "What?"

"Not Bill. He didn't ask you to do anything because you're Chinese."

"Well . . ." I said.

"In fact, if I understand it right, he asked you if *you* wanted *him* to get off the case because he *wasn't* Chinese."

"Well," I said again, wondering if the defensive note in my voice could possibly be put down to the morning's excitement, or tiredness, or something. "And?"

"Oh, nothing," Mary said. "Just trying to keep all the facts straight, in case someday you want to look at them again."

I was saved from having to answer by a detective who came by and dropped a file on Mary's desk.

"What's that?" she asked.

"Forensics report on the Mott Street bomb," he said. "Came in while you were busy."

"It's Patino's case," Mary said, picking up the file.

"I know. He's going back there later—he has an appointment with that young guy, Tan, now that he's seen this. I just thought you'd like a look."

Mary nodded, perusing the paper stapled to the inside of the folder. "Thanks, Liebold." The other cop walked away. Her eyes still on the file, Mary said to me, "Those three aren't going to trial, you know. Their agency will spring them one way or another. I wonder why they're digging in their heels and refusing to admit to the bomb, when they don't care what else they say because they know there's nothing we can do about it?" She dropped the folder wearily on her desk. "Nothing that tells me much. C-4 explosive— that's some Army thing—and a time-delay detonator."

"Nothing we didn't know."

"Well, the C-4. Our guys thought it was something more conventional."

"No, you knew that. Warren Tan told me, when I was over there."

"I don't see how he could have. It takes them a few days. This just came back."

"But he . . ."

I trailed off as Mary's eyes met mine. "Oh, my God," she said.

We jumped up and charged out of the Squad Room together.

It couldn't have taken us two minutes, fast-walking the Chinatown streets, to reach the basement office of the Chinese Restaurant Workers' Union. The door was ajar, as it had been when I'd come here the morning after the bomb, when Warren Tan had told me the explosive agent was a small amount of C-4 under the desk.

Inside, some things had improved. The furniture had been righted, progress made in organizing papers and piles of books. Fluorescent tubes blown out by the percussive force of the explosion had been replaced. Their too-generous light in the small, neatened room had the odd effect of eliminating shadows, so that everything seemed clear, open, available, but nothing was quite the way you expected to see it.

Except, maybe, Warren Tan, his face pale, dark circles under his eyes, sitting behind one of the newly reorganized desks with papers in each hand.

He looked up as Mary and I came in, and after a beat, he spoke. "I was expecting Detective Patino."

"He'll be along," Mary said, her eyes staying on him. I said nothing, letting her take the lead.

"We want to ask you some questions," Mary said. "I'd like you to come to the station house with us."

"I'll answer anything you like," Warren Tan said. "But I'd like to stay here. Unless you have an arrest warrant?"

"I can get one."

"You won't have to. But let's stay here for now."

I watched Mary as, after a brief hesitation, she nodded and

sat in one of the folding chairs set up across the desk. I sat in the other.

I wondered how Mary was going to begin, but she didn't need to.

"It's about the bomb, right?" Warren Tan asked, slipping some papers into a file folder. He reached over his hot plate, from which a teapot gently breathed steam into the air, and placed the folder on top of one of the piles.

"Yes," Mary said.

"When Detective Patino called to say the forensics report was in, I knew it would be soon," he said. He looked at me. "I knew I had a problem as soon as I heard myself say 'C-4' when you came in that morning. I was hoping you wouldn't catch on."

"I almost didn't," I said. "Until now."

Mary seemed about to say something else, but Warren went on. "I was desperate," he said. "I had to find a way to back the NYLC into a corner publicly."

"Why?" Mary asked.

He poured tea from the steaming pot into a large mug. Its flowery aroma filled the air as he sipped from it. "After the NYLC stopped talking to us, I could see our days were numbered. Once Chinatown workers got the idea that American labor wasn't just ignoring us, but that they knew about us and actually didn't want us, they'd lose whatever little faith they'd ever had that the union could do them any good. H. B. Yang and the old crowd would have won, just like that."

"There must have been another way," I said. "Something in the courts, some other kind of pressure. Peter said—"

"I know," he said quietly, sipping more tea. "Peter said it's not done this way anymore. Lydia, it will always be done this way." He put the mug down. "No one was supposed to get hurt. I'd called a demonstration for that night. Everyone was supposed to be there, at Dragon Garden. And I used so little explosive. So little. I didn't want to damage the building, you see."

His face darkened suddenly, as if with pain, then his features slowly smoothed out again. He took a breath and sipped more tea as he sat looking at Mary and me.

"You don't look good," I said to him. "I think a doctor—"

"I've been in and out of hospitals since I was two," he told me calmly. "I'll know when it's time." He looked around the office. "Everything here's in order," he said. "I moved the most important papers, tax records, things like that, to over there"—pointing at a file cabinet across the room from where the bomb had been—"so they'd be safe. Song Chan knows the filing system. So did Chi-Chun Ho." He shook his head. "God, I'm sorry about Ho."

"I think—" said Mary, but she was interrupted by a knock on the open door and the entrance of a tall, silver-haired man.

"Hey, Kee," he said when he saw Mary. "What're you doing here? I hear you had quite a day."

"Hi, Patino. I came to talk to Mr. Tan. There's something he needs to tell you."

The tall man looked to Warren Tan. I had shifted in my chair when he'd come in; now I turned back.

I was just in time to hear Warren, his face paler than before, say, "I think you'll have to tell him." He folded slowly forward, arms pressed against his stomach. He rested his head on the neatly piled desk. For a moment nothing sounded in the room except his ragged breathing.

Then, not even that.

Mary leapt up and grabbed the phone. She gave it her name and rank, demanded an ambulance as Patino pulled Warren to the floor and pushed rhythmically against his chest, counting, pushing, counting again. He kept at it until the sound of a siren cut through the silence, until the paramedics came charging down the stairs and, pushing him aside, tried to do what he'd tried to do.

They didn't succeed. We watched them take Warren Tan's body from the union office, not in a hurry now, Patino and Mary and I standing aside as they maneuvered up the stairs.

"My God," Patino breathed, the first words he'd spoken since Warren collapsed. "Young guy like that."

"He had a bad heart," Mary said. "Since he was a child."

Patino shook his head. "God, what a shame. Hey, Kee? What was he going to tell me?"

Mary looked at the other detective. "I don't know, Patino. He didn't have time."

"God," Patino said again. "Listen, I'll go back and start the report. I'd just as soon get out of here anyway. There's some smell, something sweet—what the hell is it?"

I moved slowly to Warren Tan's desk. I felt the side of the teapot; it was still warm. Lifting the top, I peered inside it. Long, thin leaves lay damply among small snips of twigs.

"Oleander," I said.

"Oleander?" Patino asked. "What's that? Something you people make tea out of?"

"Yes," said Mary, before I could answer.

Patino left to start writing the report at the Fifth Precinct that Mary and I would have to contribute to.

Mary stared at the teapot, then lifted her eyes to mine.

"Oleander," she said. "All I know about oleander is that we learned in Chinese school you're not supposed to eat it."

I nodded. I'd learned that, too; we all had.

"Because," I said, "it'll stop your heart."

twenty-six

h. B. Yang was at the mayor's side at the press conference.

The mayor congratulated the NYPD on breaking up a heroin
ring that threatened the stability of Chinatown, a family neighborhood
whose hardworking people contributed so much to the—borrowing
another mayor's phrase—gorgeous mosaic that was New York. H. B.
Yang himself shook the hands of NYPD detectives Mary Kee and,
balancing on crutches because of his broken leg, John Chester. The
whole thing was televised, including the mayor's thrust-jawed determination to rid the city of drug dealers, not least because of the
grudges their enemies carry from overseas, like the one that moti-
vated the mysterious man from China who shot the Chinatown drug
dealer—whose name was never used—just before the NYPD was
planning to close in on him. The mysterious man, also unnamed, had
been, the mayor was pleased to announce, captured, again by the
fast work of the NYPD, and was even as he spoke being extradicted
back to China, where he was wanted for many crimes. H. B. Yang
stepped to the microphone and thanked the members of the Chinatown community—also unnamed, I was relieved to see—who,

through their dedication, professionalism, and courage had helped so greatly in this effort. He thanked his good friend the mayor, who shook hands with his good friend Mr. Yang, and then it was over.

I switched off the TV as my mother rose from the sofa to go call Mary's mother and discuss the appearance Mary presented in front of the cameras. As I put my embroidered slippers on the shelf in the vestibule, I heard the Cantonese word for "professionalism" from my mother on her telephone perch, the high stool in the kitchen. Not naming names had not fooled her. I laced up my shoes, slipped on my leather jacket, and left the apartment to the tune of my mom discussing with Mary's mom the relative virtues of unostentatious anonymity, which enabled one to continue one's professional pursuits, as compared to crassly televised, although unarguably well-deserved, rewards.

The echo of the word *continue,* coming from my mother, gave me a warm feeling in the clear spring night. Bright white stars shone in the indigo sky and the breeze kept changing directions playfully, as though giddy from the pleasure of being able to go anywhere it wanted. I crossed Canal Street and strolled through Soho, admiring the flowered dresses in the boutique windows and the great bunches of tulips and daffodils in the fruit stands' white buckets. I ambled up this block and down that one; then, looking at my watch, I headed downtown again.

At the Laight Street building I rang Bill's doorbell and he buzzed me up. As I climbed the two flights to his apartment, where he waited in the open door, the aroma of garlic, tomatoes, and meat met me and escorted me up the stairs.

"What am I smelling?" I asked Bill, giving him a quick, light kiss. "Aren't we going out to dinner?"

"I thought you might be tired of restaurants," he said. "I cooked."

"You cooked?" I shrugged off my jacket and tried to deal with this concept. "You cooked what?"

"Meat loaf. Mashed potatoes, steamed carrots, salad, bread. Apple pie for dessert."

"You baked apple pie?"

"Of course not," he said, as though that idea was ridiculous but the rest of this was not. "I bought it at Greenberg's."

An apple pie from Greenberg's was not to be sneezed at. Still, I said, "I have to tell you I'm suspicious."

"Of my motives?"

"Not more than usual. But of your cooking."

"Fear not. It's meat loaf, food of my people."

So I sat on the couch and he brought me a seltzer with slices of lime and lemon, my usual cocktail.

"How does Mary feel about Yee, Deluca, and March metamorphosing into a mysterious Chinese assassin and vanishing from the scene?" he asked.

"She hates it," I said, "but she can't do anything about it. She got the runner-up prize, Three-finger Choi. Besides, it saves my Chinatown bacon."

"Sounds delicious. Chinatown bacon."

"You wouldn't like it. Anyway," I went on with dignity, "the really important thing is that now that it's part of the NYLC, the union's back in business, and H. B. Yang's going to have to deal with them if he wants to look good on the East Point project. That makes Peter happy, so it makes Mary happy."

"And Yang's still running dissidents for the State Department?"

"I wonder. If I were them I'd think his cover was pretty well blown and I'd go looking for someone else. And if he really has to start dealing with the union, he hasn't got so much use for illegals."

Bill poured himself a bourbon. "Did you guys tell Peter about Warren Tan and the bomb?"

"No." I looked into my glass at the ice cubes, watching the bubbles rise to the surface around them. "Not Peter, not anybody. What good would it do? It's not like someone who didn't do it is being blamed for it. And it's hard enough for the Tans, losing Warren like that, but since he was two they've known it could happen. This way at least they can be proud of his memory."

Bill nodded slowly, sipping at his bourbon. "To me that sounds very Chinese."

"Well, I sort of can't help it," I said. "I *am* Chinese."

He peered at me. "No kidding?"

I stuck out my tongue at him.

"But why not tell Peter?" Bill asked. "Doesn't he deserve to know?"

"That was Mary's call. She said he deserves *not* to know. I think she's afraid it would break his heart."

"Some tough cop she turns out to be."

"She's as tough as you are," I valiantly defended my friend.

"Uh-huh. Or you. And what about the tea? The Medical Examiner is ready to buy the idea that you people make tea out of something as poisonous as oleander?"

I shrugged. "It's hard to keep straight sometimes what's good for you and what's poison."

Bill put on a CD, a violin and piano playing together, the music, at first, a seamless whole; then each instrument took the lead in turn, and the other provided, effortlessly, it seemed, an accompaniment, sometimes a support, sometimes a counterpoint. I liked the music; it made me smile.

Bill sat in the easy chair, drawing my attention to the platter of room-temperature Brie with three kinds of crackers. I narrowed my eyes but spread some cheese on a cracker and tried it. Perfectly ripe, perfectly aged.

"My mother would have a cow if she saw me eating this," I said.

"Speaking of cows," Bill said, "tell me about the fox and the tiger. You didn't seem to like the story the way the late Duke Lo told it."

" 'The Fox Borrowing the Tiger's Might,' " I named the story for Bill. "Duke Lo left something out."

"Which was?"

"The reason the fox and the tiger went into the forest together, when all the other animals ran away. And the tiger thought they were all afraid of the fox, because the fox told him they were going to be? What they were really afraid of was the tiger, but the tiger didn't know that. Well, the reason the fox made up the story about everyone being afraid of him was that the tiger was about to eat him. When the tiger saw all the animals afraid of the fox he didn't eat him.''

"So?"

"Well, you think that worked in the long run? Sooner or later the tiger would have figured out *he* was the one the animals were afraid of. Then he would have gone out hunting for the fox again.''

Bill's eyebrows knit as he bit into a cheese-covered cracker. "I'm not sure this is a major point.''

"Oh no? If Duke Lo was the fox and H. B. Yang's the tiger, look who's left standing.''

I think he was about to admit I was right, but the buzzer on his stove went off. He put on an oven mitt—I didn't even know he owned an oven mitt—and took the meat loaf out to rest while he turned on a flame to steam the carrots. The tomato-glazed meat loaf filled the room with savory scents. Bill began tossing the salad with a dark dressing full of herbs, and I started to look forward to dinner.